I0717681

Dragonhunters

Sabrina Chase

This is a work of fiction. All characters and events portrayed in this book are fictional, and any resemblance to real people or events is purely coincidental. In other words, *I made it up*.

Cover art by Les Petersen

ISBN-13: 978-1-940006-20-8

Also by Sabrina Chase

Firehearted
The Scent of Metal
The Bureau of Substandards Annual Report

THE SEQUOYAH TRILOGY:
The Long Way Home
Raven's Children
Queen of Chaos

GUARDIAN'S COMPACT:
The Last Mage Guardian

ACKNOWLEDGMENTS

Many thanks to the fans who insisted on knowing what happened next.
Thanks also to the glorious members of STEW (Nisi Shawl, Michael Ehart,
Mike Canfield, Doreen Mitchum, Robert Kruger, Victoria Garcia, Elizabeth
Coleman, Kristen King, and Yang-Yang Wang), amazing editor Deb Taber,
beta readers Karen Meyers and Karl Gallagher, and supreme proofreader
Roger Ivie. I couldn't do it without you, guys!

And special thanks to Roy Chapman Andrews of the Central Asiatic
Expedition, who really did hunt dragons.

S. Chase

CHAPTER 1

It was a spell of great power. Even Sonam could tell that. The master's face was contorted with effort, sweat beading on his lined forehead, but Sonam made no move to help, obedient to the master's command. He glanced away from the dusty, rocky trail to the green valley below, and saw a little blue *kai-ling* fly up and then tumble back down with a high-pitched shriek. Sonam smiled with relief. The barrier was working!

"There." The master wheezed and reached up a shaky hand to the cliff wall to support himself. Foreigners were always pale, but now his face had no color at all. Sonam quickly ran to his side. "It's done." A cough wracked his frail body, followed by another, and another. Sonam pulled out the flask of medicine tea and raised it to the master's lips. The coughing stopped, but the man could barely move. "Good lad," he whispered.

"Sir should rest," Sonam ventured.

"The dead rest, Sonam. Have you warned the people?" Sonam nodded. "The ward should hold for a year at least, but it will grow weak before then. They must be ready. That magician will return eventually." He pressed a hand to his chest, wincing. "No time..." He turned his glance to the young man. His eyes were hard and bright blue. Sonam ducked his head, not presuming to meet the gaze of such a powerful shaman. "Show me your disguise."

Sonam caught the threads of his soul together and spun them in the proper way to bend light and divert the eye—what the master spoke of, in his own chopped language, as "magic." He had no metal mirror, but he could see his hands were now pale instead of brown, and his worn tunic, stuffed with silk floss for warmth, was now a thin blue jacket with narrow sleeves.

"Good enough. I'd be wary of bright sunlight and direct looks, if I were you, but it will serve. Do you have the card?" Sonam took the small piece of pasteboard from his sleeve and held it out. It read *I am mute* in Alban and Gaulan. "Remember, Aeropans do not carry things in their sleeves as you do here. You are to be commended on your fluency in Alban, but you still retain enough of an accent to be marked as a foreigner. A pity, but it can't be helped. Once you get to your destination, it won't matter and you can speak freely." He moved slowly, leaning on Sonam, his labored breathing loud in the thin air.

At last they reached the mouth of the cave. Long ago someone had sketched the outline of a *Bon* warding spirit on the wall inside, perhaps intending to return and paint it later. The red lines were faint, but the tusks and wild, rolling eyes were clear.

A mat lay in the back of the cave with the rest of their supplies. Sonam helped the master lie down, then gave him another sip of the medicine tea.

He grimaced. "I won't miss that, at any rate. Tastes like bog water. Ah, but I should not complain. It's kept me alive this long. Now, the satchel by the entrance has all my money, some letters that may help you, and the passport I altered. I've told you as much as I can of the way you must travel and how to avoid being seen by the enemy. Do you have any questions? Do not let your notion of respect prevent you. As my apprentice you have the right to ask, and given the difficult task ahead, the necessity. Do not fail your people."

Sonam could not help the tears that formed. "Must it be this way, sir?"

The master closed his eyes briefly and sighed. "Yes, Sonam. I beg your forgiveness and understanding. I ask much of you, but I have no choice. I am spent...one last thing. You will need to prove what you say is true." He took a green velvet bag from an inside pocket. "You may open it, but never give it to anyone else until you reach your destination. Only show it to another magician, and then only in great need." Sonam took the bag and stowed it away carefully. "Now I must leave you. May you have a safe journey and a quick return." He closed his eyes again. The master's face tightened, his lips opening, and then the air about him went hard and clear and his body froze, motionless. The spell that Sonam knew as the Uncorrupting Way would preserve his master until he could bring help.

Still Sonam had to hide him, to keep him safe from the evil stranger. Sonam bowed, picked up the satchel, and hesitated at the sketch of the spirit. He knelt and prayed, pleading that the spirit would guard his master. Once outside the cave and a safe distance away, he called to his soul again and the spirits of the stone. A few pebbles fell, then a stream of dirt, and finally a thundering rockslide completely hid the entrance of the cave as if it had never been.

Sonam hurried down the narrow mountain path, whispering his master's instructions like a meditation chant. *In the country of Bretagne, near the town of Baranton, at the house called Peran. Tell the mage Oron that Alastair MacCrimmon begs his aid.*

As soon as the carriage came to a halt, Gutrune von Kitren reached for the door handle and jumped down. She gathered her skirts and hurried up the stone steps to the front door. Muller opened the door before she reached it, and she had just enough time to notice how his face had aged before she saw her mother in the foyer. The light was dim, and for a shocked moment she thought her mother was wearing black. *But there was no telegram...* Then her mother stepped out of the shadows, wearing the same grey she had for years, and Gutrune's heart started beating again.

"I left the instant I could obtain leave," Gutrune said. "How is he?"

"As well as can be expected." Frau von Kitren gave a tremulous smile. "The burns trouble him greatly, so the doctor has prescribed morphia. Sleep is a blessing." Her eyes were red-rimmed, and Gutrune wondered how much sleep her mother had been able to get herself.

"Is he out of danger?"

"So the doctors believe. It is a miracle he is alive..." Frau von Kitren's voice faded. "There was some concern when his leg was removed, but now it appears to be healing as it should. Enough that he could be moved here."

Gutrune embraced her mother. "Have you had the entire burden of nursing him yourself all this time? You must rest. It is even more important you guard your health now. I will change, and then go straight to his room."

"But your journey..."

"I am not at all fatigued. I only wish I could have come sooner."

Gutrune eventually persuaded her mother to lie down for a few hours, and she made her way to her brother's room. It was dimly lit; only one well-shaded lamp behind a screen gave light, and the blinds were drawn. The air carried the sharp scent of arnica and other medications. Heinrich was asleep, and she stood for a moment by his bed looking down at him.

She had read the report of the incident and the extent of his injuries, but it was still a shock to see the masses of bandages and the missing leg. It was not clear if the explosion had been caused by poorly cast metal or an excessive load of powder, but the result was not in dispute—a shattered cannon sending flame and metal shards everywhere. The side nearest the cannon had the most severe injuries, including the burns, but Heinrich's horse, mortally wounded, had also fallen, trapping him and breaking his already injured leg so badly it could not be saved.

Heinrich turned his head restlessly, as if he were trying to avoid the pain. A large brown glass bottle of tincture of morphia stood on the table beside his bed, but Gutrune compressed her lips and did not reach for it. No amount of drugs would dull the real pain troubling him. And to ease that, he needed to be awake and alert.

"Only for a little while, Heine," she said softly, reaching for the one hand that was not swathed in bandages. She felt his fingers tighten briefly. After a few minutes his eyes flickered open and closed again, and Gutrune rang for cold water. By the time it came Heinrich was drowsily awake.

"Tru?" he asked, his voice rough.

"Yes, it's me." Gutrune removed the outer bandages from his face and began to bathe it with cold water. He winced a little, then sighed. When he opened his eyes again his gaze was more clear and intelligent. "Mother says you are healing well."

He grimaced, his jaw hardening. "To what end? It wasn't even in a battle, Tru! Now I'm a useless wreck, and for nothing! How can I live like this?"

"You can still serve, in the tradition of our family, as long as you draw breath." Heinrich made a strangled noise of frustration and looked away. Gutrune paused a moment. "I told Mother that I was delayed seeking permission to return home. You will not tell her this, but the King granted me permission to leave immediately when the news came. My delay," she said, leaning closer to speak softly in his ear, "was to seek a private audience —to petition His Majesty to allow you to take my place when you have recovered."

Heinrich stared at her, his sharp blue eyes wide with shock. "No, Tru. You can't! You fought so hard for that place...how can I take that away from you? Even if I could? It is too much. We can't *both* lose what we wanted so badly."

"You must not think I intend giving up my service." Gutrune wrung out the cloth and dampened it again in the cold water. "Recent events, which I am not at liberty to discuss, made me realize I prefer taking a more...active role than can typically be found at court. Still, His Majesty relies on me— and if you accept, it would free me to serve the King elsewhere knowing that there was a reliable person taking my place. And with that condition, His Majesty has agreed."

Heinrich was silent for a moment, thought deepening the furrows in his brow dug by pain. "You really want this, don't you, Tru? But you say, more active...is it dangerous?"

"Yes." She met his gaze calmly. "I have already had occasion to be most grateful for your instruction in marksmanship and hunting."

"Tru..." he groaned. "Exactly what have you been up to?"

"Serving Preusa. Defending Aerope. Soldiers are not the only ones who fight." Gutrune lowered her voice even more. "I can teach you what you need to know of the court. You can teach me more of a soldier's skills. The King needs us both, Heine." She closed her eyes, thinking of the dangers ahead. The horrors of the Mage War, flaring to life once again. "He needs all the help he can get."

Markus Asgaya unfolded the small brass telescope and rested it on the lichen-covered stone wall they were hiding behind. "How long has this been going on?" he asked, looking through it at the mansion. It was built in the Graeco-Roman Revival style, an architectural form appreciated by those whose activities required a great deal of peering through other people's windows, since it generally had a lot of them.

The Ostri magician detailed from the secret police to assist and, more likely, spy on him, narrowed his eyes and frowned. "Several months. First they claimed he was conducting complicated research, now they say he is unwell."

One of the other Ostri agents was ringing the bell at the door. Marcus watched as a liveried servant walked through the foyer and opened the door, speaking briefly before closing the door and returning.

"When was the last time Baron Kreuzen was seen in person?"

Another stare. "The baron attended a Philosophical Society meeting a year ago."

Well, the timing was right. A little over a year ago, the first of the Mage Guardian deaths directly attributed to Denais had taken place. Markus doubted the baron was currently among the living, but why the air of secrecy and concealment?

"I'm going to try a light probe." Markus sent the magic as he spoke. There was the inevitable protest, but it was too late. Besides, he *had* informed the man, just as protocol required. He wasn't stupid enough to think asking permission would work. The Ostri officials still suspected a subtle insult in being sent a Preusan *schutzmagus* of his unusual appearance and had only reluctantly agreed to allow him to help.

The probe reached the mansion wall before reflecting. Markus raised an eyebrow. For a mage-level ward, that was practically nonexistent. "I thought you said the baron had students with him. How many?"

"Five." A faint glimmer of intelligence surfaced in the man's eyes, and he added slowly, "they have not been seen recently either."

Markus closed the telescope with a snap. "I think you will find there are no magicians in that house now. The ward is weak. Even an apprentice would be able to cast something stronger. It looks to me as if the ward has not been renewed since the baron's last appearance. We should force entry and find out what has transpired there."

And if he had been in Preusa it would have been just that simple. But no, first the Ostri magicians insisted on confirming the state of the wards, and then they had to resolve their consternation when they discovered Markus was correct. That took up a full day.

In desperation Markus began using a combination of stealth and surprise. He would locate an Ostri official that had not previously encountered him and suddenly appear with no warning, loudly demanding instant answers to questions in tones of outrage. The combination of his bronze skin with the crisp, perfect Preusan accent left his victims so confused and terrified they would inadvertently blurt out very useful information, or volunteer to assist—especially if the assistance could be rendered somewhere else. The jagged slash of white in his black hair, clearly the result of a magical attack, no doubt contributed to the effect, and the usual barracks gossip about his parentage did the rest.

Sometimes he even overheard the gossip, which amused him greatly. Most mistakenly assumed his mother was the source of his Yunwiyan blood, and one story had her delivered to Aerope in a crate. Markus spent a brief moment calculating what manner of crate would be required to restrain his formidable mother for anything more than a day. More importantly, nothing would have protected the unfortunate individuals responsible for her imprisonment and subsequent wrath.

Eventually he learned that very little food had been delivered to the mansion in recent weeks, and no one had gone in or out since the watch had been set. After a day of this, the Ostri officials were convinced—either that something nefarious had happened to the baron, or that Markus was insane and would not leave until they did what he wanted. With Markus standing behind them, the Ostri forces brought down the ward and forcibly entered the mansion. As he had feared, only the servants were found inside.

The Ostri magicians spread out to search the mansion. When Markus made his next suggestion, the objections were loud and furious, and this time he couldn't blame them. He was forced to show his royal authorization, reluctantly granted by the Ostri Emperor, and with great mumbling the agents allowed him to proceed. He did not know all of the steps needed for a *geas*, but he had been taught enough to detect them.

All of the servants had *geasi*.

"You are certain of this?" The *Zauberamt* in charge of the Ostri magicians scowled at him, looking suspicious. "How do you know of this forbidden magic?"

"I was trained personally by the Mage Guardian of Bretagne, who came to assist us. Have you found any sign of the baron or his students?"

The *Zauberamt* grew grave. "Unfortunately, yes. We found the body of the baron in the cellars, but not his students or assistant."

Markus winced. "So, you have no Mage Guardian, no heir, and no suitable replacement at hand?"

"Herr Asgaya, you are being completely unhelpful. We are in charge here, and you were ordered to assist us." The *Zauberamt* gestured at the authorization document, his face darkening with anger. "I see no evidence of this assistance."

"Of course not," Markus snapped. "You saw no evidence your Mage Guardian was missing either. If I had not arrived it would have taken you another year to do anything about it! Denais is a serious threat—he is powerful, dangerous, and completely without scruples. The Mage Guardians were the only force he feared. He also plans to start a second

Mage War, conquer Aerope, and succeed where Guedoc failed in turning us all into slaves. This is his handiwork," he said, gesturing at the servants. "Do you want more of this? I hope for your sakes he does not return here, because he would make short work of the lot of you."

This frank assessment was met with a great deal of angry shouting. No doubt official protests would be lodged, but at this point Markus was beyond caring. Diplomacy had never been a talent of his, and in the face of such institutional stupidity, how could they expect him to avoid giving offense? Besides, he and the *Zauberamt* were in complete agreement that he wasn't helping here. Far better to return to Baerlen and report the bad news in person.

The death of the Ostri Mage Guardian was not entirely unexpected, given Denais's plan to destroy all of them, but it made the situation even more critical. Preusa still had not replaced their own assassinated Mage Guardian. Ideally, new Mage Guardians would be approved by the existing members. Since the entire membership now apparently consisted of one individual, whom the head of the *Kriegsa* loathed with a passion, it could hardly be expected that any candidate she approved would be agreed to. Not that suggestions from Preusa's old enemy, Ostri, would have been much better received, he admitted to himself.

Von Koller would be livid, but they really didn't have any choice now. Preusa would have to ask Ardhuin Kermarec for help. Again.

The longer Dominic lived at Peran, the more interesting features he discovered in forgotten corners of the grounds. The latest was an old stone fishpond, still in excellent condition, and as soon as it was cleaned up he had restocked it with fish and aquatic plants. He still felt the garden was his especial responsibility, even though he was not Ardhuin's hired gardener anymore. And now he had another use for the fishpond—as a place to experiment.

Dominic peered into the murky depths of the water, trying to catch a glimpse of Hector through the glass. He could just make out a scampering blur of white fur. Hector was always agitated during submersion, and since he was small and pale the fish regarded him as a giant offering of their usual treat of bread crumbs and surrounded him with gaping mouths. Dominic shifted a lily pad for better light. Hector was still running around, but now would pause occasionally to take in a sunflower seed for sustenance during his trial. Dominic picked up the ladle and poured more water into the balancing tank, and Hector descended into the depths.

"If you are *very* nice to me, I will replace the ladle in the kitchen before Estelle notices it is missing." Ardhuin's voice was brimming with amusement.

Dominic quickly glanced up. Ardhuin was standing in the sunlight, wearing a light muslin dress and with her fire-red hair swept up under a wide-brimmed straw hat. She was carrying a large basket of flowers and smiling at him, altogether presenting such a delightful picture he completely forgot what she had just said.

"I think it is working this time! Look, he's moving around just like he was in his cage. I think he is becoming accustomed."

Ardhuin put down the basket and looked over his shoulder. "It looks like a large pickle jar." Mischief danced in her eyes. "This is for your latest novel, a tale of underwater mice, yes?"

Dominic gave her a look of mock dudgeon. "Why would mice want to go underwater? It *was* a pickle jar, before I made a few modifications. This is just a proof of principle. See, the extra tanks attached to the jar allow it to go up and down at will. If empty, the buoyancy makes it rise, and by adding water..." he stared at the ladle in his hand, remembering. "Oh, right. I just wanted to see if it would work—it was too much trouble to go into town and get something suitable when this was right there in the kitchen."

Ardhuin took the ladle and gave him a kiss. "Even if you didn't want to have Michel get out the carriage, you could have him go and get it for you in his cart," she pointed out. "He quite likes an excuse to use it."

"Why does he keep that old thing? Is he afraid we will let him go and he'll have to go back to delivery? Or perhaps he has changed his mind about working around so much magic."

"We said he could keep it here, remember? And his horse. There's plenty of room in the carriage house. And while he may be suspicious of magic, I think he also views us as protection. For his sister, if not for himself."

That made sense. Michel was odd enough, but Amay was even more silent and fey than her brother, and Dominic had heard the whispers about her in the town.

"The carriage house isn't as roomy as you think these days." Dominic reached for the hand pump to raise the glass vessel. "It would be nice to have more space for a table or two for my experiments."

"Why not move your experiments to the house? There's plenty of room. Half of the cellar isn't even being used."

"Thank you, but no." Dominic suppressed a shudder, remembering the chilly damp and the chains of Denais's prison. "I have taken a great dislike to cellars of late."

Ardhuin put a comforting arm around him. "Of course. I didn't think...well, there is also that room next to the library. I think it is supposed to be a parlor, but it isn't as if we are likely to entertain so much we will need *three* of the things."

The tanks were now completely empty, and the glass vessel rested on the surface of the pond. Dominic bent and picked it up. The submersible exploration boat had worked quite well, once he'd gotten a few kinks ironed out. Hector capered and pawed at the rubber seal of the hatch, anticipating his freedom.

The door to the house opened and Henri, carrying a silver tray, came outside. An orange-and-white cat followed him with equal dignity—slightly marred when he noticed the suddenly motionless mouse and started stalking it.

"The post has arrived, sir," said Henri, bowing slightly. A large letter with a familiar ornate crest was on top of the pile, and Dominic immediately handed it to Ardhuin while fending off the cat from pawing at the glass jar.

"Ah, a royal letter. That explains why you felt it necessary to provide an escort, Hermes. No, you may not eat him, he's an employee." Affecting disinterest, Hermes wandered off with great nonchalance to annoy the Sangré rosebush instead. "Why was it sent post instead of with a courier this time? Maybe it's just an announcement of the new Mage Guardians. I was wondering what the delay was, after we did all that work for them." Dominic shuffled the rest of the letters, selecting one with a Baerlen postmark. "Oh, excellent. Dieter Theusen has written. He promised to update me on his new flying machine design. I still think they can get it to work someday." He started to open it, only to see Ardhuin handing the royal letter to him.

"It's for you."

It was in fact addressed to M. Kermarec, and he could think of no reason for anyone in the royal household to contact him. Ardhuin, of course, was a completely different matter. He opened the envelope. "A celebration of the cultural lights of Bretagne, is it? Gala at the palace, art, literature, drama...oh."

The back of the invitation, ostensibly blank, had a sheen of magic. Illusion. He could just make out the simple, handwritten message concealed underneath. He sighed and handed it back to Ardhuin. "Apparently a courier would attract too much notice. Her Majesty wishes to speak with you immediately on a matter of some delicacy."

CHAPTER 2

Rain trickled down the grimy panes of glass, obscuring the view even more than the dirt alone. Gutrune cracked open the casement window at the far corner of the room, just enough to allow the field glasses space but not enough to be seen from outside. From her vantage point on one of the upper floors, she had a clear view of the street below. A carriage approached her warehouse hideout slowly, as if it were searching for an unfamiliar address. She peered through the glasses—Stoller was driving, as expected, and one glove was removed. The signal.

When the carriage was one building away she reached for a large metal lever with a grip lock and pulled it sharply. She heard the low grumbling of the gate and felt it through the rough plank floors. The carriage swept in with a burst of speed. She engaged the grip lock and shoved the lever up to close the gate behind them, and descended to meet her visitors.

Down in the open stone-flagged courtyard, Stoller was carefully helping her brother descend from the carriage. Heinrich leaned on his cane and awkwardly shifted one leg from the hip, his lips compressed and pale.

"I am still...becoming accustomed," he managed. "It's not completely like a real leg, after all. Do you really think I should work here?" He looked around at the high wall of dirty windows that surrounded the court, frowning. "I can walk quite a distance now, but I don't think I can..."

Gutrune took his arm, unobtrusively supporting him. "Do not trouble yourself about stairs. I made some arrangements." She led him to the metal cage resting on the floor of the carriage room. "A small lift apparatus. It uses counterweights, so you should have little difficulty using it."

Heinrich, distracted, did not move when she tugged on his arm, instead pointing to a shadowed bay. "Why do you have a lamplighter's cart?"

She raised an eyebrow. "They go everywhere, and are not remarked on. You may find this useful in your new line of work."

"As you did, I presume?" He sighed and allowed her to guide him over the uneven concrete floor. "I must say, Tru, this place does not seem at all your style. More like a seedy warehouse."

"Good. It is an impression I have been at some pains to achieve. One

"

does not wish to draw attention," she said, smiling at his bemused expression. She showed him the central rope mechanism used to move the lift, and while she had to hold his cane for him, he had no trouble putting it in motion.

"Clever." Heinrich was breathing hard with exertion. "I was wondering how I would take exercise now."

"If you dislike moving it by hand, you can consider adding a small engine, but anything unusual or loud should be avoided if at all possible."

She had him go all the way to the highest floor, to a room unreachable by stairs. With the lift raised and locked in place, it was a very secure location. She showed him the mechanism that prevented anyone without a key from even reaching the top level, and the electric signaling device linked to the lower floors.

"A bell or a buzzer would not be suitable here, so the levers move up, and then you select the proper speaking tube with the matching number. And here," she said, pointing to a device with several gears and a long stylus resting on a horizontal cylinder of paper, "is the telegraph. It is set to record messages automatically that come over our own secret line. You can send directly to the palace at need, or indeed anywhere. This device is why, in addition to the information stored here," she waved at the bookshelves, "this room needs to be kept completely secure."

"Well, I wasn't expecting such a well-appointed office in this shabby building." Heinrich looked about at the desks and deep leather chairs as Gutrune lit several lamps. "It looks quite comfortable. You even have a little stove. No windows...oh. Of course. You are not provided something like this at the Imperial Palace?"

Gutrune smiled. "I am. And it is thoroughly searched at least once a month, sometimes more. There are...let us not say enemies, rather, adversarial factions at court. All of which would very much like to know what the King thinks of certain matters, or what he knows of them. Sometimes I am shockingly careless and allow carefully selected papers to be left in that office, if I think it would assist His Majesty's purpose."

Heinrich laughed. "Oh, very clever indeed. But is it really necessary to have such stringent vigilance even at court?"

"*Especially* at court. You must also watch that spies leave nothing incriminating behind for others to find, as well. Some would just as soon see me...us removed from favor." She considered her brother more carefully in the lamplight. He had recently started to affect a neatly trimmed beard, the better to hide the still-red scars the explosion had left on his face. It also accentuated the strong lines of his jaw and cheekbones, and for a moment she saw him as a woman other than his sister might. "There is another, more delicate danger I must warn you of," she continued, choosing her words with care. "Court intrigues are not exclusively political.

You will be in a position of power, and there are those who will seek any means to win you to their side. Even seduction," she said bluntly.

Heinrich reddened. "You should have better confidence in my character to even think of such a thing."

"I should hope so, especially since the...invitations would come from precisely the sources that would be most likely to embarrass the King should you accept. But it is not even necessary for you to agree for these sorts of whispers to cause damage."

Heinrich looked away, grimacing. "I am not likely to be a creditable topic of such gossip in my current damaged condition." He gestured jerkily at his leg. "Such attentions are beyond me now."

"I assure you, you are mistaken. Your scars will fade, and any man under the age of fifty has a distinct advantage to those court ladies swayed by a handsome face," Gutrune remarked dryly. "But this is mostly about power and influence, and you will most definitely have that. You would be quite surprised, I think, at some otherwise improbable affairs that have taken place."

"I begin to agree that you are best leaving this situation." Heinrich pulled out a chair and sat down stiffly. He winced and grasped his artificial leg to adjust it, which had shifted to an awkward position. "What other delights are in store for me?"

"I wrote up some notes you may find useful," Gutrune said, pulling out a sheaf of papers from a drawer. "The investigations I mentioned in Anatoli are turning up interesting information, and I may have to leave sooner than I planned. They should not leave this office."

He picked them up, interest smoothing the lines of pain from his face. "Does this have to do with these guardian mages you mentioned?"

"The Mage Guardians are mentioned in a general way. Now that you are cleared to know the details, I can tell you more of the specific issues at hand which must not be written down anywhere, and spoken of only in secure places." She gestured at the windowless room. "One of the mages of the Grand Armeé survived, and escaped. He goes by the name Denais now, and he plotted to destroy the Mage Guardians and ignite a war between Ostri and Preusa."

"But you said—"

"One Mage Guardian survived, from Bretagne. Denais's plot was discovered and thwarted thanks to that mage, but Denais himself escaped. When we learned that he had a base of operations in Anatoli, we sent people to search for it."

Heinrich stared blankly at the wall, the papers in his hand forgotten. "So. That is why...Anatoli? Do you intend to go there yourself?" he asked, giving her a fierce look. "Is *this* what you consider a 'more active role'?"

Gutrune spread her hands. "Someone who knows the full story must go.

Denais must be captured or killed. His plans endanger all of Aerope, Heine. And he is a very dangerous man."

"Well, why can't this Mage Guardian go then? You are a skilled shot but no magician, Tru!"

"Anatoli is where Denais *was*. We have no idea where he is now, and we must find out. The Mage Guardian of Bretagne is too valuable to be risked. We can't afford to lose her along with the rest."

The papers fell to the floor in a cascade. Heinrich stared at her in shock, eyes wide. "*Her?*"

Gutrune sighed. "And now you understand the need for secrecy."

It was not as bad as she had feared, despite the crowd of people present in the room. For one thing, Dominic was with her, and he was the ostensible reason for their presence at the soiree. For another, a gathering of artists, writers, and composers was by its nature less noisy and hectic than a ball. Ardhuin had also been surprised at how much she enjoyed listening to music when there was no danger of being expected to dance to it.

In comparison to the palace in Baerlen, the only other royal residence she had visited, the Bretagnan palace was less heavily ornate and less rigidly formal. The salon the soiree was held in had several tall, glass-paned doors that opened onto a terrace, admitting a refreshing evening breeze, and it was decorated with flowers in small, scattered vases rather than large, imposing arrangements.

The gentlemen—and the attendees were mostly gentlemen—were all resplendent in formal attire. Dominic had quite cheerfully acceded to the need for a new suit, and it pleased her to see his enjoyment of his new prosperity. She was less happy that he had insisted she also obtain clothing more suited to the occasion. She stifled a sigh, wondering if her mother had encouraged him, and made a mental note of the fashions the other ladies were wearing. Bright, jewel-like silks with lace overskirts were popular, as was pale velvet covered with floral embroidery. All far too eye-catching for her tastes—and to think she had worried that her soft yellow dress, with its full, flowing skirt, was too bright. But perhaps if she mentioned the latest fashions in her next letter, her mother would think Ardhuin was cured and stop worrying. And stop conniving with Dominic to bring her into fashion.

Ardhuin and Dominic walked slowly about the room, meeting the other notables and the members of the court. The Queen had opened the festivities earlier, but Ardhuin had not seen her recently. The Queen was rumored to be in the family way, so perhaps she had retired to rest. Would they be meeting with her, or just her advisers? The illusioned note had not given many details except that the meeting was important.

Dominic was clearly enjoying himself, and she supposed she didn't mind the soiree so much as she had expected. All she had to do was smile, murmur a few conventional greetings, and listen to Dominic's conversation. Quite a few of the guests had not only heard of Dominic's books, but read them. All of the attention was directed at him, and she could fade into unnoticed obscurity, just as she preferred.

"How much longer?" she asked, as yet another invitee, a poet this time, excused himself with a bow from their conversation.

"Soon, I would imagine," Dominic said. "The Royal Presence left nearly half an hour ago. I only hope we can escape without being missed." He grinned. "You are making quite a stir, you know."

Ardhuin started, and felt her face heat. "Is something wrong? Is this dress too noticeable?" She brushed her hand over her jonquil-yellow silk skirt.

More amusement in his eyes. "Only in the sense that it suits you very well. And no more arguing about whether you needed it or not! If you did not dress in the style of the court ladies you *would* stand out. No, I have been keeping a running count as you pass by. So far I have seen four extremely blatant stares, a dropped wine glass, and two collisions between gentlemen who were both trying to watch you instead of where they were going. I suspect one of the artists is trying to sketch you on the back of his program, as well."

Ardhuin hastily unfurled her fan. "Dominic! Why didn't you warn me sooner? We should go to another room until we are summoned. What if he remembers me?" She fanned herself slightly, concealing her face, and scanned the room for the alleged artist.

"That's past praying for, love. Think of it this way—now they will perceive you as merely the beautiful wife of this odd author that keeps getting invited to royal functions. I'm sure this won't be the only time we come here, after all."

Ardhuin tried to calm her pounding heart. "True, but...I wish there were some other way." She instinctively raised one hand to a nonexistent veil but stopped when she saw Dominic's look of reproof. She took his arm and gave it a squeeze. "Don't worry. I haven't forgotten my promise. No more shadow hats."

He covered her gloved hand with his own for a moment. "I am sorry I teased you. This is difficult for you, I know."

"Perhaps I will grow accustomed," Ardhuin said, not really believing she ever would. "Eventually. After hundreds of visits with my husband the famous author, such a favorite at the court." She smiled mischievously at the look of embarrassment on Dominic's face.

"Madame, monsieur—if you would follow me?" One of the court

servants stood before them, bowing. Dominic gave her a significant glance, and they left the salon in silence.

They followed the servant through several hallways and corridors to a small antechamber, where a Queen's hussar waited, resplendent in his dark green uniform rich with gold braid. The hussar, in turn, guided them through more hallways and finally to an ordinary room somewhere in the depths of the palace. Ardhuin was completely lost and only hoped any nefarious spies would be as confused as she was.

The hussar opened the door for them but made no announcement of their names. Inside, Queen Anne was seated at one end of a large oval table, still in her formal gown from the soiree but with her jewels removed. Seen close up, without the bevy of ladies-in-waiting and other court functionaries, she seemed quite ordinary: a short, round-faced lady with brown hair who would not have attracted any notice in a linen cap selling fish in the market. Ardhuin had the strong notion, however, observing the direct gaze and the graceful but firm way she invited them to be seated, that the Queen was very much in command and that grace could transform to power without a moment's hesitation.

I should be more like that. Ardhuin glanced at the three older men also seated at the table. She noticed that no one else was in the room, and with her growing understanding of politics realized this was a very confidential meeting indeed.

"My minister of magics, Louis Trégor." The Queen indicated the man to her left, who had long black hair and a weary expression. "And the minister of war, the Marquis de Chouchenn, and of detection, Pierre Jodoc." The Queen gestured to Trégor.

"Madame...*magistra.*" Trégor fidgeted with a monocle on the end of a black ribbon. "I regret to say that despite your assistance, our allies have still been unable to decide on replacements for your missing colleagues. Alba, for example, points out they have no reason to think Alastair MacCrimmon is dead. He has frequently made long journeys to distant locales. The difficulties with the Preusan succession you are already aware of," he said, his expression growing even more weary, "and Her Majesty was just informed the Ostri government has only now discovered their Mage Guardian is dead." He rubbed his forehead as if to dispel a growing headache. "The Low Countries, on the other hand, have so many candidates for the post they cannot decide among them. I will say, only within the walls of this room, that I fear none of them may in fact be suitable. With all due respect to those present, the Low Countries appear to prefer rank over ability."

The war minister bristled at this, but the Queen merely seemed amused.

"I do not understand this stubborn reluctance to face facts." Jodoc clenched his hands into fists on the table. "As long as Denais remains at large, *all* of the Allies are endangered. And as powerful as Madame is," he added, bowing to Ardhuin, "Bretagne cannot continue to allow her to be the only Mage Guardian in Aerope. Especially since we have not found the agents that attacked Peran. My men discovered traces of their presence near your home, and they could still be here and plotting mischief, under the control of the *geas*."

"The danger is real," agreed de Chouchenn in a deliberate tone. "We are not on such a hair trigger as Preusa, and we have taken precautions to prevent false orders to our generals. We know Denais's goals, and we need a full number of Mage Guardians to prevent them. If he uses the *geas*, what can we do?" His earlier hauteur had been replaced by real worry.

Ardhuin spread her hands. "What do you want of me? This seems to be more of a question of diplomacy than magic. Judging from the effect I had in Preusa, anything I attempt would be likely to make things worse."

At this the Queen did smile, discreetly hiding her mouth behind one small hand.

"I don't think it was *that* bad," Dominic murmured.

"Von Koller might have been convinced to throw me in the river if I was on fire, but he would require a period of reflection before taking action," Ardhuin whispered back. "And he wouldn't be happy about it."

"If we can add even one new Mage Guardian, one without the political or, shall we say, personal irritants associated with ours, the matter changes. We wish you to go to the Low Countries and assist them with their selection," said the Queen.

"They have an old custom, long in disuse, of awarding magical rank by trial," said Trégor. "They are considering reviving it for the purpose—not announced as such, of course! We have encouraged this, and said we would send our own magicians to compete to show support."

Ardhuin saw Dominic start in alarm. "I thought the purpose was to find more help, not put her in additional danger!"

"Of course Madame Kermarec would not compete herself," Trégor added hastily. "By attending as an observer she can evaluate candidates, and your particular talents, Monsieur Kermarec, would also be extremely useful."

Ardhuin considered this for a moment. "But how would my presence assist your goal? I would not be nominating or judging the trials, would I?"

"We are hoping you can advise likely candidates so they can succeed," Jodoc said bluntly. "This is allowed under the rules of the competition. However, it would produce a bad impression to have a Bretagnan helping Low Country magicians to win. You would need to be in disguise, and for your own safety as well. The competitions do not permit women to attend even as observers, and the fewer connections made between you and magic the better."

"When I was in Preusa, I went about openly at the Imperial Palace." Ardhuin's voice faltered. Who had seen her—who knew what she was?

"The knowledge that you were a Mage Guardian was kept secret from all but a few, and Preusa has much more stringent controls on information officials are allowed to mention in public, with severe punishments. Also, you had the good sense to go about in company with your now-husband, and we have encouraged the rumors that he is in fact a magician but an eccentric one who prefers to be thought merely an author."

Ardhuin opened her mouth to protest this was hardly an improvement, but Dominic merely sighed, raising a hand in acknowledgment. "A role I have played before. I hope the rumors are true about buildings in the Low Countries rarely having cellars."

"Here are the names of some promising magicians. They do not have official mage rank yet, but by our standards they are sufficiently skilled for it. Our information is not complete, and there may be others present." In addition to the folded paper, Trégor handed Ardhuin a small book, like a memorandum, bound in dark red leather. "We also thought we should have some means of communication. This has a code that can be used for telegrams."

"Though we do have agents in the Low Countries, it would be best for you to avoid them," added Jodoc.

"When does this competition take place?" Dominic asked.

"In two weeks' time," said Trégor. "We will arrange the proper invitations for yourself and a guest."

"I still think we should provide some kind of a guard," grumbled de Chouchenn, glowering at Jodoc. "It's too risky for our only Mage Guardian to be walking around without a proper escort or protection."

Jodoc shook his head. "A guard would immediately attract attention, and *magistra* Kermarec has the means to defend herself quite well. We must use the utmost discretion to not reveal our weakness."

"I regret the necessity of imposing on you in this way," the Queen said gently, giving Ardhuin a direct look. "But for the reasons my advisers have stated, it *is* necessary. Do your utmost to find a mage acceptable to the Low Countries and yourself."

She rose, and everyone followed suit. De Chouchenn opened the door, where two hussars waited outside. The Queen left the room with her guards.

"I will escort you to your carriage," said Trégor, to Ardhuin's great relief. She had been wondering how she would ever find her way back to a part of the palace she recognized.

She took Dominic's arm and followed the minister of magic. As they passed a small alcove near the room they had left, she felt Dominic stiffen.

"Who is there?" he asked sharply, nudging Ardhuin back down the hallway, away from the alcove. Trégor had whirled around, his hands raised. "No, wait! It is a...child? Shadow, Ardhuin."

Ardhuin quickly flicked the counterspell to dispel the avoidance magic present where he was pointing. A small boy, perhaps five years old, was looking at them with a combination of awe, trepidation, and curiosity. He had soft brown curls, bright blue eyes, and was clutching a toy soldier in one hand.

"Prince Hervé!" Trégor gasped, his eyes wide. "What are you doing here alone?"

"I'm not alone; I took a guard." The boy solemnly held up the toy soldier. "Marie said a magician would bring Maman a baby soon. And one of the green soldiers said Maman was meeting a very big magician tonight and I wanted to see him and the baby."

Trégor looked even more agitated. "Such an imagination...the hussars would never speak of such matters in his presence," he dithered, sweat visible on his forehead. "It must not be known the Prince was here...or you, and I dare not leave him by himself. Will you please stay with the Prince?" As soon as Ardhuin nodded, Trégor ran off.

Prince Hervé gave Dominic a grave look. "How did you see me? I hid really well. Nobody else can find me when I hide."

"You are very good at hiding," Dominic agreed, in a gentle tone, "but I am very good at seeing the kind of hiding you do. Did you perhaps hide near the hussars, too?"

The Prince squirmed. "Maybe a little." He gripped the toy soldier even harder. "Are you going to tell them about the hiding?" He took a step closer to Dominic and looked up at him, desperation in his eyes.

Dominic glanced at her, shrugging, and Ardhuin winced. Here was another dangerous matter her great-uncle had not seen fit to teach her. To many in the aristocracy, magical talent was considered...not exactly demeaning, but not something to be proud of either. She did not feel up to informing the Royal House of Bretagne that the Prince had magical talent, not when her own status was so new. They would have to know eventually, since such an early manifestation was a strong sign of power, but perhaps the revelation could be delayed.

"If we don't tell anyone, will you promise not to hide to do things you know you are not supposed to do?" Ardhuin asked.

The Prince scrunched up his face, clearly upset, but nodded. "I promise," he whispered.

"That's a good boy," Dominic said, and was rewarded by a princely hug at knee level. He ruffled the boy's hair, smiling down at him. "Your plan was a clever one, but I'm not the magician you are looking for."

"What kind of magician are you then?" Prince Hervé asked, apparently willing to accept a substitute.

Dominic bent down and gave him a meaningful look. "The kind who keeps secrets." Ardhuin stifled a laugh at the Prince's expression of sudden understanding, and Dominic winked at her.

Trégor returned shortly thereafter, with a trio of hussars. The young Prince went off with the guards without protest, only glancing over his shoulder at Dominic and Ardhuin as he left.

"I am afraid the Prince is extremely curious and active," Trégor said in some agitation as they continued on their way. "It has become nearly impossible to keep him from escaping his nurses and wandering all over completely unsupervised."

A carriage without insignia was waiting outside the side door, and Dominic handed Ardhuin in before jumping up himself.

"Poor little fellow," he murmured when the door was shut. "And I thought my life was thin of adventure at his age. He has to make do with hiding behind curtains."

"When they discover his magical ability his life will become exciting enough for anyone," Ardhuin said. "I doubt he will enjoy it, however."

"Is that why you agreed to keep silent?"

Ardhuin nodded. "He most likely discovered how to do aversion on his own, just as I discovered illusion. I hope I made the right decision. If he learns any dangerous magic before his talent is known—but it is unlikely he will encounter any here. It is a risk, I suppose, but he should be allowed the possibility of being just a child a while longer."

Dominic sighed, sinking back against the carriage cushions. "It is a pity that all that work we did to help find new Mage Guardians was wasted. I was hoping you would have colleagues by now to help with the work."

"To stop Denais?"

He shifted in his seat. "That, and...then it might be possible for you to decline to assist, if it were necessary for you to remain at home..."

Ardhuin blinked as his meaning became clear. "You want a Prince Hervé of your own," she murmured, taking his hand and giving it a squeeze.

He gestured with his free hand, his glance flickering between her face and the window. "I know you have a grave responsibility. I've known it from the beginning. I do not wish to appear selfish, but...yes."

"It is perfectly natural. You have been many years without a family."

"You do not object?" His eyes searched her face intently, a faint crease between his brows and concern in his voice.

"I suppose I never thought children would be possible for me. It hurt to even dream...no, how could I possibly object? If we can settle the Low Countries, that will at least be a start. I am only sorry my obligations impose so much on you and your wishes."

Dominic drew her closer. "We are together in this, as always—and I can write anywhere. Besides, I have always wanted adventure."

CHAPTER 3

Sonam stumbled on the uneven road, blinking to clear his vision. There was so much *green* in this place it overwhelmed him. Even the lowlands of Bhuta looked sparse compared to this. He stumbled again, fighting a wave of dizziness. Something was wrong—but he could not stop now, so close to his goal. The house named Peran was on this very road, according to the people of the town.

Perhaps it was the unaccustomed sunlight. Sonam had preferred to travel at night as much as possible, to avoid notice from any enemy that might be tracking him and to hide his unfamiliarity with the countries he traveled through. To save his dwindling funds and for even more concealment, he had removed his spirit disguise and hired on as a cook on a merchant ship. The ship he chose made the transit between the Ynde trade-city of Ghot and Alba, stopping at the Bretagnan port of Sanmalo on the way. The polyglot sailing community simply assumed he was Cathan, and Sonam took care to avoid any real Cathans who would know he was not one of them.

He had thought it would be a simple matter to once again assume his spirit disguise for the rest of his journey, but he had not taken into account the *geilo* fondness for star-metal. Master MacCrimmon had told him of trains and how to use them, but he had not mentioned they were made entirely of star-metal. His disguise was unworkable while riding them. Sonam did the best he could with the magics the master had taught him for avoiding notice, but quickly purchased local clothing so he would not have to hide so much of himself.

Sonam shivered, even though the day was warm. He had not felt well for some time, since leaving the ship. Perhaps it was the strange food, or simply fatigue. He had been traveling as fast as he could for weeks now, and the strangeness of everything around him was tiring too. Soon he could rest.

He caught a glimpse of a roof through the trees, and his heart beat faster. It was as the people described—a large house, the color of sand, with gates of the ever-present star-metal before it. The gates stood open, and Sonam walked up the drive. The air was rich with the sweet scent of flowers somewhere he could not see. He was wearing his spirit disguise, to be cautious. The high shaman Oron had never met him, so Sonam's true face would mean nothing to him.

Sonam reached out to the door, intending to knock, but the invisible power of a *namas* wall stopped his hand. He smiled, now sure he had found the right place. But how was he to make his presence known? He looked about and saw a long metal chain with a brass pendant at the end shaped like a hand. It hung from a bracket on the wall of the house, and it appeared to be attached somewhere inside.

Sonam reached for the chain and pulled. He was starting to feel faint. When had he last eaten? He could not remember. A bell sounded inside the house and not long after, the big door was opened by a dignified man with thin grey hair.

"Yes, sir?" the man asked politely.

"Please excuse, but I seek one..." Sonam desperately tried to remember how the master had pronounced the impossible name the shaman used in daily life. "Ayeves More Layss."

A look of concern passed over the older man's face. "My sincere apologies...I must regretfully inform you, sir, that Magister Morlais is deceased, and has been for over a year."

Sonam felt his knees buckle, and he could barely breathe. Dead! "But the protection, it is still strong," he gasped, pointing at the house and its *namas* wall before he recollected himself.

"I am sorry to give you such a shock, sir—perhaps Madame Kermarec could assist you? She is a close relative of the late Magister, and inherited this house from him. Unfortunately she and her husband are away at present, but they are expected to return shortly..."

It was suddenly hard for him to think. The light that had bothered him earlier was growing dim. He needed a magician. Would this female relative know of such things? There was this *namas* wall, so some magician remained here. He had to save his master.

"Who speaks now for Oron?" Sonam whispered, as the darkness in his vision increased. The old man reached out a hand, worry evident in his eyes. Sonam felt himself fall, and the darkness was complete.

Dominic glanced about the busy Reuytersalle in an agony of indecision, pen poised above his notebook. He only had a few blank pages left, and what should he choose to write about? The precise defensive wards being set up by the Prince's *magiewacht*, or their splendid formal uniforms? The carefully intricate rules for the magical duels, or the fascinating splendor of the masterwork spell competition? How could he pick? How could he get another notebook without leaving the building and missing something?

He had gathered that the Reuytersalle usually functioned as an indoor riding arena, which would explain the large, open space and the somewhat crude temporary plank flooring. It was full of people and bustle, with archaic clothing and banners and ceremonies Dominic had never heard of before now. He wondered if other countries had their own magical customs similar to this or if it was unique to the Low Countries. He would have to ask someone.

The dazzling magic of the masterworks was finally too much for him to resist. Each spell was in its own large glass case, which he could see also had protective wards. He wasn't sure if the wards were to protect the masterwork or the viewers. The first section was journeyman entries. They seemed to rely on illusion and spectacle more than power, and he found himself shaking his head at a sloppy stasis field in one entry. He smiled at himself, realizing he had developed rather exacting standards from watching Ardhuin's skill.

Then he came to the true masterworks. There were ten in all, ranged in a large circle in a separate space created by dark red fabric suspended from the ceiling beams. Dominic was grateful for this, since there was so much magic present it was beginning to all blur together for him.

One featured an automaton that danced with human grace and expression but was a mere six inches in height. Another featured an illusion of a nymph of flame, flickering about the case as if seeking to escape. All crafted with jeweler's precision and care. Still, the main effect was that of appearance.

Then he came to what appeared to be a simple, perpetually turning waterwheel. The water was real, not an illusion, which piqued Dominic's interest. Then he noticed the water ran *uphill* to the wheel and went around it and then up to a floating cloud, continuously. Dominic stared at it in complete fascination, trying to puzzle it out. He could see tiny gears and blades of stasis, all rotating together to make it seem the water was moving by itself in the wrong direction. The stasis gears had long axles held up by a physical frame at the top of the case, concealed by a strong combination of illusion and avoidance magic.

He stepped around the case near the curtain wall to get a better view of the hidden mechanism at the top, and to allow others to take a closer look at the waterwheel. And that was when he saw someone else looking up above the case instead of at the wheel. At something no one else should be able to see. Someone he'd seen at the dueling section earlier, a man in a grey waistcoat, wearing a pince-nez. *He's a scryer too.* It was strange to realize there was someone else like him.

The man had not seen him, and Dominic resolved to be more careful. As fascinating as all this magic was, he had a job to do and it would be easier if no one realized his true abilities.

He caught sight of Ardhuin in the crowd, talking to someone in a competitor's tabard. She had illusioned herself to appear as a male Atlantean journalist, complete with a brash accent and engaging grin. Dominic walked in that general direction to see who she was talking to, and to let her know what he had learned.

They had not had much luck with the list of candidates they had been given. All were competent but uninspiring. Dominic had seen much evidence of Trégor's accusation of the heavy weighting given to rank. It was much more likely to be mentioned than level of skill when competitors were spoken of by the officials. All the magic used in the duels was straightforward and, frankly, dull. He kept remembering the fight with Denais in the ruined mansion, and shook his head. None of these mages would have lasted five minutes.

He wandered past Ardhuin and the stranger, heading for an area marked off by shrubs in pots, set with tables and chairs, and offering refreshments. He took a seat and started writing in his notebook, and shortly Ardhuin sat down at a table behind his. He saw the bright flow of magic and then heard her normal, nonillusioned voice.

"I think I may have found a better candidate than the ones on the list," she said. "Talking to the top-ranked mages, I pretended to be ignorant of the spells used but eager to learn. They all think they are the best, of course, but when I asked who might be able to explain such things to me they mostly mentioned one name, Jan Kreuwel. I also asked them how the *other* contestants would rank in terms of skill, hinting that Atlantea was thinking of hiring talent for their own *ars magica* universities, and his name was universally suggested."

Dominic grinned. "Ah, they would love to get rid of him, is that it? Was that the man you were speaking with just now?"

"Yes. No rank to speak of, of course. And he was considering not even competing in the duels! He just put a masterwork entry up. He said there was no point, that 'favor' would not be shown for his style of magic and it wasn't worth the trouble."

"It's the second day of the tournament—is it too late for him to compete?"

"All competitors are entered. He just has to show up." He heard her shift behind him. "I've arranged to meet him tonight. I'm not sure how to help him, though. He seems just as good as the others, better even, but he is quite sure he will not win the duels."

Dominic sat back. "Ah, there I can help you. The judges don't like surprises, or any novelty. There is a strict list of the spells that may be used in the duels, and in some cases even the order is mandated. Also," he lowered his voice, even though he knew Ardhuin's spell was completely hiding their conversation, "there is another thaumatic scryer here. Grey silk waistcoat, pince-nez, and an amethyst ring. I saw him earlier, watching all the duels, and I have seen him speak to several of the more favored competitors."

"Are you sure?"

"Oh yes. I saw him looking at the masterworks. One of them, the perpetual waterwheel? It has a spell element far above the fountain itself. If you can't see magic, there's nothing to look at, but he was staring at it." Dominic opened up the competition program booklet, scanning the list of entered masterworks. "Aha! Interesting. That was Jan Kreuwel's entry. Fantastic command of detail."

"Hmm. I still don't see how they can skew the duels, but it's happening somehow. I suppose I should keep looking, in the event Jan doesn't work out." Ardhuin sighed, and he heard her chair slide back.

"How are you doing?" Dominic asked softly. "This must be difficult for you."

"There are far too many people," Ardhuin replied in an equally quiet voice. "But it helps, a little, to be in disguise. I am not myself."

"With luck, we will be done soon and we can go home," Dominic said, trying to cheer her.

"I will look forward to that."

Ardhuin left, and after a few minutes Dominic returned to the Reuytersalle. He saw Ardhuin a few times in the crowd but focused on keeping an eye on the thaumatic scryer and trying to figure out what the man was doing.

They met with Jan Kreuwel that evening at a small *bierkeller* near the Reuytersalle. There were several other people Dominic had seen at the tournament there as well, so meeting him there should not be too much remarked on. Still, he took care to find a booth in the back, away from the bar and the thickest crowd of patrons.

Jan was a middle-aged man with a cherubic face, sturdy build, and an infectious intellectual curiosity Dominic found very congenial.

When Dominic broached the issue of the duels, Jan waved a hand dismissively. "*Ach*, these *mijneer* mages, they all have this style of doing the thing, you understand. They will only teach their own kind, and if you do not know the high style, well, you don't win." He shrugged. "And why would I want to learn? It's not useful, at all."

"What if you could learn—and win?" Dominic asked. He saw Ardhuin come in and make her way to their table. "I saw your masterwork. It's amazing. I've never seen such fine control with so many disparate elements."

Jan's pale blue eyes widened slightly. "Perhaps I did not hear correctly, but did you not say you are not a magician?"

"Evenin', gentlemen. Might I join you?" Ardhuin's voice provided

Dominic with a graceful evasion. He kept forgetting...

"There you are! It is Mr. Talbot of the newspaper." Jan beamed. "You are perhaps acquainted, Monsieur Kermarec?"

"We have met." Dominic suppressed a smile. "Actually, we would like to ask you a question."

Ardhuin sat down and discreetly activated the antieavesdropping spell. The murmur of conversation in the *bierkeller* faded, earning Dominic another sharp look from Jan.

"And what is this question?"

"If we show you how to do the high style, as you call it, will you compete in the dueling competition?"

Jan took a deep drink from his mug. "I feel I must point out you are not even from the Low Countries, and of necessity not a *mijneer*." His round face remained calm, even if his gaze had become sharp. "How can you teach me what you do not know?"

"I am a thaumatic scryer," Dominic said bluntly. "I will appreciate your discretion with this information. I can see this high style and help you learn it."

Jan was interested, he could tell, but still hesitant. "The favored ones always win. It is not just a matter of skill. They seem to know just what to do."

Dominic blinked. "So that's what the fellow was up to! He was watching the duels to learn the combatants' styles! The other thaumatic scryer," he explained.

"I'm beginning to think these *mijneer* are in great need of a set-down," Ardhuin murmured. "If they already know who is going to win, why bother with competitions?"

Jan glanced at Ardhuin in her disguise, and then back to Dominic. "You are together in this? To what purpose, if I may ask?"

"I'm Atlantean. We don't like seeing a good man held down just because he doesn't belong to some dusty old family that hasn't done a lick of honest work in a hundred years," Ardhuin drawled. "Don't spread it about, now, but I know a few bits of magic that might be of use. Between us, I think we can give your *mijneers* a bit of a surprise."

Dominic nodded. "I agree. A tournament should be honest, and a mage's rank earned. Do you know of a place where we can work without attracting notice?"

Jan did.

They left the *bierkeller* and followed him down narrow, cobbled streets for some distance, until the city had thinned and the buildings were more widely spaced. By now it was completely dark, and few people were about. The building Jan lodged in had a back garden with high brick walls and the only other tenant in residence an elderly lady.

"Vrauwe Voorleyn is as deaf as a post," Jan reassured them. "And she enjoys a *tropj* of schnapps before retiring to bed. You hear?" The corners of his mouth quirked up.

Dominic listened, and indeed the sounds of stentorian snoring were quite clear near the house.

Ardhuin raised an eyebrow and set up wards and concealment anyway. Jan observed her with his arms crossed, his expression bland and revealing nothing.

Ardhuin chewed her lower lip in a gesture Dominic recognized as indicating deep thought, but also as one a man would be unlikely to use. Fortunately Jan did not seem to notice. "Let's begin with an attack." Her arm extended with the words, and Dominic saw the magic flare out.

Jan was surprised but did not falter. Ardhuin then coached him on his own attack. After a few exchanges his polite skepticism and doubt changed to enthusiasm. "I still do not understand your eagerness to help me," he gasped, his cherubic face now pink with exertion, "but I make no complaint. Again, if you please," he said to Ardhuin.

She flung another attack at Jan, with so much power Dominic blinked. Jan blocked it, not gracefully, but effectively.

"We don't want to destroy him," Dominic murmured in Ardhuin's ear. "What are you about?"

"Those duels are useless to determine his true skill in a fight."

"Yes, well, he still needs enough energy to stand up tomorrow or it will all be for nothing. And we still must teach him the high style."

Ardhuin sighed, and nodded reluctantly. "Let me show you some more effective parries than you are using."

CHAPTER 4

Ardhuin stifled a yawn and looked around the Reuytersalle discreetly. It was the fourth day of the tournament, and the final duels were taking place. Jan had advanced without much difficulty thanks to Dominic's information, carefully noted while watching other combatants, and their nightly coaching sessions. It had caused no little consternation among the officials, apparently, and the other magicians were now watching Jan's duels with interest. Which was a problem, since the crowds of magicians made it difficult for her to see.

Not that it mattered to her now. She was completely convinced Jan was the correct choice. He was far more interested in learning from her than in winning the tourney and had surprisingly little animosity toward the noble mages who had hindered him. Rank had not interested him either. She had added a few spells that would not be useful in the tournament, just to see how well he handled something completely new. What Jan didn't get with quick intuition he stubbornly persisted with until he mastered it.

She had sent her first coded telegram to let Trégor know what had happened so far and had gotten a response to contact the ambassador from Bretagne when the tourney was over to proceed with the Mage Guardian selection.

Ardhuin craned her neck and found a gap in the crowd that just let her see Jan's face. He looked intent and focused as he fought. His opponent was all but snarling as he went on the attack. Jan moved to counter, then his eyes widened, startled, and he dropped out of her sight. The crowd gasped, then broke out into excited shouting. Exasperated, Ardhuin tried to work her way closer to find out what had happened, being careful not to make physical contact with anyone. Illusion only went so far.

Dominic was visible ahead, looking furious, and she changed her direction to meet up with him.

"What happened?" she asked.

He stepped farther away, where fewer people could overhear. "They cheated, that's what happened. And if you hadn't taught Jan those powerful shields, he would be dead or injured."

"But cheated how? Only the competitors and the judge are allowed within the wards. Nothing can get through.”

Dominic smiled bitterly. “The judge himself. He placed a linking spell on Jan’s foot and the floor, just for a moment. Jan lost his balance. Naturally, his opponent attacked, and with full power. The judge gave him full points and the match. What can we do? Even if I make a complaint, it will be my word alone. I doubt their scryer will support me.”

Ardhuin grimaced. “Jan is still in third place, even so.”

“Will that be enough?”

She hesitated. “It would be better if he had won. It is more to convince their government, really.” Ardhuin could see Jan now, outside the dueling area. He was pink-faced again, but this time he looked more angry than tired. “I have an idea.” She took a leaf from her “journalist” notebook and wrote quickly. *The judge used a binding on you. Before the next duel, cast a light repulsion field on yourself. Any attempt at binding will cause a visible flash and won’t attach.*

Ardhuin wandered over, and with general conversation about the recent duel, shook Jan’s hand and passed him the folded note. She went on to speak to others still present, to maintain the fiction of her being a journalist, and when she turned back she was gratified to see Jan calm and with a hardened expression. He nodded slightly to her.

“He is still fighting?” Dominic whispered when she rejoined him.

“Yes. Have you noticed any other foreigners nearby? See if you can get them where they can see the next duel clearly. If they try the same trick, it will be visible to everyone now.”

“With pleasure.”

When the next duel was announced the judge and opponent were already there, and when Jan at first did not appear, Ardhuin could see a smug look on the opponent’s face, quickly replaced by shock and irritation when Jan came out of the crowd with no visible indication of concern. This time she was close enough to hear him speak.

“*Ach*, good! You are here! I am eager to begin.” Jan smiled as if he had not just experienced a defeat, and the opponent’s expression grew puzzled.

This duel was less theatrical, but she sensed even more serious to the contestants. Jan was cautious, never overextending himself but also never allowing an opening to go unexplored. Completely in the conservative model favored by the Low Country mages, some of whom were muttering to each other nearby, concerned.

Then it happened. A bright flash, this time near Jan’s knee when it was bent. Jan did not stumble. He clenched his jaw and unleashed a withering attack, completely overwhelming his opponent.

But before Jan could unleash the final blow, the judge, face scarlet with fury, grabbed Jan’s wrist. The crowd gasped, Ardhuin included. Of all the rules of magical decorum, that was one of the most stringent. No magician laid hands on another in anger—especially in a duel—and the judge, a magician himself, would know that. To use physical force instead of magic was a terrible insult to another magician—and a shocking loss of dignity coming from a judge.

Just as before, there was shouting from the witnesses, but this time it did not stop. It grew louder, and had an ugly undertone. This scandal was more than even the *mijneers* could countenance.

Ardhuin edged back, away from the increasingly angry crowd, but not before she saw Jan give the shocked, suddenly fearful judge a searing look of contempt. Time for her to contact the ambassador. She had a plan.

Markus Asgaya stepped off the train at Banhof Friedrichstrasse and heaved a sigh of relief. After experiencing weeks of Ostri imperial inefficiency, suspicion, and pompous arrogance, Preusan levels of government stupidity were barely noticeable. Even the stolid and unenthusiastic expression of the palace coachman sent to meet him was a welcome sight. Apparently the bad news contained in his last telegram had not caused too much official irritation with *him*.

Now he was back where he could finally do something useful. Markus reviewed the main points that needed to be covered when he reported, some too sensitive even for coded messages. The autopsy reports, for example. The Ostri Mage Guardian showed signs of being shackled for some time before his death—and multiple puncture wounds in his arms. It was not entirely a surprise, recalling how Dominic Kermarec had been bled for his presumed magical power when he was captured by Denais. Denais could have been extracting Kreuzen's magical essence for months. Markus shuddered at the thought.

On a more positive note, he was bound to see Gutrune von Kitren. As one of the few entrusted with the full details of the current situation, it would be logical for her to be present to hear his report. And if for some tragic reason she was busy elsewhere at the time, it would not take much effort on his part to find her at the palace. Purely to make sure she had the most current information, of course. And if he chose to regale her with a few anecdotes of the comic incompetence of the Ostri officials that, regrettably, could not be part of his *official* report for diplomatic reasons, where was the harm in that?

Markus was shown to a room where the King himself was present, as well as a handful of his council. Gutrune was not there, but in her usual place, behind and to the left of the King, sat a man with a strong resemblance to her.

Concealing his surprise as best he could, Markus gave his report. It was received much as he had anticipated, i.e., not well, but at length the council members ran out of useful questions and were dismissed. The King indicated Markus was to remain.

"I wish to make you both known to one another." He gestured at the man behind him and to Markus. "Heinrich von Kitren, formerly of our armed forces, will be serving me in his sister's place. Markus Asgaya you have heard mentioned in the accounts concerning the Mage Guardians and Denais. During your absence," he said to Markus, "I have received information that the Bretagne government has plans in action to get the Low Countries to name their Mage Guardian."

Markus hoped his reaction to the first piece of news had not shown on his face. Replaced? But where was Gutrune? Then the rest of what the King had said registered. "Does this mean their Mage Guardian is assisting in this process?"

One royal eyebrow was raised. "I am sure the Bretagne government sees no need to direct the actions of the Low Countries in their decision."

That meant yes. Markus stifled a grin.

The King stood and left the room, and von Kitren stiffly rose as well. Markus noticed he was using a cane.

"If you will permit, may I ask if Fräulein von Kitren enjoys her customary good health?" Markus asked, careful to appear nothing more than courteous.

That earned him a hard look and a grim expression. "When I last spoke with her, yes. But that was some weeks ago. While you were comfortably bored in Ostri, she has been sent to the wilds of Anatoli."

Markus blinked, feeling stunned. "What? Why? Denais would hardly return there."

Von Kitren studied his reaction, and some of his chilly demeanor diminished. "Indeed. Yet, there she is, or was at last report. It is also unclear to me why you were not sent there, and she to Ostri."

"Unsurprisingly, His Majesty holds her in higher esteem than he does me," Markus remarked with some asperity. "Have you ever had to deal with Ostri government bureaucracy? You can't shoot them even when they deserve it. And if I may be blunt, I was under orders. It was hardly a matter of my preference. You were in the army, were you not? I should not have to explain this to you."

Von Kitren flushed angrily. "It has not been so long for me to forget. But to see her placed in danger, when *I* am not allowed to serve because of my injuries, and then to hear that you...pray excuse me. I cannot be other than concerned."

"Nothing is more natural," Markus agreed cordially. "In a just world, your sister would have nothing less than a battalion to defend her and assist her in her duties. I feel constrained to point out, however, she would doubtless find them very much in her way and would manage to evade them entirely to go find trouble to involve herself in. I speak from experience," he added dryly.

"And if I asked you to explain in more detail, would I regret it?" Von Kitren's earlier hostility had all but vanished, replaced by resignation.

"Very likely. Perhaps it would relieve you to hear that she is quite capable of getting herself out of trouble as well."

Von Kitren scowled. "I would be more relieved to hear she had some assistance in this extremely dangerous hunt."

"I am in complete agreement. I will do what I can—now that my current mission is complete, I may be able to persuade them my help is needed there. Will you be willing to aid me in this?"

Von Kitren regarded him steadily him for a moment, then nodded.

The Bretagnan Minister of Magics finally emerged from the meeting room in the Hoegeyre, the government building of the Low Countries. He looked tired and irritable, but his expression cleared slightly when he saw Dominic waiting in the hallway outside.

"These *brughers* are beyond stubborn," Louis Trégor muttered, walking quickly away. Dominic followed.

"Did they agree to choose Kreuwel?"

Trégor sighed. "Eventually. It was the threat of exposure that did it." He gave a thin smile and lowered his voice. "Between hinting you were so shocked you were thinking of writing a story based on the tournament cheating and Hyeer Kreuwel's righteous indignation, I was able to induce them to see reason. I promised to use my influence to dissuade you and suggested that the position of Mage Guardian might calm Hyeer Kreuwel from lodging an official complaint against the tournament for being deprived of his rightful prize. I may have hinted the responsibilities of the post would give him little time for disturbing the existing social strata of the Low Country mages," he added blandly. "I understand he has accepted the position and has been told the Mage Guardian of Bretagne will consult with him shortly."

"Well, that's one good consequence of that mess. Will news of the cheating scandal get out, do you think?"

"None of the Low Country mages will spread it about, certainly. While it would be preferable to have no notice taken at all, I do not think we could have done the thing *without* the scandal. The suggestion to make use of it was a good one. Do you intend to remain long here?"

"At least long enough to get Hyeer Kreuwel started and to look over the previous Mage Guardian's laboratory," Dominic said. "We can begin this afternoon, if he is agreeable."

"Good. A message will be sent. I concur that he is well suited to deal with both Preusa and Ostri, so I will return to Bretagne to put those negotiations in motion," said Trégor. "My thanks to you both for this service. Her Majesty will be pleased."

Dominic left the Hoegeyre, and walking briskly through the center of town, soon found Ardhuin in the lobby of their hotel, still in disguise. Both her real self and the illusion raised an inquisitive eyebrow.

"Success," he said, grinning. "Your plan worked. Jan has been chosen."

Ardhuin gestured, and the noise of the lobby faded. "Excellent. Serves everyone right. And von Koller thought *I* was stubborn! It occurs to me, however, that even if we cover the essentials, Jan may need to visit us for further instruction. I never bothered to set up the house wards for magical guests; perhaps because I never thought to have guests of any kind. It will take some consideration."

Intrigued, Dominic asked for additional details on the types of warding Ardhuin was thinking of, and they discussed the matter until a message was brought to them from Trégor indicating Jan would be pleased to meet with his colleague at Schulyer Colfax's laboratory within the hour.

Dominic was quite eager to see the laboratory. Colfax was famous for magical devices, but Dominic had only seen the obscurer the Mage Guardians used for shielding conversations from eavesdropping.

"Will you need to take down the wards?" he asked.

Ardhuin shook her head. "There should be very little active magic present, save his devices. It has been over two years since his death."

"What happened? Was Denais involved?"

"I suppose it is possible," Ardhuin said dubiously, "but Schulyer Colfax was even older than my great-uncle. He had a stroke, and for some reason had not named an heir himself. Perhaps he thought there was no further need for the Mage Guardians."

"Or perhaps he was prevented," Dominic mused, feeling suddenly cold. "It would not take much for a *geas* to simply prevent him from doing so, would it? Denais might well feel old age would take care of the rest."

Ardhuin was silent, a small frown on her face. "Perhaps, but...I would think that Colfax, having fought in the Mage War, would be watchful for any such attack."

The laboratory was located on the grounds of a fortress, one of the few remaining *Ringschluess* that had survived the Mage War. It was a long, single-story brick building with few architectural ornaments besides a pair of large, arched windows near the entrance. A coach with a crest indicating royal business was waiting outside when they arrived.

"Hmm. I suppose they will object to your presence here either as a reporter or my wife," Dominic observed. "How shall we manage this with discretion?"

"I will follow, and reveal myself inside." Ardhuin gathered a thick cloud of avoidance and shadow about herself.

Dominic jumped down from the carriage. Jan was standing outside, looking bright-eyed and curious. "*Ach*, it is my good friend Kermarec! I am hearing there was involvement from Bretagne in this."

"Shall we go inside? Your colleague will be here presently," Dominic said. The official in the coach looked disapproving but said nothing. Dominic opened the door for Jan, leaving it open long enough for the dark cloud of Ardhuin to enter as well.

Inside was a dusty foyer, a few desks and chairs, and a single large metal door worked with a sigil Dominic vaguely recalled. As Ardhuin had predicted, there were only traces of magic visible from what must have been powerful wards.

"You are involved with these Guardians, I take it," Jan observed, as he first tested the door, then opened it carefully.

"Rather intimately," Dominic said wryly. "I am afraid there is a considerable need for secrecy, unfortunately. We apologize for the necessary deception."

Now inside the workroom, Jan turned to give him a quizzical look. His eyes widened as Ardhuin dropped the cloud of shadow, and then he gaped when her illusion disappeared as well.

"Hyeer...*Vrauwe*...?"

"I am Ardhuin Kermarec, Mage Guardian of Bretagne. My great-uncle, Yves Morlais, was the mage Oron and Mage Guardian before me. Thank you for accepting this post. We are in grave need of your help."

Jan continued to stare at her in stunned silence. He eventually managed to say, "Help? From *me*? And you were Mr. Talbot? And Kermarec, so you are also..." He glanced at Dominic.

"My wife, yes."

"Please excuse, but there is much to think on all at once." Jan looked about blindly, found a chair, and sat down with a thump. "First I learn of these Mage Guardians and that I am invited to join, and then Vrauwe Kermarec is one of these most powerful mages...and I am thought to be of such caliber?"

Ardhuin smiled, and Dominic was amused to see how Jan Kreuwel immediately sat up straight again.

"Yes, you are. I wish we could have done this differently, but matters are desperate. We are the only ones, and because I am...what I am, the other governments resist letting me advise them in selecting their own Mage Guardians. So you see, you are very much needed at present."

Jan gave her a look of alarm. "Only myself, and you? Of...how many? What happened that replacements are needed everywhere?"

Ardhuin glanced about the workroom. "We should probably not discuss this without wards. Do you wish to set up your permanent wards now, or shall we use only defensive wards for the moment?"

Dominic had been examining the workroom too, wondering if any of the devices were powerful enough to interfere with casting wards, and a flash of power caught his eye. "One moment. What is that?"

It looked like a spiderweb of power, just a few strands, but enough to remind him of the webs that had been set near Peran by Denais's agents. One end was anchored to a rafter above the center of the room, and the other...

The other end was shielded in shadow, flickering with magic, and held an oblong shape. The shape of a bullet.

"Dominic? What is wrong?" Ardhuin said, sounding alarmed.

"Don't cast any wards," he gasped. "There's a trap. Just like the king's assassination..." he pointed at the shadowed bullet. "It is aimed at whatever cuts the thread of power."

Ardhuin's face had gone white. "So whoever tried to use this laboratory again would be killed."

With Jan's assistance, Ardhuin set up powerful shields for each of them, then cast a stasis field around the bullet. While the stasis field cut the thread triggering the trap, it also prevented the bullet from going anywhere.

"You were not so surprised that such a thing would be here," Jan said grimly.

Ardhuin shook her head and cast a powerful defensive ward around them. "Let me tell you about Denais."

Dominic had feared Jan's initial enthusiasm would vanish in the flood of bad news. While it was plain he was appalled at the danger, he grew more determined the more Ardhuin explained.

"This is a bad business," Jan said at last. "There is much work to do, and you have been doing it all, hey? No more!" He nodded emphatically.

In the next several hours Dominic carefully scanned the entire workroom, pointing out every shred of remaining magic. They found two more traps and several devices, which Dominic piled on a table in the foyer. Ardhuin helped Jan set up his permanent wards and told him what was known about Denais.

"We stopped him in Preusa, but I am certain he had plots elsewhere," she concluded.

"And here, I think," Dominic added. "Those traps are fresh. Certainly more recent than two years, correct? Denais must have planned for the eventuality that someone would be named Mage Guardian here and would naturally come to this workshop to begin work."

"Yes, and this is not a place many would need to come to," Jan agreed. "In Preusa there were those inside the government that plotted with Denais, no? I fear this may also have happened here."

Dominic took out his watch, grimacing at the time. "It is late. We should meet here tomorrow for the two of you to continue. Besides, I want to examine those devices more closely," he added.

"Please take what you wish," Jan invited him. "I am very much in your debt and will have little leisure for such things for some time," he added, shaking his head.

Dominic accepted his offer with alacrity, selecting the three that most intrigued him, and with Ardhuin shielding herself in shadow again, they took their leave of Jan Kreuwel.

"I hope he does not regret his decision." Ardhuin yawned sleepily in the carriage.

"We did give him much to think about," Dominic agreed ruefully. "I think he will rally in time. He appears to welcome a challenge."

"Then he should be ecstatic," Ardhuin said dryly. "Oh well, we did what the Queen asked of us. And Jan is much more diplomatic than I am. I can see him doing well finding the rest of the Mage Guardians, and then it will be easier for everybody. And we will make sure everyone understands the importance of naming an heir as soon as practicable."

"I agree completely." Dominic put his arm around her waist and kissed her. "And you should set an example, speaking of heirs..."

"There is no guarantee any of our children would have talent." Ardhuin's cheeks grew red. "And an heir would need to be able to replace me immediately. Even I did not show any ability until I was seven."

"Very well, a temporary stopgap is permissible," Dominic conceded, "but I am quite willing to make several attempts to find you a worthy successor—while hoping they will have many years before they will be at all required."

"Such noble self-sacrifice," Ardhuin teased. "I had thought your experiences with young children had not been tranquil, or had you forgotten? Didn't some of your students set their house on fire?"

"Only a carpet. And that was before I made the acquaintance of an expert in magical wards," Dominic pointed out. "All you have to do is stay ahead of their ability to *remove* wards, and the difficulty is trivial!"

The carriage pulled up before the hotel, and they wearily got out and made their way inside. The clerk at the desk looked up as they entered, looking worried.

"Madame, Monsieur...there is an urgent telegram for you."

Dominic took the flimsy envelope and opened it, puzzled.

"Who would send a message here? The ambassador knew where we had gone..."

The telegram was uncoded, and from Bretagne. From Baranton. Please return soonest possbl incident related previous employer enemies H. Lebonne.

"It's from Henri," Dominic managed. "*Now* what has happened?"

CHAPTER 5

Denais's hideout in Anatoli had been a bandit's lair a hundred years ago, and before that some sort of outpost during the furthest extent of the Graeco-Roman Empire. Some of the carved marble from that period showed up incongruously in the stone walls and outbuildings. The main stronghold was built in the midst of a collection of reddish rock pillars that jutted up from the top of a hill, making use of them as walls. This made it quite secure, but also rather stuffy. Gutrune von Kitren stepped outside the stone building she had been searching for a breath of fresh air and considered what to do next.

Denais, or more likely his *geas*-enslaved people, had cleared out anything of use from the hideout before escaping. A few scraps of paper had been found, but none had any new information. The Preusan military magicians were finished with their search, and the first group had already left to make the long journey home. Gutrune was making one last attempt to find some clue as to where Denais had gone. She did not want her first foreign mission to be a failure.

There were signs that many people had lived here recently. The hideout itself was not large, but surrounded by a fairly extensive stone wall. Within the wall were a barn, a handful of small houses, and a burnt wreck that had shown signs of magic and had probably been a laboratory of some kind.

She went to the barn. The stalls were ordered and clean. She wondered if they had all been used, and walked into each in turn. Other than the fact that they had been used, it was impossible to tell how recently. Two of the stalls had grain still in the feed boxes. Quite a lot of grain, actually, and it had been left long enough to have gone moldy. Why had it been wasted like that? Why had so much been left? At a guess, it represented at least three days worth for a working horse.

Gutrune left the barn and walked back up the path to the hideout. Looking up, she saw remnants of a roof on the top of one of the rock pillars. A lookout post? It would give her a view of the terrain, and perhaps some ideas.

After a search she found the narrow, wooden steps to the lookout. In some places it was simply a series of ladders, none too sturdy, but she made it to the top eventually, glad she had decided to wear her hunting costume.

which allowed such activity. The view was breathtaking, looking down to a series of forested hills and a narrow valley with cleared fields and grazing cattle. She could see foot trails outside the walls, and the main road that led to the tiny village a few miles away.

A flash in the nearby forest suddenly caught her eye. Gutrune did not move her head to look, instead leaning on the parapet of the lookout as if she were still admiring the view of the valley. The flash had come from the top of the next ridge, an ideal location for anyone wanting to keep watch on the hideout. If she recalled correctly, there were more rock outcroppings on the other side of that hill. She yawned ostentatiously and turned to go down, but once she was no longer in sight descended as quickly as she could.

One of the smaller buildings had been set aside for her personal use. She entered, relieved that Stoller was nowhere in sight, and quickly gathered her game bag, a candle, matches, and her triple-barreled rifle. After double-checking the ammunition in her bag and taking another look around for Stoller, she headed for the gate at a quick walk.

She had argued vehemently with Heinrich about Stoller, but Heinrich had insisted, to the point of refusing the post, that the former soldier go with her. And Stoller's understanding of his instructions was he went *everywhere* with her.

"Going hunting, miss?"

Gutrune stopped, closing her eyes briefly and taking a deep breath.

"Yes, Stoller. There is no need for you to accompany me."

He stepped away from the wall where he had been standing. "Your pardon, miss, but you won't want to be carrying all the game you're bound to find in the hour before sunset," he said with a perfectly straight face.

"I can't wait for you. As you say, there is little time. I only intend to track and observe."

"Which is why you are carrying the triple, naturally. I understand some of the sheep around here can be vicious."

He fell in one step behind her as she walked on. Gutrune sighed. "I take it as a precaution, since despite what you and my brother think, I do consider my own safety. The prey I track is human."

"What, have you found one of the criminals? Why not call in the soldiers?"

"Because I want to know where he will go. I believe someone is keeping this place under observation," she told Stoller. "I saw a flash from field glasses on the ridge to the southeast."

"Very good, miss. What's the plan?"

"We find a good watch point and wait for twilight."

She had her own field glasses, and once they were in the woods made sure that she had a good view of the slope of the hill but no chance of reflected sunlight. A small, rutted track that in this area qualified as a road was a few yards away. While they waited, she told Stoller about the grain.

"You think they left in a hurry, perhaps?"

She shook her head. "That much grain? It looks like the servants had been under orders to feed the horses, and did so even when those two horses had left but the others had not. I think this watcher was in place before the rest of Denais's people abandoned the outpost."

Light was fading fast. It was not a night with a full moon, and Gutrune began to fear she would not be able to see anything when the watcher did come in view. But her eyes adapted, and before all light had left the sky she saw a human figure move furtively out of the forest, running for the rocky outcroppings on the slope.

She tapped Stoller on the shoulder and got silently to her feet. She needed to keep the watcher in view but not alert him with any noise. She walked quickly but made sure to slowly shift her weight in each step.

Then she saw a thin beam of light. A lantern? Now she did not need to go as fast, and it indicated the watcher was not suspicious he was being followed. She could see light reflected by rock walls now. He was going into a cave of some kind. She glanced about, noting as many landmarks as she could in the twilight, and sank down behind some bushes.

They waited silently for some time. Listening closely, she heard a horse nicker and she smiled. One of the missing two horses? She stood up, gripping Stoller's arm to indicate he should stay, and quietly moved up to the cave entrance. Enough of the lamplight shone for her to see her way, and she cautiously peered around a boulder where the light was coming from.

The cave was large. Large enough for a cart, two horses, and several barrels and boxes stored along the walls. A man was loading boxes in the back of the cart, which was already nearly full. He had a long mustache like the locals had, but he looked foreign.

As she watched, she noticed something odd. The man would load some boxes, freeze for a moment, shudder, and then unload a box and take it to a different part of the cave. This happened several times. All the boxes that were removed appeared to have a splash of white paint somewhere on the surface. Soon he was finished and was lashing an oilcloth cover over the boxes and taking the nosebags off the horses.

Gutrune moved back as quickly as she could without being detected.

"He's leaving now," she whispered to Stoller. "I need you to go find us some horses and alert the few remaining military magicians to come here."

"But they won't be able to make it in time!"

She shook her head. "No, I want him to leave thinking he was undetected. Eventually he will have to go to Denais or one of his subordinates to report. He's leaving some boxes behind, though, and I want them searched. Go, and if I am not here when you return, I will be following the cart."

Stoller grimaced, unhappy, but finally nodded his head and ran for the bandit fort.

The buildings deep in the mercantile section of Baerlen were tall enough to block most of the faint twilight, creating deep shadows. Markus walked down the rough, cobbled road, glancing from the corners of his eyes to make sure he was not being followed. The short summer nights were not, Markus reflected, conducive to skulking around. He had taken a cab to an innocuous location a few streets over, but now he was on foot and surrounded by avoidance magic. Hopefully that would be enough.

The street was deserted, and his destination, a familiar warehouse, showed no lights or other signs of occupation. Markus drifted up to the small side door and tapped lightly.

"Who?" whispered a harsh voice.

"Markus." The door opened into darkness. Markus stepped inside, then dropped the avoidance spell when the door had shut again.

He heard the scrape of metal, and a slim beam of light shone from a shuttered lantern. Heinrich lifted it up and looked at him. His face was hollowed by the shadows, and something more. "Come with me."

Markus followed him to a metal cage lift, which Heinrich pulled up, past two floors and into a closed room.

"Your message was quite mysterious," he said lightly, trying to figure out what was going on. "A fortunate thing I had been here before, or I doubt I would have found it in the dark."

"That was intentional." Heinrich pulled a lever with a jerk. "I don't want any of my men to hear this."

Ah. Like that, was it?

"I got a message from Gutrune. At least, I think it is from her...only she and Stoller know the code for the secret telegraph line. I also got a message from Stoller, saying he had been unable to find her. So they can't be together. I am...concerned she may be in danger."

Yes, this was bad. But first things first. Any help they could provide would take days if not weeks to reach her, but Stoller was presumably much closer. "May I see this message? If we can be reasonably certain it is not faked, we can simply direct Stoller to that location."

Heinrich grimaced. "That's just it—there is no location in her message. I could try tracing it, but that would be noticed immediately." He rummaged through the papers on the desk. "Here. This is the decoded message."

Heinzen, Korda recently in Anatoli. Spy watching base heading Parsia. Unable to follow. Watching cargo left behind. Alert Ynde, Cathan agents watch for Aeropan male 5'9" slender build dark mustache shipping several large wood crates. Track, do not intercept.

"Well?"

Markus put the slip of paper down, thinking furiously. "Do you have an atlas?"

Heinrich did not, but he did have a map of the region surrounding Anatoli. Markus frowned, trying to remember where the countries mentioned in the message were located.

"We know she was here with Stoller." He pointed to the location on the map. "The message mentions Parsia, and that she can't follow. Knowing her resourcefulness, that indicates to me the method of transportation is such she cannot hide or stow away or follow without being seen. That leaves," he tapped another location, "here. Somewhere on the coast of the Turjik Sea. Most likely the spy is using a small boat."

"So you think she did send the message." The lines of strain on Heinrich's face eased marginally.

Markus nodded. "Those names—one is a missing student from Ostri, the other is the baron's assistant, also missing. I know she saw the report I sent, asking if anyone had seen them. It is not general knowledge they are missing, or would have any reason to be in Anatoli. The enemy, certainly, would not want to encourage us to make the connection."

Heinrich shifted in his chair, fingering some of the papers on the desk. "She'll do something reckless without Stoller there to stop her. How can we find her if she decides to follow anyway?"

"Fräulein von Kitren has more sense than you give her credit for," Markus observed, raising an eyebrow. "She *did* say she was unable to follow, after all."

"How can you be so calm about it?" Heinrich slammed his hand down. "Can you think of nothing useful to help her?"

"Tell Stoller to look for her at the main port," Markus said.

"What makes you think she would stay? Yes, yes, she won't follow, I agree. But if she were to leave, to return to Preusa..."

Markus shook his head. "Firstly, she will most likely wait and watch to be certain of the boat the remaining cargo leaves on, and its heading. Then attempt to learn as much as possible of the contacts made there. Finally, wait for someone to show up to hand off her intelligence to. She makes no mention of leaving. You do have a means of contacting Stoller, yes? Give him the information to pass on to her."

"Is there nothing else we can do to help her?" Heinrich's voice was low and weary. "I fear that if I report this I will be dismissed as merely having a personal concern. But it is not just...my sister. If she is correct and this is a spy for Denais, going to report, it's the only lead we have on him."

"Ah, the simple military mind at work." Markus smiled at the irritation that flashed in Heinrich's face. "Please do not take offense. You are being *far* too direct and logical about this. The first rule for getting that bunch of old sofa cushions to do what you want is to make them think it was all their idea. And in my case, that I don't want to do it. My suggestion is this: find a plausible excuse to send me to the esteemed Mage Guardian of Bretagne, Madame Kermarec. Say there is...something she needs to see in person. The crucial thing is to include 'to offer any needed assistance' in my orders. She and your sister are good friends, you know. I am sure that once I explain matters, she will see the need for me to go to Anatoli and find Fräulein von Kitren, and what can I do but agree?" He grinned and had the satisfaction of seeing Heinrich sigh and shake his head, a small smile beginning to emerge.

"There are times when I think my sister chose the easier task. I should show you the rest of Stoller's message. They found some hidden equipment and he is having it sent back here. I expect it should arrive in a few days. No doubt something in it will merit the attention of the Mage Guardian."

"Excellent! You may also wish to make use of the fact that Herr von Koller hates Madame Kermarec even more than he hates me, if you can imagine. A delicate hint that she is considering coming to Baerlen to help would do the trick, and to finish it off mention I am relieved to be back and have no wish to leave again. But we will need a better place to meet and plan, if possible. I have no plausible reason for constantly visiting warehouses."

Heinrich nodded but kept staring at the map. "Yes, I see. I will make arrangements. I confess, though, I find it curious you are so willing to take this burden on yourself. I had not expected this level of assistance...and I must ask myself your reason." He looked up at Markus without expression.

Markus winced internally and steeled himself to show only mild exasperation. Simple military mind, eh? "Please don't tell me you suspect I have a personal interest in Madame Kermarec. I barely managed to convince her now-husband I had no untoward intentions, and it will be most unhelpful if you stir that hornet's nest again. Although she is, of course, quite worthy of admiration," he added with a grin.

Heinrich, unfortunately, was not distracted. "Your pardon, but I could not help but notice your eagerness to assist...personally."

Yes, sometimes he wondered himself. Yet, there it was. That didn't mean he felt an obligation to explain himself to a suspicious brother. He picked up Gutrune's message again and stared at it for a moment before dropping it back down on the litter of papers on the desk with a sigh. "Besides facing Denais myself, and knowing how dangerous he is," Markus gestured at the slash of white in his hair, "we have fought him together. The

Kermarecs, your sister, and I. There is a bond. I will always be willing to assist any of them at need."

The carriage had not even completed the turn in front of the house before the front door opened and Henri came down the steps at what was, for him, a quick pace.

"All seems well with him, at any rate," Ardhuin murmured. "If a trifle agitated."

"The wards are still strong too," Dominic said, sticking his head out the carriage door. "Let's find out what happened, shall we?"

Henri was already busy apologizing. "We didn't know what to do, madame, and even if we could bring him inside, it didn't seem wise, with him being a foreigner and all."

"Perhaps you should start at the beginning," Dominic interrupted. "Who is this foreigner? What has he done? Michel was worried enough to speak two entire sentences, but he was thin on detail."

Henri straightened and visibly composed himself. "He came to the house asking for the old master, sir. I'm afraid I gave him quite a shock when I told him Magister Morlais was dead. He seemed quite horrified. If I had known he was so ill...then when I suggested he could leave a message, he gave me such a desperate look—asked who now spoke for Oron, and collapsed! He had looked like an ordinary gentleman at first, but I suppose he must have been using magic because now he looks like a Cathan, and I can't understand a word he says."

"He's still alive?" Ardhuin asked, gathering up her skirts to descend from the carriage. Illusion, which meant a magician. Looking for her great-uncle, and expecting to find him here. But who would know of Oron and *not* know he had been dead for over a year?

"Yes, madame. We have him in the cottage, which seemed best until you could return and form your own opinion. Estelle has been caring for him and says his fever has broken, although he is still quite weak."

Ardhuin exchanged glances with Dominic. He was frowning.

"Very odd...I suppose we should take a look at him. When did he show up, Henri?"

"Five days ago, sir."

"Well, I suppose it might be connected to our adventures in the Low Countries, but it seems unlikely," Dominic mused, offering his arm to Ardhuin as they walked toward the old gardener's cottage.

Ardhuin stifled a chuckle. "Sending a feverish Cathan in disguise does not sound like something irritated *mijneers* would do for revenge, but really, I never could figure out their process of reasoning."

The cottage looked much tidier than it had during Dominic's residence.

Michel, the former carter, and his sister, Amay, lived there now. They were still wary of the magic of Peran but strangely willing to work there, and they had painted and planted flowers and generally made the cottage look quite charming.

"I hope Michel is not too disturbed by all this," Ardhuin remarked, reminded of their coachman's aversion.

"Well he was rather chatty, for him." Dominic knocked at the door. "But perhaps he just wants his house back."

Estelle, their housekeeper, was inside. She seemed quite relieved to see them.

"The poor lad has something troubling him. I do hope you can help," she said. "And he has *not* been eating well. It's no wonder he fell ill." She gave a disapproving sniff.

"Is he infectious?" Dominic looked alarmed.

Estelle shook her head. "Worn to the bone, and his foreign clothes, too." She led the way back to the tiny bedroom.

There was hardly room for three extra people, or even the bed. Ardhuin stood in the doorway and studied their unusual visitor. He was asleep, but restlessly. He had heavy black hair, ragged and unevenly cut, and skin a warm tea brown. From what she could see, he was slender in build and not very tall either. His face was gaunt.

Dominic had been staring at the man, and when he looked at her he gave a slight shake of his head. No *geas*.

"Do you recognize him?"

Ardhuin shook her head. "Of course, if he had been in disguise earlier..."

The man shifted on the bed, groaning. His eyes flickered, then blinked open, staring at her, then at Dominic. They held no sign of recognition.

Dominic picked up the glass of water beside the bed and helped him drink. "Are you feeling better? Can you talk with us?"

"Dono? Albanais?" The man's voice was rough, and he spoke with a strong, choppy accent.

"Do you understand Alban?" Ardhuin said in that language. His eyes brightened.

"Yes, miss. I have more words."

"What is your name?" Dominic asked. His Alban was rusty, but he could manage.

"Sonam, sir."

"Just Sonam?"

Sonam nodded.

"I am told you came seeking my great-uncle. That you knew both of his names. What did you wish with him?"

Sonam gave her a bleak look. "My teacher told me to go to this one,

Yves Morlais. But he is gone. I do not know what to do.”

“Your teacher. A magician?” Dominic asked. Sonam nodded, warily. “What is his name?”

“Forgive. I am not to say, there is danger.” Now Sonam looked frightened. “The servant said, Oron’s house now belongs to his female relative. Are you this one?” he asked, glancing at Ardhuin. “Do you know who speaks for Oron?”

Ardhuin hesitated. It was risky to reveal too much when she knew nothing about Sonam or who had sent him. The *geas* was not the only way to ensure obedient service, and it was possible Denais knew she would watch for it and use something else. “Yes, I know. But there are powerful enemies who would also like to know. How do I know you have not been sent by them?”

Sonam nodded. “Yes, very bad enemy. So my teacher tells me, not to say his name unless I know. My teacher gives me this to show to magicians.” He glanced at Dominic.

“Yes, please show me.”

Sonam reached inside his shabby, odd-looking jacket and took out a cloth drawstring bag. He tugged on the opening until the bag was completely open, a circle of cloth held flat on his hands. In the center was a dull silver metal box with heavy inscribed decorations. A dark blue stone, polished but asymmetrical, was mounted in the center. It did not appear to have hinges or any means to open it.

“Interesting. A stasis field, but only around the top.”

Ardhuin inched her way into the room to stand behind Dominic, placing one hand on his shoulder. She got a shield ready in front of them both, then tightened her grip slightly as she removed the stasis field. The little box jumped, the lid coming free, and she leaned forward to see what was inside.

It was an animal skull, only a few inches long, delicate and strangely familiar. It had many sharp teeth, a long snout, and slanted eye sockets.

Dominic started. “It’s magic! The creature itself was magic? But how…there was some other creature you mentioned, that had magic,” he said, turning to look at Ardhuin. “That fossilized scale, from the expedition.”

“A dragon,” Ardhuin breathed. “But this is not a fossil. It is still bone. And so small!”

“Wait, wait.” Dominic put both hands up to his head. “I know I’ve heard something about this. Or read it. That book, *Drakon Atlantea*…no, wait. Dragons in Asea. Why is that familiar? Connected to Baerlen somehow.”

Then she remembered. MacCrimmon. He had gone to someplace called the Tian Shan to look for dragons, and they couldn’t find him.

Ardhuin squeezed Dominic's shoulder again and left the room. He followed her out.

"Did *MacCrimmon* send him?" he asked, his voice low, when she explained what she had guessed. "He's still alive?"

"MacCrimmon may have sent the box, but what if it was stolen? Sonam could still be an agent of Denais, trying to attack us. Did you notice anything else unusual about that box?"

Dominic shook his head. "The only magic was the stasis, now gone, and the traces of magic in the skull. Magic I don't recognize. Why would MacCrimmon want to contact your great-uncle specifically, instead of the Mage Guardians in general? Were they close friends? Why the secrecy?"

Ardhuin felt herself go cold. "Because for some reason he thought the others could not or would not help him. Perhaps he knew or suspected the others were dead."

Dominic was silent for a moment, his expression worried. "We still don't know for sure Sonam was sent by MacCrimmon. Even if he was, he won't answer questions except from Oron's heir, and I doubt he'll believe you are Oron's heir without a lot of proof."

"And if MacCrimmon didn't send him, we don't want him to know." Ardhuin sighed. "I wonder...can we use the Justice rose without causing suspicion?" And did it have any open blooms? She couldn't remember.

"I should think so. Even when I know what to look for, it isn't obvious. We can have Estelle bring in a bouquet, as if to brighten up the room, and return later."

The Justice rose had one bloom just beginning to open, fortunately. Ardhuin picked a few ordinary roses to surround it and they put Dominic's plan in action. While they waited, Ardhuin searched her great-uncle's papers to see if MacCrimmon had sent any letters, or other reason for him to want to speak to Oron, but found nothing. Dominic found the volume of *Drakon Atlantea* and skimmed it for hints.

When they returned, Sonam was awake and regarding them warily. He had returned the little box to its bag, which was resting on the table by the bed, next to a vase with the roses. Given the tiny room, the rose was quite close to Sonam. He would be unable to escape the magical effects with it so near.

Best to ask some questions he would be more willing to answer first. Ardhuin smiled at Sonam. "Do you know the name of the creature that came from? My father is a naturalist, but I have seen nothing like it."

"It is...I do not know the word in this language. My people call it *kai-ling*," Sonam said.

"Where are they found?" Dominic asked, engaged in trimming a lamp.

Sonam frowned, a puzzled expression in his eyes as he rubbed his throat. Good, the rose was working.

"You must have traveled far." Ardhuin sat in the chair so she could watch Sonam's reaction. "Did MacCrimmon send you?"

Sonam gasped and choked, clawing at his throat. His eyes went wide, staring at her as he struggled to breathe.

"You won't be able to lie," Dominic said. "You can be silent if you wish, but you can't lie. It's clear you recognize his name. Is he still alive?"

Sonam closed his eyes, swallowing hard. "Yes." Then, gathering strength, he stared at Dominic fiercely. "I will not say where he is. It is a hidden place. I will only tell the one who speaks for Oron. You can kill me, I will not speak!"

He really is alive. Ardhuin felt a sudden rush of relief. Yes, there was Jan, but now she knew there was another experienced Mage Guardian. Somewhere. Now she had to convince Sonam to trust them.

"I am sorry, but we needed to be sure. Those dangerous men that threaten your teacher are not the only ones. I am in danger too." She stood and invoked the *gloire*. Through the shimmering golden wall of magic, she met Sonam's startled, suddenly comprehending eyes. "I speak for Oron. What message does Alastair MacCrimmon send? Why has he sent you instead of coming himself?"

"He is very sick," Sonam whispered, closing his eyes as if in pain. "He built a powerful *namas*...magic wall around the valley, to protect it. He had no more strength left, and the enemy was still there. After the wall he used the magic...I do not remember the name. He lives but does not breathe. And then I hid him. He told me to come here, seek help. That Oron would hear the hidden words and come." He drew a deep, almost sobbing breath. "It took many months to travel here from the Sky-Holding Mountains. Now I am sick too. How will I return in time?"

Dominic raised his head, staring at Sonam. "Wait. Hidden words? Hidden where?"

"He said he had hidden words. I do not know. He said...he said Oron would remember the place." Sonam's expression grew more and more distressed, and he turned his head restlessly on the pillow. "Please. You must help him!"

Dominic stretched out a hand. "We will do our best. But without..."

Ardhuin drew in a breath. Even MacCrimmon could not send a message so far and leave it here, in Oron's house, nor could he expect Oron to go where he was just to find out what he wanted. But MacCrimmon *had* sent the little dragon skull. She picked it up. A magic creature would naturally have residual magic in its bones. Perhaps a trace more would be hard to detect. Her great-uncle, presumably, would already know of such a trick. He had not mentioned it to her—but she had Dominic.

She turned the skull over in her fingers. At the base of the skull was a hole where it had once connected to the spine.

"Do you see anything unusual there?"

Dominic peered at the base of the skull. "No, only the same—wait. A little bead, very bright. I don't recognize the spell, though. It's so small."

Brightness, to Dominic, meant power. What spell was both strong and small? That MacCrimmon would expect her great-uncle to know he would send?

Then she remembered. She'd thought it was just a parlor trick, something he had done to amuse her. A way of catching her words as she spoke them, putting them in a bubble, and then letting them go when she gave the signal. It had never failed to entertain her, all those years ago.

"Listen carefully. It will only work once." Ardhuin focused her power, giving it the slightest ringing pulse to break the bubble.

A weary, rough voice echoed from the dragon skull. "Yves. Sorry, but I'm calling in that favor now. I'll do what I can to keep the people here safe, but it won't last forever." The words were interrupted by a hacking cough. "And neither will I," the voice continued, sounding even weaker. "It's not just for them, though. It's Compact business. I don't dare say why, even in this message. You get here, you'll know. If this gets out, it will make Guedoc look like an apprentice. I'm counting on you, Yves. If you can't come yourself, for God's sake send another Guardian or all hell's going to break loose."

The little town on the Turjik Sea was named Baftu, and that was about all that Gutrune had been able to discover in the few days she had been there. The locals were poverty-stricken and sullen, rarely talking and when they did, their dialect was so thick her few words of the language were useless.

She had managed to find some of the baggy peasant women's clothing, including a large kerchief to hide her unusual hair. It was not a perfect disguise, but it did allow her to buy food in the tiny market without attracting too much attention. To prevent her pale eyes betraying her foreign origin, she kept them lowered or squinted.

A broken-down and abandoned shed, which apparently had previously housed goats, served as shelter. It also had a view of the local telegraph office, so she could see when the lone government official left for his very long luncheons or went home for the night. Then she could pick the crude lock on the back door and send her own messages. It was too dangerous to be seen in the telegraph office itself, especially before the spy and his gear had left the town. She could not be sure he did not have other confederates watching.

If Preusa sent the assistance she requested, she could blend in with the crowd and do more. At present, however, there was not much she could do. She'd give them a week more, then she would have to move on. Best to tell them that now.

A drizzle of rain fell on the muddy street outside. An hour passed with no sign of anyone, not even a trudging fisherman. The telegraph officer opened the door, grimaced at the rain, then stepped out and quickly locked the door with a heavy, old-fashioned iron key before hustling down the street for his lunch.

Good. He'd be late coming back, too, to avoid the rain, knowing there would be few customers waiting for his return. She waited a few more minutes to make sure the man would not return for something, then began to ease silently out of the collapsing shed. It was awkward breaking in every time she needed to use the telegraph, but easier than in the other smaller towns where she had needed to tap into the line itself and risk discovery.

A familiar-looking man appeared in the street, wearing Aeropan clothes and carrying a large satchel. He stood in front of the closed telegraph office and looked up and down the street. Gutrune drew in her breath. Stoller.

She put her fingers to her mouth and gave two short, sharp whistles. Stoller's head whipped around, and he quickly made his way to the shed.

"How did you find me? I was just going to send a message."

Stoller smiled. "This is the third town I've been to. Your brother gave me a list. Said, find the telegraph office and look around it. Are you well, miss?" His eyes widened momentarily when he edged into the shed, and he coughed.

"I think there were goats," Gutrune said. "Are they watching the ports as I asked?"

He shrugged. "They got the message, but they didn't tell me more than that. I brought some clothes for you, and money. I figured you might be needing them. Your brother said to tell you he's sending some people as soon as I confirm your location."

That might actually be good news. Stoller didn't have a codebook, so they would not send coded messages—and a "no" would not need to be coded.

"What did you do with the rest of my gear?" Gutrune asked. She still had the original load of ammunition she had taken with her to the cave, and the rifle hidden in a bundle a peasant woman might carry, but a pistol would be useful now.

"Left them at the last big train station, to be sent for. What's your plan, miss? Wait for reinforcements?"

Gutrune thought wistfully of the clean clothes in the satchel, but only for a moment. She had work to do, and now that Stoller was here, she could do it.

"The spy kept his gear in a building near the dock. He only took a few boxes with him, and maybe there will be other information there. It's guarded, so I'll need a distraction to get inside."

Stoller cast his eyes heavenward and gave a resigned sigh. "I'll arrange it, miss."

CHAPTER 6

Dominic opened the double seadragon doors to the library and went over to where Ardhuin was seated at the big desk. She was puzzling over a rough sketch, biting her lip in thought.

"Still working on the wards? I thought you cast new ones when we brought Sonam in."

She looked up, blinking at him. "Well, yes, but that is just temporary. MacCrimmon's message means we will have guests again soon, whether we like it or not, and Henri can't come get me every time he needs to let someone in. Estelle would like Amay to be able to come to work earlier than I like to get up, too." She smiled mischievously.

Dominic put an arm around her shoulders and kissed her cheek. "You mean before noon?"

"Court business tires me. Besides, you seemed quite content to stay yourself."

He affected a look of high dudgeon. "How could I leave you alone and defenseless?" Ardhuin laughed, and he grinned.

Henri entered the library carrying his tray. "Telegrams, madame."

"Your use of the plural disturbs me," murmured Dominic. "At this rate, we may as well simply pay the postboy to come by every hour."

Henri bowed. "I have already taken the liberty of tipping the lad a few guilders, but it was quite unnecessary. He appears delighted to have the frequent necessity of coming to the house."

"Truly? I hope the rumors about frogs haven't started up again," Dominic remarked.

"I couldn't say, sir." Henri bowed again and left.

"I'll help you decode them," said Dominic, pulling up a chair.

"Oh, thank you." Ardhuin sighed. "They are both rather long, but I suppose that is to be expected with Sonam's news. One from the Ministry of Magic, and one from Detection."

"I'll take the Detection one." Dominic reached for a blank sheet of foolscap and a pen. "I suppose as annoying as it is to have a station in Baranton, it would be even more awkward to wait days for a reply." Not that they would have been allowed to do that—the only real alternative would be for them to return to Rennes, and Ardhuin would dislike that exceedingly.

When both messages were legible, Dominic was relieved to see that the respective court ministries had stopped objecting to the invocation of the Compact and started providing useful information. That had taken two exchanges of telegrams. Sonam had been able to provide enough detail that they had a better idea of where MacCrimmon was and how long they had before the vital stasis on MacCrimmon wore off.

Dominic finished his decoding and handed the marked-up sheet to Ardhuin. "So, they are still discussing what to do. Any word from Jan?"

Ardhuin shook her head. "I asked the Ministry to alert him, but they do not mention doing so. I already took the precaution of sending him a letter under magical seal. It will take longer to get to him but is more secure. How is Sonam today?"

"Much better. Still fretting about the delay. He is right to worry—I don't know how he managed to get here so fast all by himself, and a large distance on foot. This valley of his is halfway around the world!"

Dominic had managed to find some useful maps rolled up and stuffed in an inlaid chest of drawers in the library, and they were now spread out on a large table. Bhuta, the country Sonam nominally came from, wasn't even depicted. From his description of his travels, however, it was far to the east of Aerope and north of Ynde, in the rugged foothills of a massive mountain range. Ynde was not completely mapped itself, except near the Trade Cities on the coast, and anything beyond Behng or Jikar involved a great deal of dotted lines and blank space.

"How on earth did MacCrimmon ever hear about it? I've never come across the name Bhuta, have you?" he asked.

"Actually, yes. I thought it was a city in a legend, though. I think it was my brother who mentioned it in a letter when he visited Naipon. He loves tales of hidden cities, buried treasure, and the like." Ardhuin shook her head with a smile. "He'd be quite envious to hear I had met a real Bhutanese."

"You know, there is something odd about Sonam. Did you notice he hardly blinked when he learned you were a mage?"

Ardhuin tilted her head, the pen in her hand forgotten. "You are right— it seemed a commonplace thing to him. Did my great-uncle perhaps tell Alastair MacCrimmon...but no, Sonam did not know to look for me in his place."

"Perhaps he will stay long enough to tell us more about his home before he returns there. I hope they come up with a plan soon to rescue MacCrimmon." Dominic shuffled the pile of telegrams that had accumulated. "His message sounded quite urgent. But I suppose one cannot expect rapid decisions from government ministries. It's unlikely we'll be getting any more messages tonight, at any rate. I think I will spend my time before dinner looking at the devices Jan gave me. Oh, that reminds me...the *infusion* of magic into an object. Is there any reason one could not infuse only a part of a spell?"

Ardhuin looked intrigued. "I imagine it would depend on the spell itself, but to what purpose?"

"Oh, say magefire. If the spell was in an object but not to the point where the light appears, and then the missing part of the spell in another infused object brought into contact...a nonmagical person could have a magical light at need. Or one of your illusions! Think how useful that could be." He waved his hands, getting more excited the more he thought about it.

Ardhuin caught his hands in her own, smiling at him. "All this from Schulyer Colfax's devices? He would be impressed."

Dominic nodded emphatically. "He did amazing things—but I think we can do even more. Come take a look. I still haven't figured out—"

One of the library doors opened slowly, and Sonam's dark head peered around the edge.

"Do you need anything?" Ardhuin asked. "Are you well enough to leave your bed?"

Sonam came into the library, a curious figure in bare feet and a dressing gown so large it wrapped around him twice and trailed behind him. "I hear your voices, and wish to know what is decided." He looked at them with some anxiety, and then his eyes went wide as he took in the richness of the library. He stared, a puzzled frown on his face, at the spiral staircase to the second level, with the seadragon curled around the central post.

Dominic sighed. "They have decided to make a decision, but nothing more at present. Please do not be distressed. We want Mr. MacCrimmon back and restored to health as much as you do. I am certain they will take action soon."

Sonam nodded politely, but Dominic could tell he was not reassured.

"He has made himself very sick, protecting the valley. He was ill before he did his great magic and it made him much worse. We wish him to be well again...but if you take him away, who will defend us from the evil strangers?" Sonam spoke softly, his eyes lowered.

"No doubt the rescuers will deal with them, too, to retrieve him safely," Dominic said, trying to sound confident. "But your valley appears to be quite remote—I wonder what these evil strangers want with you? And, now that I think about it, how did MacCrimmon find you in the first place?"

Sonam smiled. "My teacher seeks the ancestor to the *kai-ling*, the *maru otakan*. So he followed the magic, *na?* The magic is everywhere in the valley. He spoke with amazement of it, that people use it for everyday things. He said that in Aerope, only certain ones have magic. It is true, we do not always have it as strong as you do, but my teacher says it is only a matter of learning your ways."

"Everyone has magic where you come from? Even women?" Ardhuin asked, eyes wide with surprise. Sonam nodded.

Well, there was the explanation for his lack of surprise at Ardhuin's talent. Dominic was seized with a sudden wish to visit this strange, magical valley. What had made it so unusual?

In the distance, he heard the front doorbell. "What, *more* telegrams? I wonder if they decided what to do? The poor postboy must be getting weary by now."

Henri appeared in the doorway. "A messenger from Preusa," he announced.

Dominic exchanged an astonished glance with Ardhuin. "Now what?" he asked. "And why are they coming directly to you rather than going to Rennes?"

"Well, it can't be a messenger from von Koller, then." Ardhuin rubbed a hand over her forehead, wincing. "This is becoming tiresome. I really need to adjust the wards. It's probably just an announcement of their choice for Mage Guardian, though you would think a simple letter would do..."

"Let them in, and I'll go down and be polite," Dominic offered. Ardhuin smiled gratefully, and he saw the magic flow from her to the ward at the front door before she turned back to Sonam.

Dominic descended the big stairs quickly, eager to return and not miss any of Sonam's descriptions. Then he saw who was standing in the foyer, and he came to a sudden stop.

"What are *you* doing here?"

Markus Asgaya grinned at him. "Do try and contain your delight. I hope I do not arrive at an inconvenient time, but the matter is of some urgency."

Dominic narrowed his eyes. "Why didn't you give your name?"

"I wanted it to be a surprise," Markus replied, his expression bland but eyes twinkling.

Dominic folded his arms. "What do you want?"

The levity vanished from Markus's face. "Gutrune von Kitren has traced Denais's people—we believe to his new location—and she is in grave need of assistance."

"I am sorry to hear that, but we have our own difficulties at present. And doesn't Preusa have its own Mage Guardian by now? There must be someone else she can send."

"I was not clear. She is already there; she is asking for help to be sent to her." This was said with something of a snap. Then, with difficulty, "You may not be very fond of me, but surely you do not have a grudge against her?"

"No, of course not." Dominic hesitated, wondering how best to proceed. It was unsettling to see Markus, usually in full command of himself, unable to produce sardonic wit. It made it ever so slightly harder to be irritated with him. "Perhaps you were not informed...there has been a startling development in the last few days. One of the Mage Guardians is still alive—Alastair MacCrimmon. His student came all the way from Asea to beg for help to rescue him. Apparently he's in a bad way, and in danger. I want Denais finished off rather badly myself, but surely it would be better to have an experienced Mage Guardian to help with the endeavor? Besides, it is high time Preusa stops using my wife to run all their errands rather than taking up their share of the work."

He caught himself, feeling his face heat, and took a deep breath to calm down.

"MacCrimmon, alive?" Markus's eyes went wide. "That is wonderful news. But where is he?"

"North of Ynde, in the mountains. Someplace called Bhuta."

Markus shook his head. "I'm not familiar with the name."

"I can show you generally on a map..." Dominic caught sight of Henri hovering in the background and resigned himself to the inevitable. "Henri, please inform Estelle we will have another guest for dinner. And I suppose you think you'll be staying the night?"

Markus summoned up his usual grin. "I knew you couldn't bear to part with me so soon."

Ardhuin looked around the dinner table, amusing herself by imagining her mother's likely reaction to her strange guests. Sonam had joined them, looking awkward and uncomfortable in his conventional Aeropan attire. He formed an interesting contrast to Markus—for while they both had bronze skin and black hair, Markus was tall and angular while Sonam was small and wiry.

Since Sonam's Gaulan consisted of only a few words, conversation was primarily conducted in Alban with side discussions she translated for Markus or Dominic when their vocabulary ran out. Sonam ate hungrily, only slightly hampered by the unfamiliar utensils and menu, and abstained only from the wine.

"...so apparently this fellow was watching Denais's old headquarters in Anatoli to make sure everyone had left before running back to report, and to bring some bulkier items left behind. Fräulein Von Kitren discovered him as he was preparing to depart and took it upon herself to follow him." Markus leaned back in his chair and observed a drop of wine descend down the side of his glass.

"But that's what I don't understand," Ardhuin protested. "I thought she was fixed at the court. Why was she in Anatoli in the first place, and why is she tracking people all by herself there?"

Markus gestured widely, setting his glass down and shaking his head. "I can understand following the spy, that's too important to miss—but the rest, frankly, eludes me. And eludes her brother, who seems to be taking her place at court. In confidence," he added, speaking quickly in Gaulan, "he is the one who arranged for me to come here on official business. He is worried," he added, switching back to Alban.

"But all by herself? I can't imagine the King allowing that," Ardhuin protested.

"Well, there was that fellow...Stiller? No, Stoller. Family retainer of some kind. But he'd been sent to arrange delivery of some baggage they found, left behind by the spy. Which reminds me. They found something interesting when it got to Baerlen and they went through it. A notebook with sketches and designs. With the name Schulyer Colfax inscribed inside."

Dominic, who had been uncharacteristically silent throughout the meal, sat up at this. "Colfax's notebook? But that implies...we looked through his laboratory, but it would be hard to know what was missing. Besides, we were primarily looking for traps. They must have stolen the notebook when they set them!"

Markus frowned. "Traps?"

"Several. Very similar to the one used in Baerlen, for the bullet that nearly killed the King."

"But why would they go to the trouble of setting traps when Colfax was already dead?" Markus asked, looking perplexed.

"Perhaps Denais was making sure no one would take his place. It was only for magicians," Ardhuin added. "The traps were triggered by anyone casting wards."

"I wonder why they wanted the notebook," Dominic mused. "I wish I could take a look at it. It might explain some of the devices we found."

Markus grinned. "You are in luck. I brought it with me, and some other items they found. Official business, consulting with the Mage Guardian." He nodded at Ardhuin.

"Or you could continue on and leave them with Jan Kreuwel, who has taken Colfax's place," Dominic remarked. "You don't want him feeling left out, do you?"

"Much tidier to stay with the same Mage Guardian we started with, rather than switch midway," Markus said cheerfully. "Perhaps he would like to assist Sonam with rescuing Mr. MacCrimmon instead? So, where exactly *is* he, anyway? You made it sound like it was the ends of the earth."

"Sonam, can you show us more precisely on a map?" Ardhuin asked quickly. She wasn't sure why Markus was teasing Dominic, or even what he was teasing him about, but Dominic's expression was becoming more and more stormy. A change of scene, and perhaps topic of discussion, was advisable.

They repaired to the library after dinner. Sonam was willing but unable to assist, being, it transpired, not familiar with maps. While he puzzled over his route, Markus left his inspection of the library to come and observe.

"This is meaning a river, yes? There was a big river, to the salt water, and then I take a small boat to the trade city where I find the steamer," Sonam said.

"So where did you come to the river? Or did you follow it all the way from Bhuta?" Dominic asked, tapping the map.

"Oh, now. This is highly interesting." Markus examined the map more closely. "That is where Sonam comes from? Where MacCrimmon is trapped?" Sonam nodded. "Truly in the middle of nowhere, isn't it? I didn't know those mountains extended into Cathai from Ynde. Blast, the map ends right where I need it..." He rummaged through the other maps piled on the table, finally finding the one he was looking for. "Now, *here* is where Denais had his hideout in Anatoli, east of the Middle Sea, and somewhere on the coastline of *this* sea the spy took a boat heading north, we think, to somewhere in Parsia. Isn't that interesting? What are the odds we've got one destination instead of two?"

Dominic stared at the map, shock visible in his eyes. "My God. You are right. It could be a coincidence, however. Of course Denais would want to attack MacCrimmon, though I still don't see why he would go all that way for the purpose when..." his voice trailed off, and then he went pale. "Sonam's people. They all have magic."

Ardhuin suddenly understood, and her blood ran cold. "Oh no. Not that." She took a deep breath and tried to compose herself. "Sonam, you said there were attacks. What happened? Were people killed?"

"For a time, people would disappear. Sometimes we would find them dead later. But the killing stopped after a month I think."

"Did they have any injuries? How did they die?" Dominic leaned forward, looking grim.

Sonam lowered his eyes. "They were..." he drew a finger across his throat.

"And there was no blood."

Sonam snapped his head up, startled. "Yes, it is true. How did you know?"

Dominic rubbed his forearm with one hand. "I have seen it done before. Well, I think we know where Denais is."

"Perhaps, but it is possible it has only been done by those Denais has trained. We are still missing the baron's students."

Dominic raised a skeptical eyebrow. "Denais would not share the knowledge of extracting power with anyone. He likes to keep such things to himself, I think."

"Ah, but the *geas* is an effective way to prevent lapses in loyalty, and he has never been shy about using it. The baron's servants had them, and discovering that was the only thing that made the Ostrians listen to me." Markus rolled his eyes.

The library door opened and Henri stepped inside. "Shall I serve coffee here, madame?" Ardhuin nodded, and he left only to return shortly with the coffee service.

Dominic spread the maps out farther to consult both at once. "I suppose it would be good to know if Denais is actually there or just directing them." Then, noticing Markus indicating Henri in agitation, he made a dismissive gesture. "Don't you remember Henri? I can understand you not recognizing Estelle, since she was a statue the last time you saw her, but he was alive…oh, well, maybe he was unconscious when you showed up. Henri was once a prisoner of Denais and has several extremely well-founded grudges against him. If anything, he knows more about him than we do."

"Indeed, sir. And if I may…during my involuntary service, I was able to learn some of his habits which may be of use, if you are desirous of locating him. He is a very particular man with regard to his personal comfort. He would go to a great deal of trouble and expense to obtain a certain kind of tea he referred to as Silver Pearl, not commonly found in Aerope. I can furnish you with a description if you wish, as well as some other items he was known to favor." He had the sternest, hardest expression on his face Ardhuin had ever seen.

"Thank you, Henri. That would be very helpful," she managed to say.

Markus frowned at the maps. "That kind of intelligence is quite important, but it is equally important Denais does not obtain the same information about us. Just looking at this area tells me a group of Aeropans is bound to attract notice, and the closer they get, the more noticeable they will be. It's one thing to go to a port city, but what excuse would cover wanting to travel to these remote hinterlands?"

Dominic looked up with an expression of delighted surprise. "I know! Expeditions! Scientific expeditions. They travel everywhere. But how are we going to find one going the right way?"

Markus shook his head, smiling. "Don't think so modestly. You are involved in government subterfuge now, and the larger the better. We merely need to concoct a sufficiently convincing fake expedition and persuade a well-known explorer to support the deception. We already have a native guide." He gave a graceful bow to Sonam. "Our respective governments can provide funds and transportation, I expect, but where can we find someone both already known for such expeditions and willing to assist us? Discreetly?"

Dominic rubbed his chin, staring off into the shadows of the library. "I think I know the man to ask," he said. "My publisher. The editor of *The Family Museum*. I shall write him immediately."

Ardhuin frowned. It was a neat and tidy solution, but why did she feel it was not enough? Not *fast* enough. Because...because Alastair MacCrimmon had not sounded merely worried, but panicked. An experienced, senior Mage Guardian was frightened by what he had found.

Dominic was looking at her with concern. "You do not approve?"

"I think perhaps we should go to your publisher in person. Now," she said slowly. "And visit the palace as well. I have the feeling we are still in ignorance of the true peril. As unpleasant as the essence extraction is, it did not give Denais limitless power. It did not take the massed magical armies of Aerope to defeat him in Baerlen. This must be something far more dangerous. I fear...I fear we do not have much time."

CHAPTER 7

Everything was taking far too long. Denais gritted his teeth and forced all emotion away from his face. He had come too far to let impatience ruin his plans. It was necessary for the *anban*, the government official in charge of travel documents here, to think him just another Aeropan merchant. He could not simply kill the man, for another would eventually take his place—and besides, he wanted the *anban*'s active assistance. Using compulsion was too dangerous here. His sources indicated that the Cathan court magicians had a rudimentary method of detecting *geasi*, and higher government officials paid quarterly visits. He could not be sure a magician would not accompany them.

He wrinkled his nose as a mild breeze brought dust and the scent of human sweat. A little, wiry man grasped the shafts of the two-wheeled carriage and drew it as if he were a horse, but not as fast. There were no Aeropan-style carriages here, and even if there were, it would draw too much attention. No, this is how a merchant would travel, so he would do the same.

The man in a threadbare black cassock seated next to him in the carriage glanced at him now and then but said nothing. Denais had ordered him to be silent. He was there to translate and facilitate the business Denais needed to transact. Naturally, he required a *geas* to be at all trustworthy. In addition, he was the lone missionary in this district, evidently because he was in disfavor with his order. He would not be missed when it became necessary to dispose of him.

The *anban*'s compound was presumably more elegant than the rest of the town buildings, but Denais could perceive no difference save, perhaps, size. Everything was dusty, few green plants were in evidence, the servants in faded dark blue cotton. He got out of the carriage and walked up the steps to the main door, leaving the translator to pay the carriage man.

The cool interior was a welcome relief, and Denais noted some tolerable pieces of porcelain on display, but nothing truly splendid. Perhaps the *anban* had taste but lacked the income to indulge it. All the better for his plan.

A servant escorted him to a large room with a polished wood floor. Two cushions were placed before a low table, which was furnished with delicate eggshell teacups. Opposite the table was a dais, with a curious couch for the *anban.*

The servant spoke, and Denais turned to the translator.

"You may speak. Tell me what they say."

The translator, Frere Ignatius, cringed, nodding. "He says to kneel and seek the wisdom of the representative of the Throne of Heaven."

No. There were limits. "Tell him I am unable to kneel due to injury. Use whatever language is considered polite."

This did not go over well with the *anban*, but two drum stools were brought to replace the cushions.

Denais brought out the small lacquered box from his coat pocket, laying it on the table before him. He lifted his chin at Ignatius, who began the usual obsequious blather that was expected when handing over a bribe. The translator had explained earlier how such matters were considered routine by government officials, especially out here on the border of the decaying empire. It was expected that they would supplement their income, not lavish and frequently not paid, with what was termed "squeeze." Denais did not care what excuses were used; it was enough that the institutional venality offered him the opportunity to get what he wanted.

"The *anban* wishes to know the business the foreign visitor desires guidance on." Ignatius winced at the expression in Denais's eyes. "This is how it is phrased, your lordship. It means nothing."

"Tell him I am planning trade routes to the Cathan Empire. Other Aeropans also wish to trade this way, but they are grasping thieves and will try to hide their trade and avoid the customs tax by using other cities, with tax officials not as wise as their superior. I have nothing to conceal, and so I will always bring my goods through this city, paying the full tax. I would be most appreciative to learn that the wise official will refuse travel documents to such lying foreigners, who may also conceal that they intend to trade. Word has spread that they may even use their own corrupting magic in this effort, which I know the wise official will detect and punish."

The little lacquered box was removed while Ignatius translated, and shortly thereafter a servant whispered in the *anban*'s ear. The *anban* showed more interest in what was said then. Denais smiled inwardly. Yes, he had guessed correctly. The official was corrupt, and the bribe had been sufficient. It had been a delicate balance between just enough—and so much the official would become too interested and want a percentage of the business.

As it was, the hint of "taxes" was enough. With a few more exchanges, Denais and the *anban* had reached an understanding. Another "gift," and exclusive tax right on the fictitious trade goods, and the *anban* would forbid all other foreign travel beyond the frontier. It was further hinted that the general posted to this region was favorably disposed to the *anban* and would enforce this edict strictly, even if the foreigners somehow evaded the border crossing. The *anban* gestured with a carved ivory rod, signaling the audience had ended.

It was not an ideal solution. The quickest route to Aerope was through Ynde, but the trade cities there were older and more law-abiding. The concessionary areas on the coast of the Cathan Empire were more accommodating, especially if you had money to convince the *tongs* to look the other way. Unfortunately, there were other unscrupulous Aeropans in these concessions that would notice, and try to take advantage of, any unusual traffic. By closing off the border, he could keep them from following and possibly discovering the valley.

And it would not do for anyone to learn of it. Especially not anyone who might mention it in the hearing of those familiar with the Mage Guardians. Denais clenched his hand about the handle of his walking stick. No, he would not make that mistake again. First he would gather power— and with access to the peculiar resources of the valley, he could do that. Then he would return to Aerope and finish the war on his own terms. This time, he would destroy *all* the Mage Guardians before they knew he was even in their midst.

He would leave nothing to chance. "One more thing." Ignatius gave him a look of pure fear, and the *anban* actually frowned. "I wish to warn of a certain very dangerous foreigner who may assist these thieves. A woman of demonic appearance, who is rumored to be a witch. Her evil is such it has turned her hair as red as burning coals."

The *anban* snapped a reply, which Ignatius translated as a contemptuous dismissal of the possible danger presented by a woman, and a foreigner to boot.

"Send to the official in charge of allowing entry passes and ask, and he will say the same," Denais replied, confident that his agents had already made the necessary arrangements with the government. "If you should see the red-haired foreign woman here, imprison her in iron immediately. And it would be best—for everyone—if she were never allowed to leave."

Early morning light filled Dominic's new workroom, now comfortably cluttered with tools and sketches for new contraptions. He had risen early after a troubled sleep and decided to spend a few moments with his latest device, which, if it worked as intended, would capture an image and make a small illusion of it. Seeing Schulyer Colfax's laboratory had given him many ideas, but this was one he thought he could actually make work.

Dominic placed the metal piece against the scale drawing he had made, checked the dimensions, and sighed. Everything looked correct, but the mechanism still wasn't sliding properly. One of the edges was rather sharp from being cut—perhaps it was catching somewhere. He rummaged for a file on the workbench to make adjustments.

Hermes, who had been sleeping in a tightly curled ball in a nearby armchair, raised his head and looked at the door. Moments later a knock sounded.

"Come in." He had been hoping for Sonam, but instead Markus entered.

"Ah, there you are. I will not keep you if you are busy..." Markus spared a puzzled glance at Hector the mouse, in his usual home in a hanging birdcage. "I only wish to inquire if the Lady Magus at all wishes me to ascertain how matters stand in Anatoli, but it appears she has not yet risen? Of course, if you knew her mind, and she does so desire, I will leave immediately."

"We did stay up quite late discussing matters," Dominic observed mildly. "The telegram has been sent. Until we learn what Her Majesty's government decides, there is not much action we can take. And they did not know our suspicions of Denais's current location until just now." Markus turned away, picking up and studying the devices from Colfax's lab, ranged on an empty bookshelf. He glanced out the window before resuming his restless wandering through the room. Dominic watched him for a moment before continuing. "Besides, it is much more likely that your government will send you with the expedition to Asea."

"But that's—" Markus broke off with a sharp gesture.

"By the by, didn't you say you had Colfax's notebook? I'd like to take a look at it. Those devices came from his laboratory."

"Of course." Markus left, returning with both a large folio notebook and a pasteboard box. "You may also be interested in these. They were found together, and some were illustrated in the notebook."

Dominic took the box. The devices inside were small, intricately made, and bright with magic. He could hardly see the individual fields to distinguish them. He shook his head, sighing. "I wish I could have met the man. He was an artist. I wonder, though, why Denais's people took these and not the others. How were they found, anyway?"

"Fräulein von Kitren found them," Markus said. "In the process of tracking the spy watching the old hideout."

Something in his voice drew Dominic's attention away from the fascinating pages of the notebook. It was as if he were speaking each word carefully. When Dominic looked up, Markus was staring out the window again, his face somber. Something was seriously wrong—and Dominic recalled that Markus had not been his usual self the previous day.

And then Dominic remembered something Ardhuin had said to him, in Baerlen, when he was uncertain of her affections—and, he had to admit, somewhat resentful of her friendship with Markus. *I think his interest lies elsewhere,* she had said, with a faint smile. In his relief at realizing Markus was not a rival he had forgotten the full implication of her words.

Ardhuin had never met Markus Asgaya before coming to Baerlen. How would she know whom he was interested in, unless it was someone she had met there? And who else had they met?

Gutrune von Kitren, now somewhere in Anatoli. Where Markus was quite evidently desperate to go.

Markus turned to face him, apparently feeling the weight of Dominic's gaze. His expression was devoid of amusement, and fatigue deepened the lines at the corners of his eyes. It would seem he had not slept any better than Dominic had, and for much the same reason. What would he feel, if Ardhuin were the one in danger in a remote place? Gutrune was more experienced at intrigue, but that only meant she was more likely to seek it out. Markus was being remarkably calm, given the circumstances.

The twinge of sympathy for Markus surprised and startled him. "Reflect, if you will, that if it is decided to send anyone to Sonam's valley, it would be easier to have Fräulein von Kitren meet them en route rather than track her from her last known location. I have the impression she is also impatient to take action."

"Very likely." Markus sighed. "But there is no certain information, and so much could go wrong..."

"Well, you aren't going be much use to her riding off in all directions," snapped Dominic. "Think about what *will* help her, whenever you get there. I shouldn't have to tell you this."

Markus dropped into an armchair, fortunately the one without Hermes, and sank his head into his hands. "It has become difficult to think rationally about this." He looked up. "And I am astonished you would be willing to give advice on...such a topic, given the sometimes hostile tenor of your opinion of me. Perhaps deserved." He held up one hand as if to forestall objection.

"Regardless of my opinion of you, Fräulein von Kitren is a dear friend of my wife's—and so naturally I share your concern about her safety and will do what I can to help in that matter. Moreover, if my guess as to the root cause of your concern is correct, and...the interest is mutual, any worries of your possible future intrigues would be greatly diminished," Dominic said dryly.

Markus managed a brief grin. "How true. Or in any event, short-lived. However, you anticipate more than I can at present. I am not entirely certain how to proceed, should the opportunity be provided."

Dominic raised a skeptical eyebrow at him. "You cannot be serious. With your address and charm?"

"The lady in question, I am sure you will agree, is not the sort to be persuaded by flattery and frequent bouquets," Markus said. "What you are kind enough to refer to as my address and charm may even be a handicap."

"She does indeed seem to be a lady of good sense and considerable intelligence," Dominic agreed blandly. "This will make your task more difficult, will it not? I would also advise a handsome pistol in lieu of flowers."

The expression in Markus's eyes grew speculative. "Would you? Advise me? You admit the task is somewhat daunting, given her...unconventional interests. You would have a much better insight into successful tactics to employ."

Dominic shook his head. "You cannot expect me to betray any confidences, even assuming she would—"

"No, no, of course not!" Markus waved a hand. "I merely meant that having spent time in her company, and of course from what your wife may have mentioned in idle conversation, you would have a better understanding of her mind. And while my happiness is of little interest to you, my...call it, close supervision, surely is?"

"Indeed. Although I remain to be convinced that the lady's happiness would be a result, I would not presume to contradict her. If you can convince her, my conscience will be clear."

"Your support, though tepid, is appreciated," Markus murmured. "Now, what service can I offer you in turn? We all know Denais has to be dealt with, and naturally I will do everything possible to aid Fräulein von Kitren, but..." he cocked his head, glancing at Dominic. "You spoke with some heat about other Mage Guardians. I doubt there is much I can do to influence such decisions, but perhaps I should ask why it troubles you so greatly. While Denais is a threat, and a serious one, he is the only one to appear in many years. Once he is dealt with, it is unlikely her services will be in such high demand."

Dominic cast about desperately for an acceptable excuse to convince him. "All this sudden travel is quite uncomfortable. It never ends. We are assuming Denais and MacCrimmon's threat are the same, but what if they are not? All that effort for nothing."

One dark eyebrow was raised, radiating skepticism. "This, from an enthusiast of expeditions? If I had to guess, I would say the two of you enjoy travel very much."

"Well, it's one thing to read about expeditions but quite another to constantly embark on them personally. I also enjoy quiet home life, and you are familiar with my wife's aversion to crowds. And...and my writing suffers from the distractions."

Markus's gaze sharpened. "Your writing. I've read it, you know. I don't recall many long scenes of tranquil domestic bliss, but quite a bit of adventure. Imagination can only do so much—you need to temper it with facts now and then. But I noticed your expression changed when you mentioned your home life. Are you still concerned? From my observations your wife is completely devoted to you, and you must admit I have some knowledge of these matters. Or is there something else amiss?"

"No!"

Hermes, awake and annoyed, jumped down from his armchair and stalked off with an irritated snap of his tail.

"You perhaps dislike your wife's involvement with the Mage Guardians, at any level? We do need her help, rather desperately at the moment. Only consider how difficult it would be to replace her, when we have not yet reached the full complement even now."

"It is an obligation she feels most strongly. I would not ask her to relinquish it. It is just..." *This is a highly improper conversation, but he is a rather improper person...and perhaps the only help I can find.* Dominic turned back to the workbench and stared down at his tools. "I would like to be assured...that others would be available and could respond to an immediate need. So that...should the occasion arise where...my wife might not be able to...for a period of some months, perhaps..." He closed his eyes, hoping the heat in his face would quickly fade.

"*Gott*, do you mean to say you have not yet..." Markus's tone of utter horror made him quickly turn his head. "Well, no wonder you are so irritable!"

"Oh, don't be an idiot! That is, the *only* thing my marriage lacks at present is the expectation of setting up a nursery. You will excuse me from going into detail, but magic is involved." A very, very improper conversation. What had he gotten himself into?

"Ah." Markus's eyes brightened with curiosity, then with a visible effort he cut short what he was about to say. "Very well. We both have extremely commendable goals of considerable delicacy and great importance. Shall we be allies, then?" He extended his hand.

Dominic glared at him, then reluctantly grasped the hand just long enough to shake it. "We are allies." If he didn't end up pushing Markus over a cliff, that is.

CHAPTER 8

The hired carriage deposited them outside the stone building housing the offices of *The Family Museum*, across the river from the palace in the center of Rennes. The day was quite warm and the sidewalks crowded, and Ardhuin was glad to enter the shade and quiet of the building.

Dominic looked about with considerable interest. "Strange that this should be the first time I visited after all my dealings with them, and when I do come it is on a matter unrelated to my writing."

"Unrelated to your current writing, perhaps, but I am sure the trip will provide many likely ideas to pursue." Ardhuin was surprised at how prosaic the offices were—worn carpeting, scratched wainscoting, and plain wooden doors with the names of various departments written on them. It did not seem to match the professional appearance of the magazine itself.

After Dominic introduced himself and mentioned his appointment to a desk clerk, they were escorted to an office with a door lettered "Editor." M. Sambin was a tall, stooped man with a full beard and a tendency to squint, but he leaped to his feet and greeted Dominic warmly before inviting them to be seated.

"So, I see your talents have received notice in high places! Now what's all this about getting an expedition together to go to Asea? You have writing to do, you know."

"You did get the telegram, then? I know it can't be a large affair on short notice, naturally, but I have a great interest in seeing the area for myself. I am sure it will generate many ideas."

Sambin leaned back in his swivel chair, fussing with his beard. "Yes, but why your own? Bové is already doing exploration there."

Ardhuin tightened her clasped hands on her reticule, feeling nervous. Why was he raising objections? What would they do if he turned them down?

Dominic persevered. "Now seemed like an ideal time, and since we are free to travel, why not? I don't want to wait for Bové's next trip; that could be years from now."

"No, no. Didn't you know? He's here now, to raise funds and get supplies."

"What?" Dominic's eyes widened. "Bové is in Bretagne?"

Sambin smiled, the corners of his eyes crinkling. "He's in Rennes. And here you are, with funding. I see no reason we cannot come to an agreement, eh? I sent him a note asking him to come."

The editor pulled out a folder from a pile on his desk and started discussing book plans with Dominic, who grew more and more worried in expression as the grandiose schedule grew.

"I am flattered by your opinion of my productivity, but I do require a few hours of rest every day," Dominic said, grinning.

Sambin chuckled and waved a hand. "Oh, very well. Still, if you can let us know what projects you *do* plan on completing, we can work on the cover and illustrations ahead of time. And it would be ideal to have something new for Solstice...but if you are determined to go off adventuring instead, what is to be done? Madame, can you not persuade him to delay?" He gestured to Ardhuin.

"Only think of what marvelous stories he will write on his return," Ardhuin replied soothingly. "After all, there will be other Solstices. And I am sure you will understand he requires new ideas from some source. Did he mention submerging mice in our fish pond? I shudder to think what he will come up with next."

Intrigued, Sambin demanded further details of the fish pond experiment and started scribbling notes for a proposed article, when a peremptory knock sounded on his door, followed by the entrance of a man with lowering brows and a frown on his hard-jawed face. His light brown hair was cut short and his skin weather-beaten and brown with sun.

"Sambin, the most damnable thing! That idiot *still* hasn't—" he started, looking at Ardhuin, and a faint flush appeared. "I beg your pardon, madame. I did not realize..."

"Ah, Bové, you got my message! Allow me to introduce Dominic Kermarec and his wife. He has brought to my attention a most interesting prospect—that may solve your funding issues."

Bové looked nonplussed for a moment, then his eyes cleared. "Ah, the story-writing fellow. You aren't planning an expedition to the center of the earth, are you? Because I'm a trifle tied up at the moment with this Asea matter, and I've never been partial to caves," he added with a small smile that just turned up the corners of his mouth.

"No, no, not that," Dominic stammered, shaking his hand eagerly. "Although I would like to ask your opinion...you must know I have read the accounts of your previous travels with great interest. In this case, it is your Asea expedition we would like to join. The Crown has most generously made available a fund of twenty thousand guilders to allow me to pursue my research there, and I had thought I would need to arrange the whole matter—but if we could join you, that would be infinitely preferable."

Bové's eyebrows shot up. "Twenty thousand? And you *want* to go to Asea? I see no reason we cannot come to an agreement, then. And there is no time to lose. Now, you said 'we.' You intend to take a party with you?"

"At least four. My wife and I, a translator, and a fellow...researcher." Dominic faltered, for Bové was shaking his head sadly.

"I am sorry, but this is no place for a lady."

Ardhuin sat up. "But...I have been on expeditions before. In Yunwiya and elsewhere. My father is the naturalist George Andrews, of Atlantea."

"Asea is much more dangerous. I cannot allow the risk, even for money I am in desperate need of," Bové said bluntly. "The risk of bandits is constant. Much of my expense is in hiring guards. I am also concerned for the stability of the Cathan government. It is ancient and riddled with corruption. There is much unrest that could flare up at any moment. If it gets much worse, I shall have to pull my own people out." He rubbed the back of his head, looking out the window as if he were expecting bandits to show up there too.

Ardhuin exchanged a worried glance with Dominic. She had to go to Asea; that was the whole point. Bové, however, was firm and probably correct in his refusal. He didn't know about her magic.

Her magic would have to do. Ardhuin ducked her head, hoping to look disappointed but acquiescent. "Perhaps your...friend, Mr. Talbot, would be willing to go in my place, then. I know I would feel better about your going if he did."

She saw the glint of understanding in his eyes. Then Dominic grimaced. "An awkward situation. It could be several months...before I return. Are you certain? I do not want you to be uncomfortable...on your own." She nodded. "Very well, I will ask him."

Bové was looking at them both, his gaze sharp. "One moment. I don't believe, Monsieur Kermarec, that you explained why you are so intent on this journey. Please don't attempt to convince me this is merely something to do with your stories. Not only are you suddenly willing to leave your charming young wife behind, *she* is permitting you to do so without complaint! What story is so urgent as that? And the Crown is bankrolling this little adventure, too. If your plans include any spying, I must beg you to reconsider. The Cathan officials are already suspicious of our expeditions. I won't risk our expedition for that. If the government needs information, it must get it another way."

"I have no interest in spying." Dominic sighed. "With your permission, Monsieur Sambin?" He took out one of the small devices from Colfax's laboratory, giving Ardhuin a meaningful glance. He fiddled with the device, then set it on the desk. As soon as he did so, Ardhuin released the obscurer spell. "Now we can talk without being overheard. For your ears only, gentlemen, yes, there is a different purpose to this trip. It is important to the security of Bretagne and even Aerope that I get to Bhuta, and speed is essential. I regret, but I cannot tell you more than this."

"Bhuta, eh?" Bové stared at him. "We had no plans to go that far."

Dominic shrugged. "Then we will have to continue on our own once you reach your destination. The researcher in my party is a magician skilled in defense."

Bové scowled, saying nothing.

"I will worry every day my husband and I are apart," Ardhuin said, putting a hand on Dominic's arm, "but I know why he must go—and yes, it is important enough for that sacrifice. Please do what you can to see he gets to Bhuta safely."

"Madame Kermarec, I will do whatever lies in my power to accomplish this. I only hope that someday he may write one of his stirring tales of adventure so I may know what all the fuss was about," he said, with an echo of his roguish grin. "Well, if the funds are available, there is no reason for delay. Can you be ready in a week or two, Kermarec? It takes a dam— er, *deuced* time to get out there, and we've got a lot to do before the winter storms start up."

Bové stayed only long enough to give Dominic the name of his hotel and a recommendation for where to find the gear he would need for Asea, and then he left as impetuously as he had arrived. Sambin was not as cheerful, but apparently determined to make the best of a bad situation.

"I suppose the sooner you leave the sooner you can return, eh? Now, don't forget to write. And send me that schedule before you go! If you have the time to send a few letters with local detail, we can publish those to keep the readers curious in your absence. Oh, and..."

Eventually Ardhuin had to resort to remembering a fictitious appointment to let them escape. It was not entirely false, since they did need to report to the palace at some point.

Outside, Dominic grimaced and rubbed his forehead. "I thought it was too good to be true, Bové already in place and visiting—but how will you manage? This will take at least a month of travel, if not more."

"You could not persuade him to change his mind...and I imagine there will be a point where Monsieur Bové can't make Mr. Talbot return, even if he should wish to. This opportunity is too good to be missed—and we do need to act quickly. Poor Sonam will worry himself into becoming ill again —and I don't like this talk of winter storms, either. We'll just have to make the best of it." She stepped back into the hired carriage. "Let's visit the place Bové mentioned before we go back to the palace."

Dominic nodded and gave the directions to the coachman. He got in and sat down beside her. "Are you thinking Mr. Talbot also needs to be supplied? Your illusion will not suffice as it did before?"

"It was something Sonam mentioned, the reason he wore Aeropan clothing—that it was easier to maintain a smaller illusion, especially traveling by train. If we go by steamer, the same problem may arise, and it can't be expected that we will always be able to have private sleeping accommodations." Ardhuin rummaged in her reticule for a notepad. "I will give you some rough measurements for Mr. Talbot, and then..." She sighed. "I hope the Queen can supply a very discreet tailor to make the necessary adjustments."

Gutrune aimed the narrow slit of light at the base of the pile of crates. Stoller had not had any difficulty in providing an opportunity for her to slip inside the dock storehouse, but she wanted to complete her search as quickly as possible just in case the watchman came back early from dealing with the "drunken foreigner." In the darkness, she could hear the lapping of the waves nearby. She was surprised at how many of the crates from the cave in Anatoli were still here. Had the boat been too small? Would the spy return for the rest?

She had little time in any case. When Stoller had gone to get the rest of her equipment, he had returned with a telegram. It was in code, directing her to the port city of Aleksandri to meet with "friends from the late campaign." She would have to leave soon to arrive by the specified date.

She shifted the shuttered lantern to look more closely. Some of the crates had labels, and the address was the same on each. Pirazzi Imports, Napoli, Roma. One of the smallest crates had broken slats, apparently from being dropped on one edge. A little more damage would not be noticed. She would have to be careful not to make too much noise, however. While Stoller was on watch to prevent accidental discovery, the cottage where the watchman lived was close by.

From a small leather satchel she took a slim pry bar. Using the edge, she carefully widened cracks near nails until she could pull away more slats from the side of the damaged crate with only a few creaks. The opening was large enough to remove large handfuls of the straw used to cushion the contents, a number of rough-fired clay pots with lids sealed with heavy twine and red sealing wax. Each pot was the size of a small stein, and scratched into the surface were the words "salis mineralis."

She took one out and examined it more closely. It was heavy, but otherwise unremarkable. She put it down and reached in again. This time when she pulled out a jar she heard a faint clink, and rummaging deeper found a broken shard. It was covered in a coarse, gritty substance, presumably the mineral salts. Gutrune brought her fingers to her nose and cautiously sniffed. Sour, and with a slight oily feel.

Well, if the crate was this damaged, it was unlikely the recipients would be suspicious that the contents were less than expected. She replaced all but one of the jars in the crate and replaced the straw and the loosened slats.

All of the labeled crates held clay pots, apparently identical to the one she had pulled out. It might be good to check the contents. There was no guarantee the contents were the same, after all. Gutrune took out a small, slim knife and cut the twine holding the lid in place. The contents appeared to be caked, and she poked at them with the point of the knife.

The gritty powder puffed explosively away from the metal, spattering her face. She jerked away, knocking the lantern on its side. The grit burned her eyes and nose, and she twisted sharply to bury a series of violent sneezes in the crook of her arm. Damn! Had the watchman heard that? She opened her streaming eyes. The lantern had gone out when it fell, and she felt about to find it in the dark.

Her fingers brushed the metal—only it felt wrong. Instead of the expected hard surface, it felt pliant as leather...and yet she knew it was the lamp. A sudden wave of dizziness washed over her, and she felt her heart pounding hard in her chest. Not right, not right. The dust...was it some kind of drug? Now the blood in her veins flashed hot and cold in rapid succession.

Light. She had to have light, to see her way. To get out. She fumbled for the little metal case of matches in the pocket of her hunting jacket, feeling frantic. She couldn't have lost it. If she couldn't light the lamp again, she...

There was light. Faint, blue-white light. Coming from her hands. Shaking, Gutrune raised them up. Rivulets of light, like water, flowing over her skin. There was no heat, no pain. She knew what it was, but it was impossible. Magefire. But how could she, who was no magician, conjure magefire?

Perhaps she was merely hallucinating. The effect of the drug, nothing more. Stoller...Stoller would not be affected.

Imaginary or not, the light let her find her way to the door without stumbling. She tugged the door open and ran outside, hands held before her, looking for Stoller. But when she found him, he stared at her in horror. And then she knew it was not hallucination. The magefire was real.

It was true that matters were dangerous and urgent. It was true that the safety of Aerope depended on the success of their efforts. And yet to Dominic, smelling the brisk salt air and watching the bustle of preparations and the varied ships in the port, it was the fulfillment of a dream. He was going on an expedition!

And not just any expedition. They were going with Bové himself, and to speed them on their way, the Bretagnan government had made available a navy steamer to transport them and their supplies to Aleksandri. And that was only a waystop! He never thought he would get as far as Geapt in his life.

"You look as if you were about to swim out to that launch," Markus remarked, walking along the pier toward him. He had changed from his Preusan *schutzmagus* uniform of black to a more ordinary dark suit.

"I am quite ready to begin the journey, I admit. Oh, the Ministry of Magic forwarded this message." Dominic searched his pockets for the telegram and handed it to Markus. "From Fräulein von Kitren. It seems everyone has agreed to combine forces on the assumption that Denais will likely be in the same place as MacCrimmon, and Preusa will send a detachment of mountain-trained soldiers. Will she be able to join us without, er, attention?"

"I am sure she will find a way," Markus replied. His voice had a distant tone as he read the message carefully. "I am relieved to hear the message of our sailing reached her in time—I believe we have her brother to thank for that. Although he might not be pleased to learn where she intends to go next. As to the details...I believe your friend Mr. Talbot will be willing to assist her."

"Do be careful and stop smirking," Dominic hissed as quietly as he could. "If your amusement gives the game away, we'll be on our own in the middle of nowhere. Talk of something else. For example, the mountain detachment from Preusa. They do not join us?"

Markus shook his head. "They don't gear up quite as quickly as we do, and they have to take another route anyway. The Cathans absolutely forbid foreign military in their territory, so they have to go north through Ynde. We still don't have all the necessary permissions from the independent *rejahs* outside the Trade Cities, but it should just be a matter of time, and perhaps bribes." He grinned. "The story is they wish to map the mountain passes and conduct weather observations."

"From what Sonam was telling us, they should have plenty of weather to observe." Dominic glanced down the pier. Still no sign of Ardhuin, who was getting a last-minute briefing from a Bretagnan government official. He crouched down and opened the small leather satchel at his feet, taking out the brass and chryselectrum device inside. The first working prototype of his imager, which had a few remaining problems but still functioned much better than his earlier attempts. Iron could still cause interference with the field, but here on the wooden pier, that should not be a difficulty.

"Oh, what have you there?"

"Well, it will eventually be an automatic illusion generator, at least I hope so. Right now all it does is capture a view, and not a very good one. Iron interferes dreadfully, so I wanted to get an image before we board the steamer."

Markus leaned closer. "How does it work? Is this all your own design, or did you modify one of Colfax's devices?"

Dominic snorted. "Modify? I still can't figure out how Colfax did what he did. No, this is all my work, with Ardhuin's help for the magic, of course. I wind up this key here, and then aim, and press this lever..." He performed each action as he spoke it, pointing the device, for lack of a better object, at Markus. A faint cylinder of magic flickered about him and vanished. "And then this lever displays the image."

A grainy image of Markus's surprised face hovered over the brass central plate of the device. It was quite comical, and Dominic resolved to save it if at all possible. Then if Markus became difficult to deal with, which was a virtual certainty, Dominic could threaten to show it to Gutrune.

"Astonishing." Markus stared at the image, then at Dominic. "How did you even think to...and how does it know what to capture?"

"It only preserves the image in a defined field, and since I can see it, it's easy for me. Not so for others, I agree. It needs work."

"Still." Markus looked off into the distance. "Think of what this means. You worked magic, yet you are not a magician. What other devices like this could be made, performing what other spells? What are the limitations? I'd be careful who you mention this to."

Dominic held the device closer to his chest, hands protectively wrapped around it. "Why?"

"Illusion is a harmless spell, for the most part." Markus's grin faded. "There are more dangerous magics, and many more people who want them than can perform them. We keep an eye on our own—the Mage Guardians are the most extreme example of this—but who will watch the machines?"

"I—I suppose that is true. I would..." A carriage pulled up near the dock, and Dominic saw a familiar magic-shrouded figure emerge. "Oh, good. My...that is, Mr. Talbot has arrived. Now we can leave."

CHAPTER 9

Ardhuin carefully looked about from her bunk, listening for any sign that the others were awake. All were still. Even the lieutenant had stopped snoring, a profound relief. How such a small man could make so much noise amazed her.

She slipped to her feet and reflexively checked her hands. It was hard to tell in the faint light, but her illusion was still holding up well. It had taken some arranging to get a cabin far from the steam engines, and even then both Markus and Sonam had proven useful in maintaining the deceit, since Dominic could always see through the illusion. What they had settled on was preserving illusion primarily for her head, and aversion for the rest of her, since it was much less disturbed by iron and moving engines.

There was no getting around the fact that the ship was not large, and not set up for the comfort of passengers. Most of their group had taken over the junior officers' quarters, with six tight bunks. Dominic fretted, but there was no other way. Ardhuin had to contrive to wash in privacy. "Mr. Talbot" was also prone to seasickness, another way to avoid scrutiny. It wasn't for very long, she told herself.

In the cramped washroom, she inspected her illusion and decided Mr. Talbot needed to look a trifle pale today, due to his illness. She made the necessary changes and then focused her magic, hard and sharp, at the metal pendant around her neck. That would preserve the illusion even if she were unconscious or sleeping, another handy idea of Dominic's.

Taking advantage of the early hour, she climbed the gangway to the deck and admired the view, breathing in the fresh salt air. The sky was cloudless and crystalline, and she could see distant islands that looked like dark, low clouds on the horizon. She took out the notebook she had brought with her and found a place out of the way of the sailors to sit.

Preusa was providing military assistance to go after Denais, but they would have to scout out the situation and get that information to the Preusan troops for it to be of any use. She nibbled her pencil, thinking of what she could do. First, of course, was getting to MacCrimmon and releasing him from his stasis. He would have the best idea of what needed to be done. It was curious—Sonam had an instinctive understanding of magic and considerable power, but larger and more complex spells apparently had only been taught to him by MacCrimmon. Was there no established magical instruction in Bhuta?

The breeze, the cries of the seabirds, and the vibration of the engines, more felt than heard, muted other sounds. She did not know Dominic was there until he put a hand on her shoulder.

"What do you find so engrossing?"

"I am merely attempting to figure out what needs to be done first, once we get to our destination. However long that takes." She sighed.

Dominic shaded his eyes with one hand, looking out over the sea. "We're supposed to make Aleksandri today—at least, that's what Bové was told yesterday." He sat down beside her. "Then it's a day or so to arrange the overland transportation to Sudr Abaya, and another ship voyage to Kiantan."

"You are sounding like quite an experienced explorer," Ardhuin teased. "Are you enjoying your first expedition?"

He leaned back against the hull of the ship and glanced at her. "Well, I do miss my wife."

"I'm given to understand she misses you too." Ardhuin leaned forward, quickly looking about. No one was in sight. She quickly cast a strong aversion field, sound damping, and a light sensing fog—not a ward; that would cause too much comment if it was triggered and create exactly the kind of notice they wanted to avoid. Now she would know before anyone came in view, and they would not be aware of detection.

She leaned back into Dominic's arms, his cheek against hers. "Ah, much better," he murmured. "I only hope our accommodations will be more...flexible once we reach Cathai."

"Certainly there will be less iron about." Ardhuin snuggled closer. "I will be able to maintain much larger and more complex illusions—but there will still be difficulties. Poor Dominic..."

"Yes, poor Dominic. He will need a great deal of sympathy, when circumstances permit." He tightened his hold about her. "Assuming he is still in his wife's good graces after all this extremely uncomfortable travel."

"Since it was all her fault to begin with, I imagine she will be both understanding and appreciative of his sacrifices. It is a pity that the necessity for speed precludes comfort."

"It will be that sooner over and done with." He stroked her hair softly. "At least we are together. Despite Bové."

Ardhuin chuckled. "Oh dear—it just occurred to me, with Gutrune meeting us in Aleksandri—how will we contrive to hide *her?*"

"I am quite certain she will be equal to the task. Especially with our help," Dominic said firmly. "Now, before we are interrupted I have a much more important matter to attend to..."

It did not involve much talking. But it was, Ardhuin agreed, quite important. It did not seem like much time had passed, but the sudden, startling blast of the ship's whistle made her realize the sun had risen significantly. The whistle was repeated and followed by the sounds of running feet.

"I suppose that means we're coming in to port." Dominic reluctantly let her go, and Ardhuin dispelled the magics that had been concealing them.

They went to the deck railing. A dark, thick smudge was visible on the horizon, and getting larger. The sea, previously empty, now sported several sails and even a smoke plume from another steamer.

"Ah, there you are!" Markus joined them at the rail, his eyes bright with amusement. "Bové was looking for you, Kermarec. I informed him you had sought solitude to write, and then I asked in turn if Herr Talbot had returned from inspecting our gear in the holds. He should now believe you have been on opposite ends of the ship for hours."

"You are too obliging." Dominic glared at him. "Unnecessary, but obliging."

Markus grinned. "Merely ensuring that suspicious thoughts do not enter the worthy Herr Bové's head, should he begin to notice the two of you seem to disappear at the same time and cannot be found. We still have several weeks that will be spent in his company, after all." He took out a pair of field glasses and handed them to Ardhuin. "There is an excellent view of the ruins of the ancient Eskelion lighthouse from here, if you would care to take a look."

Dominic's expression lightened. "Oh, the melted one? I heard that an Alban team was doing excavations there. They are investigating the theory that the destruction was caused by purely natural forces, not magic."

"They think the light was not magical, then? But what natural source would be as bright?" Ardhuin peered through the field glasses. The lighthouse was quite easy to locate, with the runnels of molten glass covering the ancient stone like a web. She had only seen illustrations of it before. It was the oldest artifact known to be connected with magic— although if Dominic's story proved true, that might change.

She handed the glasses to Dominic. "Can you see magic from this distance?" she asked.

"I suppose, though I would think after thousands of years it might have faded a trifle...oh." He lowered the glasses, looking perplexed. "Well, I can see *something* magical there, but it's larger than the tower itself. How strange! I wonder if the excavation is connected? I wish we had time to visit them."

More people, sailors and passengers, were coming up to the deck now. "I believe I will go below and see to my gear," Ardhuin said. Time to stay out of sight, at least until the engines stopped.

"And I should see Bové and find out what he wants from me." Dominic handed the field glasses back to Markus, glancing wistfully out at the ancient lighthouse.

"I'm sure it will still be there when we return," Markus said cheerfully. "And they would be delighted to learn about your observations, but first things first."

Ardhuin soon had her personal belongings—or rather, Mr. Talbot's—packed and ready to be carried ashore. The cabin's porthole had a view of the docks, and while she waited she watched the unloading begin. The local laborers wore dusty, faded robes and turbans, and apparently were unable to do anything without a great deal of shouting and gesticulation. One load of baggage nearly escaped when the net bag hanging from the dock crane slipped open, but a quick-thinking fisherman in a low, flat boat intercepted it and helped get it back on the dock, for which he was rewarded with a few tossed coins.

Dominic came in while she was watching another load smash into a cart, followed by yet more shouting. "So, Bové has arranged for us to stay at a caravanserai just outside the port district. We can leave the ship whenever we like."

She turned away from the porthole. "They don't need us here?"

He shook his head. "I rather got the impression we would be in the way." He grinned. "Not to mention the officers would like their cabin back, I imagine."

She checked her illusion. As she had expected, with the engines quiet it was clear and sharp. "By all means. I hope this place is easy to find. Aleksandri appears to be utter chaos, and I suppose we won't be able to read the signs."

"You assume there would be any signs. Besides, if we get lost, we merely need to follow any string of camels we see."

Ardhuin grabbed her carpetbag and followed Dominic out of the cabin. "What if they are leaving the city instead of entering?"

"Not at this hour. Apparently the city shuts down around noon, when the heat is greatest, and no one would be foolish enough to depart then."

At the foot of the narrow gangplank, Sonam and Markus Asgaya were already waiting. Sonam was looking about, wide-eyed with amazement. Markus was also looking about, but with a crease of worry between his brows.

The heat was like a blow once they were away from the water. Ardhuin could feel sweat trickling down her back, especially underneath her custom-made undervest that assisted in converting her silhouette into one more suited to maintaining her male disguise. It served its purpose, but now more than ever it was particularly uncomfortable.

The port city featured only a handful of Aeropan-style buildings, mostly constructed by trading companies. The rest were a motley collection of mud–brick structures, stacked up on each other apparently at random, with striped cloth awnings over dark, shaded doorways. They passed through a small market with hammered brass pots and bowls laid out on threadbare rugs, melons, chickens in cages, and fruits Ardhuin did not recognize. The sharp, pungent smell of spice filled the air. There were also a handful of women present, swathed in long, filmy cotton veils in shades of blue and green.

Markus leaned forward. "If you have not already done so, I would recommend light personal wards, very close. This is the kind of place to expect pickpockets to appear, especially for foreigners like us."

Ardhuin did so, including Dominic in her casting, and translating the warning to Alban for Sonam. He just smiled.

"I will do so, to spare their effort. I have nothing worth stealing." He turned his head to stare at an old man with a wispy beard and no teeth, eyes pale with cataracts, casting illusions for a crowd of ragged children. They appeared to be illustrating a story the man was telling in a high, cracked voice, a story of heroes and demons.

The crowds made their progress agonizingly slow, not to mention aromatic, but eventually a taller building, surrounded by palm trees and separate from the jumbled structures of the city, came into view. It had one large main gate and a colonnade inside and out to provide shade. In the center of the large courtyard was a fountain with a deep, wide basin. Men with camels waited their turn to water their animals. It was just as crowded as the marketplace, but not as noisy. They went inside and found an open spot in the shade.

Markus glanced about again, looking even more worried. "She said she would meet us without fail," he murmured, low enough only they could hear. "I saw no one that could be her, even disguised, at the docks."

Ardhuin had to wait for her eyes to adjust to the shadows after the bright light outside. Several of the Geaptan locals wore pieces of Aeropan clothing, a vest or a shirt, but one man was wearing a jacket despite the heat. He was shading his eyes, even though he was in the shade, and had brown skin like a local but looked familiar. She didn't see anyone remotely like Gutrune.

"Over by the third group of columns." She leaned close to Markus. "Doesn't that look like Stoller?"

He glanced over without moving his head. "Yes, it does, if Stoller had been spending time in the sun. Shall we nonchalantly go visit the date seller nearby and see if you are correct?"

"Yes. If for no other reason than hunger," Dominic commented. "I am told the meal will not be served until evening."

"I can understand not wanting to cook in this heat." Ardhuin mopped her forehead with a handkerchief. "But food would be good. And water."

The dates were fresh and delicious. The man who looked like Stoller faded back into the darker section of the colonnade when they approached but stayed within earshot.

"I wonder where our friend is." Dominic spoke clearly, but not loudly, in Preusan. The man glanced sharply at him, then gestured.

They strolled idly in the direction the man had indicated, eating their dates and admiring the exotic architecture. This was the section where the camels were stabled, and their noisy grunts and moans filled the air. They also covered quiet conversation.

"Thank God you made it," the man said in clear Preusan.

Ardhuin peered at his face more closely. "Stoller? What happened to you?"

Stoller made a face. "We were attacked leaving Anatoli. We had to use disguises to get this far. Someone must have seen...but you'll want to hear all that somewhere else." He glanced about. "Where is your room?"

Markus frowned. "Where is your mistress?"

"Not running about where she can be seen, sir. She'll be by when it's dark. It's a bad business and getting worse, and she needs to be careful."

"Not reassuring," Markus muttered, pacing a few steps. "By nightfall, eh? That's late for planning. How do you intend to join our caravan?"

Stoller sighed. "We've got one of those damn camels. We can generally get it to go where we want. Say you've hired us to carry your more delicate equipment or some such. If that doesn't work, we'll just join another caravan going the same way; lots of travel to Sudr Abaya."

He seemed reluctant to talk and worried, glancing about fitfully. With nothing else to do and the heat still oppressive, they decided to retire to their room and try to sleep. Ardhuin merely dozed fitfully, unable to find a comfortable spot on the lumpy and stale-smelling bed. Then the rest of the expedition team showed up, loud and noisy. It wasn't until the sun went down and the temperature began to lower that she felt able to sleep—and that's when the food arrived. She sighed and gave up.

Aside from the lack of silverware, the meal was delicious. Chunks of spiced lamb on a bed of saffron rice, eaten with sections of flat bread, and mint tea occupied everyone's attention to the exclusion of conversation for some time. With immediate hunger satisfied, the members of the expedition discussed the next stage of the trip, the caravan master they had hired, and how many camels would be needed for the travelers.

Ardhuin protested. "Why can't we ride horses? From what I've seen, a camel has all the sweet temper of a mule with a hangover and the grace of a three-legged bull. It would likely refuse to go where I wanted just from spite."

One of the junior researchers, Simons, grinned. "Yeah, they can be pretty bad—but they like to follow the others. Not much steering needed, and you get used to the motion after a while." He waved his hands in a swaying manner.

Ardhuin, in her character as Talbot, winced. "Please. I've just gotten off the blasted boat. What this place needs is a nice railway. Or horses."

"They need too much water." Bové took the hookah pipe from his mouth and gestured. "We could use horses, but then we'd need yet another camel just to carry water for them. The wells are too far apart on the quickest route. Don't let him fool you, Talbot. It isn't nearly as bad as being at sea."

Ardhuin affected relief, to general amusement, and the topic changed to visiting a nearby inn that featured music and dancers. "Wearing nothing but a few scarves and a handful of spangles!" Simons added, enthusiastically. "And flexible as cats. I don't know how they do it. You should go, Kermarec. Doesn't get much more exotic than that, and you could put it in your books! Don't worry, we won't tell your wife."

Dominic raised an eyebrow. "And when she reads it in my book, what am I to say? Or did you think she doesn't read them? No, I think I'll pass this time. I still haven't written down all the exotic details I saw this morning, and you want to leave early, I believe?" He glanced at Bové, who nodded.

"Yes, as much travel before the heat as possible."

Simons looked at Ardhuin. "What about you, Talbot? You don't have a wife to worry about, do you?"

Ardhuin smiled. "Not at all. But I didn't get much sleep on the ship, and now you are promising me more of the same tomorrow. I'd better rest now while I can. The dark beauties will have to dance without me."

"You're missing a treat." Simons shook his head sorrowfully. "They've got some pretty girls in Ynde, but we aren't going that route this time. The Cathan women—well, the locals seem to like that style of thing, but their dancing is like doing calisthenics very slowly inside a large winter overcoat, and they aren't nearly as pretty."

"Or perhaps your reputation preceded you and they took precautions to protect their ladies from your hairy *geilo* advances." Bové rose from the low couch. "The local *ras shaq* dancers are distinctly inferior to those in Lankhor —and before you embrace any of them, I would suggest you remember how many sailors have done the same."

"Oh, pfui!" Simons rolled his eyes. "What an old woman you're turning into."

"You're going too?" Dominic asked Bové.

"Yes, that's where most business is done. I have to meet with the caravan master. It's a social expectation," he added, grimacing. "Geaptans think it bad form to get straight to the point. A simple yes or no can take hours."

Markus and Sonam also made excuses to remain. As the others prepared to go, Dominic got out his writing materials and set up on a low table. Ardhuin went back to the sleeping area. It had two windows, originally shuttered against the sun, and she opened one and looked out. Lamps dotted the darkness, and faint moonlight created darker shadows of palm trees and buildings. It appeared most of the inhabitants had already gone wherever they were going, and few people could be seen in the street.

"See anything?" Dominic came in, followed by Markus.

"No. I wonder if she will come tonight or wait until we are out of the city." Ardhuin turned away and took a seat on a bed. Dominic took her place at the window, gazing at the night scene with an air of fascination.

"Stoller wanted to know where we were staying, remember? So I think —" Dominic jumped back with a gasp, stumbling and putting up an arm. A dark figure, black robes swirling around it, vaulted through the window.

Stoller warned us. Attackers, already! Ardhuin snatched power and narrowed it to a single lance, trusting Dominic to see it and dodge, and lashed out.

"No!" Markus lunged and interposed himself just as the magic left her hands and smashed into his shield, knocking him and the black-clad figure to the floor.

"What the hell do you think you are doing, Asgaya?" Dominic untangled himself from a small table, glaring.

Markus appeared stunned, and was catching his breath. The black figure was struggling to stand while staring up at Ardhuin with pale, wary eyes.

Pale eyes. "Gutrune?" The figure froze. Ardhuin hesitated, uncertain.

"Your school friend wears another face," Dominic said meaningfully. The pale eyes swung to him, and then the figure reached up and pulled the black scarf concealing their features.

"Secure?" Gutrune whispered.

Ardhuin gestured, putting wards and shielding for sound around them. Then she dropped the illusion on her face. "Is that better?"

Gutrune leaned back against the wall, breathing hard. Her face was the same unusual brown that Stoller's had been, but her golden hair was unchanged under the scarf.

"What's wrong?" Markus was staring at her, his hands clenching and flexing. "You look like hell—that is, you appear fatigued."

She gave a mirthless laugh. "Stoller and I have been on the run since Anatoli. I do not know if Denais's people knew they were being watched, or if they discovered what we had found. The disguise was the only way we could get here unnoticed, and I did not wish to bring you to their attention as well, or I would have found a less startling way to arrive." Her breathing had evened by now, and she gave Ardhuin a slight smile. "You really must give me the name of your tailor. I feel I may be in need of his services."

Something in her voice wasn't quite right. Shaky. Gutrune looked up sharply, reaching for something in her robes, and Ardhuin saw Sonam standing in the doorway staring.

"No, it's all right—he's with us." Ardhuin adjusted the magic to allow Sonam to enter. "This is Sonam. MacCrimmon sent him to bring help. That's why we're here."

"But Denais is…"

"Undoubtedly they viewed it as too sensitive to tell you using the usual means, but we believe Denais or his agents are the ones MacCrimmon needed help to deal with," Markus said smoothly. "I can give you all the details later, if you wish. Now, who is chasing you? Have you seen them here?"

"Not since we entered the city. It is harder to track here. With your help, it should be possible to evade them when we leave." Gutrune shifted. "Herr Kermarec. Do you see anything…unusual about me? Something only your talent can see?"

Ardhuin blinked. Did she fear some kind of tracking spell had been placed on her?

Dominic's brow wrinkled as he looked at her. "What am I searching for, a *geas*? I don't see anything like that."

"Nothing of that order." Gutrune closed her eyes. "I don't know what to tell you to look for. All I know is this." Her voice was measured and very even. "I opened a container left by Denais's spy. It was full of a substance that looked like oily sand. I used my knife to see if anything was hidden inside, and it sprayed up into my face. My lamp was knocked over and went out. And then," she held up her browned hands, "there was magefire. No one else was there to cast the spell. It took nearly four hours for the light to fade, and it did not return. I did not notice any other effects."

A stunned silence filled the room.

Finally Dominic stirred. "Where did you find this container?"

"In a warehouse. It was one of several in a crate. It seemed…dangerous. Too dangerous to risk a message that could be intercepted. I altered the label of the crate so it would be shipped to my brother, and alerted him to watch for it."

"Good. Although it would have been interesting to see it for ourselves, we have more than enough to do here," Ardhuin said.

Gutrune looked up at her. "I kept the opened container with me."

"Even better!" Dominic brightened. "Is it with you now?"

"Hidden. I or Stoller guard it at all times. I did not want to bring it to you without knowing more."

Which was probably wise, but now they needed a way to both get to the hidden container and not cause questions if the other explorers came back early. What they settled on was an illusion to make it appear as if "Mr. Talbot" were asleep, and Markus and Sonam remaining behind while she and Dominic went with Gutrune out the window. Markus raised several objections to this plan, but even he had to admit there was not much time and was overruled.

With levitation and shadows, they escaped the room unnoticed. Gutrune, swathed in her black native robes, led the way. Stoller saw her and stood, while an unusually ugly camel snorted and burbled in the background.

"What, did you not find her, miss?"

Ardhuin did a quick check for observers and cast more protective magic. The casting felt odd, as if she were back at Peran near the ley lines. Like something was pushing or resisting her magic.

"Oh." Dominic was staring at the angular camel harness, in the back recesses of the alcove. "Is that..." he pointed.

"You can see it?" Gutrune snapped her head around.

"It's...very bright. It looks like..." He swallowed hard. "You're sure it isn't liquid?"

Gutrune shook her head. "Like sand, or salt. You can see it through the leather?"

Dominic nodded, his face pale and drawn. "It reminds me of the essence Denais...extracted. It is magic. Pure magic."

Ardhuin walked carefully up to the harness. The magic was buffeting her like a strong wind. Even she could tell where the container was hidden, but she could not force her hands close enough to uncover it. Stoller had to reach for the flap of leather on the underside where it was concealed.

The simple clay jar was unremarkable in appearance, and as Gutrune had described them, the contents looked like salt or sand.

"What should we do with it?" Gutrune asked.

Ardhuin took a deep breath. "Keep it away from iron. That's probably what made it spurt up at you, when you used your knife."

"But should we get rid of it?"

She shook her head, trying to think of all the implications. All of the problems. With a sinking feeling, she realized this was something only the Mage Guardians could deal with. Gutrune had said there was more. She had only found one crate. What if there were others? What was the source? If she was right, the substance in the ordinary clay jar could destroy Aerope in a way that would make the Mage War seem small.

"Keep it hidden where it is. Don't let any magician near it if you can, and don't mention it to *anyone.* Do you understand me? Not the Preusan government, not your brother. Don't tell anyone else what happened to you." Despite the desert heat that still remained, she shivered.

"Ardhuin—what's wrong?" Dominic was looking worried.

Despite the wards and protections, she gestured them closer. "You were right—it is magic. *Magic anyone can use.* Mage-level magic. And if Denais has it..."

Gutrune's eyes went wide with horror. "*Gott*. He must be stopped. *This* must be stopped. And the source..."
Ardhuin nodded. "The source must be found."

CHAPTER 10

Otto Korda walked through the circular doorway in the stone wall, steeling himself for the brief moment of strong resistance from the ward. It parted to allow him to enter as it always had, but he wondered if it had recently gotten harder to push through or if it was merely his imagination. Even Denais could not put such a delicate restriction on a ward—could he?

He reviewed the list of commands as he approached the lake pavilion. Do not speak until commanded to do so. Keep your eyes lowered. Never question orders. It was a long list, and he must never forget any of it. Especially now.

It was early, and a veil of mist still covered the lake, muting the colors of the water lilies and even the brilliant colors of the peacocks searching for insects on the far shore. Denais was seated on an ornate chair facing the lake, sipping tea. One of the local servants, incongruously dressed in the Aeropan style, stood rigidly at attention to one side holding the teapot, her eyes focused on Denais for the signal to approach and refill his cup.

Denais appeared pensive, a sharp line etched between his brows, and his gaze focused on the lake. Not propitious. Otto stopped on the path just before the steps to the pavilion and waited, unmoving.

"Korda. Where is the mineral essence shipment? It should have arrived by now."

"No one has come, my lord." Otto could feel the palms of his hands getting damp. This was the risk, that Denais would begin to notice too soon.

"What of Kunstler?"

"He left Anatoli but has not yet arrived here."

Denais sipped his tea for a moment, gazing at the lifting mist. "If the mineral essence is not here in two weeks, I will leave for the valley that day. Korda, you will accompany me. Go and prepare what is necessary for the journey."

Seething, Korda bowed and left. He could not disobey, but the last thing he wanted was to go even farther from civilization. Denais had taken all of the Ostri captives to Asea, to prevent them from being recognized. Korda hated Asea. Che-ing province was bad enough, but Bhuta was even worse. No Aeropan supplies could be had at any price, and the locals were scrawny, dirty, and hostile. It would also make it nearly impossible to direct his own plans. He would have to make certain to give his own people the latest instructions before he left.

At first his only motivation had been revenge. Baron Kreuzen had been a hard master but a fair one—and Korda could not forget the baron's last desperate efforts to defend his people when he could have escaped. That had been the hardest thing, to see him wounded and in chains when there was nothing anyone could do to free him. They all had been put under the *geas* by then.

At first Korda hadn't understood what was happening. It was one thing to read about the terrible magical compulsion used by Guedoc in the Mage War, but now he had both seen and felt it. All he could do was watch and suffer. It did not take long for him to realize the full extent of Denais's plans. Not just an army of slaves, oh no. That would leave too much work for Denais, for each slave would need his *geas* placed by the master himself.

Instead, Denais had picked a handful of the students with the power and skill to do the *geas* themselves, and taught them the forbidden spell. Since they were already controlled, they could be trusted. All he needed was a victim for them to practice on—Korda.

He had been manacled with special chryselectrum-lined iron cuffs, and his *geas* removed. He'd lost track of how many times it had been placed on him, removed, and placed again. He'd memorized the list of commands, felt the vise on his mind after the few brief moments of freedom. He'd heard every step of the instructions. If he'd only had the power, he could have cast a *geas* himself. But no, he was just an assistant—not even strong enough to be considered a full magician, never mind a mage.

He'd learned to hate Denais then, with every fiber of his being. Dreaming of revenge was the only comfort he had, the only thing that kept him sane. That someday he'd be able to destroy Denais, wreck his plans, and never feel the cage of fire on his mind again. Korda found himself rubbing his wrists as he walked away from the pavilion, still feeling the weight of the cuffs. He forced himself to stop before anyone noticed.

But no one was watching. He remembered his own private hell, when he had also sometimes deliberately looked away when under the *geas*. They must be doing the same. Even Denais could not force you to betray something you hadn't seen. And then one day, to his very great surprise, the *geas* vanished. The mineral essence that Denais prized so highly had freed him—he still wasn't entirely certain how. Long after he was no longer used as a test subject, Korda had been ordered to remove a jar of the essence to Denais's workroom, and a few grains had fallen on his face when he lifted the jar up to place it on a shelf. He always thought about fighting back when the *geas* was placed, and nearly every waking moment—and suddenly the pressure on his mind was gone. Denais, supremely confident of his abilities, never thought to check that it was still there—and it was not so hard to pretend.

It had been more difficult to find a way to destroy Denais's plans until he realized all he really needed to do was subvert them. Take over the slaves, reroute the supplies, change the deliveries of the mineral essence. He'd discovered that a very simple layer of command, a light *geas* covering the one Denais had set, was all that was needed. Those under his control saw him as issuing commands by Denais, and the original, more powerful *geas* did the rest.

Now in the palatial main house Denais used as his headquarters, Korda called servants to him and issued curt orders—some for Denais, some for himself. Sometimes Korda wondered if he was allowing himself to be seduced by the promise of power, power he had always wanted, but then he found new resolve. It was a good thing to destroy Denais, wasn't it? As long as he *was* destroyed, did it really matter how it was done? Korda had not enslaved these people; he was preventing Denais from doing more. He was protecting them. He'd free them in the end. When he had everything he needed.

But first, he must not be discovered. Not before his plans were complete. Denais must not know his slave was free.

Stoller emerged from the dusty crowd carrying a cloth bundle and made his way to the shaded alley Gutrune was hiding in.

"Got rid of the lot and found what you asked for." He dumped a bundle of clothes on a low wall with the air of a man relieved of a burden. "Even with all this, we have a little left over. Would you believe that thrice-damned camel went for thirty-six *seqim*?"

"The only way that miserable creature could be worth so much is as dog meat." If she had been asked what the transit of the isthmus had been like, she would be unable to describe it in much detail. All of her time and attention, and that of Stoller, had been devoted to dragging the camel the right direction, biting and kicking the entire way. It was a miracle it hadn't completely lost its load, although it had dropped it more than once.

Stoller shrugged. "We'd better leave before the dogs get sick, then. Stupid beast will be completely indigestible, I'm thinking. Will they do?"

Gutrune held up the jacket, nodding. Her black robes were gone, no longer needed. They would be conspicuous instead of concealing on board the Atlantean packet ship that would take them to Cathai. The timing was fortunate, as the dye she had used for her skin was fading. While she and Stoller had been able to avoid the other camel drivers on the journey, it would be harder to remain unseen on the ship.

It would be more comfortable to travel simply as unconnected passengers. The only difficulty was other unconnected passengers. There had been no sign of pursuit lately, but she could not be easy.

Gutrune also wanted an opportunity to talk privately with Ardhuin, which had not been possible during the caravan. She still had the occasional nightmare in which her hands blazed with magefire as she tried to escape nameless enemies in the dark. They would disappear entirely, she was sure, if Ardhuin could tell her how to counteract it.

Their ship was the *Amabel*, one of the Bosta sailing ships designed for speed. It was tall with sleek and narrow lines, and it had an unusually large number of masts to carry all the sails it required. It stood out in the dusty harbor like a society lady dressed for a ball. Most of their fellow passengers were Alban or Aeropan, dealing with imports or business in the Trade Cities, but enough Geaptans and Beduns were present her current disguise was unremarkable.

She and Stoller boarded in the evening, close to sailing time. She wanted to make sure she was not being followed. The expedition members were already embarked, and once she felt the ship shift and roll as it left the harbor, she went in search of them.

It was habit now to stay in the shadows, to watch a place carefully before she proceeded. Thus when she saw Dominic Kermarec standing at the rail, she did not immediately join him. He was speaking in a low voice with some agitation, and when she moved closer she saw Markus Asgaya partly concealed by an open hatch cover—and she wondered if he also was hiding in shadows now.

She heard his voice but could not distinguish the words. Dominic made an exasperated sound and darted a glance over his shoulder. "How would I know?" he snapped. "There really is something pathetic in your coming to me for guidance. My experience is singular and highly unique, and you cannot expect me to help you succeed as I did."

Markus chuckled, and he also glanced about before leaning forward to speak even more quietly to Dominic. Gutrune faded back, her curiosity piqued. What secret could Markus and Dominic have in common that they would want to conceal from the others?

Gutrune made her way through the narrow corridors, edging to the wall to avoid a group of Cathans hunkered down. She did not know where the expedition's cabins were, but if she found some of the members nearby, she could follow them. Only the group involved in the Mage Guardian project knew who she was, so she would still have to keep her distance and not ask them questions.

Eventually, after much wandering and pretending to be in search of the steward, she found Ardhuin. Even though she knew Ardhuin was wearing an illusion, she had to keep reminding herself to look for "Mr. Talbot," a raw-boned Atlantean man, rather than the shy woman with blazing red hair.

It was still uncanny how a trace of Ardhuin was still visible in the illusion if you knew where to look.

Ardhuin glanced at her and kept walking past, but Gutrune saw the shimmering fog that sprang up around them and knew it was more concealing magic, making it safe to follow her to her cabin. Once inside, Ardhuin gestured with graceful command—more magic—and her shoulders slumped with relief.

"Oof. I hope I never see another camel again." The illusioned face showed chagrin. "But you had it much worse, leading one. However did you manage?"

"Extract of bitumen, on a rag concealed in my turban veil. It deadens the sense of smell." Gutrune hesitated, embarrassed by her discomfort. "If it is not too much trouble, would you..." she gestured at Ardhuin's face.

Mr. Talbot gave his engaging grin, and then Ardhuin's familiar features replaced them. "Of course. I forget myself, since I don't often see my reflection. And Dominic can see through it anyway, but he still dislikes it."

"Understandable," Gutrune murmured. "It would explain the occasional lapse in his usual cheerful nature. We have not had much opportunity to speak since I joined you, and I hope you will permit me to ask some questions of a more personal interest." Ardhuin nodded, looking concerned. "It is...the mineral salts. I am sure the effects of my accidental exposure have faded, however...can you think of any way to...prevent it from happening again?"

"I have not had an opportunity to study it, beyond the first time you showed it to us," Ardhuin said apologetically. "And given its power, I would want strong wards and no distractions. It is very dangerous, as you know. It appears to me, though, that mere proximity is not a problem. You were able to carry it without ill effect?" Gutrune nodded. "Well then. My first guess is the mineral salt must be ingested somehow—either swallowing or breathing it in. If you were to cover your nose and mouth, that would give you a measure of protection."

"When it hit me, it felt...as if I were about to explode," Gutrune whispered. "Is that...is that how you feel? With your magic?"

Ardhuin sat down on the bunk beside her and clasped Gutrune's tightly gripped hands with her own.

"No. Not at all. What happened to you was a different matter entirely—abnormal and extreme. Tell me—when I cast illusion on you earlier, did it feel at all uncomfortable?"

Gutrune, puzzled, thought back and eventually shook her head.

"Good. That means you have not been sensitized. Please do not worry. You don't have to handle everything on your own now. You have three magicians and a scryer to help you." Ardhuin's hand tightened, then relaxed. "Now, I must speak on another delicate point. How much of what happened to you have you reported to Preusa?"

"Very little. It seemed dangerous to mention even in coded telegrams. I changed the shipping address on the crate for my brother to intercept it, but I warned him not to open it."

"Good." Ardhuin hesitated a moment, a faint flush growing on her face. "I must ask you not to reveal anything more. To anyone—and impress upon Stoller and Herr Asgaya that any information about the mineral salts must be kept secret. This is a dangerous development, and the more I think about it, it must be the danger that MacCrimmon feared so greatly. I hope you do not feel that I am asking you to compromise your loyalty to the King." Now her face was quite red, and her eyes were lowered. "I know you do not take your service lightly. But I also have a duty, and in this case, I believe I must conceal the nature of the mineral salts completely. For the safety of Aerope."

Gutrune smiled. "The King gives me great latitude for the performance of my duties. If it is for the safety of Aerope, there is no conflict in what you ask."

"Well, if a conflict *should* develop, can I count on you to warn me first?" Gutrune nodded, and Ardhuin gave a hesitant smile. "Now, what exactly happened to you? You only gave a brief description, but I would like to know more. If you don't mind."

"As long as there is no repetition, I can—"

The door to the cabin opened, and Dominic came in. "Why is there..." he gestured vaguely, then caught sight of Gutrune. "Oh, there you are! We were wondering...that is, I believe Herr Asgaya wanted to speak with you." He smiled at Ardhuin. "Ah, that's better."

Seeing Ardhuin's answering smile, Gutrune rose. "I should see what he has to say, then. We will speak later of my experiences."

Ardhuin nodded without removing her gaze from Dominic, and Gutrune left the cabin after first making sure the corridor was clear. She had not spent much time with her friend after her marriage—just letters— so she had not realized how Ardhuin lost focus when Dominic was present. And he did as well, she mused. It would be better to return when Ardhuin could give her full attention, and, she admitted, she wanted her friend to have a few moments of privacy. It could not be easy for her being in disguise for so long.

She found Markus on the side deck with Sonam, having a somewhat abbreviated conversation with their limited common vocabulary. While Markus had a crease of worry between his brows, the closer they got to Bhuta, the more animated and cheerful Sonam became.

"No, not like bird. No wings! But yes, go in sky." Sonam moved his hand in a sinuous fashion. "*Kai-ling*, like this."

Markus gave him a skeptical look. "That doesn't sound like any dragon

I've ever heard of." He saw Gutrune and his head snapped around.

"Some shadow, if you would be so kind." Gutrune wished she could avoid magic entirely right now, but they needed concealment.

"At once." Markus gestured, and the blurry fog sprang up around them. "I don't like this separate boarding plan; I'm always afraid we'll miss you."

"It's better that we avoid connecting myself with your group as long as possible. I will have to travel with you once we reach Cathai. Is that what you wished to speak to me about?" Seeing his blank look, she added, "Herr Kermarec mentioned it when I saw him just now."

"Oh. Yes. Yes, indeed. Er, what was the latest information you received from Baerlen?"

Gutrune raised an eyebrow. "Other than extremely brief telegrams, the most recent intelligence reached me in Anatoli, at Denais's hideout."

They were speaking Preusan, and after a few minutes Sonam gave a quick nod of his head and wandered off.

"Right. Your brother was quite worried about you not getting the information you needed. He insisted I get you caught up. Firstly, the military detachment was delayed in their departure. They are now two weeks behind us, and that's if there are no further difficulties."

"What delayed them this time?"

He shrugged. "Apparently it was decided to take some experimental apparatus—the details were not available. Or they were too sensitive to divulge to me," he added, grinning.

Gutrune frowned. "You make light of a serious matter. The timing of their arrival could be crucial to our success."

"True—but there are always ways around obstacles. I imagine they will be more forthcoming if you make the request, or your brother does, and he will find a way to tell you."

"It should not be necessary to play such games," Gutrune muttered, frustrated. Markus showed no sign of diminished calm, and she wondered at it. Was he so inured to the vagaries of the court?

He gave her a sidelong glance. "If we had not played games, as you phrase it, we would have nothing. It's a bloody miracle they decided to send as many as they did, but your brother knew exactly which officers to ask. It was impressive to watch." He looked out over the water for a moment. "Does it bother you? All the intrigue," he clarified at her questioning glance.

"There was a time I would thrive on intrigue, but I find I have less patience for it on the receiving end," she said dryly.

"Why did you leave the court, then? Did you step aside for your brother's sake?"

She shook her head. "This career has its own rewards, despite the difficulties and discomforts. I am glad Heinrich is doing so well, but he is not...it was merely an opportunity to serve us both."

"And do you ever think that you will tire of this, as well? Would you ever consider giving it up for something else?"

Gutrune folded her arms. "No. Why would I, when this is what I always wanted? The freedom..." she caught herself. "The King's service is always paramount. But I can do so much more here."

"Of course, and you do it well. You have quite a talent for disguise, matched only by your skill in tracking information." It seemed to Gutrune that his expression, which had been mobile and animated, changed and became less open. Less reflective of his emotions. Guarded. She wondered why. Perhaps Heinrich had asked him to persuade her to come back to Preusa and the court.

"I have always enjoyed the hunt." She turned to leave.

Markus cleared his throat, and she looked back. "I saw this in the market before we boarded." He reached into an inner pocket of his jacket. "I know you prefer your pistols, but in this part of the world they can draw too much unwanted attention—and we are trying to avoid notice."

He held out a knife in a plain leather sheath. Gutrune took it, suddenly uncertain. Perhaps she had misjudged him. The blade was narrow and covered by the dull watermark of damascene. It felt light and balanced in her hand. "Excellent craftsmanship. I can indeed make use of this. Thank you."

"I live to serve," Markus said softly as she walked away.

Ardhuin frowned, focusing intently on keeping everyone slightly levitated while simultaneously casting the wards. It was fortunate, in that respect, that the cabin was not large, but that made it awkward for everyone that needed to be inside while it was cast. Dominic, Sonam, Gutrune, and Markus formed a tight knot in the small clear area between the bunks, while Ardhuin stood against the door.

"There. That should do the trick. I feel much better about keeping the mineral essence in here—but I am still not sure it is a good idea."

"I can still see it quite clearly," Dominic said. "I suppose the iron we packed around it is not enough."

"It definitely made it easier to cast the wards. I doubt we could do anything to shield it completely. You have not noticed any...other effects?" Dominic shook his head. She knew it was dangerous to leave the salts in the hold, where anyone might access them, but it was also dangerous to expose Dominic to their effects. She would simply have to keep a watchful eye on him and make sure he was not concealing anything from her.

"I hear that we have caught an early trade wind, so we may even make up some time." Markus folded his height with some difficulty to fit in the lower bunk. "Now, there is something that doesn't quite fit. If everyone in Sonam's valley can use magic, why can't they defend themselves against Denais?"

"We do not know magic for fighting," Sonam explained after a few unfamiliar words were translated. "For us, magic is...an extra hand. To help with work. Children use it for games, and for festival dances."

Ardhuin thought a moment. "But you use powerful magic—are there no others like yourself there?"

Sonam gave a quick, unhappy smile, his eyes downcast. "I have learned your way of making spells. Many say it is not...that the spirits prefer the old ways. Also, the custom is the warriors fight, and they have iron—they call it star-metal. They do not like even our magics around their weapons."

Ah. This could be difficult.

"You told us MacCrimmon had protected the valley with magic," Dominic said, brows knitted. "They did not object to this?"

"The people were fearful." Sonam spoke in a soft voice, his gaze averted. "They wanted a shield to protect them—but it was not an easy thing to agree to."

"Understandable." Ardhuin sensed he did not want to discuss the matter any further. "So, let us see if we can help Gutrune with her disguise. I thought if you had a piece of that metal you use, Dominic, we could try that."

"You mean like your pendant? Wouldn't she need magical ability to use it, though?" He lifted a skeptical eyebrow.

Ardhuin shook her head. "I think if I use enough power, I can infuse the entire spell. I was wondering if we used a bit of the mineral salt, it would act like magical power." She saw Gutrune's face go a shade paler and hastened to reassure her. "It would all be bound together with the spell. It would not, er, contaminate you. Would you be willing to make a trial?"

Gutrune nodded, but slowly. Ardhuin looked at her, not sure if she should say anything. Gutrune's jaw was set, her eyes narrowed. It would seem she was reluctant but determined.

"I believe I still have a few bits of the alloy left, stored with the imager in the event a repair was needed. In the left compartment, under the bunk." Dominic pointed, and Markus swung his long legs up to the bed. "Aaah— that's also where the salts jar is. Would you mind holding it for a moment? I just need this box..."

Markus contorted himself again to move various pieces of scrap iron away and reach for the clay jar, and Dominic rooted in the compartment.

"It looks so innocuous, for so much trouble." Markus hefted the jar to get a better view, just as the ship rocked sharply. The jar slipped from his hands and fell with a hard thump into the box Dominic was lifting up. Gutrune stepped back sharply, her face white, and she instantly pulled a fold of her jacket over her face.

"Is it broken?" Ardhuin leaned over, ready to shield Dominic if it proved necessary.

"No, but almost as bad—the lid came loose. The twine was frayed." He squinted. "I think a little spilled out, but not much. It's hard to tell."

"Here, let me." Ardhuin reached in and carefully lifted the imager out. The risk of exposure was less for her than Dominic. "Oh, one of the levers is bent."

"The alloy works well for magical infusion, but it is softer than I like." Dominic grimaced. "I can't tell if the salts damaged the spells. It's all mixed together, and so bright." He reached into the box again. "But this looks unharmed. We can make your illusion charm, and maybe use up any of the spilled salts."

A few grains were still in the bottom of the box. They resisted levitation, sliding free when she tried. In the end, she used the end of an ivory toothbrush to gather them together, then laid the small piece of metal on top.

When she invoked the spell, the surge of power was a jolt. Ardhuin caught and held it, clenching her teeth with the effort to keep it in place. It almost felt as if it were trying to escape, like a landed fish.

"What...illusion do you...want?" she managed to gasp.

"The one you cast most recently," Gutrune said instantly. Ardhuin focused the image in her mind, shaped the structures and the illusion that covered them, and slammed the magic into the metal.

"Well. That was...instructive." She wiped her forehead. She held up the piece of metal, and Dominic studied it for a moment.

"Very strange. The spell is there, and so is a web of...I suppose that is the power. But why does it not give you the illusion?"

"I made it only for Gutrune. The base structure will only fit her, so it would be useless for anyone else."

She held it out. Gutrune reached for it, keeping it as far away as she could, but the instant her fingers touched it, the illusion sprang up around her.

"Oh, well done!" Markus sat up, hitting his head on the underside of the bunk with a muttered curse and slumping down again.

"It feels no different." Gutrune sounded relieved. "And to remove it?"

"Wrap it in something thick, and keep it away from your skin. If we had any silver tissue, or chryselectrum..."

Gutrune gave a small smile. "Either of which would advertise the magical nature of the charm, no? I will find a means to hide it, then." She put her hand on the doorknob of the cabin.

"Why don't we have Herr Asgaya accompany you, so you can have an avoidance shield as well as your new illusion," Dominic suggested in a suddenly bright tone.

Gutrune lifted an eyebrow. "There is no need to inconvenience him so."

Ardhuin took her place at the door, opened it a crack, and peered out. "Completely empty." Gutrune smiled her thanks and slipped out.

When Ardhuin turned back, Markus was making a silent face at Dominic, who was shrugging. Both turned bland, innocent faces her way when they noticed she was staring at them.

"It's a pity she left before seeing your imager in action," Markus said. "I think she would have enjoyed it—but no, business first."

Dominic scowled. "I hope it still works. What will we do if the spells are damaged too? Can we remove the extra magic, or will I have to make it again from scratch?"

"There is only one way to find out." Markus grinned encouragingly.

Dominic fiddled with the device, pressing various levers and turning a dial before holding it up, aiming it at Ardhuin. He pressed the main lever, but instead of the usual loud click, it rattled for a moment. Ardhuin stepped forward to examine the device, but the rattling suddenly stopped.

"Oh, blast. The main spring must be misaligned...but did it capture an image?" Dominic pressed the other control, the one that displayed the image.

Instead of the frozen instant of illusion, a series of images, following closely on one another, showed a small, ghostly Ardhuin first in profile, smiling, then turning her head to face the viewer with a concerned expression.

"Do it again." Markus was staring at the image intently. "That was fascinating. Almost real. A true illusion. Wouldn't it be remarkable if you could also capture sound?"

With a start, Ardhuin remembered the magic MacCrimmon had used for his message. "But we can do that already. What are you thinking of?"

Markus waved a hand. "Oh, anything...a recorded message that would be secure, and proving the identity of the source. Or a famous singer." He grinned.

"Bah. What would be the use of that, when you would have to arrange to hear the singer anyway to create the image?" Dominic grumbled, shoving the imager back in its box. "Far easier to just get a parrot. Now I'll have to completely redo it, and when will I have the chance?" Another roll of the ship made him lose his balance and stumble against the wall. "Certainly not here."

His eyes widened and his irritation vanished, replaced by a look of fascination Ardhuin was beginning to recognize. "I wonder...how far down do waves go? If I made a larger submersible that could travel under water..."

CHAPTER 11

Dominic sat at his tiny desk and wrote furiously, trying to get all of the rich details down while they were fresh in his mind. He could rearrange them to suit the story later. He was vaguely aware of an empty sensation in his stomach and idly wondered if he had not heard the summons to lunch, or if he had merely forgotten to eat again.

"We've stopped, but this isn't Kiantan."

Bewildered, Dominic looked up from his writing. For a moment he was disoriented, missing the birdcage with his pet mouse, then remembered. He was on a ship thousands of leagues from Peran, and this was not his desk but one in the tiny passenger saloon. Markus Asgaya was standing beside him, a small line of worry between his brows.

"Supplies, perhaps?"

Markus shook his head. "The whole journey takes two weeks at most. This ship is provisioned for months. Ho, Bové! Do you know why we are stopping?"

The expedition leader sighed. "New customs requirements, I hear. The Cathan government is paranoid about foreign influences, some times more than others. Our arrival appears to have coincided with the high tide of officialdom. It shouldn't be too bad, at least this direction. They might want a small bribe to let all our supplies through. No, it's going back that they are dangerous. I've had to wait months for them to release our specimens, on some trumped-up pretext."

"Ah. How charming that such disparate cultures have bureaucracy in common," Markus remarked. "I feel quite at home."

Bové laughed and went back to his planning. Markus took a seat in one of the overstuffed and slightly threadbare armchairs, and Dominic went back to work. Only to be interrupted a few moments later by the arrival of the ship's purser, a harassed-looking man with sandy hair and freckles.

"Got some messages waitin' for you at the trade station, sir." He handed Bové several slips of paper. "Oh, and one for you, Mr. Asgaya."

Markus took it, one eyebrow raised. "Now who would be sending anything to me here? Oh. Him. Of course." He tucked the message in an inside pocket of his coat and stood, giving Dominic a significant look before leaving the saloon.

Dominic sighed, blotted the few new lines he had added, closed the inkwell, and folded up his work before leaving the saloon himself. Markus was on the open deck, frowning at the sea and the longboat leaving the ship.

"Well?"

Markus didn't look up. "It's from her brother. I'm to pass on a message, in code, naturally. If he can find out where this blasted ship is going to stop before I do even when I'm on it, you would think he could also find a way to reach her directly."

Dominic tried to hide his smile. "She hardly knows herself what new alias she will find useful, and it is not the sort of thing she would want to communicate. It is much better for him to send to someone traveling under his own name, and who would be expected to get foreign telegrams."

Markus made a grumbling noise. "I suppose."

"So, have you made any progress?" Dominic returned Markus's narrowed stare with his most bland expression. "Did she like the knife?"

Markus leaned his elbows on the rail and dropped his face on his hands. "Yes, yes, you were right. Of *course* she liked the knife. For all I know she's used it already. I don't think it is a wise tactic to pursue, though. It only encourages her."

Dominic rolled his eyes. "I think you need to ask yourself why you find yourself drawn to her if you disapprove of what she does. Of all the ladies at the Preusan court, you chose her. Why? Her impeccable society manners? Her frivolous conversation and fondness for gossip?" Despite himself, Markus grinned. "Do you imagine she will ever sit contentedly at home, having tea parties while you have adventures?"

Markus straightened up. "Well, when you put it that way...no, I don't see her deriving much enjoyment from a society tea party."

"Well, what *do* you want?" Dominic threw up his hands in exasperation.

The brief amusement in Markus's face vanished. "What I can't have, most likely. It is a common refrain."

And now Dominic was feeling sorry for him again. "You certainly can't expect conventionality—but it can still work. Ardhuin and I manage quite well."

Markus bared his teeth. "Fräulein von Kitren's devotion to duty is complete and her notions of proper behavior strict."

"Sorry, this *is* the woman who launched herself through an upper window of a caravanserai in full Bedun garb, correct? At midnight?"

"I was referring to the sort of...arrangement of convenience and understanding that can take place—but which she would regard as an insult, and rightly so," Markus said, his offhand manner somewhat strained. "But then, an arrangement that she would agree to, assuming permission would be obtained from her royal employer, it only removes one difficulty and replaces it with another. A difficulty you yourself have encountered—and I am not a monk."

Dominic frowned at him. "Neither am I."

Before Markus could respond, intrigued curiosity in his eyes, something caught Dominic's attention. Something bright was in the longboat, now returning to the ship. Something magically bright. A chill of fear washed over him.

"That inspection Bové referred to...does it involve magic?"

Bové did not know, but the purser, more current, did. "Yes sir, they are dead set against any foreign magic getting in. Seems they think it will corrupt their own right and proper magic, what's been approved by the emperor and such."

"You mean they forbid magicians from entering?"

"If they don't do any magic, who's to know?" The purser shrugged. "It's new. All they told me is they are looking for any magic equipment and spells, and anybody with 'em won't be let in."

Dominic and Markus exchanged quick, startled glances. "What are we going to do? That longboat must already be here," Dominic said, feeling panicked. The mineral salts alone would be enough to get them in trouble, but if they could also detect the illusions on Ardhuin and Gutrune...

"You go find your wife. I'll find Bové and get him to delay the inspectors." Markus turned quickly, then gasped and stepped back.

Bové was standing in the doorway of the saloon, staring at him with a hard expression in his eyes. "What's going on? What are you hiding? Don't imagine I'm going to help you smuggle contraband, because—"

"Oh, don't be ridiculous," Markus snarled at him while shoving Dominic toward the door to the cabins. "This air of outraged innocence does not become you. You knew when you saw who was funding us that we weren't off to pick daisies. Get going—we don't have much time!" he snapped at Dominic over his shoulder.

Dominic ran. What could they do, even if he did find Ardhuin? They'd have to use magic to hide, but that would be detected, wouldn't it? *Not if we know what they are detecting first.* Back in Baerlen, with the students—even they didn't have universal detection devices, and in the Cathan empire, famous for its reluctance to make use of modern magical science, how would they be able to do better? The detection device had to be fairly strong for him to have seen it at such a distance, but it might be highly specific.

After a frantic search Dominic found Ardhuin coming back with Sonam from the hold where their baggage was stored. Dominic quickly described the problem.

"Sonam can remove his illusion," Ardhuin began, but Sonam shook his head.

"To see one of my people, here? They will notice and remark on it.

Perhaps forbid me to travel. I should not show my true face to them."

Ardhuin rubbed her forehead, wincing. "We need to find out what they are using. If there is a way to hide from it, then we will know what to do."

"We definitely need to hide Sonam, the mineral salts, and the imager in the cabin. Any other magical equipment in the hold we can deny, but those things will give the game away. But they will search the entire ship; where can we hide them?"

Sonam's eyes brightened. "I hide outside the ship! On a rope. When they go, I climb up."

"But they will see you," Ardhuin protested. "There are people in the boat the inspector came on, for one thing. This ship is out in the open water with no concealment."

Dominic suddenly remembered his experiments in the fishpond back home. "But if he were underwater, they could not see him." He turned to Sonam. "Can you make a...a ward, like a bubble, that contains air to breathe, and submerge?" Sonam hesitated, then nodded quickly.

"I saw some rope back in the hold," Ardhuin said. "I think you are small enough to fit through the porthole in our cabin—can you take down the wards? We can't leave them up, I suppose."

"I can do this. They will not find me." Sonam darted off.

"We had better go. Have you seen Gutrune?" Dominic asked. "She's got that illusioned charm now."

Ardhuin thinned her lips. "The best thing we can do for her now is find a way around that magic detector."

Since he had nothing to hide, Dominic went first through the ship, looking for the inspection team, while Ardhuin followed behind concealed in shadow. He found the Cathan inspectors in the passenger saloon, arguing with the purser through an interpreter.

"What do you mean, you have to check all foreigners on board? Why? We have their names and nationalities here on this list, and that's been good enough for years!"

"We must see face, to not let criminal inside our borders," the head inspector insisted. "All person on ship."

They wanted to check everyone, and Dominic could guess why. The purser's face was becoming progressively more flushed as he argued, so this must be a completely new regulation, or one invented by this official. He shook his head. Another problem, but a minor one. He focused on the carved ivory staff, bright with magic, carried by the inspector's assistant. At a gesture the assistant held it horizontally before him and walked about the saloon.

Dominic squinted. The staff generated a cloud of magic about itself, and when it encountered anything with magic, a gem inset in the staff flashed. Dominic saw it detect the philogiston light, and how the cloud shrank away from the phlogiston.

He faded back to where Ardhuin was hiding, under the cover of the ship's officers summoned to help the infuriated purser explain they couldn't remove the lighting and it would stay on the ship no matter what. He explained what he saw in a whisper. "It looks a little like the sensing field you once cast," he added. "Is that what they are doing?"

"It is possible...did it look like this?" Ardhuin created a little ball of magic. Dominic shook his head. "Or perhaps like this?"

The second attempt was a much closer match. Dominic went back to the saloon, waving one finger behind his back when the inspectors were looking away from the doorway. He saw the flash of magic go by his head, and the silvery light encased a brass spittoon in the corner.

When the assistant with the staff went by, it did not detect the magic on the spittoon.

"Ha!" Ardhuin had a fiercely triumphant gleam in her eye. "It's just checking for a field that isn't like itself. And it isn't strong enough to go through a field. All I have to do is put up a layer of magic like the detector's around everything we need to hide."

"Did you hear what he said? They are checking the passenger list. If Sonam isn't present..."

Ardhuin nodded. "I have an idea. I think you should find Gutrune now, and tell her to go to our cabin without them seeing her."

Dominic left to deliver the message and to check on the inspection of the goods in the hold. When he returned to the cabin, the inspectors were already there. He took a deep breath and continued forward. Magic was bright everywhere inside. "Mr. Talbot" was encased in multiple layers, protecting the illusion concealing Ardhuin, and a complete illusion showed a sleeping young man in the lower bunk with the appearance Sonam wore when illusioned. He looked tired and ill. Gutrune was there too, leaning against the wall, face impassive.

"He's been seasick," Ardhuin explained, after the officials started suggesting a quarantine. "Nothing serious."

After the officials left, Dominic stood in the doorway, watching other inspections. Every Aeropan passenger was examined, but especially the few women—and Dominic saw one lady with sandy hair being escorted out by the officials, protesting loudly that she had done nothing wrong.

Dominic watched her go, frowning. He decided to go up on deck so they would know when the inspectors had left. It took them two hours, but eventually they did. Bové came up as their longboat pulled away.

"They've never done anything like this before." He took a pull on his pipe, face impassive. "I certainly got the impression they were looking for something. Or someone."

"Yes. I wonder why?"

Bové gave him a long look. "So do I. Apparently that something, or someone, isn't on this ship—or is well hidden. And as long as that situation continues, I won't ask awkward questions." He pointed the stem of his pipe at Dominic, his eyes narrowed. "I don't know what you're up to, and it's probably better I don't. Maybe there's more to you than meets the eye. But you want to be careful. I heard what Asgaya asked you earlier."

"What do you mean?" Dominic felt a sinking feeling.

Bové smiled. "I just realized—I don't recall that you received any messages from your wife since we left Bretagne. I hope all is well at home?"

The ramp flexed disconcertingly as Dominic stepped on it, but it remained intact and in place long enough for everyone to depart the strange square-sailed boat that had taken them from the clipper to the foreigners' dock. Even that was not land, but a huge floating building in the harbor of Kiantan. Only after they had been given official government passes would they be allowed to set foot on the territory of Cathai.

"It's bigger than Peran," Ardhuin whispered, following close behind him.

Beams jutted out from the sides, carved with square geometric designs on every surface. Small paper lanterns hung from the ends of the beams, with—Dominic peered underneath—actual burning lights inside.

"Aren't they afraid of fire?" he wondered.

"Very much so." Bové, leading the way, turned his head to speak. "And even more afraid of plague. Foreigners and their ideas are, of course, considered a form of plague. Hence the isolated barge and the purification lamps."

"Is that what the markings mean? I thought they were just decoration."

Bové smiled. "The inscriptions very prettily warn of evil emanations and uncouth behavior."

Ardhuin paused to admire a carved wooden door featuring a stylized Cathan lady and something that was either a small, extremely shaggy horse or a large, enraged dog. "Why, if they fear fire, do they not use philogiston for light?"

"Because philogiston is Aeropan magic, and as such viewed as a threat to Imperial order." Bové stopped at a set of large, red-lacquered doors and rapped sharply with his knuckles. A small, older man opened the door a crack, looked at him, and impassively opened the door wide enough for them to enter. The room inside was dark, but with gleams of gold from gilded decorations on every surface, even the ceiling.

Bové spoke enough Cathan to deal with the several layers of bureaucracy and was apparently familiar with all the procedures. Each member of the expedition was brought forth, scrutinized, and a description written on a long slip of paper with a slender brush. Even that was not enough, for the slip of paper had to be taken to yet another bureaucrat where, for a fee, a red, square stamp was inked on the slip and the whole rolled up, tied with a black silk cord, and placed in a wooden cylinder.

"Don't lose these," Bové said, handing them out. "If you're found without them, the penalty is severe—and they will likely beat you in addition just to make sure you get the point. And don't get them mixed up, either."

They left the floating building for another boat, this time through a guarded gateway. Kiantan harbor was crowded with ships, mostly the square-sailed Cathan boats with high decks. On land, the crowding was even more noticeable. The streets were jammed with people, most of whom were carrying huge piles of goods either on their backs or balanced on the ends of poles. Although Dominic felt quite conspicuous, standing a head taller than the local Cathans and so differently dressed, the carriers paid no attention to them. They were instead yelling at each other, apparently to get out of the way.

"Something smells delicious," Ardhuin said.

"Probably pork." Bové gestured at a street vendor who was cooking meat on skewers over a tiny charcoal firepot. "They eat everything but the squeal, so be careful."

Markus was looking about at the noise and crowds with a slight frown. "Where are we headed?"

"The White Jade Pavilion." Bové gestured down the street to a building of four stories. Unlike the rest, which had paper banners dangling from every surface with Cathan script written on them, it was simple and plain. White paper screens covered the windows, glowing from the light inside. As they got closer, Dominic saw an old, bent man wearing the loose Cathan clothes in dark blue with gold medallions open the door, bowing, for two patrons.

"Nicest fancy-house in Kiantan," Simons said, grinning. "Although I still prefer the Aleksandri girls."

Markus, Ardhuin, and Dominic started, and Bové rolled his eyes. "Yes, they do provide that kind of hospitality if you ask for it, but plenty of respectable businessmen go there merely for tea, music, or in our case, a temporary headquarters. This kind of tea house...well, it isn't a concept that translates well outside Cathai. It saves us time in the long run. Mother Long knows everyone and everything that is going on in Kiantan and can facilitate any additional needs before our departure."

"For a price," grumbled Simons.

"And for that price, we are left alone," Bové said. "Mother Long dislikes anyone interfering with her customers." He glanced at Dominic. "It is also safer for Aeropans. Many locals feel it is perfectly acceptable to cheat and steal from foreigners. Especially if they think you do not know the customs."

The White Jade Pavilion certainly appeared respectable, despite its reputed side business. Dominic saw nothing tawdry or suggestive—but perhaps he was simply unaware of what a Cathan would consider beyond the bounds of propriety. They were served dinner in a large private room that had, unusually, full-size chairs instead of the low benches he had seen everywhere else since arriving in Cathai. It would indeed appear the owners were accustomed to Aeropan preferences.

The meal was delicious, but Dominic was hard put to identify the sauces, spices, or even the meat involved. Near the end Bové gestured to one of the pretty young serving girls and whispered to her. She bowed and left, returning shortly thereafter carrying a tray with a porcelain teapot and several delicate cups. She set the tea down on a side table, and a few moments later an older Cathan woman entered the room.

She was wearing a short jacket of pink silk embroidered with white chrysanthemums and a pleated green skirt with a flat panel in front, also richly embroidered. Small gold pendants dangled from ornaments in the complex style of smooth loops of her jet-black hair, arranged like a coronet.

Bové rose and bowed to her in the Cathan fashion, which she returned. "Gentlemen, for those of you who have not had the pleasure, allow me to introduce Mother Long. We have a few new faces," he said to her, introducing Dominic, Markus, "Mr. Talbot," and Sonam, using the name he had acquired among the expedition, Sam.

Mother Long maintained a polite but distant expression as she acknowledged them, but her eyes looked at them sharply. As she poured tea and handed the delicate cups out, Bové asked jovially, "What news? Does all go well with your house?"

"It has been an uncertain year," Mother Long answered in perfect Gaulan. Her answer appeared to sober Bové. "But we have no cause to complain. Our visitors remain faithful, for now, but there is word that the Cabot shipping house thinks of moving their warehouses to Naipon. It would be sad to see them leave."

Bové sipped his tea thoughtfully. "We were stopped before Kiantan, for inspection of our cargo."

"All ships with Aeropan passengers are being stopped," Mother Long said, her face serene. "There is no mention that foreigners are unwelcome. Yet. It is thought someone is being looked for, but no one knows who it is. Asking would be, perhaps, unwise. The orders go most high."

"I do not recall any interest shown on my last visit—but perhaps I was not paying attention."

Mother Long folded her hands in her lap. "The orders have only been in place a short time."

"Well, I hope official curiosity has been satisfied concerning my expedition, at any rate. We have much to do."

"One hopes the usual arrangements will be sufficient?" Mother Long lifted one elegant eyebrow. "With, of course, the addition of your new friends."

Bové waved a hand. "Yes, yes, of course. Unless the road has become more dangerous."

Mother Long shook her head. "It is much the same as last year." She rose from her chair and left the room.

As soon as the door closed Bové let out a gust of air. "Damn. I wonder if this will be the last trip."

Dominic blinked. "But...it sounds as if nothing has changed."

"From what she just told us, the government is getting stranger. Cabot does perhaps twenty to twenty-five percent of the shipping here. If they are thinking of leaving, things are bad. And if the road is just as dangerous as before...well, that's even worse. The government got a lot of complaints about the bandits and swore they would increase patrols and replace the provincial governors. Either nothing happened or the bandits won. The government's been shaky for a while, but this could signal the end. Don't talk about this outside the White Jade, do you understand? Mother Long's people are very discreet, but there are informers everywhere, and it's so crowded anyone could be listening in without you knowing."

After the remains of the dinner were cleared away, musicians came and played strange long-necked string instruments with a nasal tone, while more tea was provided along with bowls of small fruits, none of which Dominic could identify.

Their rooms were located on the top level of the pavilion, and from an elliptical comment from Simons, Dominic had the impression this level was reserved for those guests who did not intend to make use of the services provided by the White Jade's *other* serving girls. Their suite had a central area in common and separate sleeping alcoves behind heavy curtains. The beds themselves looked like little pavilions, with steps and railings and even canopies.

Markus left to find Gutrune and Stoller, while Ardhuin and Dominic admired the furnishings of the room.

"I've never seen so much carving...and why do these huge beds have such tiny rolls for pillows?"

"I'm just glad to be well away from bunks on ships," Dominic said fervently. "And cramped cabins."

"How long do we stay here?" Sonam asked.

Dominic shrugged. "I'm not sure—at least a week, from what Bové was saying. It sounded like Mother Long is arranging the transportation for the expedition as well as most of the bulk supplies, and she would have no reason to be in a hurry."

"Well, if she knows everything and everyone in Kiantan, perhaps we should ask her about the items on Henri's list," Ardhuin said. "If we can't leave right away, we should make good use of the time we have."

"An excellent idea," Markus said as he entered the room, followed by Gutrune and Stoller. "But how will this help us find Henri's former employer?"

Ardhuin sat on one of the carved wooden chairs. "If we ask where such things could be found, as we stroll about the city, then we could ask the shopkeepers. If we can understand them..." she said slowly. "Bové could, but he might wonder why. Sonam, can you?"

He inclined his head. "Enough, I think. But hearing me speak, they would know my accent is not from Aerope—let us ask Mother Long to write down the Cathan script for the things we seek. Also, if they think we do not speak their language well, they will not guard their speech in our presence."

Dominic went to his trunk, already placed by the efficient pavilion servants in the main room, and opened it. "I have the list here somewhere...we can give it to her in the morning."

"Why not now?" Gutrune gestured toward the door. "Mother Long is, I believe, still welcoming guests below."

"A point." Markus rubbed his chin. "And the night is young."

Dominic copied the list on a fresh half sheet of paper he found in a drawer of the suite desk, and Markus departed on his errand.

"We have obtained some better maps of the region." Gutrune reached into an inner pocket and pulled out three rolls of heavy yellow paper. "From the Donesta monks, so the names are in Romai and Cathan—but they assure us the geographic information is accurate. It seems one of the monks' missions is introducing improved agriculture to better the lot of the poor."

Dominic spread the maps out, holding down the corners with various porcelain figurines and lacquer-ware boxes when the maps showed an inclination to roll themselves back up again. "Ah, this is much better. What route do you advise, Sonam?"

Sonam studied the maps, tapping one area with a finger. "It is best not to cross here. Desert, and dangerous people. We would need to carry much water and fodder for the animals. If we can find a boat that goes on shallow rivers, that would be longer, but safer. This place here. I know traders go through there, and strangers are less noticed."

While Sonam discussed various options, Dominic got out his pen and ink and carefully noted the names Sonam gave, matching the local language rather than the ones already on the map. During this discussion Markus returned and joined them standing around the table.

"I doubt we will be able to help ourselves to much of Bové's supplies, so we should also think about what we need to find on our own. And the return trip too."

"The Preusan reinforcements should be able to help with that," Gutrune remarked.

Sonam looked up. "And my people, as well."

"I am more concerned with any additional magical inspections that we may encounter." Ardhuin was frowning. "We need to get to Bhuta without detection before we worry about our return."

"Do you think there will be someone looking for us specifically?"

She shook her head. "They have border crossings for the provinces as well, I understand. For taxes and such. I suppose we should assume any government interaction has the risk of the magic detectors and shield accordingly."

"I wish we knew exactly what they were looking for," Dominic murmured. "If Denais has the cooperation of the Cathan government, this journey will be very difficult."

"Then we must merely disguise ourselves as government inspectors," Markus said, grinning.

Dominic gave him a disbelieving look. "Under a strict vow of silence? None of us speak Cathan, remember."

Markus waved away this minor detail, opening his mouth to presumably make more amusing suggestions, when a knock sounded at the door. Ardhuin gestured with a faint, glittering wave of magic, dissipating the sound shield and shadowing Gutrune and Stoller, and then Dominic opened the door.

Outside was one of the pavilion servants, who bowed and held out a black tray with a folded sheet of paper. Inside was his list, and the sheet that covered it had a list of names. Shop names.

"Mother Long wishes to speak with you tomorrow," the servant said. "This one would be most happy to show you to these places before that."

Dominic blinked, surprised. "That is very kind of you, but surely we can just get directions and not inconvenience you so greatly?"

The man permitted himself a small smile. "To those of Kiantan, the names of streets are already known—and to put up a sign would be foolish and unnecessary. To assist the foreign guests without this knowledge is our honor. But in this case, Mother Long has ordered this."

"Why is that?" Ardhuin asked slowly.

The man bowed again. "She is concerned for the safety of her guests. This is what she wishes to discuss, where others cannot hear."

CHAPTER 12

Gutrune was glad they had taken the trouble to get Cathan clothing as part of their disguise. As crowded as the streets were, it was impossible not to collide with anyone, and the illusions were purely visual. She and Stoller, attired as servants, trailed Sonam in his Aeropan disguise—and the three of them followed the larger party of Ardhuin, Dominic, Markus, and the guide. She had suggested it, mostly to see if anyone was interested in Ardhuin's group, or if it was merely general curiosity about Aeropans.

At first the strangeness of Kiantan was overpowering, but slowly she became accustomed—and started noticing things. Most of the people were very thin and their clothing faded and patched. One building, better maintained than most and with soldiers on guard, had a wooden rack with severed heads in varying states of decay and signs underneath them, presumably listing the crimes committed by the deceased. The locals kept their gazes studiously averted, and indeed left an unusual amount of space free in front of the building, unlike the crowded street.

The day grew hot and the smells of the city overwhelming. Gutrune and Stoller remained outside when the others went inside the shops on the list, to avoid any watchers who might notice and make a connection between the two parties. She or Stoller kept an eye on the street during these side excursions, giving a sign to the other when it was time to move on.

"The shop before this, I heard the clerks talking," Sonam said at one point, when they were alone. "They remarked that this foreigner was not sick like the other one who had asked for Silver Pearl tea this week."

Gutrune nodded. "So, we may be close. Why did they think he was sick?"

Sonam shrugged. "The word they used—it is for fevers. Or for those addicted to the dream-smoke. Thin, and shaking."

She had been watching for Aeropans anyway, and now looked for those who looked ill. None appeared—but perhaps they would not be out in the heat in their condition.

"See if you can get a better description of this man," Gutrune whispered to Sonam at the next opportunity. "Say you are looking for a friend you have heard is in Kiantan who also likes what you are asking for, or something of that nature."

She continued to search for Aeropans, but now she noticed a Cathan keeping pace with them, always at a distance. She noticed him at first because he did not look as thin as the others, but as she observed him from the corner of her eyes, he also had a hard, unfriendly look about him.

She rubbed her fingers lightly over her jacket, checking that her knife was still in position and could be reached quickly. Perhaps he merely disliked Aercpans—but why follow this group in particular?

It was now late afternoon and there were only a few more places to check. The man was sometimes hard to find, but he was always there—crouched down near a street vendor, eating, or watching acrobats balance whirling plates on long poles. He never kept the same position but always kept them in view. *He's too good at this for an amateur. He's been trained.*

When they finally turned back to the White Jade Pavilion, she leaned close to Stoller. "Go in with the others. Tell them I've seen something I want to keep an eye on." The man had made no hostile moves, but perhaps he had been instructed merely to follow them. If he attempted to enter the pavilion, however, it would be an indication of danger.

Stoller set his jaw but did not attempt to argue. While Ardhuin's group went in the main entrance, Gutrune followed the others to the small side street that gave them concealed access—and she doubled back, standing in the shadow of the building to watch the street before the pavilion.

The man stopped at the door, and her heartbeat accelerated—but he merely spoke briefly to the doorman and then turned away, back the way he had come. Gutrune took the opportunity to cross to the other side, where an old woman was selling hot noodles. Since she only had so many bowls, many people were standing about her cart, eating. Watching to see how much the others paid, she simply handed the woman the same number of the thin silver coins called *yuer* without saying anything. It worked.

She ate her noodles slowly, even more so when she saw the only cleaning that was done between customers was a quick rinse with hot water. Stoller had evidently told the others quickly, for she saw Dominic and the form of "Mr. Talbot" appear at one of the large open windows on the second floor. They were looking down at the street, but she was not sure if they could see her.

And then the man reappeared. He was wearing different clothes now and a broad straw hat that hid his face, but he hadn't changed his shoes—one of which had a distinctive splash of mud on the heel—or the way he walked. Gutrune handed her bowl to the vendor, ready to move again, and looked up at the pavilion window to see if Dominic and Ardhuin were watching.

Dominic was *staring* at the man, shock written plain on a suddenly pale face. She was afraid he would point and give the game away, but instead he spoke, turning back while gripping the rail. Ardhuin spun away back into the darkness.

Well. They knew something important about the man, so she should keep following him. He made a complete circuit of the pavilion, stopping and looking up at the neighboring buildings several times. Twice he let fall something that looked like a small rock from his pocket. She waited until he had walked on before getting closer to it. Hesitating, Gutrune finally picked it up in a fold of her sleeve, reluctant to pick up anything unknown with her bare hands.

Now he was walking at a quick pace, and they soon were in an area well away from the foreign section. The buildings were even more worn and signs faded. Gutrune kept her head down and shuffled as the locals were doing. There was very little sign of business—or beggars. That was even more evidence she was in the poorer section of Kiantan, and she was very much aware that her illusioned face, while completely Cathan, was of a Cathan that had regular meals. She was going to attract notice when the inhabitants realized how out of place she was.

She did her best to avoid everyone's gaze and kept going. Her quarry seemed to think he had shaken off any pursuit and was walking with a relaxed posture. He felt safe, it seemed, and when she saw him go into a shabby, two-story building she was sure of it.

Gutrune faded back behind a stack of rice-straw-covered barrels and considered what to do next. It was starting to get dark—could she find this place again in the dark? Should she try to get inside the building or just peer through any available windows?

"If you dislike that hovel I would be happy to destroy it for you," a familiar voice said in quiet Preusan.

Gutrune spun about, startled. "Herr Asgaya. Why would I want to destroy it?"

The shimmering not-quite-shadow effect faded, and she could see him grin. "Well, you were frowning at it rather fiercely."

"I was thinking what to do next, but since you are here, it is much simpler. One of us can stay on watch and the other can get—"

He grinned even wider. "Simpler still, we *both* stay here and make sure that quite interesting individual doesn't feel the urge to run off. She gave me a tracking token." He held up something that looked like a coin. "When we stay in one location long enough, the other three will join us."

"Is that wise? He only appeared to be following us, nothing more. She should be careful of risking herself."

Markus leaned closer, all but murmuring in her ear. "Your instincts, as always, were correct. He has a *geas*."

A chill washed over her. They had come closer to Denais than they realized, then. And it made sense now for Ardhuin to come.

"Is that what Herr Kermarec saw at the window?"

Markus nodded. "And more than that. He said the spell looked...odd. He wants a better look at it, and you know it must be interesting to let him agree to his wife taking a side trip to this slum. Now. With your assistance, I would like to cast a triggered perimeter around this building so he doesn't escape before they get here."

"How can I help with magic when I cannot cast it?"

He chuckled, and she felt the breath on her cheek. "All you need to be able to do is walk around the building. I'll attach the spell to you, and...what is it?"

At the mention of attaching magic Gutrune had flinched, but only a little. She had thought it was not enough for him to see, but he had. "I am...wary of magic. Magic in contact. It does not matter," she said forcefully. "It must be done, and quickly. Do not mind my hesitation."

A strong hand gripped hers briefly. "Think of it only as a thread you draw behind you. I will attach it to your sleeve, then." Gutrune nodded, ashamed of her weakness. "There. Go quickly—I am not quite as powerful as your friend, and maintaining it takes effort."

Gutrune ran. The street had emptied of all but a few, and they were not paying attention. She scrambled over piles of garbage and even a low roof to make the circuit complete, startling a stray dog hunting rats and a ragged girl who cast a frightened glance at her and quickly darted inside her home.

"Excellent." Markus looked strained but pleased when Gutrune returned. "Now all we need to do is wait."

"Unless he moves again. What is our plan then?"

"I'll go with you, of course. We can't let him get away, and the others need to find us."

This was quite sensible, yet Gutrune was aware of a flash of irritation. Remaining in the shadows, doing nothing but waiting, did not appeal, but neither did she wish Markus to follow her. Even though he would be very useful and had made no attempt to persuade her to stay behind. There had to be something she could do to help before Ardhuin showed up.

"Would you be able to cast the shadow spell on me after your recent exertions?"

Markus quirked an eyebrow. "Easily. It was only holding the triggered circuit in abeyance that was a strain. Like holding a weight at arm's length, what begins as a trivial effort rapidly becomes unbearably difficult. As long as we don't get involved in a major magical duel tonight, I can assist. You...you don't mind this?"

She forced herself to speak. To face her embarrassing weakness. "I have...developed an aversion to magic that touches me. It will not prevent me from doing my duty."

He grimaced. "Your duty...but you do not seem to mind the illusions she has cast for you."

It was true, she did not—and it surprised her. The illusions Ardhuin had placed on her felt more like armor, like protection and safety, but they were still magic. "I trust her completely. Now, the spell?" She wanted the uncomfortable questions to end. She wanted to move. She wanted Markus to lose the sudden expression of wondering surprise.

"At once, my lady." He gestured, his face quickly returning to its usual sardonic amusement. "Good hunting."

Assured that she could examine the exterior without attracting notice, Gutrune took a leisurely tour. The upper story had a balcony, but it was sagging and in poor repair. The windows were larger on that floor, where the ground floor windows had sturdy wooden bars and would be difficult to get through even without them. Faint light shone through the paper screens of one, but only in one section, telling her light was actually coming from an interior door. She listened but could hear nothing.

The darkness at last defeated her. There was nothing else she could see that would be useful.

"There you are," whispered Markus. "I was just about to go and find you."

Gutrune frowned, suspicious. "You said you needed to remain in one place to be found."

The corners of his eyes crinkled with suppressed amusement. "Precisely. And I was." The deep darkness behind him shimmered and and faded revealing three familiar figures. "Now, how shall we proceed?"

Dominic had seen enough of the section of Kiantan they found themselves in to know it was the poorer quarter, but he hadn't realized just how poor. Any pavement on the street, if it existed at all, was deeply buried in muck. Further, from the aroma, someone was keeping a pig. Possibly several pigs. He hadn't liked the hard and desperate expressions on the inhabitants either. It was a very good thing they had magic to conceal themselves.

And they still should not let anyone catch sight of them, even the person he intended to capture.

"We need to capture him unawares, and as silently as possible so no one else here knows."

"I believe he may be alone," Gutrune said, her voice low. She gestured at a building farther down the narrow, filthy street. "I heard no voices when I scouted his location. There are three doors on the ground floor and an open balcony on the level above. The lower windows are all blocked with bars, so it is unlikely he can escape that way."

"So, do we block all but one door or split up?" Ardhuin asked.

Markus frowned. "The second floor is not so high—he might try to jump from there if he thinks he is under attack. I think Fräulein von Kitren should start from there and prevent his escape. Of all of us she is best at silent movement."

From what Dominic could see in the darkness, Gutrune was startled by this praise. "I doubt I could climb silently. Not when the wood is so worn."

Ardhuin's illusioned face smiled. "A little levitation can solve that problem, I think. So what will the rest of us be doing?"

It ended up being fairly simple, once Gutrune was lifted up to the second floor. The lower doors were sealed magically, except for one. Ardhuin put up a magical shield, and Markus carefully opened the door.

Ardhuin had also cast magic to dampen sound, but something alerted their quarry. Dominic felt a sudden vibration on the floor, as if from footsteps, and he caught a glimpse of a man darting from an interior room and up the steep, narrow stairs.

Dominic fought back an urge to shout and gestured frantically at Ardhuin. Surely she had some magical means to stop him before he escaped! He heard a startled gasp, a thud, and then the man fell backward down the stairs, arms clutching his stomach. Gutrune was standing at the top of the stairs with one hand still clenched in a fist.

"Isn't she wonderful?" Markus whispered to Dominic, watching Gutrune help Ardhuin blindfold the now securely bound man.

Dominic rolled his eyes. "Completely charming. Now, a true gentleman always offers to carry a lady's prisoners, don't you agree?"

Soon the man, still struggling, was securely fastened to a chair in a shabby room lit by a smoking oil lamp. Dominic didn't need it to see what had intrigued him earlier, but he stared closely anyway. It was so odd it took him a few minutes to understand the magic he was seeing. "I knew there was something strange about him," Dominic said. "It's not just a simple *geas*. It's in layers. How is that even possible?"

Ardhuin looked at him, her brow wrinkled in puzzlement. "What do you mean, layers?"

Dominic waved his hands, trying to find the words to explain what he was seeing. "Well, there's one *geas* that looks like...like the others I've seen. It's compact, smooth, uniform. Pretty much identical to the ones I saw that Denais cast. But he's got another one on top of that, and it looks rough and patchy. Not...not as well done, I suppose. But he definitely has two. Why would anyone do that?"

"Perhaps when we remove them he can tell us himself." Ardhuin moved behind the man and took his head in her hands. The man jerked, making a stifled cry—the first sound they had heard from him. Then both layers of magic that had been controlling him vanished, and he began spitting out a torrent of angry words in Cathan.

Sonam blinked, hesitating. "He is swearing destruction of all Aeropans.

That he will not allow his people to be enslaved. He is angry that so many merchants come and sell to the nobles, and they tax the poor to get these things."

Ardhuin shifted. "Ask him his name. Ask if he remembers who put the spell on him."

Sonam spoke and was answered with more angry words. Sonam spoke again, more forcefully, responding in the same way to the man's angry question, and the man's demeanor suddenly changed. No longer struggling against his bonds, his head lifted and he was silent for a moment.

"My name is Pei-an," he said in heavily accented Gaulan. "Is what he says true? That you took that devil spell from me?"

"Yes," Ardhuin said in her disguised voice. "We are hunting someone that uses it for bad purposes. We would like to know if the one who did this to you is the same person."

Another silence. "I will help you do this, even though you are foreign dogs. To kill a tiger, use a snake. He was a *wuxai lein*, tall and thin. He chose me to serve him because I speak this language."

"*Wuxai lein* is a way of saying magician," Sonam added.

Dominic raised an eyebrow. "Well, that certainly sounds like De—like the one we are looking for. How old was this man?"

The blindfolded head shook. "Not old. My age."

Ardhuin looked at Dominic in consternation. "Not old? But..."

"He does not look his age, certainly, but he is clearly older than twenty," Dominic said. "Do we have more like him to worry about?" He turned back to Pei-an. "Are you a magician?" Pei-an shook his head, and Dominic believed him. He had seen no sign of magic about Pei-an other than the *geas*. "What instructions were you given when the spell was placed on you?"

"To go to this place every week and obey the commands given to me by the *geilo* there who had the lord's orders, with his sign upon them. To do nothing to harm the interests of the lord or defeat the orders. Then..." the anger in Pei-an's voice faded, replaced by confusion. "I had not remembered until now. Another *geilo* came, and told me an order from him was the same as seeing the lord's order and sign, and I should obey what he said."

Ardhuin's eyes narrowed. "Did this man touch you when he said this?"

Pei-an nodded, a sharp, jerky motion.

"Well. I think we know where the second *geas* came from," Dominic said. "But who was this man? What did he look like?"

Pei-an snorted. "He is short, and his face round. The hair on his head fades away, and he speaks Gaulan like a dog barking." He imitated the accent, which sounded vaguely Preusan.

"Very curious," Ardhuin murmured.

"We cannot stay here long," Markus said. "Let us finish questioning him, and then we can discuss what we have learned. Now, what were you doing today? Were you ordered to follow any Aeropans, or those in particular?"

"Those ones. I was given descriptions from a government document for each man. I was to see what they did and place spell-stones about the place they slept."

Gutrune held up something small that glowed faintly with magic. "I saw him drop this near the pavilion." Ardhuin smiled.

"What then?"

"I was to go back for more orders concerning these people. They did not say to me, but to others, to go to Baiyueh and stop them there, in any way. They were to kill them if they could not stop them. Others were to go farther along the route to Garze if they escaped Baiyueh."

"Did you hear why these people were to be stopped?"

Pei-an shook his head.

Ardhuin, Dominic, and Markus went off for a whispered consultation while Gutrune stood guard over the prisoner with her pistol.

"We can't just let him go," Markus protested. "You heard him—while he hates the people who put the *geas* on him, he doesn't like us much either."

"The cities he mentioned...that was the route we were going to take to Bhuta!" Dominic blurted. "How did they know?"

"I want to know how they got our entry paper descriptions." Markus frowned. "It sounds like Denais has spies in the government."

"Denais may have spies he doesn't know about," Ardhuin said. "A second *geas*—and it sounds like it was to circumvent the first in some way." She was silent for a moment, glancing at Pei-an. "Yes, he does not like foreigners, but we did free him. I think if we offer him vengeance as well, he will at least refrain from betraying us until he gets it."

Markus grimaced but made no objection.

"I don't know that we have much choice." Dominic thought the matter over. "He still doesn't know *we* are the ones he was following, so he can't tell anyone."

"Thank you for this information," Ardhuin said to Pei-an when they returned. "We will hunt the people who put that spell on you. However, if you reveal that the spell is broken, they will know we are here, and it will make it difficult for us. Will you pretend to still be under their control? At least to the point of going back for orders?"

This Pei-an did not like, but was persuaded with promises a message would be sent when it was safe for him to stop the pretense.

After removing his bonds and setting a vital stasis spell on him that would wear off in a few hours, they left hurriedly. Soon they were back at the pavilion. Dominic had completely forgotten that Mother Long had asked to speak with them, but the servants had not.

She met with them in a room entirely furnished in red lacquer, even the ceiling. Her usual calm expression had a grave cast, and she half opened and closed a fan while looking at each of them in turn before she spoke.

"Monsieur Bové perhaps has mentioned that I find many things needed by my guests—but especially information. In this case I come to you, for I have heard things I do not understand. It seems the government is searching very hard for certain Aeropans, and among them is said to be a woman with red hair. I have told those involved there are few foreign women here, and none with such hair, but they still wish to search. I regret, but I cannot stop them completely. I can only delay." Mother Long stood and gave them a serious look. "Perhaps you know of such a person. I advise you, if so, to warn her. There is great danger if she is found."

CHAPTER 13

Ardhuin woke the next morning bleary-eyed and still tired. Someone was talking in a loud and cheerful voice in the main room—Simons.

"On your feet, get moving! Come on, trice up and move out! We're only waiting for you, you can nap on the road."

"For the love of God—it's not even daylight yet!" Markus sounded as irritated as she felt. "Is this your idea of a joke? Bové said it would take a week or more, and we just got here."

"Ha! Mother Long is *amazing*. She's already got all the pack animals arranged, and the transportation. Maybe she's a magician? We just found out—Bové was surprised too. Now he wants to hurry to catch the train. It doesn't run every day. Come on, gents! Can I help you pack?"

No. The fear woke her like a dash of cold water. No one should open her trunk, with the highly specific magical equipment.

"Go help someone else. I find it hard to believe everyone is waiting on us, if you only found out just now," Ardhuin grumbled as she dressed hurriedly, making sure her illusion was in place before she opened the curtains on her palatial bed. "Failing that, you and your cheery morning attitude can find a cliff and jump off it."

Simons just laughed, but he did go away. Which was a good thing, Ardhuin discovered, as Dominic had forgotten his cravat in the bedding and she was already wearing hers. They had all stayed up late discussing the information Pei-an had given them, and then she and Dominic had decided to take advantage of the temporary privacy afforded by the closed rooms. Even though she was so weary she could drop, she did not regret it, especially now. It was unlikely they would have another opportunity until they reached Bhuta, and perhaps not even then.

The only one of their group to appear even tepidly cheerful was Sonam, always glad to be moving faster. Dominic looked ragged, rubbing his forehead.

"Someone needs to go tell Gutrune of the change in plans. I hope she can follow with so little notice."

He hadn't even finished before Markus was headed for the door.

Ardhuin wished her head didn't feel like it was full of cotton wool.

Perhaps she would not feel like she had just missed half a conversation. Why, for example, was Dominic grinning?

He saw her looking at him and the grin vanished.

"What are the two of you up to?" And Dominic was conspiring with Markus? Definitely odd.

"I'm not up to anything," Dominic protested, his gaze furtively avoiding hers.

"Ah. So *Markus* is up to something. Why..." Her brain was waking up. "Oh no. Dominic, he can't be...*now?* Could he *possibly* pick a worse time to pursue his interest in Gutrune? Denais could be in the city for all we know!"

Dominic held up his hands in a calming gesture. "When would be better? She does tend to be off on dangerous adventures on a regular basis. And somehow I find I cannot fault his timing. It worked for me." He had a tinge of color on his high cheekbones.

Ardhuin sighed, shaking her head, and went up to him, draping the forgotten cravat over his shoulders. "Yes, I suppose it did. But only consider, love. You were captured, tortured, and had a mansion collapse on you in the process. Do you really want that to happen to Markus? Well, I suppose you might," she added, remembering Dominic's earlier prickly reaction to Markus.

"A little torture might put a dent in his annoyingly smug attitude," Dominic conceded. "However, I wish to state for the record he approached me for help. I did not instigate this in any way. Now, if something equally humiliating and painful *should* happen to him, I will view it as the judgment of Heaven, and enjoy it."

"As long as he doesn't get too distracted. Or injured. Think of Gutrune, if not him. And us—we need everyone to be alert. Someone, if not Denais, has found us, and if Pei-an is correct, they even know where we are going."

"Ah, but we are leaving much earlier than they expected—and if nobody in the expedition knew, how would they? If we get to Baiyueh before they do, knowing won't help them."

At which point Markus returned. "All is in order," he reported cheerfully. Ardhuin observed him with care and decided some of the cheer was an act. She should probably see if Gutrune was in need of support, or distraction. "Now, have we decided what we are doing after Baiyueh? We will have to part company with Bové at some point, and if we need to take a different route, that would be a good place for it. I know he said communication there is sporadic—so anyone wishing to do us mischief would have difficulty communicating our change in plans to their confederates."

"It is best to stay on the caravan routes as long as possible," Sonam said. "The desert is dangerous, especially to those who do not know its ways. I have not traveled it myself."

"Then we stay with the expedition beyond Baiyueh and pick a likely spot. Perhaps at the river past Garze; we'll have to split off there if not earlier."

"I wish we knew where Pei-an is." Ardhuin was suddenly full of doubt. "While he seemed to be telling the truth, he might decide to change his mind."

Markus gave her a half bow. "Anticipating this, I surreptitiously inserted the token you gave me last night into the lining of his coat. There was a handy hole," he explained. "If he has not found it, you can track him with that. At least we will know he is not following us himself."

Pei-an, or the token, was still in the same general area they had left him in. She thought he moved about a little in the next few hours, but not in their direction. They left Kiantan by rail, on a train painted a bright red with gold and blue embellishments that did not conceal the fact the locomotive was rather old and not very powerful.

"You'll want to find seats on the very last passenger car," Bové told them as he directed, in shouted Cathan, the disposition of a large number of horses in the open cattle cars. "I am afraid the boiler on this thing has a tendency to explode. Oh, and Mother Long asked me to give you these." He handed Dominic a brown paper parcel. "She regretted being unable to say good-bye in person. You seem to have made a favorable impression on her." Then he leaned closer. "Was this...accelerated departure made possible by your powerful friends in Rennes? Or you?"

Dominic shook his head. "How could I? No, of course not."

Bové frowned, his forehead creased with worry. "It's very strange. It's almost like she wanted us out of the city as fast as possible."

They wedged their way through the crowd of passengers, Ardhuin clutching her essential carpetbag closely and dodging as best she could a man with ducks in cages, stacked like plates and dangling on either end of a pole, and old women with bundles of cloth. Eventually they secured seats as close to the end of the train as possible, hard wooden benches with no cushions. In fact, parts of the floor were missing and it became clear these holes were used generally for any and all refuse, and in some cases as latrines.

"How long do we stay on the train?" Ardhuin asked, warding off an angry duck that had gotten its head free of the cage just enough to peck at anyone in range.

Simons shrugged. "If the engine keeps up steam, six hours. If not..."

Markus glanced out one of the windows, which was broken. "Perhaps we will be lucky and the engine will explode. So, what did Mother Long present us with? A kind gesture, to strangers like us."

Dominic wrestled with the parcel, which was tied securely with heavy twine. Inside were smaller packages, also wrapped but in finer white paper with threads of floss mixed in. "Oh, they have our names. Here, Sonam, that's yours." Ardhuin was handed one with "Mr. Talbot" in delicate script on the outside. "Well, that's an excellent choice." Dominic held up a pen covered in deep cobalt-blue enamel, shaded with green and traces of gold. Sonam had been given a pierced silver-gilt incense burner, and Markus a piece of carved jade.

"I'm not quite certain what it is supposed to represent, but it is quite pretty." He held it up to the light and turned it. "And you?" He glanced at Ardhuin enquiringly.

She opened the small, flat package. Inside was a beautiful ivory comb, the top edge carved cleverly to show a dragon partly concealed in clouds.

Ardhuin looked closer and felt herself grow cold. Wound in the tines of the comb was a single strand of her long, red hair.

She knows. In a faint voice, she said, "I think I have discovered why Mother Long was so eager to help us on our way."

Dominic jumped down from the highly regrettable train, remembering just in time not to reach up to help Ardhuin descend. Although the locomotive had only broken down once, the trip had been agonizingly long —for although they all needed to discuss the implications of Mother Long's revelation, there was no way to do so in the crowded train. Even if the iron had not interfered with magic, there was simply no way to cast any spells without discovery.

The other members of the expedition had joined them en route, so they were now a party of ten. The newcomers were all experienced members of Bové's team, young, confident, and sun-bronzed. They greeted Bové and Simons with great enthusiasm and appeared to accept Dominic and the others, but he could sense their doubt and curiosity about the reason for their presence.

Now they had finally arrived at Baiyueh, they could at least decide what to do next. Ardhuin was scanning the crowd, and while her illusion maintained an even expression, he could see her real face looked worried.

"Do you see anything?" She shaded her eyes with one hand.

He shook his head. No sign of *geasi*, or of any other strong magic. Markus had placed himself in an alcove of a stone building near the train station and was also warily alert—and was using avoidance magic to conceal himself.

Bové appeared, and Dominic made his way over to him.

"We need to hire pack animals," he said when Dominic asked his plans. "I hired our riding horses in Kiantan, because the ones here are bad. We'll need camels to carry the gear, though. Oxen and carts would be cheaper, but they are slower and the carts break down too often where we are headed. Bad roads. Grangier will see to the animals. I have to go see the *anban* about our travel papers. We should be able to leave tomorrow morning. We've made better time than I hoped." He nodded to Dominic before moving away to speak to Grangier.

"Camels, again?" Ardhuin had come up beside him. "Gutrune will not be pleased."

"These look different." They were not as leggy as the ones in Geapt and had shaggier hair.

"They look smarter and just as ill-tempered. I suppose I should...oh, there she is."

Dominic looked about as if he were a dazed foreigner and saw Gutrune and Stoller making their way through the crowd. By pretending to be jostled out of the way, he and Ardhuin managed to end up beside them. A brief flare of magic told him the sound barrier was in place, and he quickly explained the new difficulties. "We should travel together from now on. Going the same route will be hard to conceal anyway, with fewer travelers."

Gutrune continued to watch the crowd unobtrusively, and her usually calm expression seemed grim. "Very true. At the moment I am more concerned about the number of soldiers about. They seem to be harassing people for no reason."

"Oh, they have a reason," Stoller muttered. "They're shaking 'em down. And that one, over by the gate? Pretty sure he's an officer, and he lets it happen. We'd best get well away. I don't like the feel of this."

The horses were unloaded by now, and Ardhuin noticed the soldiers beginning to look that direction. If Bové had needed to import good riding horses to this location, they would attract notice. She couldn't just shield them all with avoidance magic now that the soldiers were focused on the horses—she needed to distract them with something else first.

The man with the stacked duck cages walked by, and she brightened. After being pecked by one of his ducks for ten hours, she deserved a little revenge. "Stay close, and get ready to get the horses," she whispered. And then she sent a sharp, quick burst of magic.

The duck cages suddenly fell to the ground, the line holding them to the pole frayed and broken. Angry quacking multiplied, and a flock of frightened ducks flapped and struggled through the crowd, followed by the shouting duck man, who did not notice none of the cages had actually opened. While he and others chased illusionary ducks, the soldiers' attention was diverted and they laughed, pointing at the scene.

Only then did Ardhuin use a light casting of aversion, with another layer of illusion to make the horses look shabby and tired.

She grabbed the lead rope of one horse. "Where do we take them?"

Bové, looking confused, pointed. "There's an inn down that road. The camels should already be there. I'm off to see the *anban* about our travel stamps now, if you've got the horses and baggage."

Dominic winced. "Oh, damn, the baggage. Simons, can you get that?"

"Yes, yes, but these greedy porters want ten *yuer* just to go the length of the street! It's highway robbery!" he protested.

"Pay them twice that if they get it out before the soldiers come back," Markus hissed. "This is not a good time to be a difficult foreigner—haven't you noticed? They were about to take the horses. Now get moving!"

They managed to get to the inn without being stopped, but only because Ardhuin caused more distractions and in one case arranged for a runaway cow.

"This isn't really going to help." Dominic panted with effort as he brought the last horse in to the courtyard of the inn. "The soldiers will be able to find us here easily."

"If they are looking for us, yes," Markus said, peering out the gate to the street. "I had the impression they were mostly throwing their weight around and looking for bribes."

Sonam had been silent and somber ever since the train had stopped, but now he spoke up. "I heard them speaking of rebels. They are set to watch the rail line, to make sure it is not sabotaged."

"So, they might not go out of their way to bother us." Dominic grimaced. "If our luck holds."

"If we have luck, Herr Bové will return quickly with the permits and we can leave today," Gutrune said.

Markus glanced back, then returned to his scrutiny of the street. "I see him now—and his expression is not propitious."

Bové was, in fact, furious. "No permits. The *anban* refused to even see me! It's not for him to say yes or no to our travel—the permit simply records our route. I've been coming here for over seven years and I've never been treated like this."

"What do you plan to do?" Markus asked.

Bové threw up his hands explosively, making the horses start and toss their heads. "I don't know. Perhaps I should talk to the judge—he's known me for years. Maybe he can explain what is going on. I don't like it," he said, looking out into the courtyard. "I thought it would be quieter out here, away from the city, but it looks like it's getting bad all over. And if they start fighting..."

"But there are soldiers here," Ardhuin blurted, feeling shaky. What were they doing in the middle of a revolution?

"Whose soldiers?" Bové said cynically. "That's the problem. If they are the provincial governor's, *and* he's loyal to the emperor, they might enforce the law and accept our passes. At least as far as the town gate. There's a general in charge of the border based near here, and his troops. Past that it's local warlords and bandits and forces loyal to the other governors that have decided maybe the emperor should be removed. The *anban* has his own police force, and they may be at odds with the government forces. Maybe he just wants a bribe," he added gloomily. "Or thinks we have weapons he can confiscate. Aerope limits the amount of modern rifles sold to Cathai, so they are much in demand. Hey, Grangier, Pichon. Hide half the pistols and all but two of the rifles in with the supplies, and don't forget the cartridges."

"Only two?"

Bové grimaced. "They know we have them, but not how many. Losing one or two is acceptable if we can get out of here. I'm going to try the judge now. Stay here and keep a low profile." He strode out into the sun and dust.

"I'm thinking we should hide a few items of our own," Dominic said. "Suitably disguised."

Moving quickly, Ardhuin and the others gathered all items that might be deemed suspicious, including Gutrune's three-barreled rifle and other weapons. Removing bags of sugar and flour from the crates, she illusioned the hidden items to blend in and cast another illusion on the removed supplies that went to take up space in their luggage, so they looked like innocent items. Sonam burned a series of random-seeming dots on the crates so they could find their equipment again.

As she worked, Ardhuin was aware of a growing noise coming from the street.

"There's a squad of men coming this way, with sticks," Stoller reported after going to take a look. "I don't like the look of them."

"There is not time to run," Gutrune said. "If it is a squad and not a mob, someone still has control. I suggest that most of us remain in the open to deal with these people, but that one or two stay concealed as an emergency reserve."

Dominic's face was pale, and he was breathing fast. "Sonam. He's the only one of us who understands Cathan. And—"

"Gutrune," Ardhuin said. He looked at her, startled and beginning to protest. "She's better at this, Dominic. We can't *all* hide. Besides, they might not be looking for her and Stoller. I'll disguise Stoller as Sonam and vice versa."

He still didn't look happy about it, but the men in uniform were already entering the courtyard. She did the illusion and a heavy dose of aversion before levitating them to the upper rafters of the stable. Suddenly the door slammed open and the stable was full of angry, shouting men. One of them looked at each of the expedition members in turn, and Ardhuin was suddenly very glad she had disguised Stoller. They were pushed and prodded out into the courtyard. The few Cathans were allowed to remain, but all the expedition members were escorted out of the inn and, after a long walk in the sun, to a large stone building near the center of the town.

There, they were unceremoniously shoved into a large room with a few tiny, barred windows and an iron-bound door. The only light came from the windows, but it was enough to show Bové seated on a rough wooden bench.

He looked up, his expression resigned and weary. "Well, so much for that. It turns out the judge was found politically inconvenient and imprisoned by the governor. Had I known that, I would not have claimed he was a friend of mine. I'm afraid we're in a bit of a sticky situation, fellows."

"Your original plan of bribery won't work?" Markus inquired.

Bové snorted. "All my ready cash has been confiscated, on suspicion of being criminal gains or some such. We're going to need more than I had on me to get out of this. And then there's getting out of Cathai, period, which will probably require even more bribes. I am very much afraid the government is in the process of collapsing."

Ardhuin wandered around the large cell. The walls were thick stone that looked like granite. The floor was stone as well, with a scattering of dirty straw. In one corner there was a malodorous bucket, but besides the few benches there was nothing else. Since the windows showed sky, they must be on one of the walls of the building.

"But why are we imprisoned instead of just being expelled?" Dominic asked. "Are we being accused of a crime?"

Bové shook his head. "More likely to await events and use us as a bargaining chip, either way. This is the governor's armory, and his troops brought you in. He seems to be still loyal to the Empire. If the governor changes allegiance or loses a battle, the reason to keep us vanishes. If we can't bribe our way out, we'll have to send a message to the trade city representatives of Bretagne or some other Aeropan government. They can apply pressure we can't. But it will take a while."

Ardhuin inclined her head at Dominic and walked over to the other wall. Markus and Stoller joined them, and she set up a light sound-confusion spell.

"Well. I think this is where we should part company with Herr Bové," Markus said. "Not that I wish him to remain a prisoner, but we certainly can't wait to be released in the usual way."

"Abandon him? After all this?" Dominic was starting to look angry.

"He isn't going to want to go to Sonam's valley, Dominic," Ardhuin said, "and we can't really take him either. Will he be able to continue his expedition, with the country in the state it is in? We would have to leave him soon even if this hadn't happened."

Dominic set his jaw stubbornly. "We should at least ask him. Going our own way is a little different than leaving him in a dungeon!"

"And it's not to be expected our sudden disappearance would make his captors happy with him either," conceded Markus. "I would certainly prefer everyone on the other side of this wall. Shall we speak with him?"

When the matter was explained to him, Bové was at first bewildered, and then angry. "What? Breaking out will make us hunted men. You have no idea...it will be an affront to their authority, and regardless of who they ally themselves with, they will chase us."

"Herr Bové, you know as well as we do your days of adventuring in Cathai are drawing to a close. At least until this troubled time passes. How important is it to you to make one more expedition? How long do you think it will take before you can safely travel again?" Markus was radiating pure sympathetic concern, and Ardhuin watched with admiration. You would think his only motive was to help Bové.

Bové stood and kicked the wooden bench. "Damn it, that's the thing. It'll be a civil war when it goes, and it hasn't really started yet. It could take ten years. If this is the last—well, I've got to get those bones from the Fire Cliffs. They are too exposed—won't last ten years where they are, that's for sure. It's out...well, it's out where even the nomads don't go very often, so I doubt we'd have trouble with the military. A few bandits, perhaps. We could get our samples and go, three weeks at the most. But how do you plan to get out?"

"We've got three magicians at hand. One still outside this building." Even with the sound buffer, Ardhuin spoke softly. "But if we break free, you'll be cutting off your contacts here, probably for good. Is it worth it to you? We cannot stay here long. We can try to make it seem like you were not involved, but..." she shrugged.

"Yes, unlikely they would believe that." Bové's face worked. "Damn it to hell. I worked so hard for this...I will not give up now! Yes, I'll escape with you. But let's confuse them as much as possible, eh? Can these magicians of yours help with that?"

Ardhuin nodded. "That should not be difficult at all."

They waited until twilight had darkened the stone cell. With the others standing about her so the guards would see nothing, Ardhuin knelt and placed her hands against a large stone block at the base of the wall. She let the fluctuating power of Crystalline Polythrenode vibrate through her, sensing and testing. Strictly speaking, the rock was not a crystal, but the individual granite grains were. She just had to find enough large ones to let the resonance take hold, and then shatter.

What she got was a crumbling, brittle mass that had to be kicked and then shoveled out by hand. The last section was a delicate operation, since she did not know where the hole would open up on the street. So first a small spyhole, then illusion, and then the final opening for their escape.

More illusion, to make it seem they were all still in the cell, asleep, and to cover the hole on the inside, and then they ran silently through the dark streets. They had to find Gutrune, and some gunpowder or dynamite if they could. If not, she'd just have to make it *look* like dynamite had gone off. It was crucial to their plan that no one suspect magic had been used in their escape.

Bové led the way, being more familiar with the town. Their path avoided the main streets, which tended to have uniformed men present, and instead went down narrow alleys with uneven footing. Ardhuin was sure she heard a shutter close as they approached and only hoped whoever was watching hadn't noticed anything. Her avoidance magic either had to be in one continuous shell, and they were too strung out for that, or on individuals, in which case they might lose each other in the darkness. She settled for blurriness and speed.

"We're nearly at the inn, and no sign of Gutrune or Sonam," Dominic whispered. "I hope they are all right."

Ahead, Bové held up a hand and they hugged the walls. Now she could see what he had seen—more soldiers, leaving the main courtyard. They did not seem alert or tense, more like they had finished a hard day's work and were planning to return home. They left, leaving the inn apparently unguarded.

"I suppose one of us should see if it's safe to go back," Markus murmured, then stopped, his head jerking up. "On second thought, someone is trying to discreetly get our attention."

It was Gutrune. Her illusion remained unchanged, but from Dominic's expression, she had taken some damage—and she did seem to be favoring one leg.

"It is good to see you—I was afraid we would need to break you out of the armory."

"Were you seen? What happened to Sonam?"

Gutrune smiled. "He is with the horses. At least we were able to save them...they took everything else. *Everything*," she said to Ardhuin, significantly.

Including her magical gear. All of their luggage. And worst of all, the magical salts. She exchanged a horrified glance with Dominic and Markus. If it were discovered and used by the combatants, the region would be devastated. The secret would be bound to get out. And they would want more...

Bové sagged against the wall, his eyes closed. "That's it, then. I can't continue without the supplies—and even if we had the money, you can't get that stuff out here. Who took it? Did you see?" His eyes snapped open and blazed with anger.

"They appeared to be soldiers, with the dark blue uniforms with black belts. They had several carts. They took the road to the northeast. I followed them to a large camp with a wooden palisade, but it was guarded and I could not get inside."

"So. *Not* the governor." Bové stared out into the darkness as if he would track them, lips compressed. "As I feared. One of the local generals has set himself up as a warlord and wants any Aeropan weapons and gear he can get his hands on." He spun back to Gutrune. "What do we have, besides the horses?"

"Water skins. A few bags of food we managed to get on the horses. The weapons we have on us." Gutrune's voice was cool. "What do we need? What is our plan?"

Bové was silent for a moment. "We shouldn't talk here. Let's go to the horses."

The horses, and Sonam, were in a dusty, rocky ravine that had a thin trickle of water just deep enough to drink from and a few ragged pine trees. Sonam's face lit up when he saw them approach.

"I believe you are quite determined to keep going, even with this latest disaster. Am I correct?" Bové looked at Ardhuin, Dominic, and Markus in turn. Ardhuin nodded. "Well, I'm becoming desperate myself. Here is what I propose. There is a certain well-known bandit leader in this region. Kungam. I've...encountered him before. Word is he keeps the terms of any agreement, so I suppose you could call him an honest criminal, but still—he is a thief and a brigand, and he kills easily."

"Are you proposing to hire this man?" Markus said. "What would prevent him from stealing from us, again?"

"Only his reputation for honesty, as I said. We have nothing to hire him with, except the information about the location of the warlord's camp. He would be more interested in striking at his enemy and capturing *their* supplies, and would have less interest in ours."

"We have few options," Gutrune said after a moment of everyone deep in thought. "Regardless of which direction we travel, we will need either money or supplies. If the military is in open rebellion, it will be equally dangerous to traverse their territory."

"I agree." Dominic got to his feet again. "When can we leave for this bandit's hideout?"

"It isn't safe to camp here; it's too close to the town. We should ride as far as we can tonight." Yet Bové made no move to the horses. He turned his head sharply and stared at Dominic. "But first...I hope you realize my warnings were in earnest. The danger is greater than I supposed when we spoke in Rennes. If I have any reason to think your wife may be planning to join us here, I will not take you to Kungam."

Dominic sighed and carefully did not look in her direction. "Bové, I give you my word. My wife is not traveling to meet me, or wandering about by herself anywhere in Cathai."

Some of the tension left Bové. "I am glad to hear it. Now, I must ask, although it is clear you do not wish to speak of it. Who are your magicians, and are they willing to fight in this raid?"

"Asgaya, Talbot, and Sonam. And these two…er, Hentzau and Graustark, are not magicians but are…well, call them a kind of soldier."

Ardhuin stifled a laugh. Hentzau and Graustark was the name of a Baerlen bookstore.

"Excellent! It will be much easier with our own men—and we can make sure our gear is rescued. The moon will be up soon; we'd best be off."

"There is still one more thing," Ardhuin said hesitantly. "To cover up our escape, since we don't want them looking for magicians—do you know where we might find some explosives?"

"A pity we didn't know they kept gunpowder here when we escaped," Markus murmured as he and Gutrune ducked into dark shadow near the armory. "It would have saved us the extra trip."

She turned and glared at him. "If you cannot be quiet, go back to the horses. I do not need your help."

It was probably true, but he felt no compulsion to admit it. "It will be faster with my assistance, and the others cannot afford to wait long for us."

Gutrune made no response, possibly because she agreed but more likely to stifle conversation. Markus sighed quietly. It was probably also not politic to point out if he had not accompanied her, Stoller would have definitely insisted on coming along.

The moonlight was quite bright now, making the streets risky but the shadows deeper. He had learned a little of Ardhuin's aversion magic, and the delicate degrees she employed, and he decided it was worth the effort now. Just enough to divert the eye, long enough for them to move out of sight of any watcher.

The armory was quiet. The guards had not yet discovered their prisoners were nothing more than illusions or that there was a gaping hole in their thick stone walls. According to Bové, the gunpowder stores were located on the top of the armory, in a separate wooden structure for safety. Should a random spark set it off, at least the blast would not destroy the entire building. They needed to get up there without being seen and then set off enough to conceal their escape tunnel.

An idea occurred to Markus. "We should set off the whole store, if we can. It will look like the action of the military, perhaps, striking back against the governor's police."

"And blow ourselves up with it? Too much effort, too much risk."

"I can do a delayed fire," Markus said. "I wasn't planning on that much sacrifice."

"You would still need to get up to the roof yourself, no? Not worth it." She made a sharp gesture.

The armory was, unfortunately, designed to prevent persons of ill intent from entering. The walls were high and smooth, with only a few windows. The gate was guarded even now.

"So, hypothetically, if you were here by yourself—what would you do?"

"I would be able to hear myself think instead of wondering why the person supposedly helping me was incapable of silence." Gutrune gritted her teeth. "But since you insisted on coming, why not use your magic to lift me up?"

A fair, and painful, question. "Because I am not nearly as powerful as your friend. A smaller object, perhaps—or something that would not be damaged in a fall. I could not be sure of levitating you so high with safety. Lowering is much easier than lifting." When it looked like she would protest, he added emphatically, "No. Let us find another way. Do we have any rope?"

"Not long enough, no. All I have is this." She indicated the long sash that wrapped around her Cathan clothing.

In the end they combined magic and the sash, a barred window with a ledge, and a wooden flagpole. Markus boosted Gutrune with strength and a little magic high enough for her to grab the window bars, swing herself to the ledge, and then use the sash to help him reach the ledge as well. From there, he used pure magic to lift her to where she could loop the sash around the flagpole and pull herself to the roof.

It was agonizing, not being able to see what she was doing. Almost as agonizing as being forced into quite close contact on the small ledge, where her illusion had no effect at all on what she *felt* like. Moreover, he could not dwell on that brief pleasure because he had to be alert to catch the gunpowder and, eventually, her. It was most unfair. And what could he do if she was discovered?

After what seemed like hours but probably wasn't, he heard a faint grating noise but could see nothing. More mysterious sounds, some that sounded like something being torn, but still no sign of the sash, which was the signal. Then he saw a darker shape descending slowly down the wall. When it was close enough, he saw it was a small wooden cask, attached to sections of the flag formerly on the pole, which had been cut in sections and tied together. He grabbed the makeshift rope, gave a tug, and the full weight of the cask hung in his hands as the end of the rope fell on him. It was not long enough to reach the ground, and he did not want to risk the noise, so he tied one end to the bars of the window.

Then he saw the sash, and he braced himself with his magic ready. He could not fail...he *would* not. Gutrune swung over the edge of the wall and, still holding the sash, let herself fall. He did not attempt to hold her in place, only to slow her fall—and when she passed the ledge, he caught her and allowed himself to fall as well. They landed hard, and he quickly reached up to untie the cask before they ran off.

"Where is the tunnel?" Gutrune whispered, breathing hard.

Markus searched for landmarks. There had been a watering trough and a broken flagstone with weeds growing in the cracks...

"There." He trailed his hand across the stone to find the edge of the illusion, and pointed.

Gutrune took off her Cathan jacket, put it over the cask, and used the pommel of her dagger to crack the wood. A small trickle of gunpowder sifted out. She left a careful trace over the stones to the hidden tunnel, then tucked the cask inside.

Markus reached in his pocket for some matches and handed them to her. She stiffened, then reached for them, taking one from the box and striking it on a flagstone. The trail of gunpowder flared, and she jumped up to run. Markus raised his hand, forming the magic for a fireshell. Hoping it would work. The flare of light flashed like lightning, heading for the roof, and he ran after Gutrune.

The roof of the armory exploded with a roar. Fragments of stone flew by them, hitting the walls as they ran. *I do hope the horses don't break free*, he thought. They would just have to steal more if they did.

"Was that really necessary?" Gutrune snapped.

Markus grinned. "It isn't polite to keep all the explosions to yourself, you know. Especially when I was so helpful."

"Helpful? Blowing up the entire powder store is helpful? We were just supposed to cover up the escape!"

"We did. With rubble. Besides, now the police will be too busy to chase us and will blame the warlord for this. With luck, they'll attack him."

"With our luck, they'll attack him the same time we do and we'll be caught in the middle." They had reached the horses, which were nervous and wide-eyed but still tied up. Gutrune turned back toward the armory, which was burning and giving an orange glow to the sky. "Oh, very well. It was quite effective, I suppose."

Markus bowed from the saddle. It was a grudging admission, but he was not complaining. "Milady, if you wish, the next building explosion is yours."

CHAPTER 14

Dominic gazed over the open, grass-covered plains with disfavor. He was tired, sore, hungry, and quite sure they would soon see troops of some variety coming up over the rolling hills to attack them. The opportunity to ride had rarely come his way when he was a student, and not much more often since his marriage. He was greatly regretting it at the moment. Markus and Gutrune were of course completely comfortable in the saddle, and Ardhuin soon regained her childhood skill. The only one of the party that was worse off than him was Sonam.

They had been traveling two days, avoiding the heat by riding early in the morning and late at night—and also to avoid being seen. Yet here they were in broad daylight, and not even moving particularly fast.

Dominic nudged his horse toward Bové and it grudgingly accommodated him. "Isn't this rather open for us to be traveling like this?"

Bové shook his head. "We are close now. It is better that they see us coming, and that we do not pose a threat. Kungam is not a fool and has many enemies. I have heard that the general in question had Kungam's entire family killed on the pretext his father had been embezzling government tax money."

"So that is why you are so sure he will help us?"

"He will be strongly predisposed to do so, let us say. If we can convince him the benefits outweigh the risks. He does not have as many men as the general does, nor a strong defensive encampment."

They continued on for an hour or so, and Dominic noticed some dark shapes appearing on distant hills that just as quickly disappeared. He hoped they were scouts from the bandit camp, and not soldiers.

Cresting the next rise, he saw the camp. It consisted of a few shabby wooden buildings, mud-brick walls, and large felt tents with many long, narrow streamers fluttering in the wind. The encampment was bordered by a shallow river on one side and steeper hills in the back.

"Will they allow us to enter?" Markus asked.

Bové smiled grimly. "If they did not wish us to approach, we would be dead already."

Following his example, they dismounted outside the ring of tents and led their horses as they entered. The inhabitants wore heavy tunics and boots, very different from the usual attire of Cathai, and had hard, bold expressions—but made no effort to confront the strangers. All were openly carrying weapons, either long daggers tucked in belts, antique-looking flintlock rifles, or spears with red tassels hanging from the ends of wicked, multi-edged blades.

A long rope strung between two sad-looking trees served as a general tie-up for the horses, next to a curious arrangement of several vertical reed walls, standing all by themselves, with carpets in front of them. A stony-faced woman came out of a hut with a huge, battered copper kettle and served them salty tea and grimy rice balls in exchange for a few of the coins they had managed to save from the soldiers. The rice balls were surprisingly good, and Dominic was glad of the food. His outlook brightened considerably now that his stomach was not growling.

Ardhuin shifted on her carpet. "So, when do we go see Kungam?"

"We don't." Bové sipped his tea slowly. "He sends for us. He already knows I am here, and if I have come I wish to speak with him. It is how it is done in these quarters. You cannot hurry them and it is worse than useless to try."

Dominic was simply glad to not be on a horse for a while, although he hoped he would not have to walk very far either. As much as he was enjoying adventure, there were some crucial aspects he had not been prepared for. Perhaps it would become easier—Bové did not appear troubled by any of the physical discomforts they had encountered.

Time dragged on. No one felt like talking. Dominic found a small notepad in one pocket and borrowed a pencil from Pichon and started making notes on the local scenery, idly wondering if he could ever work in their adventures in one of his stories. *Too unlikely*, he decided. Besides, they needed to survive first.

As the shadows grew longer, he noticed an approaching figure in the distance. The local men, squatting on their haunches in small groups, looked up with interest but did not move. As the figure grew closer, Dominic could see it was a young boy carrying something thin and flat, like a book, high above his head. The boy headed straight for Bové and skidded to a stop, declaiming something with a great air of importance while holding the flat object high and waving it slightly for emphasis.

"We have our audience," Bové said laconically, and got up.

"Do we go as well?" Ardhuin asked.

"Everyone. Don't worry about the horses—no one will touch them. Unless he decides to deny us, but even then he will probably allow us to leave unharmed."

On that cheerful note, the party of explorers left the reed wall area and followed the messenger along a broad path between the tents. Their destination, a wooden building, looked very much like the tents in shape but was larger and had a small second story and a tower with a blue banner flying from the top.

The interior was dark and stuffy. In the center of the main room was a metal brazier, thankfully empty, ringed by low wooden stools. Bové shook his head when Ardhuin moved toward one as if to sit. One stool was broader and heavier than the others, but no more ornate, and it stood at the head of the room. The room itself was also plain, with no sign of the usual ornate Cathan ornamentation, although the main supports were carved. A handful of hard-faced men ringed the walls. No one spoke.

Heavy footsteps came from the back of the hall, and Kungam entered. He was a giant by Cathan standards—slightly taller even than Bové or Markus. A long scar slashed across his jaw, extending into his hairline, and his eyes were dark and hard as he looked them all over searchingly.

Surprisingly, when he spoke his voice was calm and even. A few words only, and then Bové replied.

"He is asking if the Bone Finder has come to hire," whispered Sonam. "That must be Bové's name here."

Kungam listened impassively as Bové explained how their gear had been stolen. Interest flickered at the mention of raiding, but his eyes blazed when Bové named the general.

"He has stated his terms. He wants a great deal of silver. Bové points out he cannot promise money he does not have, but when he takes his bones back he will have silver then. If Kungam wishes to place his own men with them while they get the bones and go to the port of Ghot, Bové will pay him the silver he asks and the hire of the men."

Kungam apparently had no patience for the usual Cathan method of long, indirect discussion. In a few minutes more an agreement had been reached. It was hard to tell from the bandit's stony expression, but Dominic imagined he was pleased.

Bové did not speak until they had left the wooden building, letting out an explosive breath. "Phew! He's a murderous bastard, all right, but refreshingly direct. We need to make a list of all the equipment that is ours. If we don't mention it, he keeps it. I also had to promise him all but one of our rifles."

"I hope you did not promise mine," Gutrune said coldly. "I will have need of it."

"Since you are not with the expedition, I'll do my best to see that it is not taken—but I can't make any promises. Your best bet is to find it yourself before that lot do." He sighed. "Kungam is sending scouts ahead to confirm what we have told him about the camp. We'll follow with the rest of the raiding party."

Dominic winced. More riding. He'd been hoping for a little more rest before they set out again. Failing that—he hoped Bové had included food in his negotiations.

The bandit camp made her nervous. Gutrune checked her pistol again, and the pouch of ammunition. The only other weapon she'd had with her when the police came was her knife. It wasn't much for a raid, but it should suffice until she could capture something else—or find her triple. She was determined not to let that, at least, fall in the hands of the bandits.

Markus Asgaya emerged from between the felt tents, carrying a bundle of dark cloth over one shoulder.

"Here, these are for you." He handed over what turned out to be wide cotton pants and a long, tunic-like jacket in the local style, dark blue with what had probably been white facings but were now off-white and stained.

Gutrune grimaced. "What I have will do, I think."

"Besides the fact none of Kungam's men wear that kind of outfit, you may have been seen when we took care of the armory. I've encouraged him to think his prestige will rise if it's believed he conducted the raid entirely with his own forces," Markus said airily.

She raised an eyebrow. "And the real reason?"

"It's a perfectly valid reason!" He hesitated, and the corners of his mouth twitched. "Oh, very well—there's no point in further inflaming any anti-Aeropan sentiment, such as Pei-an indulged in. At any rate, we should not make it harder to calm the unrest. We will do what we must, but His Majesty's government would take a dim view if we are careless about being seen as taking sides."

The clothes, surprisingly, were large enough to simply wear over her existing disguise, so she did so. Nothing about the bandits gave her confidence that belongings could be left unguarded for long. Then Bové came by with a water gourd, a thin bedroll and blanket, and a small bag with food. "This is for the journey—we'll eat before we leave."

Enough for the raid, but not enough for anything more. It would appear Kungam was not a trusting sort of bandit. Gutrune walked to the horse lines and found Ardhuin, Dominic, and Sonam there, also in bandit disguise. They were holding the reins of shaggy, stocky Asean horses with shabby felt-and-leather saddles.

"Where are our horses?"

"Needed by the raiders, apparently." Dominic patted the neck of his, a mare of ample girth if not height. "The scouts, so they can ride faster. Me, I am quite pleased with the change—and to have an unimpeachable excuse for keeping a sedate pace."

Bové appeared while he was speaking, and it seemed to Gutrune he was not entirely happy with the exchange of mounts. "If Kungam did not have such a reputation for keeping to his bargains, I would be advising a hasty escape in the night," he said in a quiet undervoice. "But then, he is also reputed to pay no attention to social courtesies or deference of any kind. What he has agreed to do he will do as he sees fit; our role is to follow his direction."

"He has only made himself free of our horses, which are useful to the planned raid," Ardhuin commented. "Or do you fear he will do more?"

"We don't have much more," snapped Bové. "No, the only thing to fear is something changing at the general's camp that would make us look like liars. If Kungam thinks we were sent to trap him..." He shook his head.

A shout was raised in the camp, and the bandits mounted up. Gutrune took this as the signal for them to do the same, as Bové confirmed. It was dark enough that all rode at a walking pace. The night was still, only disturbed by the footfall of the horses and the creak of leather harness, and the moon had not yet risen so the stars blazed in the sky over the plains.

After a time, she heard the distant thrum of horses at speed. Her eyes had adapted to the dark enough to see it was a small group—the scouts, returning? So soon? She shifted her jacket to make sure she could reach her pistol easily and edged her horse a little farther from the main body of bandits. If something had gone wrong, they would need to react quickly.

But then the scouts were close enough for her to see they were grinning, white slashes in dark faces, and that there was a paler, strange face among them. A captive?

As Sonam translated for them, not just a captive, but a deserter from the general's camp. He appeared resigned to death but readily answered the bandit's questions.

"He was with a large group of the general's men who were ordered to take control of Baiyueh. They left yesterday. There were rumors that the general and the *anban* were working together, but there was a large explosion and the general took advantage of the problem to capture the town for himself. This man does not want to be a dishonorable soldier, but he has kin in the town and he believes it is his duty to protect the people, not attack them in these troubled times. He has heard of Kungam and will not lie to him—or help him. He asks only that his body not be mutilated."

"Are they going to kill him?" Dominic sounded horrified.

"They can hardly let him go, to alert the camp." Gutrune knew she sounded cold but inwardly felt slightly ill.

The tall bulk of Kungam spoke briefly and made a sharp gesture. Sonam slumped.

"What?"

"He is to be tied to a stake here. If he has lied, or if we do not return, he will starve to death. If he has spoken the truth, he will be freed."

Harsh, but better than she had feared. Kungam spoke again, and Bové waved them over.

"He is planning the attack. Most of the general's forces are now in Baiyueh. The general remains in the camp with perhaps a third of his men, but they are trained soldiers and quite capable. The camp is fortified and well placed. He wishes to know what magics you can provide for the attack."

Markus and Sonam looked immediately at Ardhuin, and Gutrune smiled wryly at her startled movement. Even now, she was not entirely used to being thought of as the fearsome mage she was.

"Well defended—and still more men than Kungam has. He needs to get his men up close or even inside before the general knows they are there or that he is being attacked. I can muffle sound around a group of attackers and make those who watch think there is nothing unusual to see."

"Not illusion?"

She shook her head. "No, that would take too much power, and for what? I will need strength for the fight too. For that, I suggest the two of you focus on harrowfog and light stasis, and I will create a fire golem."

Markus had an expression of awe. "Truly? Not that I would dream of dissuading you—indeed, I hope to watch—but will this not cause precisely the kind of notice we hope to avoid?"

Ardhuin ducked her head. "Dramatic, yes, but not as effective as a fireshell—which *would* be noticed, and is much more modern and clearly Aeropan. Fire golems are quite old, and I am also hoping it will serve as a distraction while we look for our...personal gear."

Gutrune certainly had that intention, and they all knew they needed to keep the magical salts from being found by anyone, even quasi-honest bandits.

Bové merely grunted, and apparently Kungam also approved. Ardhuin glanced meaningfully to one side, and they faded back and away. She made a small gesture with her hand, and the ambient noise of the night and the bandits faded.

"I think you should stay with Dominic." She looked at Gutrune. "He'll be able to see the...what we're looking for, and you can protect him."

Dominic frowned. "And I think we should stay together. This is dangerous enough without additional risk."

"The whole point of the fire golem is to be a distraction. I have to keep it in sight to direct it. And Kungam will be watching the magicians but not you." Judging from Dominic's narrowed eyes and clenched jaw, he was not appeased, but he said nothing more.

They rode farther until the general's camp was in view. In the cover of a thicket of dense brush, Kungam made his final preparations. Two groups of men were selected for the initial attack, and a third group cut down brush as quietly as possible and arranged it in a roughly human shape to Ardhuin's directions. The bundles were not attached to a frame, or even each other. Once Ardhuin was satisfied, she waved the bandits back, and they speedily obeyed. They did not appear comfortable knowing magic was being planned, even for their benefit.

Ardhuin stood for a moment, motionless, then raised both hands in a complex gesture. The bundles of brush shuddered and compressed, rising like a beam lifted by one end, until the figure stood upright. It was hard to see in the dark, but it towered over the bandits even when it shuffled forward.

"Tell them...to follow the golem," Ardhuin said, strain apparent in her voice. "I have cast a shield of concealment in front of it. Now...the sound muffling."

Gutrune could still hear footsteps and the creaking rustle of the golem, but as they drew closer to the camp, no alarm was raised. Kungam had chosen a sector of the palisade to the south of the main gate for his attack, and when they were only a few hundred yards from the wall, he lifted a hand. Ardhuin and the golem stopped. She made more gestures, and the two groups of bandits moved away with Sonam and Markus, into what looked like impenetrable shadow—and Gutrune realized more magic was at work.

And then the golem burst into flame. Ardhuin had done something to shape the flame beyond merely burning the brush: the head had features now—tusks, and horns, and round bulging eyes of red coals. It moved as if attacking the main gate, and shouting soldiers could be heard behind it.

Very clever. They cannot ignore the risk of fire and hide behind their wooden walls. The frightened soldiers did not appear to notice, as Gutrune had, that their comrades on the wall had mysteriously vanished. Nor did they notice, until it was too late, that a small side gate had been opened through which the rest of the bandits and the expedition members entered the camp.

Gutrune ran inside and took a moment to orient herself. The side gate was for foot traffic, not carts, and led to what appeared to be barracks. It was unlikely their gear would be stored there. In unsettled times—when the general might not be able to fully trust his own men—he would keep valuables close by. She took Dominic's arm and tugged, catching Stoller's eye and pulling out her pistol with her free hand.

Three soldiers ran from the gap between two buildings, one bringing his long, brass-trimmed rifle in position to fire at them. *Get his weapon.* She shot him in the chest, sticking her pistol in her sash and drawing her knife in one continuous movement. She was running now, dodging a lance thrust by ducking, grabbing the rifle with one hand and stabbing upward at the lanceman as she rose. Stoller had accounted for the third soldier by then, and she tossed him the rifle. Without needing a word from her, Stoller put it to his shoulder and covered her while she reloaded the pistol. She supposed there were some advantages to having an old soldier for a servant, if she must have one with her.

A small noise escaped Dominic, and she looked up. He was flat against the building, face deathly pale. She resisted the urge to snap at him. For one thing, they dared not attract more attention.

"This way." She pointed. "It will be away from the fighting."

Her intended reassurance failed. "Ardhuin…" Dominic turned to go the opposite direction, and she had to grab his arm again to stop him.

"She's waiting for us," she hissed. "If you want to help her, find our luggage!"

That worked. He even picked up the dropped lance.

"Maybe we should disguise ourselves as soldiers." Dominic gestured at the bodies. Gutrune hesitated, but only for a moment. They were going to be near the most secure area of the camp, and in the darkness the imposture would not need to be perfect. They hacked the tunics free and draped them loosely over their existing clothes, since they would never have fit the larger Aeropans—and they would also be able to remove them quickly if the bandits came by.

They still moved cautiously but did not make as much of an effort to seek cover. Gutrune took turns with Stoller crossing open areas. She began to see what looked like a large tent ahead, with large iron torches around it, along with guards. Beyond it was an imposing multistory wood building that had the air of a fortified dwelling. The general's quarters, most likely, which would make the tent a likely prospect for their gear.

Their improvised uniforms would not pass muster here. Guards ringed the entire circumference, and closely enough that it would be impossible to take out one without the others noticing. A distraction, then? But what would be more distracting than a pitched battle? The guards looked nervous, but they were remaining at their posts.

No reinforcements. Their task was to guard the tent, clearly. They would rally to an obvious attack. So, she needed a secondary attack to draw attention away from their quieter entrance. If only she had her rifle…

"Do you think you will have any degree of accuracy with that?"

Stoller gave her a resigned shrug, hefting the rifle. "It belongs in a museum." It had engraved brass insets and carving on the stock. "I got the powder and bullets too. If you don't need a rapid rate of fire, miss, I can manage."

"Very well. Herr Kermarec, you remain here. Stoller and I will attack the front. When the guards here move to assist, use this to cut your way inside." She held out her knife.

He wasn't paying attention. He was staring over her shoulder, back toward the battle. "Someone using magic just ran past that building," Dominic said. "But it isn't…that is, I think it was Asgaya."

She turned as he finished speaking, hugging the deeper shadows as she moved. She crouched down, making a quiet whistle like a birdcall.

"Was that for me?" Markus sank down against the wall beside her, breathing in deep, gasping breaths from exertion. "We've taken the gate and the fire golem is wreaking havoc inside, so I thought I would try and find you and see how you were doing."

"We need your magic to create a diversion. We need to get inside that tent."

His head sank down. "Milady, I am desolate...but I am spent. I barely had enough power to cast shadow just now, and I'll pay for it later. That's why I left the main battle—I was not much use without a weapon, and there were too many angry men who had theirs and wanted to use them on me. But perhaps I can assist another way?" Trying not to let her disappointment show, she explained her intent. Markus had regained his breath by now. "A frontal assault? That is not in your usual style. And I don't care for the odds."

"Nor do I, but if we wait for Kungam's men, they can just as easily take our equipment for themselves as give it to us."

"What if it is not the right place?"

"It is." Dominic was rather pale, but still clutching the lance he had claimed. "I saw bright magic through the entrance when that guard came out, just a glimpse."

Gutrune felt her frustration build. They didn't have enough weapons, or magic, or anything to work with.

"Did you see anything useful on your way here?" she asked Markus.

He shook his head. "A barn of some kind, most likely pigs from the smell. Oh, and a kitchen. We might find some knives, or spices," he added, a doubtful expression on his face.

She felt a spurt of hope. "I have an idea."

The barn did contain pigs. The kitchen, as she hoped, had cooking oil in quantities suitable for providing for a large number of hungry men. The barn also had rope, and Dominic's lance proved to be an effective pig motivator. In short order a stampede of frantic pigs dragging leaking oil casks from ropes around their necks bore down on the hapless guards, who stared in horrified confusion at this new threat. The guards' attempts to turn the pigs only had the happy effect of tangling the ropes around one of the iron torch stands, saving Gutrune and the others the effort of setting the oil on fire themselves. For a moment, the squealing and screaming even drowned out the sounds of the battle.

The pigs diverted, all the guards were focused on putting out the fire. Gutrune quickly cut a slit in the back of the tent and they slipped inside.

"Where was it?" she whispered to Dominic. He waved, indicating a section of the crowded tent.

The tent was full of bales and boxes, but there weren't many Aeropan trunks to sort through. They quickly found their baggage in the pile, and Gutrune lunged for the box with her triple rifle. It appeared undamaged, and she quickly loaded it. Now their chances had improved considerably.

"It's in here." Dominic pointed. "Someone else needs to take it." He was squinting and shielding his eyes.

"No, we certainly don't want anyone else finding that." Markus reached in the trunk and took out the clay jar, which he wrapped in a piece of silk and tucked inside his Cathan disguise. "I'll go see how the guards are doing, shall I?"

He moved off silently in the gloom. Gutrune stood watch while Stoller gathered more of their belongings that would be immediately useful or should not be appropriated, while Dominic sorted out the gear Ardhuin would need.

Markus returned and knelt beside Gutrune. "It appears they have put out the fire. I am a trifle concerned we have not yet seen any of the others, though. Perhaps we should go and see if they need our help. Not that I can do much"—and there was a trace of bitterness in his voice—"I am no mage. It will be several hours before I can do anything." He felt at the front of his jacket, frowning. "Unless..."

Without thought, her hand reached out and caught his wrist. "No."

Markus went completely still, making no attempt to escape her grasp. So why was she still gripping him so tightly she could feel his pulse?

"With it I would not be useless." His voice was rough.

Her breath hissed out, fury flooding her. "If you use that, you have no idea what it will do to you in the end. You may not be able to cast magic at this moment, but do you think it ends here? There will be other battles— and if you have injured yourself in a misguided attempt to assist now, you will truly be useless then."

"This, from one who seems determined to sacrifice herself on the altar of duty? Who will take any risk in that service, who seeks out the most dangerous tasks? Why should I not take dangerous risks too?" He sounded as angry as she felt, and his words only enraged her further.

"I take risks because I do not want to be a sacrifice. I want to live to my fullest extent, not be kept in a velvet-lined box and only taken out to be admired on special occasions. But even then, I act in service—not for my own personal gratification. *I will not be wasted*—and you should not be wasted either." The anger had burned away, and now all she felt was a bone-deep fatigue. "Promise me you will not use the salts. You do not know...consider the source and what he has done in the past for power." Her voice shook, remembering the fevered course of the magic in her body, her mind.

She felt his free hand cover hers, warm and strong, and lift it to his lips.

"I give you my word."

CHAPTER 15

It was a rout. Even Ardhuin, inexperienced in warfare, could see that. Any vestige of fight had left the soldiers when it was discovered the general had run away, abandoning them to their fate. Pale dawn was growing visible on the horizon and dusting a few thin, high clouds with pink.

The fire golem was becoming thin and pale, surrounded by a cloud of bitter smoke, but she did not disperse it. Kungam was still striding about the camp, stone-faced. She presumed he was angry, but it was difficult to tell. The bandit did not allow any feelings to show. She, on the other hand, could not conceal her worry. Where were the others? Were they safe?

Kungam eventually headed for the central building, past a large tent with scorch marks along the front. Someone else must have done that—the fire golem had not gone that far in the battle. She heard voices, speaking Gaulan, inside the building. She stopped the golem and went inside. If it wasn't Dominic, maybe it was someone who had seen him recently.

It was Bové, soot marking his face and a crude bandage on one arm. He was grimacing, either from annoyance or pain. "Ah, there you are, Talbot. How did you fare?"

"Better than you, from the looks of it. Have you seen Kermarec?"

He shook his head. "I've had worse—at least the bullet went through. You don't want to see what this bunch thinks constitutes surgery. I often do a better job myself with iodine paste and a penknife, but it's difficult to operate on your own arm." He glanced quickly at the door. Ardhuin turned and saw Dominic standing there with Markus Asgaya behind him. He appeared tired but unhurt.

"I thought I recognized that fire golem." He smiled wearily. "We found our supplies. The important things have been accounted for."

Ah. That was a relief.

Some of the bandits were dragging forward captives wearing rich silks. They did not look like fighters—one man, in fact, was quite elderly and huddled behind the others, his eyes wide with fear. Kungam addressed them in his usual blunt, straightforward style. One snarled defiance at him but the rest were silent in a sullen, hangdog way.

Kungam gazed at them for a moment, gave an order that was greeted with laughter and cheers by his men but pale-faced horror by the captives, then appeared to dismiss them from his mind. He turned and approached the Aeropans, speaking to Bové.

Bové translated. "He says we have more than fulfilled the terms of the agreement. We may take whatever animals or gear we need from the camp, and our supplies. He also wishes to thank the magicians—and asks that the fire demon be sent away, as it disturbs his men."

"I'll dispel it now." Ardhuin headed for the door, passing the captives, who were being roped together. The old man, clutching his staff, gave her a look of pure hatred as she passed.

"Look out!" Bové shouted behind her, and she spun around. The old man had raised his staff over his head to strike at her.

Ardhuin raised her arm to block the blow, but the old man was amazingly quick—and strong. The staff struck her head hard enough to make her stumble, shattering in the process. It sounded strange in breaking, as if it were glass.

Her eyes watering, she raised a hand to see if there was any blood where she had been hit. There was sharp grit in her hair, and a piece...a piece of silvery glass. Just then she felt her hair fall loose. It was annoying, because she couldn't fix it without looking very odd to the others.

"The illusion is dispersed!" Dominic yelled. *Chryselectrum. His staff had chryselectrum.* That must have been enough to weaken her illusion. Ardhuin cast everything she could that was quick and did not require much concentration to conceal herself, but it was too late. Bové was staring at her in horror, mouth agape.

"But who...*Madame Kermarec? How...?*"

Kungam was also staring at her in amazement, the first real emotion she could recall seeing him display. *Oh, splendid. Time to disappear, I think.*

The *gloire* did not take much power, and dazzled the eye. She cast that and spun around, pulling the darkest concealing shadow she could manage, and ran. She was getting dangerously tired, but surely there was someplace she could hide in the damaged camp until it was time to leave or she was recovered enough to create another in-depth illusion? "Mr. Talbot" had been completely exposed now. Still, she could not appear as herself just yet either. How many people had seen her true appearance in that room?

She rounded the large tent before the general's quarters. The movement of fabric caught her eye—a flap? Was it an opening? The edges looked ragged. Someone had cut it. She heard voices approaching and darted inside.

Stoller looked up from filling a knapsack, startled. In the dim light Ardhuin could just make out a dark figure seated on a bale and holding a rifle.

"Gutrune?"

"She's gone to see about pack animals," Markus said. He shifted and stood up. "Is there a problem?"

I suppose you could call it that. "One of the general's people hit me with chryselectrum. My illusion was dispersed with outsiders present. Bové recognized me. I need to stay out of sight until we can leave the camp and the bandits."

Markus snarled something in Preusan that earned him a raised eyebrow from Stoller. "You are sure? How did...never mind, the damage is done. I suppose you had best stay here for now. I'll go find out how we can get you out. I doubt Bové wants to stay around Kungam any longer than he must." He handed the rifle to Stoller and ducked out through the tent slit.

Stoller propped the rifle against a wooden box and went back to work. Ardhuin saw he had already filled three other knapsacks, and went to help. It was always possible that they would have to make a run for it. What supplies did she absolutely need to take?

As she was rummaging through her baggage Dominic came in, breathing fast, followed by Markus and Gutrune.

"There's a problem." His face was grim. "Kungam is refusing to let us leave."

"What? Why?"

Markus peered out of the slit, then back inside. "Bové is talking to him now, trying to find out. Sonam...ah, here he is."

In contrast to the others, Sonam did not appear apprehensive. He had more of an expression of wanting to be somewhere else, combined with dazed confusion.

They huddled around him, voices hushed.

"Why is Kungam angry?" Ardhuin asked. "Why won't he let us go?"

Sonam was looking down at his feet, his hands twisting around each other. "He is not...angry," he managed to say. "Not after Mr. Bové convinced him he did not know you had hidden what you are. He wants..." he finally looked up, pleading, at Dominic. "He appears to believe she is a *tingri*—a powerful spirit. The one who struck you was the general's shaman." Sonam finally dared to look her in the eye. "He thinks this has angered you and made you abandon this place. He wishes to speak with you and appease you and asked Mr. Bové to call you back." His weak smile raised Ardhuin's suspicions.

Markus had been continually checking outside, and now he gave a soft whistle. Ardhuin stared at him in shock, but then Bové himself entered the tent. He was shaking with some suppressed emotion, and when he saw her his eyes blazed with fury.

"My people are hostages now, thanks to you. Do you realize your heedless, selfish actions could get us all killed? But no, you insisted on coming despite the danger. What possible reason could you have for doing this?"

She clenched her fists, feeling the nails dig into her palms. He had a right to be angry—she had deceived him. There was no time for admitting fault. She needed to be angry too, to get him to understand. To help.

"I did it because I had no choice. Because the safety of Aerope is at stake." Bové snorted and looked at the others. What he saw must have puzzled him, for he did not immediately respond. "I concealed myself to shield you and the members of your expedition. Have you not noticed how we have been pursued and attacked? The unusual custom inspection? Mother Long sending us on our way with miraculous speed? The enemy I am hunting is very dangerous and suspects I am near."

"The government of Bretagne is involved," Dominic said, quiet but intense. "You knew this from the beginning. Now you know why."

Gutrune shifted, pulling a slender piece of metal from her sleeve and laying it on a crate. Her illusion warped and faded, showing her calm, austere true face. "The government of Preusa is also. This is not the first time we have fought this man. He is a dangerous mage, a relict of the Mage War. A Gaulan mage," she added.

Now Bové was looking worried. "But they were all executed...and that was decades ago!"

"One escaped—and he was quite lively when he gave me this last year." Markus touched the white streak in his hair. "Now, it is true our presence has made your life more difficult, but it is also true we have rescued you from the dangers we have brought."

Bové made a strangled noise deep in his throat. "And how do you intend to rescue us from this? And why *you?*" He stabbed a finger at Ardhuin. "What can you do against this old mage? At least Talbot could..." he faltered.

"Ah, starting to figure it out, are you?" Markus raised an amused eyebrow. "I know it is a bit of a shock, and I really shouldn't be telling you anything—but I will say this. Young Sonam is a magician of talent. I am a *schutzmagus* of the Preusan Imperial Court. Madame Kermarec could take us both on *and* the general's camp. She was trying to keep a low profile, or we could have slept in."

Bové looked blindly around, then dropped to sit on a battered trunk. He looked haggard. "Right, then." He seemed to be talking to himself, to give himself encouragement. "Here we are. It makes no sense, but we must make do. Kungam..." His eyes widened as if he had completely forgotten the bandit leader. "Damnation. Kungam seems to want some kind of alliance. That fire golem made a strong impression, and he still wants to capture the general, which won't be easy. He saw powerful magic and he wants it for his own ends."

"We cannot take the time to assist Kungam with his personal vendetta,"

Gutrune said calmly. "And I am sure he would find other tasks in need of magical assistance."

"Can we simply escape?" Dominic asked. "Although I suppose it would be difficult to take the supplies, which was the point of the exercise."

Ardhuin sighed. "More importantly, we need to rest. It would take a great deal of magic to escape Kungam and his men, possibly more than we used in the fight."

Gutrune turned her head to Bové. "Then we need to delay. Can you do this?"

He snorted. "Oh, I can manage. The fire spirit is angry, et cetera."

"Then we will find you when we are ready to meet with Kungam."

Dominic stared at her in surprise. "What, are you willing to talk to him?"

"I would rather not have two sets of enemies chasing me all the way, and with us on foot," Ardhuin snapped. "If we can't make him see reason, we'll...oh, I don't know, take *him* hostage."

Bové left, looking gloomy. Ardhuin used one last bit of magic to illusion the slit in the tent so it appeared to be unbroken fabric, and then she curled up on a rank-smelling camel rug and tried to sleep.

She must have slept at some point, for reddish afternoon light was now filtering through and the heat was unpleasant. She summoned power—it felt strong, but she knew her reserves were not fully restored. She would just have to be careful. To that end, Ardhuin did not plan for full illusions for the meeting. She left her hair down completely, only casting a combination of the *gloire* base with aversion to make it hard for anyone to look at her. Sonam was sent to find Bové.

As she had requested, the area around the wood building was deserted. According to Markus, when the chryselectrum had struck her, her real face had only been visible for a short time and few people had been in a position to see it. Her hair, though...that might be enough. Someone was looking for a woman with red hair. Still, the fewer that saw her, the better it would be.

Inside the building Ardhuin stopped to let her eyes adjust to the gloom. Two people stood in the main room, Bové and Kungam. Kungam...she blinked. Instead of dusty boots and worn, heavy tunic coat spattered with blood, he was wearing a yellow robe with stylized eagles in applique—and his hair, drawn back tightly in a smooth, folded queue, was wet.

To one side was a low carved wooden table with several small boxes, a covered woven basket that was leaking dark liquid from its base, and a colorful pile of what looked like embroidered silk. A small brass pot gave off a tendril of smoke that smelled rich and heavy. She took a step and felt something crunch under her feet. At first she thought it was coarse sand, and then she feared it was the magical salts.

"It is the custom to purify a place contaminated by evil spirits with salt,"

Bové said, seeing her hesitate. "I am afraid he did not take kindly to that shaman's behavior. In a rather permanent, beheading kind of way."

Ardhuin had a sudden suspicion what was in the covered, leaking basket. "I see." The others had come in behind her, and she felt a little braver knowing they were there. "What does he want to discuss?"

Bové struggled to speak. She stared at him, concerned, and realized his face was turning red. "I believe I mentioned an alliance earlier?" Ardhuin nodded. "Well, it appears he has a particular kind of alliance in mind."

It clicked into place. A table of gifts, a freshly cleaned-up Kungam...

"He can't be serious," she said, just as Dominic stated forcefully, "She already *has* a husband!"

Markus Asgaya suddenly appeared to have a slight choking problem, and even Gutrune widened her eyes in shock.

"I told him that. Several times." Bové looked harried. "The people here...please forgive me, Madame Kermarec, but I must speak of things not suited for a lady's ears. Besides a...highly elastic definition of chastity, they also practice on occasion the custom of...multiple husbands. For very high-ranking women," he added in a strained voice.

Of all the possibilities they had discussed, this had not been one of them. She was at a loss as to how to proceed. Then she looked at Kungam. He had not said a word, had not even shifted his position, but was returning her gaze intently, determination in his eyes. *Aha.*

"Sonam. Why would a man want to marry a fire spirit?"

"It would give him prestige. Only a very brave man would attempt it. There are stories...but it does not end well for the men, if they forget the danger."

"What are you thinking?" Dominic was standing at her shoulder, speaking quietly in her ear.

"Kungam has no real interest in me," she whispered back. "He wants some proof he can call on a fire spirit for help. You've seen him in action— he is always quick to seize an advantage. We need something that will give the impression of that proof, yet let us leave freely."

"And reason to think that keeping your secrets helps him, as well," Gutrune murmured. "He has no difficulty enforcing discipline among his men. If he wishes to please you, we can use that."

"*I* have no interest in pleasing him," Dominic said through gritted teeth.

Gutrune inclined her head. "Only to the extent of making him useful. Perhaps we should make clear we cannot stay. That we...have important obligations to attend to."

Ardhuin waved Bové closer. "Tell him that I am here hunting a powerful enemy, just as he hunted the general, and I must go and defeat him. I have sworn an oath."

Bové translated, and to Ardhuin it seemed Kungam's intent gaze only sharpened. He spoke a few words.

"He asks if you will return when this enemy is dead."

Dominic put a hand on her arm before she could answer. "I think I have an idea. A plausible story, an excuse, might serve him just as well as your presence would."

"Ah, a very long engagement, then?" Markus grinned. His grin disappeared with a grunt and he put one hand to his side, giving Gutrune a pained expression. She just glared at him.

Dominic scowled. "Yes, something like that. You know, like the tale of the diamond mountain in *La Travaille de Fayre*? Where the fayre prince had to wear down the diamond mountain using the single tailfeather of a phoenix that only regrew once every hundred years?"

Gutrune's eyes brightened in understanding. "So, the Mage Guardian will return...once the evil that Denais has caused is completely destroyed?"

"That should take a long time," Markus agreed. "Many years, in fact, if you include the fact that he nearly wiped out the Mage Guardians. You'll need to train and work with them until they are up to snuff, in addition."

Kungam took the news with unimpaired calm, further convincing Ardhuin they were on the right path.

"He offers to help you fight."

"The enemy is a powerful magician and has other magicians helping him. Soldiers would be of little use," Gutrune said fluidly, after Ardhuin gave her a worried look. "In addition, he must not know we are attacking him. We must travel in secret, leaving no trace."

This did not go over well, but eventually it was agreed that Kungam would provide guides to cross the desert to the high mountains, and also allow Bové to hire guards from his bandits.

"So I will get my last expedition after all." Bové looked stunned. "Are you quite sure you must cross the desert? That is not an easy route—and if you did not have local guides, almost certain death. You are aware these guides will be loyal to Kungam, rather than you?"

"And your so-called guards will not?" Dominic asked.

Bové waved his hand. "They will get paid when I get the samples to Ghot. Kungam knows I have no money here; I don't mind having them along to make sure I keep my end of the bargain. And they won't be a threat until I do get money. One last thing. He wants some sort of proof of this promise. Something, I suspect, impressive."

"That would mean magical, I believe," Dominic said.

Gutrune frowned slightly. "Magical, but also personal."

Markus lifted his head. "I know the very thing! And your imager even has a beautiful subject ready to display. A thoughtful gift indeed, and a reminder of an absent love...oh, very well, I'll stop."

CHAPTER 16

The dusty, rutted road was a distant memory. Now they rode on a bare plain with scrubby grass and low brush and outcroppings of crumbling rock. There was no sign of civilization anywhere in sight, just distant mountains ahead. Even the bandit camp was three days behind them.

Dominic wished he could ride so Kungam's men were not in view, but since they were the guides that was difficult to accomplish. He supposed it was worth putting up with them to get as far away from Kungam himself as fast as possible. He heard the sound of approaching hoof-falls and sighed inwardly. Would he never stop?

"I do not understand why you cherish your black mood so," Markus remarked. "Really, we got off remarkably lightly. No real harm done, and indeed significant benefits, all for allowing one blood-soaked bandit a harmless fiction."

"It was not harmless for that shaman," Dominic said, his teeth clenched. They had managed to dispose of the severed head without the guides noticing, but it had taken some magic to accomplish.

"From what Bové was saying, it merely hastened his inevitable death. Kungam had no intention of letting any of that lot enjoy a quiet retirement. You do not fear he will attempt any attack on Madame Kermarec, I trust? He is not such a fool, and she is more than capable of defending herself against the entire bandit camp." Markus tilted his head, giving Dominic a speculative glance. "Or is it another kind of threat you fear? Kungam is a fine specimen, agreed, but I find it hard to believe you would doubt your lady's affection."

Anger surged through him. "It pleases you to jest," Dominic snapped. "Do you have no other way to beguile the tedium of the journey save tormenting me? Of course I do not doubt Ardhuin. And you—your recent particular attentions are a complete novelty. How can you possibly understand my sentiments? I never loved any woman before Ardhuin. It is completely incomprehensible to me to think of not loving her, or loving another. If she had not...if it had not been my very good fortune..." He could not continue speaking.

It did not help that he still did not feel completely worthy of her—and this most recent incident had only heightened his sense of relative uselessness. So he could see magic. What good was that in a fight? What was he truly contributing to the success of their endeavor?

"Do you mean to say...not even one mild amorous adventure? Did the university you attended have a strict religious rule?" Markus seemed genuinely taken aback and a trifle shocked.

"No such thing. Or my friend Phillipe would have been expelled his first year." Dominic stared straight ahead, hoping to be left alone again.

"I...see. I did, in fact, misread the situation. If it is any consolation, I truly believe the bandit king was merely trying to gain his own local advantage by association, and nothing...nothing more. Which is why I thought it humorous. Now that I understand your sentiments, I can understand your black looks and will say nothing further on the subject. Ah, here is Sonam coming back from his scouting."

Dominic was very glad for the change of subject and greeted Sonam, coming over the grassy dune towards the rest of the riders, with enthusiasm. "When do we reach the Taklamakan Desert?" he called.

"This is the Taklamakan," Sonam replied, bobbing his head with a small smile. "There—they mix with the clouds, but the Sky-Holding Mountains are visible, with snow on their tops. We are very close now."

Dominic squinted, but all he saw were distant white clouds on the horizon. "I had thought there would be sand dunes and such in the desert, like in Geapt."

Sonam smiled wider. "Perhaps a few, but the wind does not leave them long."

"Bové did mention the windstorms as being powerful." Ardhuin rode closer, and he smiled at her. As infuriating as Kungam's behavior had been, he did owe him one favor. She had no further need of her illusion magic, and while she still wore the clothes of her male disguise for convenience, it was a relief to see her face clearly again.

"Is wind alone truly dangerous?" Gutrune was behind them, but her hearing was good.

Ardhuin nodded vigorously. "In Atlantea, in the interior, the wind-funnels can be devastating. There is one town that built entirely underground after the second time it was destroyed."

Dominic was intrigued. "Truly? I think the Family Museum had an article that mentioned them, but I have never seen one."

"Neither have I—I've never heard of them outside Atlantea, at least not the big sort. They look a bit like the dust-travelers, but *much* bigger, and they hang down from the clouds." Ardhuin pointed to the side. "Oh look, there goes one now."

The dust-traveler drifted across the ground ahead of them, a narrow, spinning cloud of airborne sand and leaves, prompting muttering and warding gestures to avert evil from their guides. Kungam had been true to his word and provided camels, horses, provisions, and guides for their travels. Dominic was sure the guides considered themselves Kungam's representatives as well as protection, but besides keeping an eye on them there was not much to be done. None of them knew how to cross the Taklamakan desert, and he was not sure how the bandits could know which way to go. Besides, they always kept a considerable distance between Ardhuin and themselves, so after the first few days his concerns subsided.

"You have been quiet since we left the bandits. I hope that you are not still unhappy about what happened there." Ardhuin spoke in a low tone meant only for his ears.

Dominic sighed. "Since we are away, I suppose not—I have been thinking about Bové. From what I had read I had thought of him as supremely competent, able to handle any eventuality on an expedition—but then it's a rare hero that survives a meeting in real life. Editors can do so much," he added, grinning.

"Or perhaps you learned so much from his example, and also from your own experiences that he did *not* have, and you are just as much an adventurer as he is." Ardhuin smiled back, clearly proud of him.

He gave a surprised laugh. "What? I can barely stay on a horse, I cannot make myself understood to any of the people in Asea, and in any fight I am of most use by staying out of the way."

"You do not give yourself credit. He knows virtually nothing of magic, and you are a mage-level thaumatic scryer. Besides, this is your first trip outside Aerope; do you really think Bové reached his familiarity with Asean customs and languages so easily? He has been traveling here many years, has he not?"

"True, but..." It was a startling thought. Was he really being an adventurer, right now?

"I am glad Kungam didn't bother you too much." She leaned forward in the saddle, almost whispering. "But do you know of anything troubling Markus? He's been nearly as silent as you."

Dominic spared a quick glance at Markus, riding ahead with Sonam and one of the guides. "No, but it makes a refreshing change. I only hope it continues." He gave Ardhuin a quick kiss. It was, he considered, what an adventurer would do, and her answering smile and flush of color rewarded him.

Something was coming into view ahead that was not a feature of the landscape but clearly man-made. Sonam looked back at the others and pointed, indicating they would go around it to the right. As they got closer, Dominic saw it was made of stone. A round tower with a curved top ending in a segmented spire, the whole perhaps fifteen feet in height. There may have been carving on the base long ago, but the wind and sand had scoured it almost completely away. Tied to the spire were long scarves with ragged ends, in various shades of faded blue.

"What is it?" he called out to Sonam.

"It is an *obo*. They are a kind of shrine," Sonam said. "People leave the scarves as gifts for the spirits, to make them happy to live in the shrine."

As they went around, Dominic suddenly felt a sudden twitch inside, a familiar but disturbing sensation. It was very brief, and he puzzled over why it had felt familiar. When had he ever felt something like that before? And why did he feel surprised to feel it here?

The rest of the day's ride was uneventful. They stopped early to set up camp and allow Gutrune to go hunting, and she returned with two small gazelle-like creatures. The fresh meat was supplemented by dried fruit and tough, leathery cheese curds with a tart aftertaste.

"Do we have any idea what we will encounter once we get to Bhuta?" Markus asked after staring into the fire. "We are getting close enough to begin our planning."

Sonam spread his hands. "I can say how I left the valley, but it has been many months. I only hope we can reach it before the protections my teacher set have faded." He looked off to the horizon. The impossibly high mountains were visible now, backlit by the setting sun. Sonam started to describe the valley, scratching in the dirt with a rib bone, interspersed with questions from Markus and Gutrune. Ardhuin was listening, but they had already determined neither Sonam nor MacCrimmon were certain of the source or extent of the magical attacks. A powerful magician had been seen there, however.

It was, Dominic reflected, understandable to worry about the dangers they faced, which were considerable. But it was also true that the night sky blazed with stars overhead, that he was thousands of leagues from Bretagne in a place where he never thought he would be, with someone he never thought he would ever meet. Dominic decided he was enjoying himself.

Ardhuin woke feeling achy and sore. Sleeping on the ground was not comfortable, but she'd thought she had become accustomed. The sky was a strange color, a dull, gunmetal blue with thin threads of red clouds near the rising sun, and the air humid. Simply standing up made her break out in a sweat. She was very reluctant to start traveling again, and from what she could see the others were in a similar mood. Even the guides were irritable, kicking and swearing at the camels, who were refusing to rise to their feet.

One of the men eventually came to Sonam and delivered an emphatic speech, complete with sharp, chopping hand gestures. Sonam looked frightened.

"They say there is a storm coming," he translated. "A *zhur-i-khnat*. Very bad. They want to head for a place with deep ravines that will be safer, but we must go fast to get there in time."

Dominic frowned. "Won't ravines be dangerous when they fill with water?"

Sonam shook his head sharply. "This storm is not with water, but sand. It picks it up and carries it with the winds. They usually do not come in this season. If they had known, they would have gone a different way. This way is shorter but too open."

They moved quickly. Now Ardhuin was aware of an oppressive feeling in the air, an itchy feeling on her skin. The horses were skittish and difficult to handle; even Dominic's easygoing horse had to be held so he could mount. The camels changed their minds and decided instead of staying hunkered down they would do their best to run away. The delay was making the guides frantic, and when the group finally was able to move, they set a quick pace.

They traveled for hours under that same oppressive, dull sky. Ardhuin wondered if perhaps they had avoided the storm—she felt no wind—but the guides had not slacked the pace for an instant. The only time they stopped was to give their horses water, and even that was rushed.

Something caught her attention, and she turned in the saddle to look behind where they had been—and nearly screamed. What looked like a giant wall was moving slowly but inexorably across the plain, following them. How high was it? How would a ravine possibly give them enough shelter to survive?

They kept going. They passed a group of three *obo*, one much bigger than the others and with its spire mostly broken off. It had fragments of blue tile on its dome, and the base of the spire had jutting projections, like wings. Dominic stiffened as they went by, suddenly turning and staring at the *obo*.

"So that's it! I think...it feels like the ley lines back home. Are these shrine things causing it? But I don't see any magic..."

"Ley lines are natural, and they occur everywhere. Why do you think the *obo* would cause them?"

He grimaced. "Because every time we come near one, I feel ley lines. So perhaps they are markers? But you said the ley lines move."

"They do, usually...but not very far. How strange, since the *obo* are obviously very old." Dominic shrugged, and Ardhuin concentrated on following the camels, who had gotten ahead. The air was getting dusty, and her eyes stung. She refused to look back at the looming wall of the storm.

"We are losing visibility," yelled Markus. "How much farther? I don't want us lost in this dust."

"They say we should take rope, tie together," Sonam called back. "We must not stop here, we will die. Put cloth over your mouth and nose, and for the horses too."

Everyone dismounted. Ardhuin ripped up one of her few remaining shirts to breathe through. The storm...where was the storm? She couldn't see it—and then she realized with a wave of fear that the wall had already passed over them. The wind was mild, but she could barely see the camels only a few yards ahead. If they had not stopped and tied themselves together, she might already be lost.

The dust got thicker. How could the guides know where to go? Any landmarks would be lost in the murk, even the sun was diffused and impossible to pinpoint overhead. They needed to see.

If the dust was out of the way, they could. Dust...her great-uncle had set a cleaning spell on Peran, many years ago. Dust and crumbs on the floor were wafted away. If she remembered how it went, how it could be modified here...

She gripped the stirrup of her horse's saddle in one hand, trusting it would follow the others, and concentrated. Light magic, but over a large area. Nudging aside the sand in the air, not allowing any more to enter. Was it her imagination, or could she see Dominic more clearly now?

"Oh, that's much better," he said, and coughed. "It's your doing, yes?"

Seeing the clear space, the others congregated, and Sonam called to the guides ahead to join them. The camels milled about but made no attempt to leave the dust-free dome Ardhuin had created.

"This is a big help." Markus wiped damp grime from his face. "How much of an effort is it for you? Can I help maintain it?"

A gust of wind swirled through them, and Ardhuin staggered. "It's not that much...power. But a large...area, I had hoped...we could see where to go."

"Well, let's get everyone closer for now. Maybe we can wait this out."

Sonam shook his head, looking grim. "The storms can last for days. We must keep moving and find shelter. Even a large hill would help a little, but we need that ravine or something like it."

"I think Sonam mentioned an area with ravines," Dominic said slowly. "If we were headed in the general direction, would it be enough?"

Sonam discussed this with the guides, who nodded emphatically. "Yes, there are many in that place. They think they still have the right heading, but with no way to check we can easily go astray."

"Which direction?" Gutrune asked. The guide pointed. "Do we have a compass?" There was an awkward silence.

"Of all the things we neglected to bring..." Markus sighed and wiped his face.

"They do not work very well near the Sky-Holding Mountains," Sonam said. "It is perhaps not important."

"It would be rather useful *now*," Markus snapped. "What can we do? Keep going in a straight line and hope?"

"I think I may have an idea." Dominic untied his rope. He looked nervous. He darted away from the line of travelers, into the dust.

"No! Dominic! What are you doing?" Ardhuin struggled with her own rope, then stopped and extended her power the direction he had gone. He was already returning, coughing.

"I thought I felt it...and it is there. The ley line. It is different than ours, it feels very...sharp? Narrow? It's going that way," he pointed, "which is not that far off from the direction we need to go. I can track that."

"But Dominic..." her voice trailed off. "You would need to stay in contact for a long time. It's too dangerous."

He looked at her grimly. "It is too dangerous for us to even be discussing this. I don't have to stay in it the whole time. Just now and then, to make sure we're on course."

She wanted to argue, but he was right. There was no time. She tried to think of a way to protect him, but how could she do that without blocking his sense of the ley line?

Their travel soon became a delirious nightmare, putting one foot in front of the other in a dome of uniform pale reddish dust. It sometimes seemed they were not moving at all; even the rocks that appeared looked the same. Every so often Dominic would leave to check their direction— now with a longer rope, at her insistence—and sometimes they had to correct course. He was starting to show the effects of the ley line, too. He was seeing things that weren't there, rambling in his speech, but he remembered enough to continue guiding them. She hoped...she prayed he would not get so ill this time, but it was a feeble hope. *I can't lose him. Not when I'm the reason he's here.*

Keeping the shield up and moving took all of her concentration. The familiar pins-and-needles sensation of overextension made itself known— but what could she do? She had to keep the protection up or they were truly lost.

Hours of walking. She was hanging on to her horse's saddle to keep upright, letting it pull her forward. Her mouth was so dry she could not speak.

Then she heard a shout ahead. It sounded frantic—or excited. She could barely understand Sonam when he ran back to her. All she knew was it was not the promised ravine, yet they had stopped. Then what he was saying got through her fatigue.

"They see a wall! There is a wall ahead!"

CHAPTER 17

Gutrune half pulled, half dragged Ardhuin in the break in the wall the guides had found. It provided enough of a shield that with Ardhuin's magic, they could see other shapes in the cloudy air, shapes with the unmistakable look of buildings. Most of the ones they checked at first were either half-filled with sand or collapsed debris, or roofless. But as they kept going, the buildings were less damaged—and eventually they came across a large one that was mostly intact. There was even room for the animals.

"Do we stop here?" gasped Ardhuin. She staggered and braced herself against a wall. "Dominic...where is Dominic?"

"Over here." Marcus gave a hacking cough. "He's not making sense. Watch out; there's a hole in the floor. Here, I'll make some light."

The pale blue ball of magefire flared up. Dominic made a strange whimpering noise, like a stifled scream, and Ardhuin's head snapped up.

"Move away from him. Now!"

Markus stared at her and stepped closer to the door. Dominic stopped writhing and looked about with an air of delighted wonder.

"So beautiful..." he whispered. "Where are you?"

Gutrune felt the hair on her neck rise. Something was, indeed, very odd about him. And Ardhuin, even more oddly, made no move to go to him even as tears left muddy tracks down her dust-covered face.

"What's wrong with him?" Gutrune whispered.

"The ley line overexposed him to magic. Any magic now, however slight, will cause him great pain." Ardhuin's voice was thick with tears, her hands clenching. "He wanted to be useful."

Dominic turned his head as if searching. Even though Ardhuin was in shadow, as soon as he looked her way, an expression of pure joy suffused his face.

"Oh, there you are. I was afraid I had lost you."

"No, you haven't lost me. You will never lose me." Still she made no move, although it seemed every muscle was taut.

"What is it?" Gutrune spoke softly in her ear. "Why do you not comfort him when he is so distressed?"

Ardhuin swallowed hard. "In this state, he is...not quite rational. He won't notice anyone else. Please—" Her voice broke. "I ask so much. I know you must be as tired as I am, but if it were not for Dominic we would never have made it here safely. We need...he needs to be alone. As far from everyone else as possible."

"Then I and my magefire will go find a place distant but secure, and you can arrange more conventional lighting." Markus turned and ran off.

"You are far away again," Dominic told Ardhuin reproachfully. He was trying to walk through a fallen stone block and appeared quite puzzled why he could not.

"I know, love. Just a moment longer."

The raw pain in her voice spurred Gutrune to action. Sonam had already understood the problem and explained it to the guides. One of them gathered scraps of bone-dry wood and started a fire. The other was making rough torches with wood, the torn cloth they had used as masks, and some fat saved from the gazelle kill. It smelled horrible, but it gave off enough light to see the room they were in.

"Success," Markus gasped, running back. "That is, if you don't mind a bit of climbing. Part of the ceiling collapsed. There's even a door, of sorts."

"Dominic. Dominic, let's go." Ardhuin stood next to him, but when he didn't respond she gingerly put a hand on his arm.

The effect was electric. His head snapped up, and he made a sound between a moan and a cry. He wrapped his arms around Ardhuin tightly and buried his face in the crook of her neck, tugging at her collar with his fingers.

"Too far away..."

Markus was staring at them with wide eyes. "I'm thinking we'd better move quickly, then. You have light, good. Bring their bedrolls and some water," he said, pointing at Gutrune. "Anything else you need?"

"Spirits, if we have any. It...mitigates thaumatic shock." Ardhuin slipped one arm free and turned, pulling Dominic to follow Markus.

Did they have any? It wasn't something she had brought. But as she gathered up the bedrolls Stoller handed her a flask. "Schnapps. I'd say warn them but from the look of him he won't even notice."

Gutrune jogged to catch up, following the glow of the torch ahead. The stonework here was in much better shape than the exterior, but she still had to watch her footing. Dust fell through the hole in the ceiling, and she could barely make out the sky in the gap. The sun must be going down, then. They had indeed reached their shelter just in time.

Markus passed several openings in the wall until stopping before one that still had fragments of a wood frame in the doorway.

"Here. I think it will serve—and while the door is no longer attached, it can be propped up as a temporary measure."

Ardhuin was too exhausted to speak and merely nodded as she went inside. Dominic was murmuring insistently, oblivious to his surroundings. Markus took the gear Gutrune held, placed it inside, and wrestled the old door over the opening.

"And just in time too." He wiped his forehead, stuck the torch in a crack in the wall, and turned to leave.

Gutrune frowned, at a loss. It did not seem right to leave them there alone, but she was not sure what would be of assistance. "Is there anything I can do to help?" she called, only to find a firm hand grasping her elbow and pulling her down the stone hallway.

"I know you have the best intentions, but I strongly suspect we would only be very much in the way right now." He summoned magefire, and it revealed a tired and worried expression. "Recall that this exposure, or something similar, happened to him before. If Frau Kermarec says isolation is best, even in our current circumstances, she must speak from experience."

Her temper flared. "I can't simply walk away when my friend is in grave distress, when her husband is terribly ill in the middle of a desert with no help for hundreds of miles!"

"It is not abandoning them to do as she asks. I know you would do anything to help her now—I feel I owe Herr Kermarec myself for...well, for not understanding his situation. But we all agreed to undertake this task, dangerous as it is, for equally important reasons." He sighed, his shoulders sagging. "It is never easy to see those you care for put themselves in danger—but sometimes there is no choice. The best we can do, I suppose," he said slowly, "is to see their effort is not wasted."

Gutrune felt her anger fade, replaced by even greater fatigue. It was suddenly hard to think, even though she felt she must. Something Markus had said...was important. Something she needed to understand, something potentially dangerous. A thought surfaced, only to disappear before she could grasp it fully, and the fragment made no sense. Markus was dangerous?

She shook her head. She was too tired. Markus was watching her with concern, and she did not want to discuss anything further with her thoughts in such confusion. She forced herself to turn away. She would rest and then if Ardhuin needed her she would be ready.

The fourth time a camel kicked him awake Markus gave up and took his bedroll into the stone hall. He ought to have been so tired he would sleep through it—and perhaps he had, other times—but now the camels were getting restive and noisy, making it difficult to fall asleep again. And even when they were quiet, they still stank.

He'd thought all he truly wanted was to be out of the storm to be comfortable, but no. Sonam had passed on the information that two of the water bags had leaked and were now completely empty, and the guides were afraid because they had no idea where they were, and thus could not find the water sources they knew about. Plus something about ghosts, but the guides were apparently more afraid of the storm than the ghosts. They did pray a lot and had asked for protective spells. It appeared they thought anything connected to Ardhuin was a good defense, as Markus found her discarded jacket carefully folded and placed across the threshold. Markus had also allowed them to think the magefire was protective, so now he had to keep one going at all times.

He drifted off to sleep, despite the chill and the hard stone floor, and only woke when he heard footsteps coming from the far end of the hall. There was enough daylight now he could just make out Ardhuin, her long red hair in a loose braid, disheveled and drooping with weariness.

Markus was alert instantly. "How is he?"

She sighed. "Better. I think the schnapps helped...but he can't be moved. Not yet."

"No fear of that. The storm shows no sign of letting up, and I am told these things can last up to a week. Sonam is of the opinion this will have a shorter duration, fortunately."

"Is everything all right?" Gutrune had emerged from the main room, rubbing her eyes.

"I wanted to get some food while Dominic is sleeping."

Gutrune gave Ardhuin a critical look. "I suggest that you are in need of rest yourself—you do not look well. Let us bring what you need. I apologize for not thinking of it last night, but I also have a lantern. If you must still avoid magic near him..."

Ardhuin gave a tired smile. "Thank you. Yes, that will be useful." She handed over the canteen she was carrying and turned back.

Markus tossed the canteen in one hand. "Well, this could be awkward. Herr Kermarec is most definitely in need of water, being ill, but there is not much water for anyone at the moment."

Gutrune nodded but seemed abstracted. He knew she was not attending when she also nodded to his joking suggestion that they go through their supplies to see if a bottle of wine had gotten packed by mistake.

Sonam was standing by the door, looking outside. He had taken up the task of casting a wind shield at the entrance so they could leave it uncovered for light and air, which, with all the horses and camels, was increasingly necessary. Fragrant only began to describe it.

"How much water can we spare for the sick?" Markus asked.

"The Guardian...I hear her say, alcohol helps the sickness?" Sonam said, with a bit of translation assistance from Gutrune. "The guides just now have told me, they have brought *qui-me*. It is made from milk, fermented.

This can be used instead of water, perhaps?"

"If they are willing to share, it is worth the attempt. I shall make a note on the next adventure to be sure to bring an adequate supply of brandy, but I did not realize it was so crucial." Even this attempt at humor was not noticed, and he felt his good spirits diminish. What ailed her? Well, aside from narrowly escaping death in a desert sandstorm, that is, but they were alive at the moment, were they not? Matters were not yet desperate.

Gutrune retrieved and lit her lantern and picked up the package of food, mostly dried fruit and nuts. Markus retrieved the bag of *qui-me* before she could add it to her burdens.

"You will need some kind of light on your return, you know. The footing is quite uneven." No response, but no objection either. Markus continued to make idle observations on the curious structure they were sheltering in, the nature of sandstorms, and how it all reminded him of a youthful trip to the seashore where he had done his best to stow away on a fishing boat.

"Ardhuin?" Gutrune called softly when they reached the door, now set ajar. She gave no indication she had heard a word of what he had said.

An equally quiet voice bade them enter. Gutrune shifted the lamp to a narrow slit and crouched down to get past the door. Markus followed.

Ardhuin was seated on the ground by Dominic, who appeared to be asleep. He was very pale and turned his head restlessly as if unable to find a comfortable position. Ardhuin took his hand, which had emerged from under the blanket as he tossed, and Dominic instantly quieted with a small sigh.

"Sonam suggested trying this," Gutrune whispered, indicating the *qui-me*. "It contains a slight amount of alcohol—and we need to conserve our water." She explained the damage that had happened during the storm.

"But there is water here," murmured Dominic, startling everyone. His eyelids flickered, opening slightly. Markus discreetly stepped back into the deeper shadow. There was no need to agitate him in his current state. Although he did not sound as...hallucinatory as he had the previous day, he still made no sense. The entire building was bone-dry, not even showing signs of insects.

"What do you mean? Where?" Ardhuin, strangely, was taking his feverish statement at face value.

Dominic gave a small smile. "When we had to climb up the rocks...there was a bright sign. Like this." His free hand sketched a shaky spiral with a long tail. "I smelled water there. And heard it. It was moving..." His voice faded and his eyes closed again.

"When he is overexposed to strong magic, as he was, his...other senses become incredibly acute," Ardhuin said. "I know it sounds strange, but if he smelled water, it is there."

"Then we will look for it."

Gutrune got back to her feet. Markus dodged out of the room, hoping to prevent his sudden blinding insight from becoming apparent. *All* of his senses, eh? How very amus...no. With a sinking feeling, he realized he would have to remain forever in official ignorance. While it would have been the height of rudeness to indicate his understanding to Ardhuin of what precisely had happened the previous day, he could not even subtly twit Dominic about it in private—even apologizing would be counterproductive.

And either Gutrune had phenomenal self-control, or she had led a more sheltered life than he thought possible at court. No, that was unlikely. Given her character and situation, though, her knowledge was bound to be predominately theoretical.

"I suppose the place where we 'climbed up the rocks' is the section where the roof fell in," Markus observed. He wasn't expecting an answer, so he was surprised when Gutrune spoke.

"I have not seen any signs, bright or otherwise. Yet he was clearly seeing something last night that fascinated him on the walls."

"So...magic, then. Interesting. One wonders what people lived here. More importantly, how can we see what he did? Perhaps there will be only one way to go, and it will not matter."

With magefire, the area of the roof-fall revealed an unfortunate plethora of possible routes. The hall widened here, which had perhaps weakened the roof in the first place, and several avenues opened up from it.

"Why would anyone want to embed magic in a wall? And how could it possibly last so long?" Now that he thought about it, hadn't Dominic seen magic in the ancient lighthouse in Aleksandri? It would seem the ancients knew a few things they had not seen fit to share.

"Perhaps the people here had similar gifts to his—and these markings would only reveal themselves to those intended to see them, and not to outsiders." Gutrune ran her hand over the stone wall, studying it. At least she was talking with him now.

Magic, and magic that persisted in an object. Ardhuin had embedded illusion in a metal charm. He did not have the skill to do that, but did he need to? Magefire was a very simple spell and took little power. If some material had already been infused, would it be more amenable to further adjustment?

"I'm going to try an experiment." Markus hoped they were distant enough that the magic would not discomfort Dominic.

He placed his hands on the wall, closed his eyes, and summoned power, concentrating on the magefire spell, focusing his entire attention on sending that and nothing else. An indrawn breath from Gutrune made him open his eyes again, and he grinned. As he had hoped, faint glowing traces of design were now visible on the section of wall he had touched.

"Well. I hope we find this spiral soon, because there is more wall than I have power." Markus felt his optimism returning. Gutrune was examining the design with a look of wonder.

"How very strange...I have never seen anything like it."

It took three more tries, but he found the spiral at last. He was eager to go looking at once, but Gutrune with great prudence insisted they let the others know what they were about. Markus supposed it was a good idea for people to have some idea of where to start looking if disaster struck.

The first thing he noticed when they returned was light in the passageway under the spiral sign. Stone elements that he had thought were merely decorative, a kind of column capital shaped like a simple flower, now glowed with a soft, pale gold light.

"The magefire looks different," Gutrune observed.

His earlier adventurousness had vanished, replaced by wary caution. "That's because it isn't magefire. I didn't do that—at least, not directly." It would be just his luck to have awakened the ghostly inhabitants with his magic. Perhaps the magic he'd used had...percolated through and activated them? "And a very good thing. I can rest up. Something tells me we'll be needing more magic shortly."

The passageway was not very wide and had no side openings so far. It was also sloping downward. He looked back and could just make out a gentle curve as well. The spiral? The stonework was in good repair, and with little debris or sand the path was easy. He wished he could see ahead better or had a sense of where they were. When everything looked the same, how could they tell?

Identical, that is, until they came to an impressive metal gate. It completely blocked the passageway, which either ended or the lights were not working beyond it, judging from the darkness he saw through the bars. Markus grabbed the gate and shook it. It did not even creak.

"Bah. Iron. It feels very well secured, too, so I doubt we can just batter it down. But is it worth trying?"

Gutrune fingered one of the bars, looking thoughtful. "I believe so. Look." She pointed. At the base of the bar, where it met a crosspiece, it was rusted. The gate had further traces of rust, all on the opposite side of where they were.

"Fascinating. I suppose there must be water somewhere, then, or there used to be. Now, how do we get past this?" He tapped a section he had first taken for a decorative element, made of interlocking metal plates. "Presumably this is a lock of some kind. I see no place for a key. Maybe we can simply batter this instead of the whole door? A pity it is iron, or I'd have more options."

Gutrune reached into her jacket and pulled out her pistol. "I suggest you step back, Herr Asgaya."

The noise in the narrow passageway was quite loud, and the acrid smoke was thick. It took two shots, but eventually the lock gave way—and Markus saw, looking at the fragments more closely, that they showed even more evidence of rust. The gate was stiff, but with both of them pulling they eventually got it open enough to slip past.

"Well, that's...disturbing."

Gutrune turned to look at him, one eyebrow raised. "What?"

"Two things, actually. One, there's an air current moving the smoke away, beyond the gate. Secondly, it just occurred to me the people here must have had a good reason to put this rather substantial barrier here, and maybe it was to keep something out." He pointed to a bar that was visibly bent, with deep gouges on the side. "Perhaps you should reload before we continue."

The passageway continued perhaps a hundred yards, now with niches every few feet and more debris underfoot. The glint of metal caught his eye, and he bent and picked up a section of mail made of metal scales. A few feet farther away was a human jawbone. As they kept walking, more fragments of human remains were visible, crumbling away, and then they came to another gate, similar to the first only much more severely rusted and warped off its hinges.

He could feel a breeze now, chilly and damp against his skin. Beyond the ruined gate was darkness. The story told by the skeletal remains and the smashed gate were clear—a violent story. But how long ago? Would whatever had wrecked the gate still be here?

We need that water.

Markus pulled a piece of the gate free that was relatively undamaged by rust, long and sturdy, and propped it against the wall of the passageway.

"That's for re-barring the upper gate, in the event," he said, trying to convey a nonchalant attitude. "I'm going to see what's out there now."

Gutrune nodded and took a position against the far wall, covering the opening with her pistol. Markus considered a moment, then picked a spell primarily used for entertainment, a falling shower of silver light.

It glittered in the air and was reflected back by a dome of rough rock that also glittered. A cave? White projections like icicles decorated the surface, but it did not feel cold enough to be ice. A stone platform led from the passageway to an edge with pillars. Indistinct shapes like boulders were scattered in one section of the platform, and in another, a large pile of bones.

Nothing moved. No sign of life, no noise except the whisper of the breeze, and perhaps...the lapping of water?

They waited in silence but nothing changed. No sound. Markus fired the silver shower again, and the same scene was revealed. Cautiously, they ventured out, Markus casting a large globe of magefire above and before them.

The pile of large bones was a creature with a long, sinuous neck and scimitar-like teeth. The water they found at the base of the platform, which looked very much like a dock. A large half-circular opening could be seen on the opposite wall of the cave, certainly large enough for a barge or small ship. From the existing stairs down from the platform, which ended well above where they should, and watermarks on the cave wall, the water level had been much higher in the past, but there was still plenty for their purposes.

Gutrune insisted on checking, so Markus held on to one hand as she dangled from the lowest step to dip her handkerchief in the water, and then pulled her up. She let the water drip into her mouth and tilted her head thoughtfully.

"Well?"

"Very cold. It tastes pure." She used the handkerchief to wipe her face free of the ever-present dust. "We should tell the others immediately. The horses especially are feeling the lack." She tugged her hand, still in his grasp, but he did not let go.

"One moment more will not make a difference."

The old impassive, emotionless expression that he had learned to hate returned to her face. "Is it important?" Cool and distant, precisely as if she were discussing the weather.

Well, he had spent considerable time at court himself. "Perhaps," Markus said lightly. "We are a small group, relying heavily on each other. I have noticed something has disturbed your peace of mind since last night. You have never been, thank God, of a garrulous disposition, but you are taking that virtue to a dangerous extreme, don't you think? If something troubles you, it must be a serious matter. It is not easy, traveling as we are, to find opportunities for confidential discussions, which is why I mention it now. Perhaps you do not wish to confide in me—but compared to our colleagues I have relatively few worries of my own at the moment and have no other wish than to be of service." He let go reluctantly. Gutrune pulled her hand free and went quickly and silently up the stone stairs. "And running away won't help," he called after her.

Gutrune stopped. He followed her up the stairs to the stone dock and waited.

"It is a purely personal failing. A weakness." There was a tremor in her voice. "There is nothing any of you can do to help me. I know that...you would help, if it were possible. What else can I do but keep it to myself? I...made a choice, a long time ago. I made it freely, I do not regret it—and I must accept the consequences."

"A long time ago, and you have learned nothing since? Nothing has changed; you have not gained new information? What an amazingly prescient person you must be. Or bloody stubborn." *I'm not exactly setting a new standard for diplomacy here, am I?*

"Oh, leave it be!" The words sounded wrenched from her, raw with emotion. She turned as if to confront him, her hands clenched into fists.

"I can't." She rocked back on her heels slightly, eyes wide. Markus was surprised at his own vehemence. "You are in pain. I can no more ignore that than I can stop breathing." Saying it, he realized with a chill that the two things were, in some level of his mind, the same. *Enough. We can't both be serious at the same time.* "Unless, of course, my breathing is the problem? In that case I will have to request a delay, merely until we have finished our original task—and then you can proceed with smothering me. Or shooting me, if that is your preference."

"I shall consider the matter carefully," Gutrune snapped. She closed her eyes and sighed, her head sagging down. "No, I don't..." She was silent for a moment, then raised her head again, looking out at the cave and the water. "I thought I could evade the rules. Step outside of them. I thought the price of my freedom was...giving up all of the privileges the rules provide in exchange. It was not hard at first." Her expression grew puzzled. "But when Ardhuin came to Baerlen as the Mage Guardian—she simply smashed through the rules as if they did not exist. I told myself it was because of her power. They feared her, and how would they dare to enforce the rules against someone like her? Yet what I have seen since...Herr Kermarec does not love her because he fears her. I do see when my opinions require change," she said, rounding on him indignantly. "But what have my observations taught me that I can apply to my own case? I do not have great power and never will. But when you said..." her voice faltered, but she set her jaw and continued, "Never mind. Even if another such admirable man existed, and we understood each other as they do, we could not do what they have done."

A time of miracles. I am jealous of Dominic Kermarec. "Is that what you want?"

"Perhaps," she managed to say with dignity, a flush of color on her high cheekbones. "But it is not possible. I have sworn to serve the King. That is why I have been...preoccupied. It is only a momentary weakness and will pass."

"But if it could be accomplished..."

"Is that what *you* want?" She gave a slight gasp, putting a hand over her mouth as if to trap the words, watching him warily.

"Yes." And there it was. Admitted freely, in a dank cavern under a forgotten city, with both of them grimy with travel and the least elegant they had ever been in their lives. It seemed strangely appropriate.

Her color deepened. "But I cannot—that is, even if we could keep it secret from the King, I would not do so. I would have to seek his permission to marry—and he would never countenance the...kind of connections you have...it is *reputed* you have had at court."

He felt a breath jerk out of him as if he had been punched in the gut. It felt like that too—but Gutrune had every right to point out his behavior. He had not been celibate in the slightest, and now, like she, he was regretting his choice.

"No, that was not what I had in mind, although I can understand the misapprehension." His throat was tight, and it was very hard to speak. But he had to. "You are not the only one to have limited options available to you. I invite you to consider...the reaction of the family of any of the eligible young ladies at court...should I have presented myself as a prospective suitor," he said softly. "Like you, I suppose, I believed it better to not even consider something I could not have—and instead pursued a poor substitute."

Her gaze softened. "I am sorry." She reached out, hesitated, then rested her hand on his arm. With careful deliberation, he covered her hand with his own.

"Among the people whose opinions I value, my interesting parentage made no difference," Markus said, attempting lightness. And since there were so few of those, it was natural to want to keep them close. "Do I have your permission to try, milady?"

"How do you think you can succeed?" she wondered.

"I have the strongest of motivations. And since you mention Herr Kermarec—I feel constrained to point out he did not begin as a fearless adventurer and prospective consort to mages, but as a mere tutor with no notion of his special talents. Love can create a determination even mules find excessive."

A small smile briefly disturbed her mouth. "In other words, you will persist regardless of what I say."

"I would not dare oppose your will."

She met his gaze steadily, once more calm and collected. He had achieved that much, at least.

"When we have done what we set out to do in Bhuta, you may try."

He gave a deep sigh. "Thank you." He carried her hand to his lips with his most graceful bow, then tucked it through his arm as they walked back to the passageway. "A trifling matter of rescuing MacCrimmon and stopping Denais, then. I will set to work at once, milady."

Gutrune shook her head, but she was, just barely, smiling.

CHAPTER 18

Dominic braced himself on his elbows, waiting for the wave of dizziness to pass. He was doing better—*much* better than last time, but he still found it tiring to sit up for long periods. The storm had finally stopped, so he was the only reason they still remained in the ancient lost city.

"Ah, good. You're awake again." Markus came in the room, carefully cradling something wrapped in a blanket. "I know you wanted to go down to the water cave, but perhaps this will be an acceptable substitute. We really should take something back with us, and I'm hoping you can select the most interesting pieces."

"Pieces? Of what? I thought you said there were only bones and wreckage down there." Dominic watched with interest as Markus knelt and unwrapped the blanket. He had been deeply disappointed he could not visit the cavern, but he reluctantly agreed with Ardhuin's assessment that he should not be exposed to more magic of an unknown type, and it seemed clear there was much magic in the structures here.

"Ah. Well, what we thought was wreckage was actually luggage. Or cargo. I wonder if they were loading a ship when that thing with all the teeth attacked."

"I wonder where that opening leads. Are there even more cities like this one? Hmm, what's this?" Dominic held up a smooth, black stone, carved in a strange, sinuous shape. It felt...hungry. He let it fall hastily and picked up another object, a chain with a pendant made of gold and something red, perhaps coral. That felt normal. "Probably just jewelry. Now this...is it a mat of some kind?"

It looked like a pile of thin, rectangular slats, woven together with thin gold wire. It looked very much like a section of railroad, if railroad were made of ivory. The slats had markings on them, on both sides.

"Some of these symbols...I remember seeing them on the walls! This must be their writing."

"Then we should definitely take this. I wonder..."

Ardhuin came in with an armload of clothing. She was wearing the flowing blue silk robe that Kungam had given her, which shone in the lamplight like a dark gem. To the great relief of all the Aeropans, at any rate, the copious amounts of clean water had permitted washing and baths, somewhat improvised. Everyone was in a much better mood as a result.

"Stoller and the guides have come up with a solution for you," she said. "They've emptied the biggest trunk and removed the lid. With some blankets for padding, you should be able to travel that way relatively well, I think. You could even sleep on the way."

"If you don't mind camels." Markus rolled his eyes. "I understand their movement can take some getting used to from what Gutrune has said."

Dominic exchanged a puzzled look with Ardhuin. *What happened to "Fräulein von Kitren" then?*

"Speaking of camels, what was that horrific noise yesterday? Were you skinning one of them with a spoon?"

Ardhuin laughed.

Markus grimaced. "The thought did cross my mind...no, we were trying to take the ungrateful beasts to the water, versus taking the water to them. They drink a lot, when they do drink. There was plenty of room in the passage for them, if they kept their heads down." He had an aggrieved expression on his face. "Not one of our better ideas. The basta—beg pardon, the camels of uncertain parentage decided they would much rather bite us. Oh yes, they could lower their heads for *that* important task."

Dominic chuckled. "I had not realized Stoller had such an impressive range of Preusan invective. He is usually quite taciturn, from my observation."

Markus raised an eyebrow. "Considering where the camel was attempting to take a chunk out of him, he was rather calm about it."

"So how did they water them?" Ardhuin asked.

"Relays of the horses, blindfolded. It took several trips, but we have enough and the water bags have been mended and filled. The plan is to leave at first light in the morning."

"Do we know where we are?"

"Sonam says he thinks he sees familiar mountains, so we should be able to get back on track."

Ardhuin turned toward the doorway, cocking her head a little to the side. "That sounds like Gutrune. She must have had luck hunting. While we still have plentiful water I want to make some broth for you." She rose and left, the silk robe whispering about her bare feet.

Markus went to follow.

"Speaking of hunting," Dominic remarked casually, "you appear remarkably cheerful of late. Am I to understand your...project has met with success?"

Markus glowered. "You need not sound so astonished." Then he grinned. "I have reached—let us say, an understanding. My lady has given me an important task to accomplish before I can claim anything, but the most important question has been answered. I am very much in your debt."

It was said in his usual slightly mocking manner, but there was a thread of seriousness Dominic had not noticed previously.

"I don't recall doing much...well, just remember that if your current good understanding fails, I wash my hands of the whole thing."

Markus's cheerfulness was unabated. "Pish. You would cheer her on and help her reload. Now, is there any more immediate service I can do for you?"

Prevented from assisting in the preparations for departure, Dominic tried to sleep as much as he could and in the intervals examined the artifacts Markus and later Ardhuin brought up for his inspection. The ancient inhabitants appeared to prefer coral and turquoise as precious stones, and were capable of intricately detailed metalwork. He wondered what Bové's reaction would be and how he was doing with his excavations. Perhaps he could identify the writing and the people who had lived here. Now that he had seen their city, apparently forgotten in time, Dominic felt a burning interest in finding out.

When he saw his new mode of transportation, he felt other, stronger emotions. Predominant among them was horror.

"Wait, shouldn't the camel be standing?"

"What, and make you climb all that height in your weakened state? Besides, we don't have a ladder." Markus, who had helped move him to the main room with the animals and gear, one arm over his shoulder, kept a firm hold of his wrist and continued on. He was shaking with laughter, which only alarmed Dominic more.

"And all the rope—well, why not put the lid back on and shut me up inside, then?"

Gutrune held blankets and a filled canteen. "You will need to be secure, after all. These should make you more comfortable."

Resigned to the inevitable, Dominic got in. He had to keep his knees bent, but he had to admit it was not too bad.

Until the camel got up.

The next three days were an unending but varied misery, only relieved by exhausted sleep—but to reach that merciful release he had to survive something worse than the camel getting to its feet, namely the camel lowering itself again. It was like being in his own slow, personal earthquake. He did not even notice how far they had come until he realized they were in low foothills instead of the flat plain, that tufts of green had become more common, and they were following a small stream.

The next morning, he woke to find their guides had gone, taking with them three camels. Beside him when he woke was a folded blue scarf, a carved soapstone cat curled in a ball, and a small silver hawkbell.

"Offerings to you, so they may cross again safely," Sonam explained, smiling broadly. "They think you are a very powerful spirit-talker, both for how you found the old city and, well," he shrugged, tilting his head at Ardhuin. "They want the ghosts to stay away on their return."

"I didn't see any ghosts, but then you wouldn't let me go down to the cavern." Dominic stood up stiffly—and then realized he had done so without stumbling. "Do you think they will try to go back to the old city and look around?"

Sonam shook his head sharply. "Without you and the lady? Never."

Then perhaps it would remain secret long enough to be properly excavated. Dominic took a deep breath, enjoying the cooler air and admiring the view. Though there was something about one section of the mountains...

"Which way is your home, Sonam?"

And Sonam pointed, exactly where he had been looking. Where magical brightness outlined the edges of a valley, enclosed by mountains like spires.

So much magic. Dominic shuddered. What were they heading for?

He could not complain. Denais rode in a succession of palanquins, horses, and litters while Korda followed on foot, in the dust. One of his shoes had developed an uncomfortable hole, and he did not have any replacements since the little space for extra luggage was only for Denais. Stinging insects and heat and the stench of dung and unwashed humans made Korda nauseous and miserable, but he could not complain. Denais still thought he was under his *geas.*

He could not complain or show the slightest indication of his true feelings, so Korda sought relief in planning Denais's inevitable demise. Every humiliation, every ounce of suffering Korda had experienced, he intended to see inflicted on his tormentor tenfold. But to have his revenge, he must find a way to strike with no warning, with no possibility of Denais's escape.

It slowly dawned on him that this horrible trip might provide a perfect opportunity. Only a handful of the bound Aeropan magicians accompanied him, who might stage a successful defense if Denais were attacked. Several men at the source of the magical salts were under Korda's actual control. If he was careful, and watched for opportunities, his path to freedom might appear. He must be ready.

Korda considered and discarded plans as he trudged through the forested foothills that gradually changed to bare rock. As the air grew thin and dry Denais stopped more frequently, always with a servant instantly starting a spirit lamp so the master could enjoy his tea while they rested. Korda and the others were allowed one swallow each of dank water from a slimy leather waterbag. He supposed he was grateful that even Denais realized the *geas* compelled obedience only to the point that the body could comply. And if he killed his bearers with overwork, his lordship would be forced to walk.

Through the mountain passes Korda discovered a new torment, for the nights were brutally cold and none of them had warm clothing or blankets. He was forced to huddle with the native servants, another insult he added to his ever-growing list. During the sleepless nights he made plans and lists of what he would need to implement those plans. Chief among these was access to a supply of mineral essence. The supply would be there, since they were going to the source, but removing enough without alerting Denais or his personal guard would be much more difficult. Then there were the interlocking excuses for the missing deliveries, or rather the deliveries that Korda had redirected.

Another long, trudging day, but shorter than the others. Denais had decided to stop early in the twilight rather than tackle a long, steep trail to the height of a pass, for his own convenience, of course. Korda was sent to a small cluster of nearby huts for fodder and extra food since their supplies had proven inadequate.

As he approached the open door of one hut a fresh-faced young girl with a shy but radiant smile stepped out. In her hands was a silver bowl of the horrid half-rancid yak's milk drink the local savages thought was a gesture of hospitality. She glanced at Korda and bowed her head but was clearly intending to go to the front of the pack train—and Denais.

Horror froze him motionless. Without thinking, Korda spread his hands before him, shaking his head. An old woman in the back of the hut glanced sharply at him, eyes narrowing. She spoke one word, and the girl stepped back inside looking disappointed. Korda watched the old woman take the welcoming bowl herself, cursing his sudden impulse of chivalry as fear knotted his stomach. Had any of Denais's people seen him? And what did he care if some native chit was compelled to provide more hospitality than she ever intended, and prevented from telling anyone afterward what had happened to her? Except...except he hadn't been able to stop the others. He'd only seen the aftermath.

She's barely more than a child. Even a savage deserves better than that. Yet fear of detection made him violent and harsh in obtaining the supplies he had been ordered to find, and he sat up the entire night watching Denais's tent, just in case. But what could he do, run? Without food or water?

Nothing happened that night, or the next few days. And then they were in the heart of the barren, rocky hellhole known as Bhuta, and the comparative paradise of Denais's facility. At least there were structures to sleep in and more civilized food.

And utter chaos. True to their orders, workers were taking wooden wheelbarrows and wooden spades to the deep pits excavated at the base of the eroded cliffs—and coming to a complete halt at what turned out to be an extremely strong ward. They stayed there until the shift horn blew, and then they turned around again. The living ones, that is. There were several gaunt, skeletal bodies along the path.

Denais was absolutely furious. Korda, on the other hand, was terrified. What had happened to the mineral essence he was counting on for his plans? And if Denais began investigating closely, he might detect the modified *geasi*.

"Impossible! Who would dare..." Denais glared furiously at the barrier. "This is mage-level work. The natives are incapable of anything so sophisticated. But who would even know—that red-headed freak fancies herself a mage, but she only left Aerope...Korda. Find out when this barrier appeared and report back to me immediately."

Korda bowed silently and walked away as quickly as he could. He wanted to know himself. Unfortunately most of the workers here were natives. Not only could they not speak any useful language, he doubted they understood calendars either. He finally found an Aeropan in the extraction facility, a large stone building with human-powered mills, dissolving vats, and extraction sprayers and dryers. All were carefully manufactured to avoid any iron. Korda looked carefully, but the machines were all idle and with no sign of recent use. He could smell the mineral essence, though. The faint sharp, sour scent reminded him how long it had been, and he found himself fingering the hidden pockets where his last remaining supply was hidden. If he could only find some here...he should have some power, just in case. It was dangerous now. But the hunger had awakened, and he found it harder to ignore.

After much prodding, the man finally answered. "At least seven months." He looked gaunt and worn, his clothing tattered. When he gestured, his hands shook like an old man's.

"Why didn't you send word?" Korda asked as much for himself as for Denais.

The man blinked at him, uncomprehending. "I had no orders to send word."

Korda's information did not please Denais, who then had him bring others to him for questioning. Since he had not been ordered to leave after doing so, Korda stayed—and learned much. The *geas* compelled certain actions but not independent thought. Most of those present had been ordered to stay and extract the mineral essence. Even though they knew something was amiss, they could not leave to send a message. Those who had left to take shipments never returned, and no message had been sent with them because the barrier had not been raised then.

The other questions Denais asked made little sense. He kept asking about a red-headed woman, and then, to one of his guard, if the Cathan authorities had reported finding the magicians Denais had warned them of.

The way he spoke made it seem that the two were the same, but that made no sense at all. Korda wondered, not for the first time, if Denais was completely sane. A woman magician?

Korda had learned a little of who Denais really was and why Baron Kreuzen had been attacked and killed. He wasn't sure of the details, only that a group of powerful mages formed to combat the Gaulan forces in the Mage War survived in some form—or had, until Denais destroyed them. Now it seemed some had survived.

After a period of brooding, Denais issued a series of rapid orders. "Kohlmann. Take a fast horse and money sufficient to travel and return. You will stop at the nearest telegraph office in Ynde, send these messages in code, and wait for a reply. If there is no reply within three days, return at full speed. You will take no more than ten minutes to eat or drink and may sleep only four hours per day while traveling. You must go as quickly as you can while understanding your primary duty is to send these messages and report back to me. Korda, assist him. He must leave within the hour."

It took all of Korda's self-control to leave. He needed to know what other orders Denais would give. Was he getting him out of the room deliberately? His pulse raced. And why wasn't Denais taking down the barrier? He would likely use mineral essence to give him more power, and then Korda would know where it was hidden.

He followed Kohlmann in silence, obeying his reluctant commands. Kohlmann was not under his control, and he realized this could work to his advantage. Denais himself was sending one of his three guards away, and now the odds had changed in Korda's favor. When Kohlmann left to get the money for his trip, Korda feverishly read the telegrams. Commands to agents in Aerope to discover if any Mage Guardian replacements had been made in Ostri, Preusa, or the Low Countries and if they had left the country after a certain date. Other commands to report any sightings of the Bretagnan group being watched for.

He hastily replaced the telegrams exactly as he had found them when he heard the sound of returning footsteps. Kohlmann was sweating, a sign he was attempting to fight the *geas*. Distracted, Kohlmann did not notice when Korda removed one of the pouches of coins from the saddlebags or when Korda cut a notch in the girth leathers. It would last for a while, but riding hard, it would eventually fail. Kohlmann would at best be delayed, and at worst killed in a fall. And even if he should arrive and send the messages, he would not have enough money to return as swiftly as he had gone. Korda would simply have to overthrow Denais before then, that's all.

He saw Kohlmann off, grimly pleased that the daylight was already fading. Kohlmann would keep riding through the night in obedience to Denais's commands, and all it would take was one stumble on the steep, rocky path. Now he was free to return to Denais. Should he use some mineral essence? The one thing he could not risk was Denais placing a working *geas* on him. He would need more power to prevent that. There were shadows moving, and he thought he could hear voices, whispering his name...

No. He had to take the risk. Until he had more, he could not use what he had saved.

When he returned, to his surprise Denais had donned a light coat against the evening chill and had his walking stick in hand, meaning he intended to actually walk. The two guards were also prepared to go out with him.

"Korda. We go to seek any sign of enemy magic. You will signal if you see anything suspicious, but do not speak. Now take that and follow us." Denais pointed to a large, heavy pack.

Korda struggled to lift it on his back, and when it shifted, a familiar sour smell wafted up. A muscle in his arm spasmed and cramped, and he nearly wept. Mineral essence. The mineral essence he desperately needed, but still out of reach. He wanted to scream.

CHAPTER 19

Sonam called out a cheerful greeting from up ahead, giving Ardhuin enough warning to lower her head and to make sure Dominic hadn't fallen asleep with his notebook out again. The yak cart did not have a smooth ride, but he was still tired enough he could sleep through the bumps. She, on the other hand, was on foot leading their horses, which were illusioned to look like ragged donkeys and carrying the supplies and gear that didn't fit in the cart. Sonam was driving the cart, obtained in trade for a few of their camels, which could not support the higher altitudes. The cart was narrow and crudely made and provided an excellent cover for their entry into Bhuta.

Once the road had cleared again, Dominic emerged from his burlap cover. While he claimed he no longer felt the sensitivity of magic, Ardhuin felt it best for him to avoid any magic at all, even mild illusion, until he was fully recovered.

"Shouldn't they be back by now? It's been two days."

"Perhaps they had to go farther than they had planned. Gutrune did mention the troops were delayed in setting out," Ardhuin said. "Also, I believe the Preusans are taking pains not to stand out."

Dominic looked skeptical. "It's not like there's a great deal of space to be unobtrusive in," he pointed out. "It's all narrow ravines and tiny valleys out here. And mountains half the size of Aerope. I wonder if I could make an imager large enough to capture that," he said, diverted. "If anyone had tried to explain them to me, I wouldn't believe it either."

They camped that night on the gravel shores of a shallow, icy river, with a few gnarled bushes for cover. Markus and Gutrune had still not returned.

"I am thinking we should not stop again until we reach my valley," Sonam said as they sat around the tiny fire. "There is danger. Here, we are travelers that no one cares about. Closer by, the attackers will be present and maybe looking."

"Isn't that dangerous too? I mean, some of these roads aren't very wide, and on the side of rather steep mountains," Ardhuin said.

Sonam dipped his head with a smile. "This is a quiet magic, of my people. We call it moon-seeing. I will keep us safely on the road. We will stop for rest, for the animals...but not for sleeping. You can also go in the cart, with the horses tied to it. It will not be so bad."

"I suppose not." Dominic sounded distracted. Ardhuin glanced at him. He was staring fixedly at the river. "Sonam, does this river come from your valley?"

"It does." Sonam looked surprised. "How did you know?"

"It has magic. Faint, but definite. I think..." Dominic got stiffly to his feet and searched the banks for a few minutes. He returned with a long branch, which he used to scrape the riverbed. Examining the end of the stick, he gave a satisfied nod. "As I thought. It's in the soil."

"Is it strong enough to affect a ward?"

He shook his head. "Just enough for me to detect."

Still, Ardhuin used extra care in setting up their defenses for the night. A ward, a layer of shadow, and another ward on top of that. It was time to be cautious.

A shuddering in the wards woke her up a few hours later. It took her a few disoriented seconds to realize it was a rather rhythmic shudder, very much like a...knock?

"What'sis..." murmured Dominic sleepily.

"Something is outside." She reached out, touching the inner ward and stretching it until it contacted the outer one. "It's magic, but it is rather weak."

"You mean someone is deliberately attacking but not enough to actually do anything? How ineffectual...oh, I know who it is. He pulled a similar stunt in Baerlen, as I recall."

Ardhuin removed the shadow, and indeed there was Markus—and Gutrune.

"It's about time you woke up," Markus grumbled when she lowered the wards.

"How did you know where to find us?"

"We were fairly sure you would follow this river," Gutrune's cool voice came from the shadows. "It was just a matter of time."

"That, and I recognized the yak," Markus said brightly. "Then I just wandered about until I tripped on something that wasn't there." There was something in his voice that did not sound like his usual cheerful nonsense, and Gutrune was grimly quiet.

Ardhuin sighed. "You don't have good news, do you." She gestured them to the fire and opened the wards for them. Then, as an afterthought, extended shadow to include their animals as well. She should have been more careful.

Markus sat down with a groan. "No. No sign of the detachment, nobody recalled seeing them—that is, they mentioned a group of foreigners some time ago but clearly no soldiers. I don't know what happened to them."

"It would seem Denais happened to them." Dominic sounded worried.

"It is possible he did something to stop or misdirect them, but there were no signs of attack either." Gutrune sat down as well, and Ardhuin could tell she was also very tired. "We must consider the likelihood of the detachment...not arriving in time."

The sinking feeling in her gut would not go away. They had always counted on the Preusan soldiers in their plans, but now it appeared it was only the five of them. Only five, three with magic, to take a stronghold of Denais's? No, there was possibly a sixth...

"Then it is even more important that we find and speak with MacCrimmon," she said. "He will at least be able to give us a clearer understanding of what we must do, and perhaps he can also fight with us."

Sonam was somber. "He is very ill. The making of the barrier was quite dangerous for him. I do not know how much he can do to help." He stared at the coals of the fire, his hands dangling loosely over his knees. "We should go now."

Markus winced. "If needs must—but our horses have done what they can do for the night. They have to rest."

"Yes. All the animals must stay, and out of sight. I know a place where we can leave them and what we cannot carry ourselves. If this Denais has stopped the soldiers, he will be hunting us now—and he is a magician of great power. Shadow and illusion will not be enough."

"He's right." Ardhuin got to her feet, feeling stiff and irritable and wishing Gutrune and Markus had taken just a few hours more to reach them. "Why not sit in the cart, while we have it, and rest until we get to Sonam's safe place. I'm sure Dominic can make room."

"I'm much recovered, you know. I will walk."

She smiled at him. "We all will, for the last section. Why don't you ride, then, if you are feeling better?"

The yak, usually phlegmatic and resigned about his work, did not appreciate being yoked up so early. Ardhuin decided to follow her own advice and rode while leading the rest of the pack animals. They would be following Sonam in the cart, anyway, and the road was broader here.

Perhaps it was her imagination, but every sound seemed magnified in the dark. Every clink of harness or creak of the wheel echoed loudly, as did the rushing water of the river. She hoped that noise would mask theirs.

The first signs of dawn were barely visible in the sky, mostly hidden by the towering mountains, when they reached Sonam's "safe place." An old man, half blind and unable to speak, lived in a stone hut half a mile from the river. He had a few scrawny goats in a large mud-wall enclosure and was quite willing to let their animals stay for a few silver coins. Sonam was the only one of the party he saw; the others stayed out of sight, hastily arranging packs and hiding, with brush and magic, the rest of their gear near the enclosure.

Sonam hurried them away, glancing at the sky with a worried expression. They were all too fatigued to move quickly, and the road was steep. Ardhuin found herself panting at the least exertion, and dizzy. She focused on putting one foot in front of the other, so determinedly that she ran into Dominic when he stopped suddenly.

"Something ahead!" he whispered urgently. Sonam stopped.

"Where?"

Dominic gestured. "A web. I have seen something like this before."

Denais. So, they were right. The path was high on the side of the mountain, with a sheer cliff on one side and a steep drop to the river below. Everything was bare rock, and a chill wind whistled down the pass. From Dominic's indication, the web blocked the entire way.

"We have to get through somehow. Even if there was another route, he'd likely have that trapped too." She looked at Dominic. "How exactly is it configured? I thought it had to be anchored on both ends."

He sighed and reached in the inner pocket of his jacket for his precious notebook. He sketched a quick diagram. "It goes up fairly high on the cliff side and angles down like this. A bit triangular, but effective. You can't really step around it." He turned his head, squinting at the path. "There's something else, at the top. Brighter. It's...hanging in the web."

Ardhuin thought for a moment. The first time Denais had used detection webs, it was just to notify him if magical items traveled from her house, and ordinary people could walk through without any difficulty. In this case, he was more likely trying to keep people out than keep watch and was less concerned with remaining concealed from the locals.

"It's probably a trap of some sort. Is there another way we can go?"

Sonam shook his head. "It would take many days—and we should not be here when the sun comes. We must decide what to do very quickly."

"I doubt Denais would leave any alternate paths open, so we may as well try to find a way to get past this," Dominic added. "Is there no way to remove it?"

"Possibly, but Denais is bound to have some kind of signal if that happens—and it would be proof that someone with advanced magic was approaching. I wish I could see as you do. I don't even know what to tell you to look for."

He scratched his chin. "Why don't you cast a little bit of what you think it is, and I can compare?"

With Sonam visibly fretting, she did just that. Needing to anchor the threads of magic to rock narrowed the options, but it still took longer than anyone liked. Gutrune had unslung her rifle and had it resting in her arms, facing up the path. Markus was watching the other direction and occasionally glancing at the sky.

"No...yes, that one is very close. The trap has little threads inside the threads, too."

Ardhuin gritted her teeth and tried again. Dominic gasped, and she glanced at him, worried and readying a magical shield in case she had triggered the trap. But then she felt it herself, in the web of her magic. It felt...*heavier*, and larger.

"Did it just..."

"Yes! The large web merged with your little one. The anchor points are still there, and the bright lump. Can you remove it now?"

She smiled. "I have a better idea." Now she had control over the web, and she could shape it to her purposes. She merged another web, more dense and stronger but designed to move at her command. She forced an opening in the middle of the web, large enough for them to pass underneath without stooping.

Dominic pointed out the edges of the hole to the others, and with great care they stepped through. Ardhuin closed the hole behind them, making sure she could still find her patched-on magic after releasing contact. They might need to do this again.

"Oh, that was very clever. And if they examine it somehow, it should look like nothing has happened. It just looks...stronger now." Dominic looked quite intrigued, and like he would welcome further time to study it. But Sonam was all but dragging them by the arm to get away, and she could see the dawn light getting stronger and angling down farther into the ravine.

Despite the fatigue, despite the thin air, they ran. Ten stumbling steps at a time, ten steps walking, ten running. They crested the top of the trail just after the bright sun became visible over the cliffs, and then they ran downhill. Ardhuin was gasping for air, black spots dancing across her vision. She could not fall. She must not fall.

For all that, she nearly did, running into Sonam. He had stopped, and it took her a moment to understand why.

"This is the place." He pointed to a slope of rubble against a cliff face. "My master is here."

His dreams had stirred slowly during his time in stasis. In one sense MacCrimmon knew time had passed, but in another it seemed he had merely closed his eyes on Sonam's sorrowful face and opened them to see him again. The first impulse was fear, that the vital stasis had somehow failed to take hold. But then he noticed how Sonam's face had changed, his expression more confident and mature, and he was wearing clothing MacCrimmon had never seen before.

His own clothing was covered in gritty dust. "How long?" he managed to say before being overcome by coughing.

"Ten months." Sonam held a canteen for him to drink. "The barrier still holds, but it is much weaker."

Good. MacCrimmon rested a moment. "And Morlais? Did you find him?"

"I sorrow to say, his spirit is one with the sky. But in his dwelling I found his heir."

"Ah. That was the risk. Yves was quite old, but somehow I never thought he would get around to dying...this heir, you have brought him, then?" His vision was improving, and he saw a young man with intelligent, bright eyes and a sharply angled face watching them in the shadows of the cave. "Thank you, sir, for coming. I assure you the need is great."

"I am not the one you should thank—although I have come to assist you, I am not a magician," the man said apologetically. He spoke Alban with a strong accent, Gaulan—or more likely, Bretagnan. "I am Dominic Kermarec. We thought it best to introduce ourselves gradually, since you are unwell and we...you could say we are uniformly unconventional and might prove more of a shock than it would be wise to expose you to all at once."

Confusion and irritation tumbled about in his mind. "I appreciate your consideration, but my health is of little importance compared to the dangers here. Where is Oron's heir? I must speak with him immediately."

"A matter of some difficulty," said another voice in the shadows. A ball of magefire illuminated the speaker, a man with bronze skin and dark hair with a startling slash of white. "If you permit—Markus Asgaya, *schutzmagus* of the Imperial Preusan Court, and just now returning is Fräulein Gutrune von Kitren...also of the Preusan Court, shall we say."

The golden-haired woman gave him a graceful nod, for all the world as if she were at a society function instead of in a filthy cave and carrying—he blinked—a rather unusual and deadly-looking rifle. She was wearing a greenish tweed hunting outfit and had a game bag slung over her shoulder. An older man with a military bearing followed her.

"We had hoped to arrive sooner, and with more resources, but your adversary has been active and was nearly successful in preventing us from reaching you at all," she said. Her Preusan accent was light and her voice cool and calm.

"Ma'am, I am astonished that a lady like yourself would be willing to make such a long and dangerous journey, or that your government would permit you to go."

This seemed to greatly amuse Asgaya, and Kermarec developed a cough of his own. The young lady herself showed no reaction beyond polite interest.

"We should be able to get the rest of our gear up the path with another trip, when it is darker. The old man will take the animals back again," she said to the others.

"And Ardhuin?" Kermarec asked.

"Arranging further protections for the entrance." Gutrune von Kitren turned her head. "Here she is now."

Another lady? And so it proved, a tall, striking young woman with fiery red hair and a self-effacing manner. Like Miss von Kitren she was dressed in male attire, which while undoubtedly sensible was jarring.

"I do not understand." MacCrimmon felt suddenly dizzy. Had he fully recovered from the vital stasis? "Why are you here? This is not an occasion for an excursion or entertainment. The danger here is extreme, and—"

"I know. The magical salts." The young woman regarded him steadily. "You aren't going to like this, I am afraid. We tried to break it to you gently...I am here because you sent for me. Yves Morlais was my great-uncle, and I am his heir." Before MacCrimmon could do more than open his mouth to protest, she gestured. The golden fire of the *gloire* surrounded her, illuminating the entire cave. "I am Ardhuin Kermarec, and I am the Mage Guardian of Bretagne."

<h1 style="text-align:center">CHAPTER 20</h1>

Dominic had to admit, Alastair MacCrimmon adjusted rather quickly to the unusual situation once he had been convinced of Ardhuin's bona fides. It was less a matter of the *gloire*, strangely enough, but her matter-of-fact summation of the traps and her method of dealing with them. MacCrimmon instantly seized on her intellect and power, appearing to completely forget her gender in his interest.

Dominic's own abilities had also come under scrutiny and appeared to greatly cheer MacCrimmon.

"A scryer! Now that's a handy thing. So this Denais fellow is behind it, eh?"

"He has extracted power from human magicians before, so it does not surprise me he learned to somehow extract it from the natural magic of Sonam's valley."

MacCrimmon shook his head. "Not natural. That is, it was created by the ancient animals, descended from the dragons, that made their home here. The *kai-ling* are their modern descendants, and their magic, while present, is much too weak to produce the residual effects of their ancestors. The cliffs, eroded and riddled with caves, were used as the dragons' rookery —and the droppings, rich in magic, accumulated over the centuries. The magic now is in the soil, in the food, and the people here pick it up unconsciously. Anyone with even the slightest trace of talent has a constant low-level source of power at their disposal." He looked down and pulled at the blanket with thin, shaking fingers. "I suspected what he was doing when I saw the mining, and my suspicions were quickly confirmed. I apologize, Sonam, for not telling you this when I sent you for help—but your innocence of the salts both protected you and made certain you could not reveal the secret."

"One wonders, then, how Denais found out about this," Markus said. "Not that it affects what we plan to do next, but as much as I enjoy travel, coming here on a regular basis would prove tiresome. I would rather no one *else* found out about the unusual properties of the local soil."

"Agreed—but if Denais regains access to the main source, that would likewise be difficult to regain control of. I chose the location for the barrier quite deliberately, and I waited until the magician in charge had left to set it up for precisely that reason. I did not know his name then."

Ardhuin stirred. "Had you heard nothing of him before? He claims to have been a magician of the Grand Armeé who escaped the impoundment. He certainly knows the war magic spells they used and makes extensive use of the *geas*."

MacCrimmon's eyes widened. "Are you sure?"

Ardhuin indicated Dominic.

"I can see it clearly. Yes, he uses it wherever he can."

"Well, that explains the single-mindedness of his people, then. But enough of this. What can we do to stop him? I regret to say I am unable to be of much assistance. Any physical exertion, even walking, leaves me on the verge of unconsciousness. Establishing the barrier weakened me even further. I am very much afraid you will have to rely on your own abilities to stop this madman."

"First we must learn where he is and what his current strength is," Gutrune said. "What forces does he have at his disposal, and can we eliminate or distract them?"

"That you will have to discover for yourselves. Anything could have happened in ten months. They were setting up some kind of structures near the river, on the northeast slope. Something to do with the extraction process—they have a waterwheel. I'm not sure what they are managing to extract, though. I had thought I had enclosed the majority of the deposits within the shield."

Markus narrowed his eyes. "What makes you think you did not?"

MacCrimmon gestured weakly. "Why, that the barrier is still present, which means Denais either was not told when it appeared or he is unable to take it down—a most unlikely case. The extraction has been going on for some time, alas. He must have a significant store of this magic power at his disposal."

"I will go and discover what has happened here," Sonam said quickly. "Is there any way for me to speak to those inside, or must the barrier be taken down?"

"Ah." MacCrimmon closed his eyes, a thin smile on his face. "There is a way, or at least there was. A tunnel that connects to a well inside the Celestial Cloud Palace and goes underneath the barrier. I put a separate barrier in the tunnel, but you should have no difficulty removing it. Be very careful that no one else sees you near it, though."

"I will use great caution," Sonam assured him emphatically. "And if sir allows, I will go now."

MacCrimmon gave Sonam directions on how to find the tunnel, his voice going fainter as he spoke. His hands trembled as he adjusted the blanket that covered him. The cave was getting chilly again.

Ardhuin moved some of the larger rocks Dominic and Markus had brought in from the landslide so they were closer to MacCrimmon and focused a blast of raw power through them until they glowed red. "We decided a fire was too dangerous here. The smoke..." she said, when she caught his curious gaze. "Stoller has seen some patrols on the paths nearby when he was bringing up more supplies. It appears Denais knows something is happening."

"There is little time." MacCrimmon sighed. "And not just Denais. You feel the cold? The snows are coming soon."

Farther down the trail and nearer the valley it was not so bare, and Sonam felt he could slow down. The vegetation gave him a little cover, and it was also not so steep making it possible to go off the path. That is what Dominic Kermarec had advised, for the detection traps appeared to only show up where people might walk, at least below the pass. If he had come with Sonam, he could tell him if the webs were dangerous or not, but this way it would not matter.

For the first time in many months Sonam had no illusions or magic about him. It felt good to be back home, and yet with his prolonged absence it seemed he had a better sense of the magical power that covered the land like mist. Perhaps it was good he had gone away, so he would appreciate this world better. So he would see with new eyes.

In normal circumstances, at this time of year the roads would be busy. Everyone would be preparing for winter, when travel was nearly impossible. Now the roads were empty and the few huts outside the barrier were showing signs of neglect. There were footprints in the dust, so he could not be the only one outside the barrier.

He continued through a grove of juniper trees, using the magic his people called large-shadow to keep watch for anyone nearby. Now he could see the edge of the Celestial Cloud Palace just above the trees, and he felt his pulse beat harder. He needed to be even more cautious now.

Using magic to make himself light, he climbed one of the trees that ordinarily would not have been able to support his weight. There, where the river widened near the base of the cliff Celestial Cloud was built on, was the foreign camp. In the months Sonam had been away, however, it had become more than a camp. No more canvas tents. Wooden buildings had taken their place, and...he squinted. Yes. A new building was right next to the rock outcropping where the entrance to the tunnel was.

Sonam waited and watched. He found other concealed places to observe from, closer to the camp. He was surprised how many Aeropans were present, at least twenty that he could see. There were also some that looked like they came from Ynde and Cathai, but not very many. They had haggard expressions and did not speak.

He saw Bhutans too. They were chained in threes and nearly skeletal. They carried picks and pushed wheelbarrows, but strangely all their tools appeared to be made of wood. One path they followed went right to the outcropping with the tunnel. Had it been discovered? Even if it had not, there was no way he could sneak past without being seen.

As one ragged group left the compound, another would come in. An Aeropan sat on a raised platform, and the groups of three would stop there while he looked at the contents of their wheelbarrow and held up one, two, or three fingers. The contents of the wheelbarrow were then emptied into a large copper vessel, and the group of workers staggered away to where a large pot of rice stood. For each finger that had been raised, a bowl of rice was handed over. Most of them got only one or two bowls for three men, and it looked like this had been going on for a while. Sometimes fights would break out, but the workers were too weak to do much damage to each other.

Sonam waited until one unlucky group wandered off, still chained together, to the edge of a covered shelter open on two sides that appeared to be their sleeping area.

"Do not fear," he whispered from the shadows behind the shelter wall. "I have come to help you."

"No one can help us. The white devils will devour our souls," the stronger of the three said bitterly. "How is it that you have not been chained as we are?"

Sonam wanted to tell him he had gone to bring powerful assistance to give him hope, but there was always the risk that this would be discovered. "I have been given the gift of a strong spirit," he said instead. "I only show what I wish them to see. Where do you go with your wheelbarrow, and what do you bring up?"

"The sour dirt," said the oldest. His voice was weak and dry, like paper rustling. "Deep down, with the dragon bones. If we do not bring the white devils enough, they do not feed us. Then we have no strength to dig and bring nothing. And then we die."

Sonam had taken some dried meat and fruit with him when he had left the cave. "Here. I have food. Will you help me defeat the white devils? I must go inside that cleft without being noticed to do this. Let me take the place of one of you when you go back there."

All the men could focus on at first was the food. Only after every scrap was gone would they discuss which one of them should be released so Sonam could take his place. To Sonam's surprise, the older man, Dezen, insisted the youngest go free.

"We are used up." He indicated himself and the other old man. "To live a little longer, it is not so important. Tsering has more to lose."

"I hope to set everyone free, if I succeed in my task." Sonam made a reverence. "I give honor to your sacrifice."

"I will fight," Tsering said bluntly. "That is how I will use my freedom."

"Better if you stay hidden, find food, and help free the others," Sonam said. "There is a big fight coming, to drive all these evil strangers out. Let the people be strong, and watchful for that time."

Tsering gave him a hard, thoughtful look and then nodded. "Yes. I could kill one, maybe two. Better to kill them all."

The chains were not made of iron, but brass. Sonam was easily able to defeat the locks with magic. Tsering vanished into the night once he was free, and Sonam curled up to rest with his arms over his head. He would have to use illusion in the morning to disguise himself as Tsering, but according to the other workers, the supervisors rarely looked at them.

Then he heard voices. Voices speaking Gaulan. His understanding of the language had improved, traveling with the Mage Guardian, and he understood most of what was being said.

"...and none of the gateways have been triggered?"

"No, my lord."

Sonam did not dare shift his arms or do anything to attract attention. The speakers were walking by the shelter for the workers now, very close. He should have used illusion—what if they saw his different clothing?

"And the power residual scrying? You have done them every week?"

"Yes, my lord. No results."

"Excellent. Whoever created the barrier is either dead or trapped inside. Clearly they cannot come out and fight for whatever reason. Korda. Has there been any sign of Kohlmann?"

"No, my lord." This voice sounded different to Sonam. It seemed to hold more emotion, or some other quality that made the speaker real, not like the rigid automatons that had spoken earlier. The voices had passed the shelter now, and he dared to open one eye.

A tall, older man with a cane was walking away. Beside him were two other men, and behind followed a man with thinning hair and a round face damp with perspiration. All were Aeropan.

The older man stopped, turning. Sonam squinted so his eyes would appear to be closed. "Take a horse and go discover what has happened to delay him. Return and report immediately when you have found him. Make no unnecessary stops. Go."

"Yes, my lord," Korda, the round-faced man gasped.

"You two, report to me in the morning. We must take the barrier down. The good ore is all within—and we need more workers as well." The older man walked away, out of sight. Korda's face worked with emotion. He looked frightened and desperate. He took one step in the direction the man with the cane had gone, stopped, then quickly ducked inside a small shed.

A few minutes later Korda peeked out the door, chin trembling, and looked about. He was stuffing some round brown sticks in his jacket. Something made him whip his head around, and his expression became more resolute.

"You there. Heinzen. His lordship orders you to take a horse and ride it on the trail to Ghot until you reach the base of the mountain. You will hold this and set it alight. It will...it will give you further instructions." Korda handed him one of the brown sticks.

Another man came in view, his eyes wide with pain, sweat beading his brow. Every motion was jerky and stiff. He was clearly fighting the compulsion, but it was no use. He slowly turned and walked away. Korda ran.

"Why did they not put compulsions on you?" Sonam asked the others.

One shrugged. "Maybe the evil magicians must speak our language to give us orders that way. Why should they? The chains are enough."

Sonam put it aside as another question to ask the Mage Guardian when he returned. He slipped out of his manacles when it was fully dark and most of the workers were asleep. He wanted to know what was in the small shed.

Inside were small wood crates with rope handles. One had its lid ajar, and he opened it. With a trickle of moon-seeing, he saw that the contents were the same brown sticks that Korda had taken. On the outside of the box was writing. "Gefärlich—Explosiv" and a symbol of flame. He took a few himself, thinking they might be useful, and pondered what Korda had done. He had ordered the man to take the horse instead of himself, and given him one of the sticks. Something that would explode. Why would he do that? Why did he not follow the orders he had been given, if he was under a compulsion?

He is not compelled, but he can compel others. This was something those in the cave needed to know. As was the fact the old man intended to remove the barrier tomorrow morning.

Sonam went farther out, to the cliffs. The *kai-ling* were sleepy now, and he found one perched on an outcropping, blinking slowly and grooming its scales. It was young, which explained why it was still active. He reached out gently to scratch the dorsal spines, and it arched its back and kittered at him, making no move to leave. When he thought it was relaxed enough, he picked it up and tucked it in his jacket.

Quickly, before the *kai-ling* warmed up completely, he took the hollow reed he had found and cast the magic to capture his words. He described the old man with the cane, warned them of the barrier destruction, and described the strange behavior of Korda. He did not mention his plans for the morning, just in case the message was intercepted somehow.

Now the *kai-ling* was very active. He finished with one last instruction that the *kai-ling* would certainly consider important, and sealed the message. "Find the red hair in the mountain." He made a series of simple illusions as the *kai-ling* watched intently. They were drawn naturally to magic, and a magic image would stay in their minds for days. "Red hair gives meat." The *kai-ling* grasped the reed in its foreclaws, kittered at him again, and took off in a rush.

Now he had to return to the chains that did not hold him so he could go into the mine and find the way past the barrier. And now, thanks to Korda, he had a way to ensure the hidden entrance was not found and that he would not be missed. He would simply blow up the mine.

Ardhuin had slept uneasily, so it was not as much a decision to wake up as to stop trying to sleep. The faint illumination of magefire still filled the cave, enough that she could see Gutrune shift and raise her head as she went by.

"I'm going to check outside," she whispered. Gutrune nodded and sat up. Ardhuin sighed inwardly. It really should be possible for her to do something without offers of help.

Nothing had changed. Her various traps and detection systems had not been triggered, and the path remained in darkness even though dawn lit the sky. Something flew overhead, briefly making a small, darker shadow, and she went back in the tunnel to the cave.

"I suppose we should start making plans," Ardhuin said as soon as she had gone through the barrier.

"It would be wise, but we should also consider waiting a few days more for the detachment." Gutrune spoke in low tones, but the others were beginning to wake. "In fact, I—" her gaze sharpened, and she moved swiftly between Ardhuin and the opening, her pistol in her hand. "Something is moving."

Something was, and it moved very strangely. Ardhuin called up brighter magefire and blinked in astonishment. The creature was long and sinuous, a curious combination of weasel and snake, and a beautiful cerulean blue shaded with purple at the edges of its scales. It was now running back and forth along the ground, raking its claws against the barrier in an agitated way.

"How did it manage to get past the illusion? And what is it?" Ardhuin had the strangest feeling it was staring at her.

"It looks like a little dragon," Dominic said drowsily. "Are you doing illusions for fun?"

"What is it?" The thin voice of MacCrimmon came from the back of the cave.

"Some little creature got in the tunnel and wants to visit," Markus said over his shoulder. "That or high altitude causes me to hallucinate. It is a rather improbable shade of blue."

"Ah, it is a *kai-ling* then. A dragonet, I call them. Its rather unusual to see one so early in the day, when it is still chilly."

Now it was trying to bite the barrier in frustration. "Seems it wants to get in," Stoller observed.

"Is it carrying anything?" MacCrimmon asked, strangely.

"Why would it...oh. Yes, it has something like a stem in one claw."

MacCrimmon struggled to sit up, and Markus hurried over to assist him. "It's probably been sent then, with a message. The people here use them for that purpose. Let it in—they are not dangerous."

Dubious, Ardhuin made a small opening in the barrier. The little dragonet wiggled through immediately, apparently able to sense where the opening was as soon as it was made. It was making a repeated *khi-khi-khi* noise in a high tone, and launched into the air, circling around Ardhuin. It made no attempt to attack, and Ardhuin reluctantly held out a hand.

It perched immediately and allowed Ardhuin to take the thing it was clutching. Dominic reached for it.

"There's something magical inside...and the creature itself has a cloud of magic about it. Oh, it's a bubble like MacCrimmon sent us—and the skull! It was one of these animals?"

MacCrimmon nodded, smiling. "Then the message must be from Sonam."

"Already?" Markus bent slightly to examine the dragonet, which flared its neck scales at him but did not attempt to leave Ardhuin's hand. "He's been busy."

They gathered about MacCrimmon's pallet so they all could hear. MacCrimmon gently scratched the dragonet's back, and it stretched and arched its neck and closed its eyes.

Sonam's voice in the message was tight and abrupt. He had much news, and none of it good.

"Denais," breathed Dominic. "It has to be him. And he is taking down the barrier...he could be doing it now!"

"I want to know more of this Korda," Gutrune said. "He does not appear to be entirely loyal to Denais—in fact, is actively sabotaging him."

Ardhuin felt a chill. "Sabotaging Denais by giving one of the *geas*-controlled commands. Is it possible that he...but Denais would hardly have taught him how to do it."

"We should certainly look out for this Korda fellow, but we have a more immediate problem to deal with." Markus paced restlessly. "What will happen when the barrier is destroyed? It sounds like Denais doesn't have as much of that magic salt as he'd like—how long will it take him to make more?"

"It doesn't matter. He is powerful enough without it to be dangerous. We have to stop him, now." Ardhuin thought hard, ignoring the fear that knotted her stomach. No time to wait for the reinforcements or to make careful plans.

"It will take him more effort to take down the barrier than it took me to make it," MacCrimmon said softly. "I am ill, but he is old. It will depend then on whether he feels it likely he will need to dispel a subsequent magical attack himself, or if he will rely on his enslaved magicians until he is recovered."

"Then I should not reveal myself until we can prevent him from using either the magical essence or his magicians," Ardhuin mused.

"Can we release the *geas*? It is likely once freed the magicians will be able and willing to assist us," Gutrune said.

"I can. Unfortunately, it is necessary to know how to create the *geas* to dispel it." Ardhuin felt her face heat, and she did not look at Dominic. "It is...not common knowledge, and teaching it is forbidden for very good reason."

The little blue *kai-ling* wriggled up her arm and nuzzled her hair, braided for simplicity. She scratched it as she had seen MacCrimmon do, but it would not be still.

"Ah. That was the last part of Sonam's message." MacCrimmon smiled. "We owe our little messenger some food in payment."

Ardhuin was glad of the distraction. "What do they eat?"

"Insects, mice...other small creatures."

"Would a sardine do?" Stoller held up a tin. "We don't have much else left. Or much at all, actually."

Another reason to act quickly.

The *kai-ling* regarded the sardine with initial suspicion, but when enticed it grasped the fish in its forepaws and took a darting bite. It then proceeded to stuff the entire sardine in its mouth.

"It appears to be acceptable. Now when—"

A distant boom echoed from the cliffs, followed shortly by a vibration in the ground.

"What, has he taken down the barrier already?"

They ran for the cave opening. Dominic scanned the valley below, looking puzzled.

"It's still there. The barrier."

"What's that?" Markus pointed. A thin column of dust rose into the air in the distance.

Gutrune was looking through her field glasses. "The location is very close to where Herr MacCrimmon said the passage was. Perhaps Sonam has been forced to defend himself." She lowered the glasses, her brows wrinkled in a look of worry Ardhuin had rarely seen on her. "Denais will be more wary now, regardless. We must act quickly. I regret to say I had been counting on resupply from the Preusan detachment. I do not have much ammunition left, and we have only three effective magicians. We must make our targets come to a place of our choosing."

Dominic's face was pale. "They will come if their traps are triggered, I think. And I can watch for any magic they send ahead. The magicians are most likely to come, and only Ardhuin can release them to help us."

Ardhuin closed her eyes, hating the necessity of what she had to say. What if something happened and she was unable to protect him? *It is possible none of us will survive this. And yet it must be done.*

"You have another task, equally important, that only you can do. Someone must find the supply of magical salts and keep it away from Denais."

Markus nodded. "Yes, we must first weaken him before we go on the attack together. The salts and the enslaved magicians first, each in our own way. Then we can take him down. And with young Sonam even now rousing the local population to action, matters are not hopeless." Markus rubbed his chin. "Better if we draw off the magicians to more than one location, the better to aid Herr Kermarec's mission."

"I may be able to find it, but I can't touch it or get near it," Dominic protested.

"That will be my job, sir," Stoller said. "I can't do much with magicians so I might as well come along with you."

"But you will need a magician yourself to trigger the traps, will you not?" Dominic asked Gutrune, looking a bit desperate.

"I can give her another magic-infused token that will be effective enough," Ardhuin said. "That will give us three diversions."

"Four." A shaky MacCrimmon stood at the mouth of the cave tunnel, leaning heavily against the wall. "If you will permit me to lie in wait here, where I do not need to walk as far. I have enough power for that."

CHAPTER 21

Dominic took out his watch one more time, knowing he was just worrying. They still had over an hour until the plan went into effect. If you could call it a plan, and every time he thought about how shaky it was, he panicked and checked the time again.

"You shouldn't do that, sir," Stoller said in a quiet voice. "It's not invisibility she's given us. Motion draws the eye, and the little click when the case closes doesn't help."

Dominic nodded, sighing. The early morning light cast dark shadows, which helped, but people in Denais's facility were going about their work already despite the earlier explosion. He had been able to scan the open areas with Gutrune's field glasses before they split up, and no bright sources of magic were visible. Unless the magical salts were deeply buried, they must be hidden somewhere in the buildings. Which meant they had to go closer. But how could they do that without being seen?

Smoke was drifting up from the center of the camp, and the smell reminded him of how hungry he was. The location was near where Sonam had reported some kind of open kitchen.

"Let's go in now. I think they may be having breakfast." Maybe they could steal some before the war started.

Stoller got up and started moving away from the clump of scraggly bushes they had been hiding behind, so it appeared he agreed. Dominic did his best to follow as silently as Stoller, with indifferent success. Several times Stoller halted suddenly or darted into concealment as they got closer. Denais had set guards, a ragged lot but armed, and they had clearly been told exactly where to patrol and to look. Once you knew that they would not vary, it was possible to sneak by. Although many of the larger trees in the area had been cut down, bushes and rough boulders dotted the landscape and slopes of the valley.

Inside the guard perimeter it was easier. While there were more people about, they also were constrained to certain areas and activities, and there were more buildings to hide behind or in some cases, underneath.

Where was the damn stuff? Was it possible Denais had hidden it in a completely different location? Ardhuin didn't think so, and Gutrune had agreed with her. The magical salts were too valuable and too useful. Denais would keep them close at hand, both for his convenience and to keep an eye on them. And Denais was staying in the camp, from Sonam's information.

More people. Dominic darted around a corner, breathing heavily, his heart pounding. Stoller had his pistol out. These people did not look like the guards and workers—they were Aeropan and walked with stiff precision and expressionless faces. They all had *geasi*—but Dominic could see two of them that had the curious second layer.

Staring at them, something else caught his eye. A building. He tapped Stoller on the shoulder and pointed. Stoller watched for a moment, then gestured him forward. Dominic ran.

He knew as soon as he looked at it that it was Denais's work. Rather than a single ward like a bubble, magic was infused in the building itself. It was better looking than the other, functional structures of the camp as well, matching Denais's known love of comfort and luxury. Fancy or not, with the magic protections there was no way he could get in. With Stoller on guard, Dominic examined the exterior as much as he could.

A nearby building, an older stone structure that had been incorporated when the camp was set up, had a low, dusty cellar with a rotted door. They hid inside.

"I'm not sure what we can do." Dominic described what he had seen. "Besides the defenses, there's something else with very strong magic inside. It could be the salts, but I can't tell for sure. We don't have much time left before the others start. What can we do besides keep an eye on it? We'll have to wait for someone with magical ability."

Stoller scratched his chin thoughtfully. "Maybe. Or we can do like the others and give the enemy something more to worry about. If it's that important, they'll come in a hurry if it's threatened, I'm thinking."

"But what can we do? It's shielded with magic."

Stoller smiled grimly. "Let's see if magic can shield wood from fire, sir."

Gutrune hid behind a large granite boulder with a band of pure white running through it, and swore. She had only twenty-eight rounds for the triple. One box had gotten lost somewhere in the desert when that miserable camel dropped its load. More had been used hunting for food. There had not been space for heavy ammunition when they made the last segment of their journey, and she had been counting on the Preusan detachment for resupply—a terrible mistake. Too late to remedy now. She would have to make every bullet count.

Dominic had pointed out the web of detection near her position. She could see nothing, but she knew where the web was anchored. Ardhuin had given her the magic-infused token that would trigger the web, and that was in her hand. In her other hand was her watch.

She had found a group of boulders that would give her cover near the web, and spent the time while waiting carving holes in a piece of wood to hold her extra rounds ready to her hand. There might not be much time for reloading, and having her ammunition set out would make things run more smoothly. Until it didn't, and then it would have to be the pistol and the knife. And no Stoller to reload for her.

You see, Heinrich? Nothing is safe, nothing is certain. Winning was...unlikely. But the more damage they did, the more it improved the chance that the detachment would succeed. It could not have been destroyed, not so completely that word would not have gotten out. Someone would come, eventually.

She spared a thought for Heinrich, and another for Markus. Perhaps it was better this way than hoping for the impossible. Kinder, in the end.

It was time. Gutrune lifted her head, forced her sorrow aside, and threw the token at the web.

He had a lovely view, not that Markus really felt he could appreciate it. For one thing, it was just possible to see the curve of the valley slope where Gutrune was, and it was too tempting to watch that location instead of the section of road where the defenders most likely would appear to attack *him.*

Markus had tapped the web assigned to him on schedule, just a light little pulse of sensing magic likely to be used for general detection. Nothing serious. No one had shown up. He was beginning to think he should try again, more forcefully.

Motion on the road, near the camp. Ah, this was more promising. He took out his battered telescope and squinted through it. A foreboding feeling troubled him. A sizable group, yes, but...weapons?

The feeling of foreboding only increased as they came fully into view. Every single one of the motley group had weapons. *What? I don't rate a single magician?*

He thought furiously. The others must have triggered their own webs by now. This could only mean the available magicians were either held in reserve, defending Denais and the magical salts, or were attacking the other triggered webs. Such as Gutrune's—and she was no magician.

That just meant he had to deal with these attackers thoroughly, and with speed.

As soon as the front row of the fighters emerged around the bend of the road, Markus let loose with a powerful blast. It hit the rock opposite the road, but none of the fighters. They stopped immediately and aimed their weapons up the hill, but before they could fire, Markus had captured the rock shards created by the blast in a cloud of magic, sending them ripping through the fighters. It was a secret *schutzmagus* spell designed to shield against mass gunfire, but Markus saw no reason not to repurpose the general intent. Besides, he had no bullets himself and didn't want to wait for the fighters to give him any.

Several of the fighters were dead or severely wounded, but they made no sound. All ensorcelled, still trying to fight. Well, he should give them something to fight, then, if they were so determined. He did not have even a tenth of Ardhuin's skill with illusion, but with the dust stirred up by his blast and the fighters running about, he didn't need to.

Two vague figures emerged from a clump of bushes farther up the road and ran. The surviving fighters ran after them, and even the wounded crawled or staggered in pursuit. In a few moments the road was empty again.

Markus emerged from behind his rock, making sure he was unobserved, and set a few powerful magical surprises for when the fighters decided to return. Now he needed to go find the enemy magicians.

The first part of their plan had worked well. MacCrimmon triggered the web outside the cave, and Ardhuin concealed herself to trap the magicians who came in response. Three came. She used the tricky but powerful Gerverin Tangle spell, which absorbed and used magic to further contract and constrain those it trapped. It was a difficult mage-level spell, and she was profoundly grateful that her great-uncle had made sure she had command of it—although she had complained bitterly at the time.

Then she tried to remove the *geasi*. Oh, the removal was a complete success. The first man she freed seemed only a little dazed and confused at first. He kept asking, "Am I truly free?" She thought he was referring to the Tangle spell, and released it. The man gave her a weary look, thanked her, then ran for the edge of the cliff and jumped. He did not even scream as he fell.

After that she left the Tangle spell on, but it made no difference. The second man she freed did not speak at all, just stared vacantly, and the third would only weep.

"It is not surprising the balance of their minds is disturbed after so long under the *geas*," MacCrimmon said. "It has been nearly two years for them, and forced to do terrible things all that time."

Ardhuin finally cast vital stasis on the two survivors to keep them quiet and to limit their suffering.

"Will they all be like this? Can we not rescue some to help us?"

He shook his head. "It is possible one with greater strength of will may be found, but the only way to know is to free them. You have little time available to you," he said gently. "I do not envy you your decision." He was seated on a rock just inside the cave tunnel. His color had improved since they had found him, but he was still too weak to walk more than a few steps. "I am afraid the fact that we do not have any likely assistance makes my request of you more urgent. Leave me. There is one final spell I can perform."

Fear and anger made her feel nauseous. She knew what he was referring to. "I can't possibly leave you to destroy yourself," she gritted out. "Someone needs to survive. I can cast a very strong ward for you—"

"No, you must conserve your power to defeat Denais. What we truly cannot risk is for me to be taken alive in my weakened condition," MacCrimmon said forcefully. "This is the calculus by which the Mage Guardians live. We are the last defense. You cannot permit him to put a *geas* on me. If you fail, I will have no choice. The most I can do is hope to take him with me."

"Then permit me at least to give you an illusion, the better to take him unawares," she managed to say. Her throat was tight.

He leaned back against the rock wall, sighing. "Very well. But then you must leave and not return. Your duty is not to me."

Korda waited and watched in concealment until he saw Denais leave his quarters, two enslaved magicians following him. One carried the rucksack still containing the two jars of magical essence, and Korda ground his teeth in frustration. He had hoped to steal that to replenish his own supply, since the main store was under powerful protections only Denais knew how to remove. The rucksack, on the other hand, had been kept inside the quarters —and Korda knew he had access there. Denais still thought he was under control.

He had no choice. He had to take the risk. The essence here he would never be able to take, but he could prevent Denais from using it. And he knew Denais would return soon after taking the barrier down. Korda drew back his lips in a snarl. Denais was powerful but old. Even with the essence, he tired. He would return to rest and to ingest the essence in protection. All Korda had to do was use his own magic to trigger a spell. A minor one; that should avoid detection. But it would set another, nonmagical, effect in action.

He felt at his pockets. He still had the packet of essence—now was finally the time to use it. He had also gone back to the mining shed and retrieved more of the explosives.

Denais was no longer in sight. Korda dropped down from the roof and walked calmly up to the door of Denais's quarters. No one who had heard the command ordering him to leave would be there, and those who were would not question his presence if he were seen. And indeed, the few people inside said nothing when they saw him. Should he try to get them out first? No, too much of a risk that Denais would become suspicious. Their deaths could not be avoided.

He was not, of course, allowed in the private rooms. No one was. But he could approach the door, and the carved chest with a surprisingly ordinary pottery bowl on top. He made sure none of the other servants were nearby, and opened the carved chest, placing all of the sticks of explosive inside. Then, with shaking hands, he took the packet of essence and spilled all but a spoonful into a sheet of paper. He creased a line in the paper, allowing it to fold, and brought it to his nose.

Korda felt the fire of power burn through him, desperately stifling the moan of agony that he could not prevent. He had never taken so much at once before. Surely he was powerful enough to break down the protections and steal the rest, the precious essence that could mean victory? But one shred of caution remained in the fire of pain, and he held back. He might well have the power, but not the knowledge. Power was not enough.

He did know how to set a trigger spell, however, and link it to a sphere of contained fire tucked in with the explosives. He closed the chest and added a light binding on the door so it would seem to stick. That would make Denais hesitate just a fraction of a second when he attempted to open the door. That should be enough. Only Denais would trigger the explosive, and he would not expect an attack in his quarters. He would die, and Korda would finally be free.

Korda left the building to wait in hiding for the sound of freedom.

Denais gazed down at the valley, now open to him once again, and smiled. The secret, he had discovered, was to use the essence to supplement his natural power—and to prevent the dangerous overdraw that could permanently damage a magician engaged in extensive spellwork. By continual small doses, he could remain at his full capability for days. The human-derived essence had fewer uncomfortable effects, but the mineral essence could be stored nearly indefinitely without loss of potency—and was far easier to obtain in bulk. At least, when he had access to the source.

How strange it was...that a simple ceramic pot had provided the essential clue to bring him to this valley. To this ancient source of power. How could he say that his exile had been without purpose? If he had not been traveling in Parsia, he would never have seen the pot, or felt the magic it contained, or traced it to this savage and primitive land. Such a small, insignificant thing to bring him to ultimate success.

Denais was conscious of a mild, burning fatigue. Bringing down the barrier had taken his full effort, even with the essence. "Doring. Do a detection scan for any additional barriers or defenses."

The bound magician gestured, effort creasing his face. He shook his head. Denais smiled, now confident his assessment had proven correct. No one capable of further defense remained within the valley. Now it was only a matter of returning the extraction facility to full production.

He turned to order the guards to begin gathering more workers and saw someone running up the road from the facility. Denais frowned when he recognized one of the minor magicians, tasked with watching over the boundary systems. The man stopped before him, panting. Denais gestured, permitting him to speak.

"The security nets have been triggered, my lord."

"Which nets?" Denais felt a thread of irritation. He should have made the commands more specific, to include important detail without becoming verbose.

"All of them, my lord."

He felt a slight chill. So, perhaps lowering the barrier had alerted the maker...but why attack now, instead of earlier?

"Report measures taken."

His irritation grew as he listened. He was already missing Kohlmann and Korda, sent for more information. A significant number of his guards were here with him instead of available to respond to the alarms. Why, it was almost as if an enemy had planned it all to take advantage.

"Doring. Open the bag." Denais did not hesitate further. He was under attack by a cunning enemy, who had clearly laid plans long in advance. He grabbed the container of mineral essence and placed a generous pinch on his wrist, as if taking snuff. The power stung a trifle, so soon after taking a prior dose, but he felt much restored.

It was unlikely there were forces present inside the valley protected by the barrier. The attackers would be coming from outside. He gathered power to do a scan for significant magical presence, and let it go. It took time for the result to become clear. There was a large but not very powerful source, but it was some distance from the valley. This must not be the main attack, then. It was meant to distract him, to keep him from noticing the true threat. And had that accident in the mine truly been an accident? Had the attack started *before* he had brought the barrier down?

That freakish chit is behind this somehow. He fumed. What had become of his agents, his trackers? How had she eluded the traps he had set? He shook his head, angry with himself. Preoccupation with irrelevancies—the important thing was, had she brought others with her? With the essence he could easily best her alone. He should have been able to do so in Baerlen. But now...

This was merely a feint. He was sure of it. Otherwise the attack would have been stronger. He had enough time to start the first batch of extraction, now that the source was available, and he would need it for the fight ahead. He had to overwhelm them with force, to give himself time to bring about his final victory.

He pointed at the head guard. "Send three men to bring the mine workers here to dig. They are to work night and day until new workers replace them. The rest of your men are to return to the facility and ensure no strangers are inside. Kill anyone who does not belong there."

The guards had no sooner turned in obedience to his order when a massive explosion split the air.

CHAPTER 22

Initially Gutrune killed the three closest when the enemy came in range, but soon she had to switch her targeting to the three *fastest*. It made no difference that she could see when their fellows dropped in their tracks next to them, they kept coming. And her escape was blocked as well. If she left the cover of the boulder, two magicians aimed bolts of fire at her position. She'd tried for the magicians as soon as she'd identified them, but they had shields. The rounds had not been entirely wasted, however. The magicians stayed at the rear, and the shields caused the bullets to ricochet—and took out their own fighters.

Still, there were too many. She fought for time, to think of how she could sell her life most dearly. If nothing else, she would take as many of the foot soldiers down as possible so the magicians could not shelter behind them again. If the others survived to keep up the fight. A huge explosion in the camp startled her, then gave her hope. The others were fighting too.

Last reload for the triple. With one round left she quickly shifted to her pistol, then took the knife in her other hand and stepped out from behind the boulder. Perhaps she would get one lucky shot...

The soldiers were armed mostly with swords, and she ducked a swinging blow to stab another in the gut. They made no sound, even in death. So when the eerie horn sounded, it was very clear, echoing over the valley.

And the soldiers halted their attack, some in midswing, and turned back to the direction of the horn. The direction of the explosion also, or close to it. They paid her no further attention, even the magicians. She was able to reload her pistol and kill several more before running out of that ammunition as well.

Perhaps there were other guns in the buildings. Perhaps she would find a good use for the last rifle round. Perhaps the others were there already, She picked up the triple again and ran after the retreating foe.

Ardhuin gasped for air, trying to catch her breath while she looked for a place to hide in the camp. She should rethink her plan. It was a safe guess that anyone she didn't recognize had a *geas*, but there were so many! She couldn't free all of them. She needed to find the magicians first—even if it was more dangerous and took more time. Magicians could sense the beginnings of vital stasis and defend themselves, and everything else took too much power.

And she still had not seen Denais.

Deal with him when you find him. Always keep moving, Gutrune had advised. They were outnumbered and weak, but they had mobility and surprise to their advantage. She'd run from the cave, both to draw attention away from MacCrimmon, and also to find fresh targets. No other magicians had arrived after the first three. She needed another lure. What would Denais order his people to attack no matter what?

Denais knew she was searching for him. She was the bait. A fire golem would certainly attract attention, but there was hardly anything to burn and it would take too much time. All she had to work with were flimsy buildings and dusty streets.

She smiled. A dust-traveler was easy to create, and then, tied to it, an illusion of herself with long red hair swirling in the wind. Ardhuin found a piece of dark cloth to cover her real hair with and let the dust-traveler go.

It brought out two men, but not close enough for her to touch them without being seen. She grimaced and moved the dust-traveler to lead them nearer—and a sudden, violent explosion blasted wood splinters and debris. She dropped to the ground and covered her head with her arms, wincing when wreckage landed on her. When she looked up, a plume of dust and smoke rose a few hundred yards away.

What was...I didn't do that, did I?

The two men, being closer, had been knocked down and dazed by the explosion. She took advantage of the smoke to run up and destroy their *geasi.* What if that had been Denais, on the attack? She should go find out— and if it wasn't, surely Denais's men would be heading there too?

Shouts came from behind her. Ardhuin whirled around. A group of men were running down the street, long curved knives in their hands. They had seen her, and she would have to fight. She could not outrun them. Ardhuin quickly formed a shield, wondering which attack would be best, when she heard her name shouted from the middle of the group.

"Sonam?"

He waved and smiled, a full smile that flashed white, and the same fierce smile was echoed in the men about him. "My people have come to help you hunt!"

So the barrier was down. She had help, but now she needed it even more.

"We're running low on matches, sir." Stoller spoke with praiseworthy calm, as if he were merely making conversation.

Dominic ran his fingers through his hair, feeling frantic. It should have been easier than this to set fire to a wood building, nicely dry. Apparently the magical protections prevented anything physical from getting near the wood, however, and his attempts at arson had so far been failures.

"We just need to find a better spot," he said to Stoller. "How many matches do we have left?"

"Three."

He stared at the back of the building, hoping for inspiration. As a nicer building it had a low stone foundation, which hadn't helped the combustion process. However, situated as it was on the edge of the cliff with a large mountain draining any rain down the side, metal grates had been placed at even spaces for drainage. And when he checked, the magical field was slightly warped next to the gratings.

"There. They must be iron. We just have to put the tinder in first, and then set it alight. It will also be out of the wind."

This time it worked. The tinder they had found, like all the wood around the valley, was extremely dry and caught fire rapidly. Dominic shoved in a few more twigs and darted off with Stoller. He stopped beside the neighboring building and turned to watch.

"I just want to make sure it will work." Stoller rolled his eyes but said nothing.

First a thread of black smoke appeared from another grating. Then a tongue of flame appeared at a window. More smoke was seeping from the sides and openings.

"Time to go, sir," Stoller said. "We don't want his folk finding us."

"I suppose not." It was clear the entire building was involved now, and the lower floor was completely in flames. "Very well, let's find the oth—"

The roar of an explosion hit him like a hammer, and then a massive shockwave lifted him up and smashed him against a nearby building.

When he regained consciousness, it was to the sound of a worried Stoller and disturbing sharp pains that told him something was not quite right. Since all of him ached, it was hard to figure out exactly what.

"Sir. Sir, you have to wake up. There are people coming. We need to run."

"I don't think I can," Dominic said woozily. His head swam, and when he tried to get up, one leg let him know in no uncertain terms it was not going to cooperate. He also could not see—everything was a bright haze of white. At first he thought it was smoke, and then he realized the truth. They had somehow blown up the magical salts, which were now dispersed in the air. "Oh, blast and damn." He pulled himself up on his good leg, trying not to whimper. He'd cracked a few ribs too, it seemed.

"I've got you, sir." Stoller pulled Dominic's arm over his shoulder and they hobbled away as fast as Dominic could manage. "Is it bad?"

"I'm pretty sure it's broken." Dominic gritted his teeth to keep from screaming with pain. "What on earth happened? We only set it on fire! Now all that magic dust is in the air and I can't see a thing!"

"Well, at least we got it." Stoller shrugged. "I'm thinking we'd better hide out for a bit, though. I saw a wheelbarrow a ways back; that would be a faster way to get you out. You stay here in this shed and rest, and I'll fetch it."

Dominic nodded, unable to speak without revealing his bitterness. He was useless, again. A burden other people had to deal with. He didn't even know where Ardhuin was. It was true that he had effectively destroyed the magical salts, he realized, cheering up slightly. Still, there had to be something more he could do to help. At least keep watch, which he couldn't do lying down.

A collection of tools was stacked in the corner of the building Stoller had left him in. He could just reach one, a curious shovel made entirely of wood. The handle was long enough to serve as a crude crutch. With considerable pain and effort, he managed to stand again.

The dust in the air was beginning to settle, and he could see the edges of buildings again. In the distance the mountains were visible. Something about them looked odd—and then he realized the barrier had disappeared.

Dominic heard laughter in the distance, high-pitched and quick. Children? He shuffled painfully to the door, but all he could see was a short, balding man in worn clothes stumbling toward the now-destroyed house. The man had an expression of ecstatic happiness on his face, for all that he looked worn and exhausted. He laughed again.

"He's gone...he's gone! I'm finally free! Rot in hell, you Gaulan bastard!"

The man spoke Preusan—and he didn't have a *geas*. Ardhuin must have freed him, and since he was Aeropan, he was probably a magician. Dominic started to move back into the shadows, but the man saw him.

"Don't be afraid, friend. It's all over." He spoke in a reassuring way.

"What happened?"

"Why, his stinking lordship set off a little trap when he went inside his house. He'll never bind anyone again. He thought he had bound me, but I tricked him. I tricked him and I put the explosives where only he would go." The man giggled, hugging himself. "Baron Kreuzen is avenged at last."

So that's why it blew up.

"Er, are you sure? I didn't see anyone go inside and I've been here for at least half an hour." Dominic decided it would be unwise to mention why he had been watching.

The man stopped giggling and his face paled. "No. Nothing else could have triggered the..." he stared at Dominic, eyes narrowed. "Who are you? I don't remember seeing you before."

"I...arrived recently." Where was Stoller?

"No. Nobody has come, that's why he tried to send *me*, because he thought enemies..." The man's face cleared a little. "Are you an enemy?" He seemed to notice for the first time Dominic's battered and disheveled state. "You're hurt. Was it the explosion? I'm sorry, but I had to do it. There was no other way, he is too strong, especially—" A horn sounded, long and wailing, and the man screamed. "He's still alive? That's impossible!"

He stiffened, looking down the street. Despite the brightness of the magic dust, Dominic could see power building around his clenched fists, a strangely ragged but strong power. There, finally, was Stoller—with the wheelbarrow—and Sonam, and a crowd of fierce men that looked a lot like him, and behind them all, a familiar red head of hair. The fear he could not shake diminished, seeing Ardhuin was still alive.

"Don't worry. They are all here to defeat Denais, just like me," Dominic said quickly. "Don't you remember her? The one who freed you?"

The man looked at him, puzzled. "Freed me? No one freed me."

"Dominic!" Ardhuin came running through the crowd. "You are bleeding! Stoller said you were hurt..."

He leaned gratefully on her. "I will admit to not feeling my best, but appearances can be deceiving." He leaned closer, whispering in her ear. "That man is a magician and has no *geas*, but he claims you did not free him."

Ardhuin glanced at the man, frowning. "I don't remember him...and all of those I freed so far are in shock or worse." She waved to the man, who was nervously sidling away. "Sir, will you not help us fight Denais?"

"You can't fight him. No one can. He is too strong. The explosives would have done it, but now he knows...now he knows you are here. I have to go."

"If he escapes again, he will continue to enslave others like yourself. We cannot allow someone who is able and willing to use the geas as he has to live. Is it not worth the danger to stop him?"

Now the man was staring at her in horror. "Not live?"

Something isn't right here. He wasn't acting normally. And then Sonam appeared from the crowd, looking as grim as Dominic had ever seen him.

"His name is Korda. I saw him. Did you get my message?"

And it all came together. The ragged magic he'd seen the man summon looked familiar, and now he knew why. "It's him," Dominic gasped. "He's been putting the secondary *geas* on people."

Unfortunately Korda also understood, and had figured it out before him.

"I had to do it! Don't you understand? He had to be stopped! Why would you kill me for that? *He* is the one you should kill, but you didn't. You *can't*. No. I'm not going to help you! He's going to destroy you all!"

And Korda ran.

Ardhuin stared blankly in the direction Korda had gone. "I suppose he wouldn't have been much use, but will he be helping Denais now?"

"Unlikely." Dominic squinted into the cloud of magic. Something had changed. Something in the cloud was bright, and moving fast. Power like he had never seen before. "Shield!" he yelled. "Incoming magical attack!"

Denais had found them.

The warning had barely been in time. Ardhuin had cast an initial large shield as soon as Dominic had yelled, and she felt it shatter an instant later —just as she had completed a more powerful one centered on the defenders. She thought she heard screaming but resolutely thrust it out of her mind.

Korda had been right. Denais had more power than she had ever seen before. More than she had ever used herself. How could she hope to defeat him?

"Where is he? I can't see a thing in this smoke."

Dominic grimaced. "There's too much of that magical salt dust in the air for me to see much either—but the attack came from that direction." He pointed. "How does he know where we are?"

"I don't think he does," Ardhuin said slowly. "I think that was an area effect spell, something like Grenat's Hammer." Now figures were approaching out of the smoke, carrying weapons. "See? He is sending in his soldiers to kill any survivors." Feeling cold, she made her decision. "Sonam. Tell your people they will have to fight the soldiers. You and I must go find Denais before he discovers we have split our forces."

"And what about me?" Dominic's grip on her arm tightened.

"I need you too." Looking at him, bloody and battered, she felt like crying—but strangely Dominic's expression lightened.

"In that case, we need Stoller and his wheelbarrow. I seem to have broken my leg."

Well, Stoller's insistence on bringing the wheelbarrow finally made sense. Ardhuin spared a thought for Gutrune and Markus, wondering where they were and if they were still alive. Sonam was giving quick whispered instructions to the men with the knives, and then he was running back. Dominic was collapsing carefully into the wheelbarrow, and Ardhuin cast a strong sound-dampening spell around them all.

Everything looked different in the smoke. If she recalled correctly, the direction Dominic had indicated was near the rough sheds and equipment that was used for extracting the magical salts, up the slope and against the cliffs, near the waterwheel. If they found the cliff wall and went uphill, they should find Denais.

She arranged the dampening spell to only block sound near the ground, so they could hear any approaching attackers, but that meant they could not speak except in whispers. Her heart was hammering in her chest, and she stared into the smoke, trying to make sense of the shadows. Then Sonam recoiled sharply and a soft grunt escaped him.

"A barrier. Denais wishes to keep us at a distance, it seems," Dominic observed.

Ardhuin grimaced. Yes, that would be like him. Trap the enemy in a shell, along with his soldiers, while he stayed outside to await events. She let her fingers contact the barrier, and thought hard. It was just a barrier of force, making no distinction of what it was excluding.

"Dominic. Can you see what kind of magic it is?"

He squinted. "Yes. Why, what do you mean to do, take it down?"

She shook her head. "That would alert him. No, I want to do what we did with the webs. Create my own bubble of force to let us out, but I will need to match the magic exactly."

It was easier than she had thought it would be. Then she recalled the dust. She was breathing in power, a little bit at a time. Perhaps that would give her an edge against Denais—but no. He was taking the magical salts directly.

Outside the barrier, the air was a little clearer. They went up the steep path to the cliffs, which were sharply eroded and streaked with white, with occasional rocky protrusions. She could tell where MacCrimmon's barrier had been, because the excavations were extensive up to that point.

"They are digging, even now." Sonam pointed.

Denais must be desperate for the salts. Ardhuin looked more closely at the workers. They had wheelbarrows too, and worked in groups of three chained together. She smiled. Time for an illusion. They would need something to get close to Denais and have any chance at succeeding.

The gaunt workers said nothing as they joined the line. Where was Denais? She heard voices up ahead, too faint to distinguish the words, but the tone of command was unmistakable. They must be getting close.

There. The workers shuffled down a deep ditch to the cliff wall, and a group of three men stood at the top of the ditch. Denais was looking at the buildings of the facility with a harsh frown, but he did not seem unduly disturbed. Neither he nor the two bound magicians next to him looked at the workers.

Move slowly. Do nothing to attract attention. She held her breath, not even daring to adjust the illusion for fear it would be noticed, and they inched away. Dominic's face was white, and his eyes were wide. Just let them get past Denais and find cover...

The sharp crack of a rifle split the air. *Oh no. Gutrune.* Ardhuin huddled against the wall of the ditch with Dominic and Stoller and looked up.

Denais was unharmed, but one of the bound magicians was down and bleeding profusely from a neck wound. He was still struggling, despite his mortal injury, to stand.

Denais gestured. A lightning bolt lanced out and struck the cliff, but before it hit, Gutrune rolled from the cliff rock she had been hiding behind and fell. The cliff face was not completely vertical, so she slid in a cloud of dust, and Ardhuin saw she was using the butt of her rifle to help slow her descent. Even so, she was completely exposed to another attack.

"Something's odd about the magic!" Dominic hissed. "I could see...waves...coming off of the lightning bolt."

No time to plan now. Ardhuin pointed to Sonam and waved him to another position. Denais might still be taken by surprise.

Denais was staring at where Gutrune had fallen at the base of the cliff. She was still moving, so presumably still alive. He levitated in a single burst over the ditch to where she was and stood, looking down at her with a curled lip.

"A gun? Against *me?*" He laughed. "Where are the rest of your sorry group?"

Gutrune groaned, shifting slightly, but did not speak.

Dominic gripped her hands tightly. "Oh God...he's summoning power for a *geas*!"

There was no time. She had to fight. She had to leave Dominic. Ardhuin kissed him, hard. "I love you," she said, and pulled away.

She needed a powerful attack and something to overcome the shield she knew he must have. She remembered her layered defense earlier and summoned power. Gesalt's Lance was the most powerful attack that might work, and she sent it three times in rapid succession—twice at moderated power and the third with all the strength she had.

Denais staggered and dropped to one knee. Bright threads of light, almost like a *gloire*, shimmered in the air, popping in and out with a noise like ripping paper. Was that a shield?

He had been staggered, but not nearly enough. His head twisted around and Denais looked directly at her. He did not appear to be injured in the slightest.

"Ah, there you are."

Shield. Not enough. She screamed as the power flooded over her, fighting to keep something, anything in place. Not for herself, but for Dominic behind her who had no defense at all except flimsy illusion. The shield contracted in the face of the attack, and she felt burning agony on her legs and arms.

Then she realized it had stopped, and she was lying at the bottom of the ditch. She could not move. Her body refused to obey her. But then she found herself being lifted up into the air, hanging limply, close before the hard, scornful eyes of Denais.

He raised one elegant eyebrow. "Is this really the best you could do? I presume this is one of yours." He nudged Gutrune with his foot.

"The others...are coming," Ardhuin gasped. The burns on her skin were a wall of pain, making it difficult to think.

"If this is the caliber of the Mage Guardian forces, I do not anticipate any difficulty. He is...oh, I do beg your pardon. *She* is of negligible use. A friend?" One hand slashed down.

Fire engulfed Gutrune—Gutrune, and someone else. A familiar shape, protectively crouched over her, the avoidance magic stripped away by the attack. Denais appeared surprised, and he had not used as much power in his attack as previously, but Markus collapsed with smoke drifting up around him.

She knew she did not have enough power to kill Denais, not with the advantage the magical salts had given him. Something Dominic had said, about Denais keeping his distance, triggered a memory. The magical duels at the Reuytersalle. Old custom.

When Denais reached out to blast Markus and Gutrune again, she grabbed his wrists.

Whenever he summoned power, she interfered with it. He was tall, but she was just as tall as he was. He was a man, but old. She was wounded, but young. And angry, and terrified. The burns on her hands were raw and excruciating, but she did not let go.

The levitation spell vanished—and she fell. She had expected that, and bent her knees and pulled backward. Denais fell with her into the ditch. Despite the impact of landing, she managed to keep hold of his wrists. It didn't matter how much power he had if he couldn't focus it.

She could hear sounds of fighting behind her, but she dared not look to see who it was. Denais was struggling to get free, his face working with rage.

"You mangy bitch, how dare you get in my way? Don't you realize I will win in the end? My loyal servants alone will defeat you!"

"I removed their 'loyalty,'" Ardhuin gasped. "Did you think I made no plans for that?" She forced herself to smile. "Where are they, these loyal servants? Have you noticed any of them missing lately?"

Denais snarled at her. Ardhuin recalled childhood fights with her brothers and slammed her forehead into his nose. He screamed and thrashed harder. She felt her grip beginning to slip, her hands wet with her own blood.

"Help me! He's getting loose!"

A wooden shovel smacked Denais in the head and shattered. "Something's very wrong." Dominic's voice came out of the shadows. "I see it every time magic is used—there is something in the dust here too."

"Dominic! Hide! Run!" Ardhuin screamed. Dominic had no defenses. It would take so little for Denais to destroy him...and here he was getting distracted.

Dirt and pebbles fell from the side of the ditch as she struggled to keep her grip. Then a body launched itself over the edge, landing on Denais with a thud.

Denais screamed, wrenching himself sharply away. He managed to pull one hand free with the effort, and Ardhuin saw the hilt of a familiar knife sticking out of his back. She tried to reach it, to push it in farther, but Denais was finally able to focus power and launched himself upward with levitation. He writhed as he floated, trying to reach the knife, but his arms could not bend far enough and his magic refused to attach to the iron.

Ardhuin staggered to her feet. Gutrune was lying in the ditch, no longer moving. Soram and Stoller were fighting the last bound magician, and Dominic lay on the ground, clutching the broken handle of the shovel, his face twisting with agony as he struggled to speak.

"Use the dust," he yelled. "Get it between you and him, with as little magic as possible!"

She didn't have much magic, so that part would be easy. She wasn't sure why the dust would help—perhaps cloud his vision? Deflect his magic just enough? Dominic seemed to know exactly what it would do, and she trusted him.

The dust-traveler magic was light and simple. It scoured the cliff face, creating a huge, thick cloud of dust.

Denais laughed. "Is that the best you can do, little girl?" He gestured. "I have had enough, I think. You cease to amuse me."

She could barely see him now in the dust. It didn't matter. There was nothing else for her to do, no one else to rescue them. She stuck out her chin and clenched her fists.

Fire bloomed in the cloud. And then smaller explosions scattered off of that. Denais's laughter turned to a frightened, frustrated scream, a scream that increased in pitch and volume until a final, devastating explosion slammed into the cliff face. A thundering roar shook the earth, and the world went dark.

CHAPTER 23

"Eventually someone will come," Sonam said, shivering. He had gotten off with only minor burns and a stab wound and was the most mobile of the survivors.

"Well and good, but how long is 'eventually'?" Dominic resumed bandaging Ardhuin's wounds with the tattered remnants of his shirt. She was so exhausted she could only manage a few words, but at least she was conscious. The air was still full of the sour scent of the dust, although a cold wind was beginning to disperse it.

Gutrune was alive but had not woken since stabbing Denais. Markus guarded her, his face a mask of pain both from his own burns and seeing the extent of her injuries. More broken bones, at the very least, so perhaps it was best she was not conscious.

Seeing Sonam's crestfallen expression, Dominic sighed. "I am sure your people will investigate, but we have nothing here, not even water, and everyone is in need of urgent medical attention. And we can't use magic."

After seeing what had happened to Denais, no one argued with him. Their situation was dire, but the raw magical dust made it even worse. Any magic of power beyond a mild illusion seemed to build up a resonance of discharge, causing a chain reaction of magical detonations. It was Denais's very power that had eventually destroyed him.

Unfortunately, it had also caused a massive avalanche that had isolated them on a narrow rock ledge. The path, and the excavations, were gone, ripped off the mountainside. Above was the cliff and high mountain peak, virtually impossible to climb. Below was another steep cliff. And it was starting to snow.

"The dust will die down in time," Markus managed to say. "The snow might even help with that."

Dominic shook his head. "It's not just the dust. The avalanche exposed fresh material, and it is quite strong here. I'm afraid we need to find another way."

"A message, then. Or perhaps you can see a section that is less magically enhanced, and one of us could slide down as she did? We can't just stay here." Markus's voice was ragged with frustration. "She isn't waking..."

Dominic crawled on one side, stifling his whimpers of pain as best he could. Stoller just looked at him in resignation, his broken shoulder and other injuries preventing him from helping. From the edge of the rock ledge he looked about, seeing if there was any way out, even a dangerous one.

Sliding was not an option. The rock they rested on went down a considerable way, and below that were some other sharp protrusions. To either side...he squinted. The view was still quite obscured from the avalanche, and the brightness of the magic interfered with his regular vision. And that patch was even brighter than the rest. He frowned. The bright patch was *moving*.

"Er, how sure are we that Denais exploded?"

Markus chuckled, then winced. "Quite sure. You didn't see the torso go by, but I never forget a waistcoat. Even with the blood and...other matter, it was quite recognizable. Denais is *not* an issue anymore. So I suppose we won..." He picked up Gutrune's pale hand and rested his forehead on his bent knees.

"The reason I'm asking is something seems to be coming this way. Something magical."

"Korda..." Ardhuin whispered roughly.

"If it's him, he's learned to levitate over mountains." Now Dominic could hear a steady, rhythmic throbbing noise, like a deep hum. Or an engine.

It grew louder, and a large, dark shape emerged overhead. A bulbous shape, like a large loaf, was held in a network of ropes or cables. It was the source of the magical brightness. From it hung an open framework something like a boat, and below that an engine with large, leaf-like blades turned in the air. He could see people moving about in the boat.

"What in the name of heaven is that?"

Markus managed a tired grin. "I haven't the slightest notion, but it is flying the Preusan flag."

A few moments later a long rope ladder dropped, followed by a familiar short man with a round, freckled face. "Ho, Kermarec! It *is* you!" Jens-Peter Oberacker called cheerfully. "We used your ideas for the ship! Isn't it great?"

The levitation ship, as Jens-Peter called it, managed to rescue everyone from the rock ledge. The rescue took several trips and some clever rigging to handle the wounded once the Preusan military doctor had done his initial patching up.

Ardhuin tried to direct them to rescue MacCrimmon, only to find he had been the one to signal the levitation ship in the first place.

"How is he?"

Dr. Kanitz shook his head. "Very weak. This high altitude has been very bad for his health. He's at the camp, where we are taking you."

Except for the noise of the engine, traveling in the levitation ship was very much like floating. The descent was gradual, accompanied by creaking noises as the canopy of the ship was compressed by pulling in the cables that ran like netting over the surface. Jens-Peter bounced from running the ship to explaining it all to Dominic.

"It's ground-up levitators! You remember the wreckage from Siebert's laboratory, how it was floating about the ceiling after the accident? Well, with what you had said in your letters we decided to try another way. What did we have to lose? And this way, the magical element is well away from the engines, and we don't have to be quite so precise. It was a bit of bother to figure out pulleys and such that don't use iron, but bronze works quite well if you don't abuse it." He broke off to yell some orders to the crew.

"You said this was just a prototype?" Dominic asked, propped up against one of the central attachments. Despite the pain of his injuries, he had kept up a constant stream of questions. Ardhuin smiled.

"Oh, we have bigger ones! They just thought this would be a better idea for the purpose. Besides being easier to hide on the way up. We're trying to keep it to ourselves for a while." Jens-Peter grinned. "I'm to captain the next one being built!"

Besides MacCrimmon, a group of elders from the valley were assembled at the collection of white tents on the narrow plain, escorted by Sonam, looking dashing in bandages. Ardhuin and the others were carried into one of the tents on stretchers.

"Why are we not in the valley itself? It's a long walk for them."

Sonam tilted his head. "There is still fighting. The soldiers that came are dealing with the guards left by Denais. They said we would be safer here until they are done."

"Did they find Korda?"

Sonam shook his head.

"I believe I may have seen this Korda, running from the valley," MacCrimmon said. "Short man, thinning hair? I did not want to stop him and reveal myself—like the others who were freed, he did not seem entirely sane."

Ardhuin glanced around the tent. A handful of Preusan soldiers and a medical orderly were inside. "Would you mind casting an obscurer spell?"

MacCrimmon nodded and gestured. "You are still fatigued?"

"Yes. Denais is most definitely dead, but this Korda appears to have learned how to cast *geasi* from him—and from what we have discovered, he has been stealing the magical salts and sending them to places only he knows. Fräulein von Kitren intercepted one such shipment, but...he has the knowledge and now the ability to do much of what Denais did. And now he thinks that the Mage Guardians will kill him because of that knowledge."

MacCrimmon winced. "I wish I had known, then. I am sorry, Sonam. We did not solve the problem completely."

Sonam made another effacing gesture. "It is difficult for me to say...the elders do not understand the danger. That if any outsider with ill intent knows of the unique nature of the soil here, others will come to steal power." He bowed profoundly. "They regard your service to them as a distasteful necessity. They thank you, but will be glad when you go. I am sorry. They owe their lives to you."

"It is not for me to tell them to change their ways—but we must find a means to protect them, and the rest of the world, despite their views." MacCrimmon smiled weakly.

So we don't tell them what we are doing. "I have some suggestions," Ardhuin said, "but they can wait. As long as we are sure there is no immediate danger..."

Her eye was drawn to the entrance of the tent and a group of people bringing in another stretcher. Markus Asgaya followed on crutches, his otherwise bare chest covered by a mass of bandages and his arms red with burns. Despite the lines of pain and fatigue on his face, his expression was much more cheerful than she had last seen. She tilted her head at MacCrimmon as Markus approached, and the sound dampener disappeared.

"She opened her eyes as they were bringing her in on the ship," Markus reported. "The doctor says that is a good sign."

Ardhuin felt a little of her own anxiety lessen. "That is excellent news. Gutrune is amazingly robust, but even she cannot withstand falling down a mountain without ill effect."

Markus collapsed on a cot with a groan. "If you would endeavor to convince her of this I will be eternally in your debt. Oh, look there. It's the little blue dragon."

It was indeed the little blue *kai-ling*, wrapped around the arm of one of the Bhuta elders. The elder came over to Sonam and spoke briefly with him, but the *kai-ling* buzzed into the air as soon as it saw her. It circled around, making a curious kind of clicking purr, until it settled on her pillow, right next to her head.

Dominic was chuckling. "I believe you have formed a friend for life, dear. There is a little image of a fish in front of it, made of faint magic."

Ardhuin reached up with her bandaged hand. The *kai-ling* shifted its head so her fingers could find the places it thought needed scratching, and it click-purred even more. "Who would have thought one sardine would make such an impression? I wonder why the elder brought it in here, though?"

Sonam smiled. "It was trying to find you and being a nuisance. This sometimes happens to the young ones. They find a person they prefer, usually someone with strong magic, and will not be driven away."

"Oh dear." Ardhuin looked at the *kai-ling* with dismay. "Will it try to follow us back home?"

"Yes, of course. Is this not desired? They are very good for sending messages, as you saw, and they are protective of their nesting places. They serve much like Aeropan dogs in that way."

"It seems your choice is bringing it with you, in some level of concealment, or having it trail you all the way back to Peran," Markus said. His words were beginning to slur as the morphia took hold. "I'm sure no one would take notice of a miniature dragon in the same colors as a festival balloon. Flying through the air, trailing your coach..."

"We could keep it in the library. Plenty of room to fly in, and perhaps we could contrive a window that could be opened at need." Dominic's eyes brightened at the thought. "And it could guard the books."

"If it doesn't *eat* them, or hide sardines in the shelves," Ardhuin protested. "And I don't want to keep opening and closing a window when it wants in or out. A cat is quite bad enough."

"*Kai-ling* are quite clever," Sonam said earnestly. "If the mechanism is not complicated, you can teach it to open and close the window itself. And they never leave messes in their nests."

Ardhuin sighed and closed her eyes. It was clear the matter had been decided for her. She now had a little dragon as a pet. Well, her great-uncle had had his roses, so perhaps she was doomed to collect magical animals. *I do hope he and Hermes will get along...*

She could hear waves splashing and smell cool salt air and feel gentle motion. Almost like being on a ship. Gutrune slowly opened her eyes and realized she was, in fact, on a ship. She was reclining on a deck chair, wrapped in several blankets, and for the first time her injuries were not a constant pressure of pain but merely an overall ache covered by deep fatigue.

At first she thought she was alone, but then she heard a slow, rhythmic tapping and saw Markus walking slowly and stiffly up and down the deck, using a cane and the railing for balance. He looked over at her and started.

"Awake, are you?" He came over and sat down on an adjoining deck chair with slow caution.

Gutrune nodded, struggling to speak. Her mouth and throat were dry. "How...here?" she finally managed.

"You will doubtless be happy to hear we are on the Bretagnan naval ship *Regina Astraea*, the royal brigantine. It appears Her Majesty is quite pleased with the lot of us. Ah, and in the Middle Sea once again." He grinned, glancing at her. "Yes, I can see you thinking it out. Never fear, the journey across the sands was achieved without a single camel, at least in your case. We unpacked the levitation ship and managed to make the transit entirely at night. We also used that extremely handy ship to get all the wounded down from Bhuta, or we'd still be in the mountains. And it's snowing there now, so we'd have been stuck for months. They decided it was worth the risk."

"Denais?" She had only fragments of memory, and she wasn't sure what was real and what was nightmare. Pain, and fire. Ardhuin fighting him, desperation in her eyes. A frantic, screamed plea—and somehow finding the last iota of strength, and her knife. An explosion, and snatches of unfamiliar faces.

"Quite, quite dead. I will not describe the scene in detail, in deference to your health and my stomach, but I was able to identify several large portions of his body. He...well, I suppose you could say he came apart. Dominic's theory is he had absorbed more power than human flesh could withstand, and coupled with the amplification effect of the dust in the air the magic discharged—without his control." Markus shuddered and closed his eyes.

"The others?" She somehow knew they were alive. Perhaps they had visited her, and in the dreamlike state of morphia she remembered this.

"Madame Kermarec is nearly restored to health, which is a fortunate thing because Herr Kermarec is frequently distracted into forgetting his leg is still quite broken. He requires constant supervision. Herr MacCrimmon is, I fear, still quite frail, and while we do not despair of his life, his health has likely suffered permanent damage. Sonam, on the other hand, is fully recovered and quite helpful with—"

Gutrune blinked. "Sonam? He is here?"

Markus sighed. "Yes. I was hoping to delay that discussion until you were feeling stronger. It's a touchy matter and rife with politics, but Madame Kermarec is, I think, losing patience with the usual way of doing things. And given that Herr Kermarec is quite determined to assist her in her plans, I have decided to ally myself entirely with them. I have seen what happens to those that oppose that pair when they get angry. Not to mention it will make my own plans much more feasible."

The change in his tone made her look up at him, and his gaze was both meaningful and steady. Gutrune turned her head and stared out over the sea. There was no use getting her hopes up. It was impossible.

"I...I know I said, when we were done, when Denais was defeated..."

"...that I could try. Well, if he was any more defeated, he'd be a string of sausages. Now, are you going to help me or not?" His smile lacked the usual trace of mockery. He seemed...happy. Genuinely happy. How could she do anything to change that? How could she deny what he asked? But how could she lie to him, even to preserve his happiness?

"Of course I will help you. I merely...that is, I do not see a clear way to do anything to the purpose."

Markus, strangely, did not seem in the least cast down by this. "Naturally. You are still far from well and that can lead to gloomy thoughts and depression. This plan she's come up with may be exactly the thing we need, and even if that doesn't work, I have a secret weapon. My mother," he confided. "Mind you, I suggest she only be deployed as a last resort, but I have no doubt she would do the trick."

Gutrune raised a skeptical eyebrow at him, and he chuckled, wincing slightly. "You are so certain she would approve of me?"

"I haven't the slightest idea," he said, clearly amused. "You can never tell with Mutti. But she is a woman of her word, as my father found out to his considerable astonishment, and she promised me when we left Yunwiya that if I ever encountered...difficulties because of my parentage, I need only bring it to her attention and she would deal with it. I do think I deserve some credit for never so much as considering using her before," he added. "Mutti does not hold with half measures. The thing is I cannot guarantee she would not reduce Baerlen to smoking rubble in the process, and I could not reconcile that with my oath of service."

She couldn't help it. Gutrune laughed. It hurt to laugh, but the image of Gnädigefrau Asgaya, no doubt a formidable if older lady, besieging the city for her son was suddenly quite vivid in her imagination.

"There, that's better." Markus was smiling again, and she realized he'd done it on purpose, to give her thoughts a more cheerful direction.

Gutrune shifted, feeling doubtful again. She couldn't move her arms, wrapped tightly in the blankets as she was and still weak. "That's all very well, but what can *we* do? I can't even—"

"You are still recovering from defeating a powerful mage. I do wish you would rest, beloved. Now if you promise not to thrash about, I will untuck you. We only wrapped you up like this because you kept flinging the blankets away, and we can't risk you getting a chill on top of everything else."

She could tell it caused him discomfort to move and realized he had left out some details in his report. "You did not tell me the extent of your injuries."

"A few burns, for the most part." He pulled the blanket free and draped it loosely over her again. "And a large number of small bruises, from the avalanche. You weren't awake for that, but we had to move quickly to escape and you and Dominic Kermarec had to be carried." He stopped arranging the blanket about her shoulders, his eyes squeezing shut for a moment. His fingers brushed her cheek. "I don't suppose you would be willing to promise me to not fall off of any more mountains?"

He was trying to keep his usual light, careless tone, she could tell, but his voice had a small tremor in it. Gutrune took her newly free hand and clasped the hand cupping her face. "Promise me that we will go into danger together, and then you can fall with me. Always."

"I promise," Markus whispered. With no evasion or conditions, like an oath. And so she kissed him, as an oath in return.

"I wonder how people usually manage," Dominic said as he floated up the narrow stairway of the ship.

"They don't," Ardhuin replied, levitating him. "They stay in bed until they heal up."

"But I'd miss out!"

For everything but the stairway, two strong sailors could carry him, but the narrowness made that impossible here. Ardhuin rolled her eyes and sighed, and he smiled at her.

"Well, we can't have that." She directed the sailors to the deck where the others were gathered, also dealing with their respective infirmities. Dominic felt quite restored, with the exception of his leg, but MacCrimmon and Gutrune von Kitren still could not move very well on their own.

Out of consideration for the sailors, Ardhuin walked ahead. The blue *kai-ling*, now named Dorje, was alternately twining about her arms and shoulders and flying above her head, and it was still viewed with trepidation by the crew. It apparently found the sea air exhilarating.

A semicircle of chairs had been arranged on the deck, shaded from the direct sun. Markus, Gutrune, MacCrimmon, and Sonam were already there, and Dominic noticed with amusement Markus and Gutrune had contrived both to be next to each other and to discreetly hold hands under cover of her blankets. He took the chair next to Markus and gave him a lofty look.

"You owe me that favor now, I think," Dominic said in a soft tone.

"I agree—and is that not the matter we are to discuss?" Markus gave him a mischievous smile. "I can only wish us both an equal degree of success in our respective endeavors."

"That will do, thank you." Dominic felt his face heat.

Fortunately, before Ardhuin could get curious and ask, Dorje launched itself into the air with a whistling cry and dove out of sight over the side.

Ardhuin shook her head. "What, again? It's going to get as big as a real dragon at this rate."

"Dorje must think it has gone to *kai-ling* heaven. First sardines, and now this! Worth the mild inconvenience of the crate, I hope."

The familiar blue-purple head rose slowly above the rail with a fish nearly as big as the *kai-ling* itself clutched in Dorje's jaws. Lashing about with effort, it managed to land on the railing, making a muffled clicking while looking at Ardhuin.

"No, you go ahead," she told it. It glanced briefly at Dominic, who seemed to be included in the pecking order, but when he showed no interest, Dorje proceeded to eat its prey, only pausing to raise its neck scales when one of the crew, bringing refreshments, came too close.

"I must say, your idea would solve a number of difficulties," MacCrimmon said. "Not the least of which is the problem of protecting the valley. But what shall we do while Sonam is in training?"

"It appears Korda is the only free agent with knowledge of the valley." Gutrune's voice was still weaker than usual. "As long as we are vigilant in tracking down any hint of the salts, and him, we should have a little time. And I believe he will be as careful as we are in preserving the location as a secret."

Markus sat up to hand Gutrune a glass and to accept his own. "And how will we recruit the necessary agents? Besides our humble selves," he said, waving a hand.

"I think perhaps going through the...sympathetic Mage Guardians will be the best way, at first. Mr. MacCrimmon will be interviewing many magicians that, while they might not be suitable as his replacement, would still be fine agents for our purpose. And Hyeer Kreuwel, I know, is acquainted with several Low Country magicians like himself that have been held back from advancement only by rank, not skill. I doubt that Preusa..."

Markus chuckled. "Yes, we may need to neglect to mention this to the Preusan Mage Guardian, if von Koller has his way. But I believe we can be useful there, and His Majesty will, I suspect, be in full sympathy with our aims." Gutrune nodded agreement.

Sonam was sitting in silence, eyes wide and worried. MacCrimmon glanced his way and gave a weary smile.

"Yes, it makes no sense. And yet we must pay attention to it anyway. This is another reason why I wish you to study with Madame Kermarec. In a different world I would be able to keep you with me as my heir-magical, but Alba would not permit you to succeed me. In this way you will learn the politics that constrain our world and may come to impact yours, as well as learn how to protect your own people despite themselves."

"I will learn. Everything that I must, to do this." Sonam nodded vigorously.

"I worry about Cathai, too," Ardhuin said. "They also have great distrust of Aeropan magic—which, sadly, left them vulnerable to unscrupulous mages such as Denais. I fear that could happen again."

"There is no call for you to go there yourself," Dominic said quickly, worry spiking. The farther Ardhuin stayed away from Kungam or anyone who could report to him, the happier he would be. He was not entirely convinced the bandit king was satisfied with his deal.

Gutrune stirred. "I would advise approaching Mother Long for advice. We know she can be both observant and very discreet."

Ardhuin nodded. "Yes, and I think she would be willing to help, if for no other reason than to keep Kiantan safe. Besides the agents, I hope to encourage...an expanded set of Mage Guardians. Not just the representatives of the original Mage War allies, but every modern nation. Atlantea should have one too."

Dominic perked up. "I would like to visit Atlantea." Markus grinned at him but thankfully refrained from commenting.

"So, we are agreed? I believe we can count on the full support of Bretagne and Preusa, and at least the tolerance of the Low Countries for this scheme."

"I suspect Ruska will also wish to join, when they hear of it," Gutrune said. "But we should be cautious. They will wish to use it for their own political ends, to spy on those they believe their enemies, even in their own country."

"As long as we are aware, we can use that motivation for our own purposes," Markus pointed out. "Now there is one crucial point that remains to be settled. I am surprised at the lot of you for neglecting it."

Dominic raised an eyebrow. "What, dashing uniforms?"

Markus laughed, lifting a hand in acknowledgment. "It is kind of you to think of me, but I already have one. No, I was thinking we need a name for this organization. You have to have a name, if only for the paperwork."

Dominic thought for a moment. Well, what could they call it? "Secret Organization #23" lacked style and distinction. He supposed they shouldn't draw attention to the fact they were looking for magical troublemakers either.

Dorje was perched on the railing again, looking slightly plumper and carefully cleaning its colorful scales after its meal. A little dragon—and hadn't MacCrimmon gone to the Tian Shan to look for dragons in the first place?

"How about the Dragonhunters?" he asked.

EPILOGUE

To Oberleiter Schutzmagus M. Asgaya, Imperial Palace, Baerlen

Asgaya, you chuckling clown. I hope you've learned how to wear shirts again; you can't act like you're in the middle of the Taklamakan Desert anymore. The newspapers do not report any uprisings or volcanic eruptions in your country, so I presume you are still in the good graces of your lady. I would have thought she would have come to her senses by now.

Which brings me to the matter I wish to address—draw whatever conclusions you please, but I wish to warn you that you have less than six months to bring your section of the Dragonhunters to full strength, since Ardhuin will *not be traveling* for some time past that date. I would prefer she not travel at all even now, although she assures me she is in excellent health. I can't help but worry, you know...

I have enclosed some of Dorje's shed scales, as I promised. The magical residue is faint, but Ardhuin claims an exposure to a cantorial resonance will attune them quite nicely for use as badges that cannot be forged. I am working on a verifier that nonmagicians can use. Dorje sheds a handful every month or so, so we should have a reasonable supply for future use. You inquire about the moving imager—I have a working prototype, and it is even better than the first. With the exception of the size, the image is amazingly lifelike. I suppose you may come and see it, and the other devices, if you like. As long as you don't stay *too* long, that is. A day should suffice.

Oh, and congratulations on the promotion. I make no doubt it gave von Koller a spasm to hear of it, so on that account alone it pleases us both.

Your co-conspirator and, I suppose, friend,
Dominic

To Monsieur D. Kermarec, Peran, in Morbihan

My dear Dominic—I am greatly relieved to learn that all your party are safely home again. I will confess to some sleepless nights on your behalf, and for your charming wife as well. And now you send me word that makes me even more curious what you were up to when we parted company. You ask if I have ever seen anything like the amulet and the symbols you sketched in your last letter. I must confess that while I have *heard* of something similar, it was in the context of what I believed at the time to be a complete myth. Yet you assure me you walked in an ancient abandoned city that appears to match the particulars of that myth, and I am forced to surmise the rest may also prove true as well. If so, I beg of you to guard the artifacts you discovered *very well*, with *all the means at your disposal.* I would say more, but I do not trust the medium of the post. Please inform me when I may pay you a visit, when I will be delighted to tell you all I know in return for being allowed to see the artifacts in person. I would also strongly advise keeping all information about the city's location in strict confidence. The risk of robbers in that region is always to be guarded against, but in this case there could be *other dangers* associated with the city.

Yours,
Emil Bové

ABOUT THE AUTHOR

Sabrina Chase was originally trained as a Mad Scientist, but due to a tragic lack of available lairs at the time of graduation fell into low company and started working in the software industry. She lives in the Pacific Northwest and is owned by two cats.

Further sordid details may or may not be available at her website, chaseadventures.com